THE GIRL WITH NOWHERE TO GO

LOUISE GUY

B
Boldwood

First published in Great Britain in 2026 by Boldwood Books Ltd.

Cover Design by JD Smith Design Ltd

Cover Images: Shutterstock

A CIP catalogue record for this book is available from the British Library.

Paperback ISBN 978-1-83533-167-5

Large Print ISBN 978-1-83533-166-8

Hardback ISBN 978-1-83533-168-2

Trade Paperback ISBN 978-1-80656-144-5

Ebook ISBN 978-1-83533-165-1

Kindle ISBN 978-1-83533-164-4

Audio CD ISBN 978-1-83533-173-6

MP3 CD ISBN 978-1-83533-172-9

Digital audio download ISBN 978-1-83533-169-9

This book is printed on certified sustainable paper. Boldwood Books is dedicated to putting sustainability at the heart of our business. For more information please visit https://www.boldwoodbooks.com/about-us/sustainability/

Boldwood Books Ltd, 23 Bowerdean Street, London, SW6 3TN

www.boldwoodbooks.com

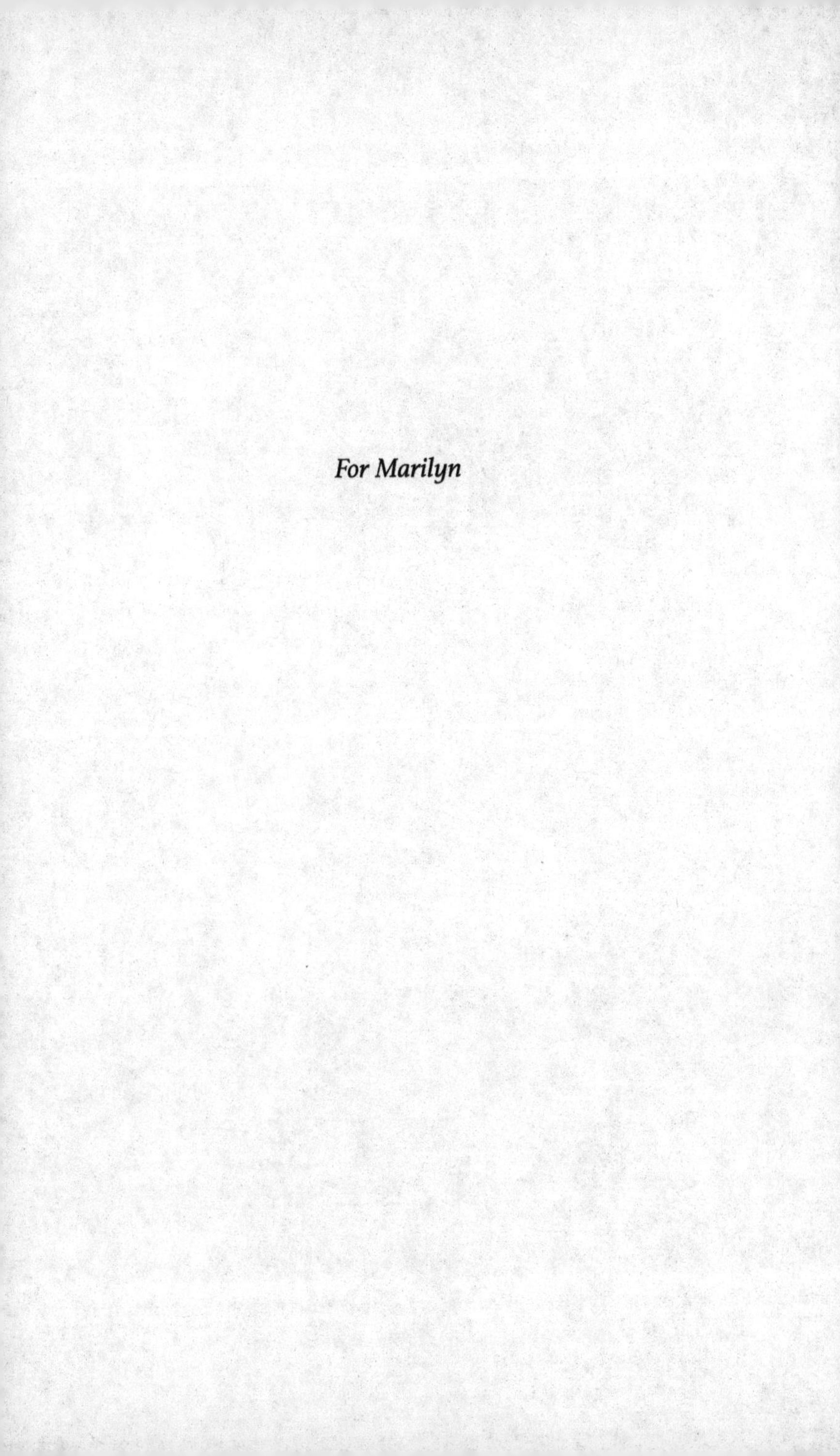

For Marilyn

PROLOGUE

Jodi Miller stirred her coffee slowly, sunlight spilling across the table. The café was quiet, the low hum of conversation and the hiss of the espresso machine filling the air. She pressed her fingers lightly to her side, feeling a flicker of discomfort she did her best to dismiss.

She forced a smile at her best friend who was watching her with interest.

'You okay?' Erin asked.

Jodi nodded, concentrating on stirring her coffee rather than meeting her friend's eyes. 'You know how, years ago, when Skye was born and I asked you to be her guardian if something happened to me?' Jodi did her best to keep the tremor out of her voice.

'Guardian and godmother from memory.' Erin raised an eyebrow. 'What, are you firing me from the job?'

'Of course not. I'm just updating my will... wanted to check you're still up for it.' She wrapped her hands around the mug, noticing how warm it felt.

Erin frowned. 'Of course I am. Not that I hope I'd ever have to step up and do it.' Her frown deepened. 'Why are you updating your will? Everything's okay, isn't it? You're not sick or anything?'

Jodi did her best to keep a smile firmly fixed to her lips. 'Everything's fine. My will's as old as Skye and I have a few investments and things I want added to it – just so all my information's in one place. You know me. I like to have everything in order.' She forced a laugh. 'The fact that my will hasn't been updated in over sixteen years suggests I'm not doing the best job of keeping things in order.'

Erin shrugged. 'As long as everything's left to Skye and you have me as guardian, I can't imagine your will needs too many changes.'

'No. Changes are fairly minor. I just wanted to check you'd be there for Skye if anything did happen. I couldn't bear to think of her being on her own or – even worse – with strangers.' She shuddered. 'That was my upbringing; it certainly can't be hers.'

Erin reached across the table and squeezed her hand. 'I'd be there for her. But just make sure that never happens. Losing you would be the end of me.'

Jodi squeezed her hand back, having to avert her eyes from Erin's, aware they were filling with tears. It was crazy to think what a difference two weeks could make. Two weeks earlier they'd sat at the same table having a drink, laughing without a care in the world. Later that afternoon she'd had her routine breast screen. Within two weeks everything had changed. She'd had her results. Had further tests and heard her prognosis. Stage IV triple-negative breast cancer that had already spread to her liver and bones. Treatment might buy her time, but not much according to the oncologist.

She'd then made the hardest decision she'd ever had to make – not to tell Erin or Skye.

Was it a selfish decision? She'd tried to convince herself that she wasn't able to tell them because it would hurt them too much, but deep down inside she knew that wasn't the case. She couldn't bear to see the pity and the fear in their eyes. It would mirror her own.

As the cancer progressed she'd probably have to tell them, but right now it wasn't something she could imagine being able to do.

She took a deep breath as Erin started to talk about her job and a promotion that was looking likely.

She was so caught up in her own thoughts she realised she'd hardly been listening when Erin asked her a question.

'Well, what would you do?'

'Do?'

'Yes. Would you move with the job or not? It's a pretty big ask, even of the UN. I know I've worked for them for years, but a stint in Yemen wasn't in the original job description.'

'Yemen?' Jodi's heart caught in her throat. Erin couldn't move to Yemen.

'It'd only be for a few months, but still, it seems pretty risky.'

'Do you have to go?' It always amazed Jodi that her friend had such an important job.

Erin shook her head. 'No, it's just an opportunity, nothing more. I can say no.'

'Say no,' Jodi said. 'It's far too dangerous. It's madness with what's going on there that they'd even think of sending you or anyone else.'

Erin nodded slowly. 'You're probably right. I've travelled a lot with my job, but right now, with all the unrest over there, I'd rather avoid it.' She gave a little laugh. 'Although it'll mean I'm destined to be chained to my desk forever.'

'Better than being shot or blown up.'

'True. Now, tell me something fun about Skye. This conversation's getting too heavy for me.'

Jodi smiled, trying to ignore the wave of fatigue that hit her. 'She's great. Such an amazing daughter. I've been so lucky.' This time she couldn't help it when tears filled her eyes. She smiled through them, wanting Erin to think they were happy tears.

'She's lucky,' Erin said. 'To have a mum like you. She hit the jackpot when she was born.'

The tears rolled faster and thicker down Jodi's cheeks. Six months. That's what the oncologist had predicted earlier that day. She had six months left of being a mum. She couldn't begin to imagine how Skye would cope. It had been just the two of them since her daughter was born.

She smiled at Erin through her tears. Thank God for her best friend. Knowing Erin would be there for Skye was the only thing that made it slightly bearable.

1

Bec Sampson manoeuvred her Mini Cooper into her late husband's parking space, the sign still marked with his name and switched off the engine. A tight ache curled in her chest that she did her best to push away. Owen had been on her mind all morning, but now she had to shove the grief aside. The day demanded her attention. A new course was starting and she had back-to-back creative therapy sessions to run. She needed to function, look like she belonged in the world. As Owen would have said: she needed to be a person.

A rap on the car window made her jump and a smile tugged at her lips as she met Damien's concerned green eyes.

She unclipped her seat belt, collected her bag from the passenger seat and pushed open the door.

'Everything okay?' Damien held the door open for her.

'Just giving myself a pep talk. Making sure my focus is in the right place. We've got a huge week ahead.'

'We have,' Damien said. 'But you also have permission to be kind to yourself. It's perfectly reasonable that your focus is elsewhere.'

Bec gave his arm a quick squeeze. 'Thanks. Same goes for you.'

She walked beside him towards the front entrance. Eight years ago, Damien had approached her and Owen and suggested opening a Melbourne branch of their Sydney-based business. Reclaim had started fifteen years earlier as a small initiative to honour her late brother, Chris, focusing on men's mental health, and it had quickly grown into a rehabilitation centre with a broader scope. Over time, they'd added all sorts of programs including several preventative ones aimed at keeping young and first-time offenders out of prison. Damien had known her since they were teenagers, had been a close friend of Chris's, and had a background in business development, which he knew would help Reclaim thrive. When he joined the business, he'd quickly become a trusted friend to Owen, too, and together the three of them had built the organisation into something far bigger than she had ever imagined.

Now, following Owen's death, she'd closed the Sydney branch and, with two reluctant sixteen-year-olds in tow, returned to Melbourne, bringing her art therapy sessions with her. The creative classes had always been her space within Reclaim – a way to help attendees process pain, rebuild confidence and reclaim parts of themselves they had lost.

Damien's voice broke into her thoughts. 'Are you still good to do the welcome and housekeeping introduction?'

'Of course.'

* * *

After depositing her bag and computer on her desk, Bec made her way to the training room. While there were plenty of students already seated, the room was quiet. That would change within a few hours of them getting to know each other.

'You ready for this lot?' Bec asked Vance, one of her regular trainers who was making final adjustments to the tools and equipment for the electrical course.

Vance finished what he was doing, folded his arms, the tattoos on his thick forearms shifting with the movement, and gave Bec a half-smile. He was a walking contradiction. All muscle, gym-built with bulging biceps and calves. It was clear to anyone that he spent hours working out, but what wasn't clear until you got to know him was that he had a heart of gold.

'Always ready.' Vance nodded towards the students who were already seated. 'Interesting mix today.'

Bec looked around the room. Fifteen of the eighteen seats were filled. It was quite likely the other three would remain empty for the duration of the course. It was always interesting to read the profiles of those who decided not to turn up, because the reality was courses at Reclaim were usually filled with people who *had* to attend. They'd be answering to parole officers, legal representatives or government administrators refusing their welfare payments if they didn't complete their side of the bargain.

Her eyes stopped briefly as she saw a girl huddled down in the second row, baseball hat pulled low over her face. She could see her eyes flitting nervously around the room. Bec felt a tug on her heart. This girl didn't look any older than her twins. Everything about her appearance, from her stained jacket, knotted hair and her mismatched shoes told the story that her experiences in life had been very different to those Bec's children had been through. Bec often thought it'd do her daughter, Zara, good to come and work at the centre. It might put a dent in her layers of entitlement.

Bec averted her gaze and cleared her throat. It was a few

minutes past the nine o'clock starting time and there was no point waiting for the three empty chairs to fill.

She raised her voice, injecting as much enthusiasm as she could muster. 'Good morning, everyone, and welcome to Reclaim.' She had to push the thought of Owen away as she welcomed the group with a broad smile. He joked that every time either of them welcomed a new group to the centre, he expected to say those words and applause to erupt throughout the room. That he imagined he was Oprah or Ellen welcoming the audience. Of course, it never did. If anything, the class would shift uncomfortably in their seats, or they'd have to stop and ask someone to remove their AirPods or switch off their phones.

It was ten minutes later that Bec left the group in Vance's hands and settled down at her desk. She found her thoughts going back to the girl on the course. She'd seen enough people in trouble to know the signs of things not being right. The girl's clothes alone had suggested times were tough. Bec wondered whether she had a support system to lean on? Did she have any family?

She booted up her computer and clicked through to the course notes, looking at the list of participants. Four females out of the eighteen booked in. She clicked on each one, grateful that three of the four had been populated with all the student's details, including photos. She stopped when she opened Skye Miller's profile. The girl looked positively miserable. Again, Bec's heart contracted as she looked at her gaunt face in the photo.

She read through the notes that accompanied the application for the course. She'd come from the Preventative Prison program. The notes were brief about what had landed her in trouble with the police, shoplifting, but she was only sixteen, so they were encouraging her to get some skills and do something with her life and hopefully not end up in prison. Bec sighed, thinking of her frustrations with Zara and how trivial they were compared to what this girl, and so many others, were going through.

* * *

As she moved through her one-on-one art therapy sessions for the day, Bec's thoughts drifted back to Skye and the electrical course. Something felt off. Her track record proved she should trust her intuition and she made a mental note to see if Damien had any more information on Skye.

For now, she focused on her current client. Tom, a reformed ex-prisoner who spoke little but let his oil paints do the talking, was at his easel, layering deep blues over fiery reds. Bec stood beside him, watching as he applied a subtle blending technique.

'You're in one of those flowing dresses again,' he said, his tone gruff, undercut by admiration. 'Looks like you should be in a gallery, not a classroom.'

Bec paused, weighing the comment. Was he crossing a line? No, she didn't think so. He was in his sixties and basically old-school. No doubt thought she should be flattered by his comment rather than consider it sexual harassment. 'Inspiration comes in different forms,' she said lightly, letting the moment pass as she turned her attention back to the canvas.

Tom lapsed into silence.

Bec stepped back, letting him continue, and studied the painting emerging under his careful strokes.

She breathed in the stillness of the room, her mind drifting back to Skye. Would the teen be open to art therapy? While it was encouraged, it wasn't a compulsory part of everyone's course. She guessed she needed to find out more about her and go from there.

The time with Tom disappeared and once again she admired

his handiwork while they packed away the canvas, ensuring it would be ready for their next session.

'Your work is really remarkable,' she said, noticing the red splotches creeping up Tom's cheeks. 'I think you should consider entering it into a competition when it's finished.'

He snorted. 'Competition? What's the point?'

'Just to share it. See what others think. Celebrate what you've created.'

'No thanks.' His words were firm but there was the slightest twitch at the corner of his mouth that suggested he wasn't entirely dismissing the idea.

After his gruff goodbye, Bec finished readying herself for her next session, her thoughts once again returning to Skye.

2

Bec's last session ran over and she was disappointed to see that the electrical class had already wound up for the day and the participants had left. She would attempt to speak to the teenager first thing in the morning.

As she pulled into her driveway, her eyes focused on the patchy grass in their new front yard. Patchy was being generous – it was really dirt with a few green blades sticking through. She groaned. She'd add fixing it, plus dealing with the overgrown flower beds to what felt like a never-ending list of chores. She was beginning to realise how much Owen had done around the home. Although the house in Sydney had had years of love and attention, whereas they hadn't been in the Camberwell house long enough to be worried that it was already falling into a state of disrepair.

She pushed the thought from her mind as she climbed out of the car, remembering her therapist's parting words as she hugged her for the last time.

'Give yourself time and permission to just be. Grief's a tricky train to ride and you need to be kind to yourself.'

Bec took a deep breath before pushing the front door open. She was doing her best to leave work at the office each day so that she'd hopefully be present for her children. It hadn't been an easy time for any of them, each dealing with their grief, and she was doing her best to make sure they knew that they were her priority. She didn't achieve it every day – her daughter, Zara, was quick to point out when she wasn't present – but she was doing her best.

She opened the door, flinching as a crash came from one of the bedrooms down the hall. Music blared. Knowing Zara, this would be her attempting to cover up whatever she'd dropped or broken.

She sighed. The house still didn't feel like theirs. They'd only been in Melbourne a few months, and some days she wasn't sure they'd made the right call leaving Balmain in Sydney's inner west. But the house in Balmain hadn't felt like theirs either. Not after Owen's death. And then she was wondering if anything would ever feel the same.

'Hey,' her son, Hugo, said, pouring himself a glass of water as she entered the kitchen. His gym shorts hung off his hips and his white T-shirt outlined his muscly arms. In the space of a year he'd transformed from gangly teenager to a tall, broad-shouldered, and – according to what Zara had reported back from the friends she'd made at their new school – *smoking hot* young adult. She forced a smile, pushing all thoughts of Owen from her mind.

'Hey, yourself,' Bec said, depositing her bag on the island counter. 'Good day?'

'Pretty good. Just got back from the gym. Went with Curtis.'

'That's great, and while I should follow your healthy lead with a glass of water, I'd kill for a wine.'

Hugo laughed and took an open bottle of Pinot Gris from the fridge and poured Bec a glass.

She took it gratefully and sank down onto one of the stools at the island. 'That's what I call good service. Thank you.'

Hugo grinned and Bec couldn't help but smile. It was such a relief to see him happy. When she'd made the decision to move to Melbourne, she knew Zara would be furious, but that her daughter would also have no trouble making new friends. Hugo, on the other hand, she'd been worried about. He was a bit of a loner, had two good mates in Sydney, but didn't make friends easily. So when he'd come back from school on his first day telling her he was going to try out a gym one of the boys had recommended, she'd been relieved. Now he was at the gym five days a week and usually met Curtis there. Curtis had also introduced Hugo to his group of friends, who seemed to have readily accepted him, and he was now more social than he'd been in Sydney. Perhaps being *smoking hot* had something to do with it, as the friend group consisted of several girls as well.

As she felt the relaxing effects of her first sip of wine, Zara's door flew open and Bec braced herself as her feisty daughter appeared in the kitchen. Tall and slim was her only likeness to her twin brother. With flushed cheeks and a dark mane of hair, she looked from Bec to Hugo and back to Bec, hands on hips, her green eyes flashing. 'Why do you always lie about everyone being dead?'

Bec put her glass down on the counter, wondering if she had the strength for another Zara confrontation. They'd been a thing while Owen was alive, but since his death their frequency had increased dramatically.

'Evening, Zars.' Bec couldn't keep the sarcasm from her tone.

Whether Zara picked up on it or not, she chose to ignore it.

'You moved us back to Melbourne, away from all my friends and everything we love, and it's not like it's because we have a huge family here or something that would make sense. We don't know anyone according to you.'

'According to me?'

Zara nodded. 'I know you're lying. To me and Hugo – about our grandparents. Tell us who they were. We're old enough to deal with the truth.' She rolled her judgement-loaded teenage eyes. 'What, were they murderers or something?'

Hugo laughed. 'You're nuts. You know that don't you?'

'We have no family on Mum's side,' Zara said. 'Dad's gone and he hardly had any family, and I hate that we're always on our own at Christmas and holidays. I'd like to have a family and I think I've got one that you won't give me access to.'

Hugo leaned against the counter. 'Leave Mum alone, would you? Just because you want more relatives doesn't mean she can magically make them appear.'

'I'm not asking for magic, just the truth.'

Hugo shook his head and turned to Bec, an apologetic smile crossing his lips. 'Mum, are you hiding a family from us?'

Bec swallowed, doing her best to keep her face neutral. She couldn't imagine what had caused Zara to be suspicious. 'Of course not. As much as I'd like to bring my parents back from the dead and introduce you to them, that's not going to happen.'

Zara snorted. 'And yet they have no gravestones and you have no photos of them. It's like they never even existed.'

Bec took a deep breath. Since they'd moved from Sydney, Zara had been bringing up family more and more.

'But you used to live in Melbourne, didn't you? You grew up here?'

'And?'

'And, you had family and you had friends. Other than Damien, there's no one from your past?'

Bec had laughed at this. 'I left Melbourne years ago. When I was only slightly older than you two. I've told you this a million times. After the house fire, I started a whole new life in Sydney. Met your dad and never looked back. The only real connection to Melbourne was Damien and the business. But even with that, it was usually Dad who'd come down to meet with him, or Damien would come to us at the Sydney office for strategy meetings.' And it had been. Bec had avoided Melbourne at all costs. She continued: 'I didn't enjoy school and, other than Damien, didn't keep in touch with any of my old friends. I can hardly look them up now. They'd think I was mad. And staying here after the fire was way too hard.'

'The fire that killed my grandparents and burnt up all of the photos that ever existed of them?'

Bec nodded, her stomach twisting as the lies rolled off her tongue. 'It wasn't the same back then. We didn't save things in the Cloud. Most photos were printed or saved on memory cards from digital cameras. All of it was burnt – I've told you that.' She decided to change tack. 'Do you really think I like that I don't have any photos of my parents?'

Zara hesitated, perhaps realising she was crossing a line, but then shook her head. 'Someone would have had photos. They had friends, didn't they?'

The fact that Zara was clever was something Bec was usually proud of, but at other times it was nothing short of annoying.

'Zar, leave it,' Hugo said.

Bec could only imagine how pale her face had gone.

Zara threw her hands in the air. 'Fine. But I know you're lying.' She calmed momentarily. She looked Bec up and down, causing Bec to tug on her skirt self-consciously.

'What *are* you wearing?'

Bec looked down at herself. The flowing linen skirt Tom had complimented sported shades of teal and mustard, layered with a tie-dyed blouse that billowed around her waist. Her bangles clinked as she tugged at the hem, and a pair of woven sandals peeked out beneath the skirt, their straps frayed from years of wear. She loved the colours, the freedom in the fabric, the way it made her feel like herself. Owen would have told her she looked beautiful, that no one else could carry colour the way she did.

Before she had a chance to respond, Zara turned and stomped out of the room.

'Sorry,' Hugo said.

Bec reached out and stroked his blond hair. 'Why are you sorry? It's not your fault she's feisty.'

Hugo shrugged, causing Bec to smile. He seemed to always be standing up for, or apologising for, his twin.

'She's really critical, that's all. You look nice by the way, but she's been on about this family thing ever since we left Sydney,' Hugo said. 'What do you think that's all about?'

Bec sighed. 'I'd say it's part of her grieving process of losing your dad. We all handle things differently and she'd like more family, I guess to compensate for what she's lost.'

'Makes sense.' Hugo grinned. 'Maybe we should hire some grandparents and shut her up. Really bad, ugly, loser ones that she'll meet once and not want anything to do with.'

Bec forced a laugh. If she produced the real ones, she'd like to think that both Hugo and Zara wouldn't want anything to do with them. But that was never going to happen.

Hugo refilled his water glass and grabbed a banana from the fruit bowl as he made his way out of the kitchen towards the hallway and his bedroom.

Tears welled in Bec's eyes. Owen would be so proud of his son. He'd stepped up since his father's death, and seemed to have taken on the role of protector, man of the house. Bec certainly hadn't expected him, or even needed him, to do that, but was incredibly proud that it was his instinct.

She sipped her wine and sighed, wondering how many times she'd wished her daughter's personality mirrored that of her twin. Life would be so much easier and calmer. But then again, was it really all that hard? She saw enough in her job to put her own world in perspective. Thoughts of Skye once again filled her head. She hoped the teenager had a bed for the night and food. A niggling feeling in her gut told her she might not.

* * *

Bec did her best to push away the uneasy feeling in the pit of her stomach as she drove to work the next morning. She hadn't slept well following Zara's outburst. Thoughts of her parents, Owen and even Skye had swirled in her mind until the early hours when she'd finally drifted off.

She caught a glimpse of movement in her rear-vision mirror as she pulled into Owen's parking spot. Skye was walking across the car park, her backpack slung over one shoulder, head down as she made her way towards the entrance. Her heart skipped a beat. This was her chance to finally talk to the girl and find out her story.

Bec hurried from the car, hooked her bag over her shoulder and took a deep breath. She wasn't sure why she was nervous. She dealt with troubled teenagers all the time and generally had a lot of success in helping them, well maybe more success with others than her own. She pushed a vision of Zara from her mind and walked in Skye's direction. She forced her movements to be slow, deliberately casual, not wanting to startle Skye as she approached.

'Hey there,' she called lightly, a smile in her voice, keeping her tone easy and friendly.

The girl glanced in her direction and nodded before averting her eyes and continuing towards the centre.

'Hey, wait a minute,' Bec called, and Skye stopped. 'It's Skye, isn't it?' Bec said when she reached her.

Skye nodded again.

Bec realised up close how thin she was. 'I'm Bec.'

'I know, you told us yesterday at the start of the course.'

'So I did. How did you find day one?'

Skye shrugged, stuffing her hands deep in her pockets. 'Okay.'

'You're early today. You know the course doesn't start until nine?'

Skye's cheeks coloured. 'I was hoping I could sit in the room until then. It's nice and warm in there.'

'You can,' Bec said. She studied the girl again, her gut telling her something was very wrong. She wondered where she was living and whether she had money for food. She was in the same grubby clothes as she'd worn the day before. It wasn't something she could ask her outright, but she could certainly offer her a meal.

'But,' Bec added, 'you can join me if you want across the road.' She nodded towards Café Bloom, which was directly across from Reclaim. 'They do a great breakfast special. My treat.'

Skye looked torn. 'Thanks, but I'm fine.'

'Really? What did you have for breakfast?'

Skye looked away.

'Dinner last night?' Bec didn't wait for the teenager to answer her; instead she took her elbow and led her gently in the direction of the café. 'No arguments.'

Ten minutes later, Bec sipped her coffee, watching as Skye

appeared to be doing her best not to scoff down the big breakfast she'd insisted on ordering for her.

'You're the same age as my daughter,' Bec said.

'How do you know how old I am?'

'I looked up your file yesterday,' she admitted. 'It's hard not to be concerned when I see kids the same age as my own in our courses. I wondered what had brought you to us for training.'

A defiant look crossed Skye's face. 'It's none of your business why I'm here.'

'No, it's not,' Bec agreed. 'But it worries me when I see someone who's only sixteen going through a hard time.' She nodded towards the plate of food. 'When did you last eat?'

'Yesterday.'

'At the course?' As part of the day, Reclaim put on lunch for the students. Bec had realised early on that several of the class participants had no money and were struggling through the day on whatever they'd managed to scrounge for breakfast, so she had made that part of the course fee. As the government were predominantly paying for the courses, it hadn't been an issue.

Skye's cheeks flushed, and she looked away.

'Do you have somewhere to stay?'

She nodded. 'Look, I appreciate you being concerned, but I'm fine. I've got this far by myself and don't need anyone's help.'

Bec leaned back in her chair. 'I'd disagree with you. You're here because your other option is to end up in juvenile detention. I have no idea what you did, and it's none of my business, but there are people at Reclaim who can help you.'

'Get a job?'

'Well, yes, we have plenty of connections that we link our students with after they complete our courses, but we can do more than that. Some of the younger people who come to us, like you, don't realise how much help is available to them. If, for example, you were at school, there are all sorts of youth allowances and rent assistance you're most likely eligible for.'

'Yeah, I know.'

Bec wasn't sure whether to push the conversation or not. She didn't want her shutting down, but she also had an overwhelming desire to help her. 'I'm not trying to pry,' she said and then gave a small laugh, causing Skye to look up. 'Actually, that's a lie, I'm the queen of prying.' She was relieved to see the corner of Skye's mouth turn up ever so slightly. Almost a smile. 'Look,' Bec said, 'I'd like to help you if you'd let me. As a mum, I find it hard not to look after our younger clients. Do you have any family? Are your mum and dad around?'

Skye shook her head and looked away as her eyes filled with tears.

'Hey,' Bec said, placing a hand on Skye's. 'I didn't mean to upset you.'

Skye shook her hand off and stood. 'The course is going to start soon; I don't want to be late. Thanks for the food.'

Bec nodded and watched as the teen hurried out of the café and across the road. The question about Skye's parents had hit a nerve. She wondered if Damien had any further information available to him on Skye, or who she could reach out to, to find out more.

* * *

The kitchen at Reclaim was warm, the scent of burnt toast still hanging in the air. Bec stood by the bench, slowly stirring her coffee.

'You look a million miles away.'

Bec jumped at the sound of Damien's voice. She took the teaspoon from the cup and dropped it in the dishwasher before turning to face him. 'Bit distracted. There's a girl in the course that started yesterday who I spent some time with this morning. Skye Miller.'

Damien took a cup from the cupboard above the bench and set about making himself a coffee. 'The young one? Skinny, was wearing a cap?'

Bec nodded. 'She didn't admit it, but I'm pretty sure she's homeless and may not have any money. She closed up when I asked about her parents.'

Damien frowned. 'There's more to her story. I don't know if I added it to the file, but she lost her mum a few months back. All the trouble she's found has been since then. I suspect it's her way of dealing with her grief.'

'Oh no. No wonder she's a mess. She needs more than an electrical course. She needs some proper support.'

'You can't take her home – you know that, don't you?'

Bec relaxed when she saw the twinkle in his eye. She'd found herself in trouble on more than one occasion for taking clients under her wing. While the situation that drove her away from her family and away from Melbourne had been very different from the young people she came across through Reclaim, she saw herself in a lot of them. Alone at a young age. Not as young as Skye, but still young.

'But,' Damien said, 'you could suggest some counselling or even direct her to that support group at Hopefield that I was telling you about. I've been a couple of times now.'

'The grief one?'

Damien nodded. 'They do plenty of funded counselling and that type of thing, but the program I mentioned previously, Echoes, is on a Tuesday night. It's impressive. The woman who's in charge… she just gets it. You need to be there to see what I mean, but everyone who goes says the same. We've all come from different backgrounds with different experiences and are trying to come to terms with our grief, but she's created a space where you feel like you belong, no matter what you're trying to hide from.'

Bec reached over and squeezed Damien's arm. 'Sorry.'

Damien frowned. 'Why are you sorry?'

'Because I've made Owen dying all about me when I'm with you. I forget how big his loss is for you, too. You were great friends.'

'It's big for everyone, Bec. But I'm doing okay. Keeping busy. Up until the last few weeks, I was coping by avoiding anything to do with Owen, but the couple of visits to Echoes have changed my outlook a little. I need to stop avoiding grief and go through the process.' He added milk to his coffee and glanced at his watch. 'I'd better get back to it. And maybe think about it for Skye, if not for yourself. I won't make tonight's session, but if you go, tell Anna I said hi.'

'Anna?'

'Anna Morrison, she's the woman who runs it.'

3

Anna Morrison did her best to ignore the shiver that travelled the length of her spine as she read through the case file in front of her. She found cases involving car accident victims unsettling, which was ironic considering it was a car accident that claimed the life of her brother, Jake, twenty-two years ago. His death was what led her to specialising in counselling people who'd been through traumatic events like accidents or violent crimes.

'Hey.'

Anna looked up as Isabella, her manager, stepped into her office.

Isabella nodded towards the file she was reading. 'Clare Fleming. I put it on your desk this morning. She's coming in this afternoon, and I'd really like you to look after her.'

Anna swallowed, doing her best – she hoped – to mask her feelings. Some cases she'd rather not even hear about, let alone work on.

Isabella moved into Anna's office and sat down across from her. 'I know car accidents are your least favourite, and while I'd usually get someone else to handle this one, there are a lot of similarities to the client you worked with about twelve months ago, Paul Jones. Similar hit-and-run accident scenario. Unfortunately this accident also ended in a fatality. Clare hasn't been able to sleep or function. Mind you, it's only two weeks since the accident, but she needs help. She's having issues with the legal process and really needs some guidance. She's also a very close friend of my sister-in-law so I want her to have the best, which of course, is you.'

Anna forced a smile while her stomach churned as she thought back to the months she'd spent helping Paul Jones. It had been a successful outcome, but it had taken an emotional toll on her. As much as she'd tried to keep her distance and remain professional, she'd found it impossible not to think about Jake and be drawn back to that night in 2003 when their family was destroyed.

'If you're not up for it, I can ask one of the others.' Isabella studied Anna's face carefully. 'I know your background makes some clients more difficult than others.'

'No, I'll be fine. I learned a lot working with Paul that will be useful when counselling Clare.' She glanced at the file notes. 'It's only two weeks since the accident?'

'Be careful calling it an accident with Clare. She's clear in her description that it was murder.'

Anna's eyes shot up from the document and met Isabella's. 'Murder?'

'The person slammed into their car, killing her husband and leaving her with minor injuries. He or she then drove away from the scene. The police are still searching for them.' Isabella stood. 'I'd better get on. I've called a staff meeting at twelve, so please make yourself available.'

'Everything okay?' Staff meetings other than the weekly update were unusual. The last had been when one of the senior counsellors unexpectedly resigned and left without working out their notice period. Another had been when a very distressed client had committed suicide. Anna couldn't remember an ad-hoc staff meeting that had ever been for good news.

Isabella pursed her lips in a grim smile. 'I was given some information over the weekend that suggests tonight's state budget is going to deliver cuts that will affect our funding. I want to give the team a heads-up before they see it and start worrying.' Her face relaxed and she did her best to smile. 'Now, if you have any trouble with Clare Fleming, or feel you'd prefer not to take her on, let me know, okay?'

Anna nodded, knowing as she did, that she'd be meeting with Clare later that afternoon and if anything, would get far too involved in helping the woman rather than handing her back to Isabella to reallocate.

* * *

While she'd done her best not to show it in the staff meeting, Isabella's news had rattled Anna. Budget cuts of in excess of a million dollars would hit the support centre hard – programs would be axed, possibly jobs lost. Isabella had promised to do all she could to protect staff, but there were no guarantees until the board met after the budget.

Anna liked to think her job was safe, but you never knew. She'd poured her heart into the centre and couldn't imagine working anywhere else. She wondered what it might mean for Echoes, the support group she ran on Tuesday nights. It cost little to run, and she'd volunteer if she had to in order to keep it going.

She glanced at the clock. Clare Fleming was due any minute.

'It wasn't a car accident,' Clare said after Anna had gone through a series of preliminary questions and allowed Clare to talk about her situation for some time. Her arm was in a sling, bruises colouring one side of her face. Despite the injuries, her silk blouse and immaculate make-up spoke of money. Her jaw was tight, her eyes sharp with anger.

'I want that clear. It was murder. What else do you call it when someone hits you at high speed and flees the scene?'

Anna had already spoken with the detective. It was a hit-and-run. No witnesses, no cameras, no leads.

'You've been through a lot,' Anna said. 'My role is to assist you any way I can, both practically and emotionally.'

'I was told you'd help with the police. They're not doing enough.'

'I've spoken with the detective in charge,' Anna said. 'They're doing all they can, but there's no CCTV footage of the other car. The police will keep us updated of any developments.'

'Developments?'

'If they find the driver.' Anna shifted the focus. 'There are also victim-support payments that may help with funeral costs and counselling.'

'That's the least of my concerns,' Clare said. 'I want publicity. If enough people hear about it, maybe someone will come forward.'

'That's something we can look at,' Anna said carefully. Putting Clare in front of cameras might not help – her anger was too raw.

'What?' Clare demanded.

'You've every right to be angry,' Anna said gently. 'But for the public to connect, they'll need to see your grief as well.'

Tears filled Clare's eyes, her first crack of emotion. 'I don't know how to be anything but angry right now. It's easier than anything else.'

Anna swallowed the lump in her throat. When Jake had been killed, she'd initially raged with anger. It took weeks for her to put that aside enough to even start to properly grieve the loss of her brother.

'It's not easy,' she said. 'But talking about Ned will help. I'd like to see you weekly and also invite you to our Tuesday night support group, Echoes.'

'Echoes?' Clare frowned. 'I don't want to sit around talking about my feelings. It won't bring him back.'

'No,' Anna said softly. 'But it might help bring you back. Anger's easier than pain, but eventually you'll have to face it, and support helps when you do.'

'I have friends and family.'

'Of course. But Echoes is different. Everyone there understands.' Anna went on to explain more about the group to Clare. 'Come tonight if you can. You'd be welcome.'

'And you run it?'

Anna nodded. 'I started it years ago when I realised what would have helped me cope with my loss.' She stood, signalling the end of their session. 'Think about it. There's no pressure. Just keep your appointments and look after yourself. It's a huge loss, Clare.'

It was clear how huge as Anna watched fat tears roll down her cheeks.

* * *

After seeing Clare back out to the reception area, Anna returned to her desk, determined to push away the chill Clare's session had left her with. At least she didn't have to think about why the situation left her uneasy. It was all about Jake. She wondered if a day would ever pass when she wasn't affected by her brother's death.

She opened her laptop and opened the file named Echoes. Everything was organised for the evening's session, but she liked to double check and remind herself of the plans for the following week so she could share them with the group. The group was one of the highlights of her week. Bringing strangers together with a common thread of loss offered them a safe place to be heard and share their grief around others who understood. She sighed. To lose the group was unthinkable.

'That was a big sigh.'

She looked up as Isabella entered her office and sat down in the chair across from her.

'Just thinking about Echoes. I'd be gutted to close that down. I'd be happy to run the sessions on a volunteer basis if it means it can continue.'

Isabella smiled. 'And that's why you're one of my most valuable assets. You work from the heart, not from the purse strings. And in fact, I popped in to tell you I'm thinking quite the opposite when it comes to Echoes. I think we need to build it even bigger. Possibly put on another session if you can do that.'

Anna frowned. This was the last thing she'd imagined Isabella suggesting.

'If we lose funding, and in turn lose counsellors and some of our sessions need to be cancelled, then Echoes allows those clients to still turn up, still be heard, and potentially meet other like-minded people to give them support. Exactly the scenario you outlined when you first set it up. The second session could be something different from grief. Possibly general trauma or life issues. Whatever we decide we'll make it available to the most people and continue it free of charge. Our costs are very minimal with the session you currently run, but it provides us with such a large client base and referral program.' She smiled. 'I'm thinking longer term here as you can see.'

Anna nodded. 'It's a great idea. I've thought a few times about suggesting we expand out what Echoes offers; I've just never acted on it.'

Isabella stood. 'Well, it's time to act. Encouraging groups into the centre is a good long-term plan too. If we get an investor, or funding allocations change and increase down the track, then we haven't let all of our clients disappear. If you have time, put something together in writing over the next day or two. Once we know the impact on our budget, I'd like to include this in our recommendation to the board.'

Anna smiled as Isabella left her office. When she'd originally set up Echoes, it was because it was something she knew she would have benefited from when Jake had died, and she believed her parents would have too. Hearing from Isabella that she wanted the concept expanded out to a larger audience was very rewarding. She had to admit that the conversation brought a sense of relief. Her job, for a start, didn't sound like it was under threat.

4

Bec had been surprised when Skye agreed to come with her to the Echoes support group Damien had recommended. She'd pulled her aside at the lunch break and apologised.

'Why are you apologising?' Skye asked.

'For this morning,' Bec said. 'I wouldn't have asked about your parents if I'd known about your mum. Damien mentioned that you'd lost her recently. I have some idea what that feels like. My husband passed away not long ago.'

Skye's eyes flicked up, surprise softening them. 'I'm really sorry about your husband,' she said. 'That sucks.'

Bec drew in a slow breath. 'Thanks. I'm going to try out a grief support group tonight that Damien's recommended. If it's any good, I'll encourage my kids, Hugo and Zara, to come along. It might be something that helps you too, if you're interested.'

Skye didn't respond.

'It's run on Tuesday nights in Camberwell. Tonight's will be followed by a free dinner at Sophia's.' Bec didn't add that the free meal would be at her expense.

'The pizza place?'

Bec nodded. 'Italian. Anyway, no rush to let me know. Just confirm either way by the end of your training today.'

She'd assumed the teenager would tell her where to go, but she hadn't. She'd agreed then and there to go with Bec. Perhaps it had been the promise of dinner afterwards, but Bec wasn't going to question what felt like a win.

Now, ten minutes before the start of the six o'clock session, Bec – with Skye beside her – walked into the large room at Hopefield Support Centre the group used. 'You okay?' she asked Skye, conscious that, other than one boy who looked slightly older than Skye, the rest of the people were more around Bec's age or older.

Skye nodded, apprehension written on her face.

They took seats to one side, and Bec watched with interest as a woman, about her age, moved away from the two older guys she was talking to and stood at the front of the room. Late thirties, maybe early forties, she was attractive with wavy chestnut hair framing her face.

'Hi, everyone,' she said. 'For those who haven't attended Echoes before, I'll give you a quick run-down of who I am and how the evening operates. Firstly, I'd like to offer you a very warm welcome. It's always with mixed feelings that I welcome our newcomers, because I know that something difficult or even devastating has led you here. You'll find many of us are still dealing with the deaths of our loved ones. Some are unable to move on with their lives; others need a place where they know they'll be understood. Everyone deals with death and grief differently, and that's what Echoes is all about, letting you grieve how you need to, but offering a support system too.

'My name's Anna Morrison, and it was the death of my brother that led me to establish Echoes about ten years ago.'

Bec sat taller in her seat.

'Jake died over twenty years ago, but for me, it's as if it happened yesterday. Don't get me wrong, I have lots happening in my life, but that loss is something I've never recovered from. For years, I had people looking at me strangely, wondering how I could still be grieving for my brother, and they didn't get that while for some time makes things a little easier, for others it doesn't. It often feels as raw as it was when it happened.'

Bec felt an immediate connection to this woman. While Bec's current grief was centred around losing Owen, she'd also truthfully never recovered from her twin brother, Chris's death. The rawness was just like Anna said. Even now, a hollow ache spread through her body as she was transported back twenty years to that night.

* * *

Her mother's scream rang out through the darkness, jolting Bec awake. She found herself on her feet, rushing from the bedroom. They'd spent the night celebrating. Her father had won his first political state seat after months of campaigning. His rise from local council to mayor, and now state government, was being regarded as one of the quickest in history, and he'd invited friends and neighbours to celebrate his success.

Other than Chris being high on drugs and making a small scene before a security guard removed him from the party, the night had been a wonderful celebration.

Bec's mum screamed again, and she ran faster towards Chris's room where the screams were coming from. Her father's heavy footsteps beat her, and she could hear him trying to calm her mother down.

'Samara, it's okay. He'll be okay.'

'He's not okay,' her mother screamed. 'He's not breathing.'

Bec reached the doorway to find her father checking for Chris's pulse.

'Shit.' He looked up at her as he started compressions. 'Call an ambulance. Tell them it's possibly a drug overdose.'

Bec raced to the phone, and the ambulance arrived in under ten minutes, even though it felt like a lifetime. Her father collapsed, allowing the paramedics to take over, but it was too late.

* * *

Bec did her best to shake off the weight of grief that thinking about Chris and Owen brought on her. She needed to be able to focus on Skye as well as her own situation. She glanced at the teenager sitting beside her, her fingers twisted together, her foot gently tapping against the leg of her chair. While Bec had her demons to face, her heart went out to this kid doing her best to hold it together.

'I'm pleased to welcome a few new faces tonight,' Anna said, interrupting Bec's thoughts. She smiled at Bec and Skye, before focusing her gaze on a middle-aged guy in the second row.

'There's no expectation to share your stories,' she added. 'This group was set up to be a safe space for all of us. And I can tell you, while you'll discover that we all have very different stories, you'll also find that we share one important fact, and that is that we've lost loved ones, and it's left a massive hole in our hearts. It might be a recent death you're trying to come to terms with, or it might be, like me, from years ago. For those of you who are new, I'll share a little more of my story with you before I open the floor to the group.'

Bec sat mesmerised while Anna described the loss of her brother. 'Jake was one of those people who never sat still,' Anna said. 'Always on the move and pushing himself. He was a state swimmer and dreamed of becoming a pilot.' She smiled. 'Spent hours building model planes and memorising flight paths. He was funny and had an infectious personality that people gravitated to. But it was all taken from him, from us, in an instant. A car accident took his life and it also changed the course of my life – and my parents' lives too.'

The room was quiet as Anna continued. 'This happened over twenty years ago, so it isn't something new, but I still wake up most mornings and have that sweet moment of bliss where all's still right in the world before I remember. I always assumed that would go away over time. That I'd wake up remembering he was gone and not having that horrible moment of recollection, but it never did.'

'You still relive it every morning?' one of the women asked.

Anna smiled at her. 'Thankfully not every morning, but it still happens regularly enough to be awful. And I know I'm not the only one who does that. Many of you in this room still have that moment of blissful unawareness before the reality hits again.'

Bec knew exactly what she meant, and from the looks on many of the faces around her, so did a lot of them. She glanced at Skye, whose eyes were fixed firmly on the floor.

'Would anyone like to share their story tonight?' Anna asked. 'And when I say story, I don't mean relaying the details of who you lost and how, although of course you are welcome to share that. Your story may be where you're at right now and what you're struggling with. You're likely to find that others in the group have gone through the same struggles and have suggestions on how to cope.'

A man, Bec guessed probably to be in his late forties, with dark hair, greying at the temples, raised his hand.

Anna nodded. 'Thank you, Elliot, please share.'

Elliot let out a shaky breath. 'I keep thinking I did something wrong, and Maddie died because of me. I can't get it out of my head. The triple-zero operator walked me through every step –

compressions, breaths – over and over, but it wasn't enough. She didn't come back.'

A cold shiver ran through Bec as silence fell across the room. Chris didn't come back either. She knew her father had done everything possible to save him, but it hadn't been enough. Her shiver turned to anger as an image of her father's distressed face entered her mind. They should never have been in that situation. If her parents had recognised Chris's need for help earlier, or listened to her when she tried to convince them, he could have been helped.

'I keep seeing her face. Her lips were so pale. I should have been able to save her.'

Anna shook her head. 'You did everything you could. Sometimes, no matter how hard we try, the situation's out of our control. You loved her and you tried to save her.'

'But I didn't.'

'Do you think she blames you for that, or would she be devastated that you believe that?'

Elliot looked up at Anna. 'Devastated, but it doesn't change anything. She should be alive.'

'I know that feeling,' another man said, staring at his hands.

'Would you like to share, Darren?' Anna asked.

'My brother called me that night. The night he took his life. I should have stayed on the phone with him. I should have heard how desperate he was. Instead, I told him to get a good night's sleep, that he'd feel better in the morning. If I'd stayed on the phone, or better still, gone over to see him, he might still be alive.'

Murmurs of understanding went around the room, and Bec found herself shifting awkwardly in her seat. This hit exactly where it hurt when it came to Chris's death. If only she'd realised how low he was. To this day, she was sure it was completely avoidable. And of course, she blamed her father. How could she not? The only thing that he'd cared about at that time was his political career. He'd put it in front of everything. He'd turned his back on Chris two years earlier, which was without a doubt one of the main reasons Chris had opted to leave this world. He'd idolised his father before then. They both had. He was powerful and important and someone they'd both looked up to.

Skye nudged her, bringing Bec out of her thoughts and back to the group. 'Are you alright? You look weird. Kinda pale.'

Bec did her best to pull herself together, realising that another woman was speaking. Her arm was in a sling and her face badly bruised.

'Anna convinced me to come along tonight,' the woman said. 'I'm Clare. My husband died a couple of weeks ago. We were hit by another car, and the driver fled the scene. They still haven't been found.'

A chill ran down Bec's spine. This poor woman was here only weeks after this had happened? She felt Skye tense beside her as well. This was more than either of them had bargained for.

'I'm not coping all that well,' she went on to say. 'I'm furious and want the driver found and thrown in jail. I'd like him or her killed, if I'm honest.'

The group remained silent, mesmerised by Clare's emotions.

'Don't worry, I don't actually plan to kill anyone, but it feels like it'd be fair.'

'Definitely fair,' one of the women said. 'Other people destroy us, and even if they do get caught, they still get away with it. They go to prison or get fined and feel sorry for themselves. How many feel that their lives have been ruined because of what they did?'

'It's good you've come along tonight,' Anna said to Clare. 'I know it wasn't easy.' She looked to the group. 'The point I made to Clare when we first met earlier today is that this group offers us a safe space with people who understand how hard grief is.

That we're not here to judge each other, we're here to support each other. Yes, Clare is angry, and rightly so, but as we all know, there's a lot more to contemplate as her grief becomes about the loss of her husband and not so much about finding the person who did this to them.'

There were plenty of nods of agreement around the room.

'We'll be here for you,' another of the women said. 'Whatever you need. We're all here to support you.'

Clare flashed her a grateful smile.

'Now,' Anna said, 'let's take a twenty-minute break. There's tea and coffee set up in the kitchen and a delicious-looking cake Darren's wife kindly sent along with him. Help yourselves, and when we come back, we're going to enjoy a guided meditation session.'

Bec looked to Skye. 'Want a drink and something to eat?'

Skye shook her head. 'No, I'm going to find the bathrooms and then maybe go outside for some fresh air. Don't worry though, I'm not doing a runner. I'll be back before the next session starts.'

* * *

After Skye went in search of the bathrooms, Bec made her way to the kitchen to find a cup of tea. She hesitated when she realised Clare Fleming had her back to her and was extracting a teabag from her cup. She took a deep breath. Clare's pain and anger were palpable and not something Bec necessarily had the capacity for.

'Can I give you a hand?'

Clare smiled. 'No, but thanks. I'm getting better at doing things one-handed. At least it's my left arm that's broken, not the right. I think I'd be in big trouble then.'

'I'm sorry about your husband. And believe me, I'm aware of how insufficient those words are.' She reached out and took a cup from the shelf and studied the tea selection.

'Thanks,' Clare said, dropping the teabag into the bin. 'And while you're right about the words, it's still nice that people try and make you feel better.' She sighed. 'It's hard to imagine it ever getting better.'

Bec nodded. She knew exactly what Clare meant. She forced herself up each day, tried her best to seem upbeat around the kids and at work, but really, she was forcing one foot in front of the other daily. The hole Owen had left in her life was gigantic and something she doubted anything could ever refill.

'Is that your daughter you're here with?'

'No,' Bec said. 'She's attending a training course my company runs, and I thought this might be good for her. She lost someone recently and I'm hoping I might be able to get to know her situation a little better and help her.'

'Hopefully you can. I wasn't going to come tonight,' Clare admitted, 'but there was something about Anna that I liked when I met her earlier today. I saw it again tonight. The way she spoke to everyone. She's set up a nice energy here. You know, sometimes you can feel it. To be honest, this is the first time since Ned died that I feel like I've relaxed a little. Maybe it's being in a room with other people who've lost as much as I have, and in some cases more. I'm not sure. You don't feel like you're the leper, if you know what I mean. Everyone's in the same situation, or like you, supporting someone who is.'

Bec nodded. She agreed with everything Clare said.

'So, what do you do for work?'

Bec told Clare about Reclaim and the training sessions they offered. She realised her mistake almost as soon as the words started to leave her lips.

'So let me get this straight,' Clare said, her voice rising. 'If this person who murdered my husband is ever found and charged, when he or she gets out of prison, assuming they even go there, you'll happily retrain them so they can get back into the world and earn an income? That employers will fling their doors open for them?'

'Only after they've served their sentence,' Bec said. 'We certainly don't help anyone before that. And, keep in mind, quite a lot of those who come to us are young like Skye. They're dealing with difficult situations and have got themselves into trouble. Rather than sending them to prison or a youth centre, they're given the opportunity to learn new skills and hopefully get placed with an apprenticeship or job of some kind.' Clare shook her head, and Bec was aware that she could only see her own situation. 'Hey,' she said. 'I didn't mean to upset you.'

'Everything okay here?'

Bec was relieved by Anna's interruption. 'I've said the wrong thing, I'm afraid.'

'Oh?'

'I run a training centre that helps people, including youths, to rehabilitate them after prison or, for some, allow them to become a constructive member of society instead of having to serve a sentence.'

Anna nodded and turned her focus to Clare, seeming to make the connection immediately.

'And you're concerned that the driver of the vehicle will be given an opportunity like this, rather than pay for what they did?'

'Other than shooting them between the eyes,' Clare said, 'there's no punishment that is sufficient to pay for what they did.' With a shaky hand, she placed her teacup in the sink and turned to Anna. 'I'm going to go. I know my reaction is extreme, but it is what it is.'

Anna placed a hand on her shoulder. 'Why don't you stay? This is something very powerful and sharing with the group might help you and them at the same time.'

Clare shrugged off her hand. 'Not tonight. I need to calm down. I'll see you at our session later in the week.'

She didn't look at Bec as she hurried from the kitchen.

5

Anna wasn't surprised that Clare had chosen to leave; if anything, she was surprised she'd come in the first place.

'I'm so sorry,' the woman who'd upset her said. 'I can't believe I didn't think that through before I told her what I did.'

Anna smiled and held out her hand. 'I'm Anna, which you already know of course. And you're...?'

'Bec. Big mouth Bec!'

'It's not your fault. Clare's in a world of pain right now. She doesn't know if she's coming or going, and the one thing she's clinging to is how much she hates the driver of the other vehicle. It's an interesting one, because if it had been a straight-out accident and the driver hadn't fled, she might still be angry, but not to this level. She'd probably be starting to deal with her actual loss by now instead of this. Mind you, it has only been a couple of weeks. It's surprising she's even getting out of bed.'

Bec nodded. She never thought she'd say it, but perhaps the way Owen died was lucky for her. He'd gone to sleep and never woken up due to a brain aneurysm that they weren't aware he had. She wasn't put in the position of someone else causing his death or not being able to revive him, like what had happened to Elliot and his failed attempts to resuscitate his wife. Owen had been away at a conference the night it happened, so she hadn't even been the one to find him. That was one regret – that she didn't get to hold him and tell him that she loved him.

'I'd be interested in hearing more about your business,' Anna said. 'It sounds like it could be quite complementary to what we do here.'

'You've met my business partner already,' Bec said. 'Damien Murray. He said to say hi by the way. He was the one who told me about Echoes and then suggested I should bring Skye along. She's one of our clients. Lost her mum recently and is going through a hard time. Your services would probably be ideal for her. I'm sure she'd be eligible for government benefits in her situation.'

'Of course,' Anna said. 'Damien's joined us for a couple of sessions.' She frowned. 'Are you his new business partner? I only ask as he did share his story with us, and the reason he was coming to Echoes. He said it was because his business partner had passed earlier this year.'

Bec hesitated. Would it ever get any easier talking about Owen? 'That was my husband. All three of us were in business together.'

Sympathy flooded Anna's eyes. 'I'm very sorry to hear that. So, coming tonight wasn't just for Skye?'

Bec shook her head. 'I can see how much I could get out of attending regularly and possibly even my kids. I'll have a chat with them and see what they think. It's not nice that everyone here has suffered, but it is nice that you don't have to pretend you're okay. Also… even though Owen's passing is still new and raw, there's something else. In fact you and I share a similar loss, because I also lost my brother twenty years ago. Not the same circumstances as you, but I do understand what it's like to lose a brother and not recover from it.'

Anna sighed. 'I'm sorry about your brother. People think I should be over it by now, but I'll never get over it. It's shaped who I am, which is possibly the same for you?'

Bec nodded. 'It's why I set up Reclaim. Chris was suffering mental health issues, and—' her voice caught briefly as it always did when she told Chris's story '—he took his life. He needed intervention and help a couple of years earlier when he was facing a rough time. He turned to drugs instead of help, and that was the result.'

'That's awfully sad,' Anna said. 'I guess at least one good thing that's come from it is that you've helped a lot of people.' She glanced at her watch. 'As much as I'd like to keep chatting, I'd better get the group started again. It's lovely to have met you, Bec.'

***

Two hours later, Anna put the key in the lock of her Prahran apartment and pushed open the front door. Except for Clare Fleming's angry departure, the evening had gone well. She'd particularly enjoyed meeting Bec. There was something she'd immediately liked about her. Perhaps the fact that they'd both lost brothers gave them a connection.

She smiled as the rapid, light patter of paws got louder and Smoko hurried up the hallway tiles. He mewed loudly when he reached her, butting his head against her leg as he circled her ankles. She scooped him up and carried him back down the hallway to the kitchen and open-plan living area. 'Miss me, did you?'

Smoko rubbed his face against hers, causing her to laugh.

'You're the best boyfriend ever, you know that, Smoko?' The cat meowed in agreement, as Anna placed him down on the floor and her bag on the bench. 'Let's get you some dinner.'

Moments later she watched as he wolfed down his food. You'd think he'd been starved for days.

When she and her now ex-husband had separated, one of the first things she did was go to the animal shelter. She loved cats. Had grown up with them and always had one or two in the house, but her ex wasn't a cat person and wouldn't budge. 'Get as many dogs as you want,' he'd said, 'but no cats.'

She should have known they weren't compatible the moment he said that. Smoko, however, was perfect. The shelter had named him, *partly cause he's grey and smoke-coloured*, one of them had said, *and partly cause he's the type of cat that you need when you want to take a break from life. He's there when you need a smoko.* Anna had loved that idea, particularly as it reminded her of her father who, like many Australians, had always referred to morning and afternoon tea as *smoko*. She'd needed time out from life after the separation and Smoko certainly helped keep her in the moment and made her feel loved when he snuggled up against her at night.

She glanced at the clock. She imagined she'd missed most of the information from the budget, which would have been handed down by now. Not that it mattered. Even if there were cuts in funding, it wouldn't be obvious immediately how the centre would be impacted.

Her phone rang as she had this thought. She took it from her bag, half expecting it to be Isabella. Her stomach dropped when she saw Willowridge flash up on her screen. A call in the evening from the care facility where her mother lived was never a good thing.

She accepted the call, expecting the worst.

'Anna, it's Marty from Willowridge.'

'Is Mum okay?' Anna realised as soon as the words left her lips that it wasn't the most gracious of greetings, but she also knew that Marty would understand. Calls from the aged care facility were rarely good news.

'Physically, yes, but she's very agitated tonight. We've done our best to calm her, but she keeps asking for Jake.'

'Oh,' Anna said. This had happened before, with her mother believing Jake was still alive.

'She's been pacing up and down for hours. We'll probably need to sedate her but I wanted to ask if you had the time to come and visit. It might help. She's trying to remember something about some friend of your father's, so you might be able to help her with that.'

'I'll leave now,' Anna said. 'See you in about thirty.'

6

Zara's frustration levels rose as she lay on her bed and stared at her computer screen. She had no idea why her mother continued to lie about her grandparents being dead, but she was determined to find out the truth. The problem was, all of the obvious searches she'd done – Google, Facebook and even Trove, which she'd never even heard of before but an AI program suggested she look at – had come up with nothing. Trove, being digital newspapers, had no record of a house fire or of her grandparents at all back in the year her mother claimed their house had burnt down.

Her mother was lying; she knew that much. She had no idea why but she had a right to know who her family were. Maybe they were criminals or in jail, or deadbeats and that was why her mother was lying. But that made no sense. She wouldn't want anything to do with them if they were, so her mother could just tell the truth. No, it was something else.

She put their names into Google again, just on the off chance something new appeared. The page was littered with hundreds of John and Mary Smiths. The more she scrolled, the more ridiculous it felt.

She stopped scrolling, anger welling inside her. Of course! Her mother had picked the most boring, untraceable names possible. Heat prickled at the back of her neck. She'd known deep down her mum was hiding something about her grandparents, but she'd never thought to question their names or her mother's maiden name, if it was even Smith. Now she was furious at her own gullibility and at her mother for treating her like a fool.

'Zar!'

She jumped at Hugo's frantic cry that was followed by a loud bang.

'Shit. Jesus. Shit. Zar!' Further crashes and bangs erupted from the kitchen as her brother continued swearing.

She leapt from her bed and hurried to see what was going on. She stopped in the doorway of the kitchen as her foot landed in cold water spreading across the tiles. Water gushed from beneath the kitchen sink.

'Turn it off,' she shouted, her voice high-pitched in panic.

'I'm trying,' Hugo yelled back. He swore again and then visibly relaxed as the water stopped gushing.

'Thank God,' Zara said, her hand firmly clasped over her mouth. She surveyed the kitchen floor, noticing the water wasn't far from the carpeted area of the home office, which ran off the kitchen. 'I'll grab towels,' she called to Hugo. 'You get the mop.'

* * *

Bec's mind had flittered all over the place during the guided meditation Anna finished the evening with. She would have loved to have lost herself in it, but didn't seem to be able to. Her mind jumped from thoughts of Owen to Chris, to Clare, to Skye and even to Anna's situation. She would have failed meditation if it were a graded subject.

When the evening was over, she turned to Skye, who looked like she'd had more success with the meditation. It was the most relaxed Bec had seen her.

'Pizza and pasta's still on offer at Sophia's,' she said. 'It's not far from here.'

Skye frowned. 'The way you spoke about it earlier I thought it was part of the night. You can't pay for another meal for me.'

'Yes I can and I'd like to,' Bec said.

'Why?'

'Because you need food and talking to you distracts me from my own issues, of which I can assure you, there are plenty. Now, I'm hungry and the way your stomach was rumbling through the meditation, I'd say you are too.'

Skye blushed, but Bec was pleased when she nodded. 'I am, thank you.'

Bec's phone pinged before she had a chance to respond. She slipped it from her bag, read Hugo's message and swore under her breath.

'Everything okay?'

'My son. Sounds like a pipe's burst under the kitchen sink or something like that. He's dealing with the cleanup.' She sighed. 'I'll need to go home and help. How about we go and grab some takeaways, and I'll drop you off at your friend's place?'

'Friend's place?'

'The friend you're staying with tonight. You seem to have all your things in that backpack you're lugging around, so I assume you're moving to somewhere new?'

Skye's blush deepened. 'Oh yeah, sorry, wasn't thinking. But no, that's okay. You've got enough to deal with. I can find food on my way to my friend's. She doesn't live too far from here. I'll see you at Reclaim tomorrow.'

Bec shook her head. 'No. I want to deliver you there. It's not safe for a sixteen-year-old to be wandering around on their own after dark.'

Skye rolled her eyes, and Bec could only imagine where she'd been at night since her mother died.

'So,' Bec said. 'Let's get some food and then I'll drop you off. I might call Hugo first. My son. Check that he's got everything under control.'

A few minutes later, when Hugo had assured Bec that he and Zara were mopping up and they'd isolated the pipe that connected to the water filter, Bec and Skye made their way across the road to Sophia's to order takeaway.

'The pizzas are sensational,' Bec said as she ordered pizzas for herself and Hugo and Zara. 'Choose anything you want.'

Skye chose her pizza, and after ordering, they moved outside to the tables that were available for people to wait for their orders.

'How did you find the Echoes group?' Bec asked Skye as they found a quiet spot to wait.

'Okay,' Skye said. 'The meditation bit was good. I'm not sure if I want to hear about other people's problems, though. I've got enough of my own.'

Bec studied the girl; it was the second time she'd mentioned not wanting to hear or deal with other people's problems, which was interesting. She gave a small laugh. 'You and I are total opposites.'

'What do you mean?'

'I do everything possible to take on other people's problems rather than deal with my own, whereas you're very aware of not doing that so that you can deal with your stuff.'

'I'm not saying I'm dealing with it,' Skye said. 'I just don't want to have to try and help someone else. That sounds bad, doesn't it?'

'Not at all. It sounds very honest. We all have a different capacity to deal with things.'

'What are your kids like?' Skye asked, a not-very-subtle change of subject.

'Same age as you,' Bec said. 'Twins. Hugo's more mature than Zara.' She smiled. 'She does her best to push my buttons.'

'Pizza for Bec,' the young guy at the register called out.

They moved inside, collected the pizza boxes and headed towards Bec's car.

'Where am I dropping you?'

'Let me grab my bag,' Skye said. 'I can walk from here. It's around the corner.'

'Nope,' Bec said. 'Not an option.' She unlocked the car and stopped as she saw Skye's face. It had drained of colour. She'd been pretty sure earlier on that Skye had nowhere to stay tonight, and now she was certain.

'Jump in. You're coming back to my place tonight. No arguments.'

* * *

Bec and Skye travelled the few minutes to Bec's Camberwell house in silence. Bec was aware she shouldn't be taking a client home with her, but it was her business, and she and Damien made up the rules. Yes, it could backfire spectacularly if Skye decided to accuse her of something, but her gut feeling was that this was a good kid sitting next to her.

'Are your kids going to be okay with me coming back with you?'

Bec shot her a sideways look, seeing the apprehension on her face. 'Definitely, although I'll apologise for Zara before you even meet her. She can be a bit full on at times.'

Bec could hear the raised voices of her children as she parked in her driveway and killed the car's engine. And they weren't raised in fun. She was sure the neighbours halfway down the street were tuning in to the angry confrontation.

She indicated for Skye to bring her bag, and she took the pizza boxes from the back seat of the car. Hugo's volume went up a notch as she reached the front door. Part of her was ready to push it open and demand they calm down, but at Hugo's words, she found herself stopping.

'Just leave it, Zar. Mum's been through enough. She doesn't need this too.'

'But she's lied to us all our lives. She said her parents died in a house fire twenty years ago. I looked up digital newspaper records and there were no house fires in Canterbury that year, or the year before or after. Their names aren't even real. I can't believe I've only just realised that.'

Bec froze.

'Don't be stupid,' Hugo said. 'She's not going to lie about their names. If she was, she'd have thought of something better than John and Mary Smith.'

A very good point, and one Bec should have thought of when she quickly made up the names when Zara had asked about her grandparents years ago.

'She's not getting away with it,' Zara said. 'As soon as she gets home, I'm going to make her tell the truth.'

Bec gave Skye an apologetic smile and pushed open the door. 'Hey, you two,' she called, adding as much enthusiasm to her voice as possible. 'We've got a guest, so how about you lower your voices?'

She was met by silence, but she could imagine the fury on Zara's face.

She entered the kitchen with Skye trailing behind her to find Zara with a forced smile and Hugo looking like thunder.

'This is Skye,' she said, stepping out of Skye's way. 'Hugo and Zara,' she said, pointing to her twins.

'Hey,' all three teenagers said at once.

Bec held up the pizza boxes. 'Food, but first tell me what happened here.' She glanced at the towels that had been heaped in a pile at the side of the kitchen.

'The water filter under the sink burst,' Hugo said. 'It was fine when I left for the gym, but there was water everywhere when I got home. I've had a look, and it has a little tap that I was able to turn off. We can still use the normal taps. We'll need to get a plumber in to fix it if you want to keep using it.'

'Thanks, Hugo,' Bec said. 'And both of you for cleaning up. Thank God for tiles. At least the floor won't be damaged.'

'Just very clean,' Zara said. She was eyeing Skye curiously.

'How about you get some plates out, Zar?' Bec said. 'Hugo, you get some drinks for everyone, and I'll quickly show Skye the spare room so she can put her bag down. She'll be staying with us tonight.'

Hugo and Zara exchanged a look, and Bec could see they were dying to know Skye's story. She hoped they, or more specifically, Zara, would be gentle with her and she hoped Zara would leave questioning her about her parents until later… until she'd had time to think up what she was going to say.

* * *

Bec was pleased to see Skye relaxing around Zara and Hugo. Hugo was being particularly kind, running through the selection of drinks that were on offer, which was slightly chlorinated tap water with the option of fresh lemon or lime, and going to more effort than usual, ensuring Skye's glass was one of the nicer ones and had plenty of ice.

'So, what's your story?' Zara said, glancing at Skye as she lifted a slice of pizza from the boxes they'd spread on the kitchen table.

'Zara!' Bec admonished.

'What? I'm interested.' She rolled her eyes and gave Skye a conspiratorial grin. 'My mum's kind of crazy. You and I know exactly what I was asking you whereas she thinks I'm prying into your personal stuff.' She turned to face Bec. 'Don't worry, Mum, I'm not interested in Skye's sex life or when her period is.'

Bec shook her head, about to apologise to Skye again, when Skye started to laugh. She looked at Bec. 'It's fine. I should probably tell you the full story anyway. You've only been fed selected bits. My story is pretty crap, to be honest. I used to go to school in Richmond, but my mum died a couple of months back, and I have no idea where my dad is, never met him, so if I go back to school, I'll end up in foster care.'

'That sucks,' Zara said. 'Why would going back to school mean you end up in foster care?'

''Cause they'll know where I am,' Skye said. 'Right now I should be with a foster family and I'm choosing not to be, and because I'm only sixteen, that's not my choice.'

'Don't you have any other family?' Bec asked, this being complete news to her, but suddenly she realised it made sense.

Skye shook her head. 'No, so I was kind of hiding out from the education department and the police, but then I got caught shoplifting and ended up with the cops anyway. I told them I'd dropped out of school, so they put me in the program at your work rather than putting me in some kind of kid jail.'

Bec had difficulty swallowing her pizza as she listened to Skye being so casual in her storytelling.

'But the cops did try and put you in a foster home then?' Zara said.

Skye bit into a slice of pizza, her eyes rolling back as she did. 'Yum, this is so good. Sophia's was my mum's favourite. We went there for her birthday every year.'

Hugo glanced at Bec; his eyes filled with concern. At least one of her two children could see this situation was anything but normal.

'And yes, they put me in a foster home, but I've chosen to stay with friends instead.'

'Cool. Are you allowed to do that?'

Skye shook her head and grinned, causing Zara's eyes to widen before she joined in the laughter. 'Nah, but they were a shitty family. I think they were looking for a babysitter for their little kids. That's not something I want to be doing.'

'You should listen to this, Mum,' Zara said. 'If you stopped lying about my grandparents not existing then I'd have options if something happened to you. But no, you continue to lie and if you suddenly aren't here, Hugo and I'll be put into foster care and be expected to raise someone's shitty brats.'

Bec stared at her daughter. Was this really behind Zara's quest to find more family? She was worried that she might be orphaned at some point?

Zara didn't wait for a response. 'So, what are you going to do then? Do you like school? Do you want to go back?'

Skye nodded. 'I'd prefer to do that than the course they're making me do. No offence,' she said to Bec, 'but electrical safety isn't something I've dreamed my whole life of doing.'

Zara snorted. 'Is that the punishment for shoplifting these days? What did you steal anyway? Anything valuable?'

Bec might as well have been having an out-of-body experience watching this conversation take place. She thought of Anna briefly, imagining in her counselling role that she had to use all kinds of clever strategies to extract information from clients, and here Skye was unloading the lot, seemingly unbothered by Zara's unfiltered questions.

Skye shook her head at Zara's last question, her cheeks red. 'Food. That's all. Nothing exciting.'

'So let me get this straight,' Zara said. 'You're hiding from your foster family and, in effect, the cops or whoever is supposed to be looking after you. You have no money and no food and can't go to school or they'll catch you and force you back to the foster family.'

Skye nodded.

Zara took a bite of her pizza, chewing thoughtfully. 'Why don't you stay here then? We have plenty of food. Mum's kind of respectable, so they probably wouldn't object to that.' She looked at Bec. 'Would they?'

Bec was doing her best not to choke on her pizza. 'I'm pretty sure there are requirements to become a foster carer; they won't let just anyone do it.'

'Don't worry,' Skye said. 'I'm not expecting you to do that. But I would appreciate it if I could stay tonight.'

'Do we need to call anyone?' Bec asked. 'The actual foster family? They must be worried about you.'

'No,' Skye said. 'I haven't stayed there in over a week. I don't think they're looking for me. My caseworker is, but not the foster family. And the caseworker can't be looking too hard, considering it's all over my file that I'm doing the course at your work.'

'Still, we should probably contact your caseworker and let them know you're okay,' Bec said.

'She'll want to bring me in if you do,' Skye said. 'Can we leave it until tomorrow at least? I don't want to have to go somewhere else now.'

Bec nodded. 'Okay, but first thing in the morning we'll let them know you're safe and check that she's aware you're at Reclaim doing the course.'

* * *

After checking Skye was settled in the spare room, and saying goodnight to Hugo and Zara, Bec was pleased to close her bedroom door on the day. She wished Owen was there to talk to about Zara and about Bec's parents. He knew the truth about them and her background, but she'd never had any intention of her children finding them if they were alive. The last thing she wanted was them back in her life or the lives of her kids.

Skye's arrival had at least brought her some time as Zara's focus appeared to have moved to Skye's problems rather than her own.

She was about to change into her pyjamas when there was a gentle knock on the door.

She opened it, half expecting to see Skye on the other side, but instead, was faced with an angry-looking Zara.

She sighed and opened the door wider as Zara pushed her way into the room. It appeared she wasn't going to have any thinking time after all.

'What are my grandparents' names?'

Bec stared at her daughter.

'Come on, Mum, tell me. I'm not so stupid that I believe they were actually called Mary and John. There's no record of any house fire in Canterbury in 2005 either. You're lying – why won't you just admit it?'

Bec let out a defeated sigh. 'Okay, fine. Go and get Hugo and

I'll meet you in the kitchen. I'm going to need a drink to get through this.'

A few minutes later Bec sat down at the island bench, having poured herself a glass of wine. She hated to imagine where this confession might lead.

Hugo and Zara appeared moments later and sat down next to her.

She sipped her wine, unable to ignore the daggers flying from her daughter's eyes. 'Why are you looking so angry? I haven't even started speaking yet.'

'Because you're going to make up more lies. Admit it, your parents are alive and you don't want me to contact them.'

'Zar,' Hugo said. 'Let Mum talk.'

Bec shot him a grateful smile as Zara folded her arms across her chest.

She took a deep breath. 'Here goes.' She looked directly at Zara. 'Firstly, you're right, I haven't been honest about your grandparents, my parents. They didn't die in a fire and from what I know are still alive.'

'See,' Zara said, looking to Hugo. 'Told you.'

'Shut up,' Hugo said, his expression shocked as he turned his attention to Bec. 'Why did you tell us they were dead?'

'They were dead to me,' Bec said. 'I've told you about my brother.'

'That he died in an accident when you were a teenager. That's true, isn't it?' Hugo asked.

Bec nodded. 'He died, but it wasn't an accident.' She took a deep breath. 'Chris took his own life.'

Her children exchanged a glance.

'That's awful,' Hugo said. 'Do you know why?'

'It's a long story,' Bec said, 'but the important part and why I left home was that my parents covered up his suicide. They told everyone he was killed in a car accident rather than facing up to the fact that they'd failed their son, and he ended his life.' As the words left her lips she expected Zara to point out the irony that she'd lied about her parents' death, although it wasn't quite the same. Her parents hadn't actually died.

But she didn't. Instead, silence filled the kitchen. Eventually, Hugo spoke. 'I'm sorry, Mum. I can't imagine how that would have been for you.'

'It was awful,' Bec admitted. 'It's something you never get over, and my way of dealing with it was to start again. I couldn't stay part of a family that would be so dismissive of the pain he was in and what it led him to. My dad shut me down any time I tried to bring Chris into the conversation.'

Bec was transported back twenty years.

* * *

'I've told you I don't want to hear his name in this house again.' Her father, Bruce's eyes flashed with anger. 'He was a coward, and I'm ashamed to have called him my son.'

'A coward?' Tears streamed down Bec's face as she confronted her father. 'You're the coward. Covering up his suicide. Not letting on that he was suicidal. If you'd paid any attention to him in the last two years, you'd know how much he'd been struggling.'

'He brought that on himself, didn't he?'

'No, you did. Everything he was suffering was your fault,' Bec cried. 'Why can't you see that turning your back on him was what killed him?'

'Turning my back on him? What you should be looking at, Rebecca, is what I did for him. My actions were to save him and look how he repaid me.'

'Do you really believe that?'

'Of course I do. I would have done anything for Chris. The same way I would have done anything for you. How I raised such ungrateful kids, I'll never know.'

The fury on her father's face had been the final straw that pushed Bec to leave. She couldn't be around a man who, in her opinion, was not only the cause of Chris's death but couldn't see himself in the wrong, under any circumstances.

* * *

'About four months after we buried Chris, I packed my bags and left. I couldn't stand listening to my dad refuse to let us talk about Chris at home. He even made my mum remove all the family photos and any mementos of him. But then, if anyone outside the family brought Chris up in conversation, he'd talk proudly about what a wonderful son he was and how much he missed him. It was awful.'

'Didn't they try and stop you leaving or come after you?' Hugo asked.

'I didn't tell them I was leaving,' Bec said. 'I was twenty, so I wasn't a runaway teen. I drove to Sydney and, up until a few months ago, stayed there. I made it very difficult for them to find me.'

Zara frowned. 'But you have LinkedIn and Facebook. They could find you easily. You have real photos on both of those accounts.'

'I do, but they don't know me as Rebecca Smith or my married surname. Rebecca Sampson isn't someone they'd be searching for.'

'What do you mean, they don't know you as Rebecca Smith?' Hugo said. 'I thought that was your maiden name. Did you change your name when you left? Or was Zara right?'

'Zara was right. Smith wasn't my surname and their names aren't John and Mary. My surname was Langford,' Bec said. 'Rebecca Jane Langford. You'll find the family quickly enough. Dad was a high-profile politician. They moved to Canberra a few years after Chris died.'

'And you've never spoken to them?' Hugo said. 'They don't know about me and Zara?'

Bec shook her head.

'What are their names?' Zara asked.

'Bruce and Samara Langford.'

Zara already had her phone out and was googling her grandparents.

Bec placed a hand over her daughter's hand and phone. 'I'm telling you this because you're old enough to know the truth, but Zara...'

Zara looked at her mother expectantly.

'...I don't want those people invited back into my life. I can't stop you from contacting them, but at the same time, I'm asking you not to.'

Zara continued to stare at Bec.

'Zar, promise Mum,' Hugo said.

Zara turned to her brother. 'Aren't you curious?'

He nodded. 'Of course, and I'll probably google them. But for Mum to leave her family is massive. She wouldn't have done it if the situation weren't terrible.'

Zara nodded slowly. 'I guess.'

Bec smiled at her son. 'Thanks.' She looked at Zara, tempted to say more but knowing it was pointless. Her daughter was incredibly determined, and it was quite clear from the defiant look on her face that she would ignore Bec's wishes.

Hugo stood. 'I'm going to bed if that's okay.'

'Of course it is,' Bec said. 'And Hugo, and you too, Zara, I'm sorry I've lied to you for so long. Let me assure you, there was a reason. What I believed was a good one and I hope that you'll both respect my wishes and not invite them into our lives.'

Bec's stomach churned as her children retreated from the kitchen, Zara not acknowledging Bec's request. Knowing her daughter, her days were numbered before she saw her parents again.

7

Marty was waiting for Anna when she hurried into the reception area of the Willowridge care home. His dark hair, sporting flecks of silver, made him look younger than his mid-forties, and the easy smile that seemed to live on his lips made him instantly approachable.

'Hey, I'm really sorry but your mum's calmed down. It might have been a false alarm, but she got very agitated earlier.'

'Did she think Jake was still alive?'

'No, which was why I was a little more concerned than usual,' Marty said. 'In many ways, she was quite accurate with her memories, but still very agitated. I went in a few minutes ago and it was like it never happened. She was reading a book.'

Anna let out a sigh of relief. 'Honestly, that's a better scenario than I was thinking I was walking into. I'll go and visit.'

With a smile firmly fixed in place, Anna walked towards her mother's room.

She pushed open the door, surprised to find her mother sitting in the armchair next to her bed with the television off and a book in her hands.

'Hey, Mum.'

Lyn looked up, a wide smile breaking across her face. 'Annie, it's so good to see you.'

Anna tensed. As much as she should love her mother's greeting, Annie was Lyn's best friend throughout her childhood and was who Anna was named after. When her mother called her Annie, she was never sure who Lyn thought was visiting.

She reached down and gave her mother a hug before pulling the other chair up close to her. 'What are you reading?'

Lyn held up the book proudly. 'One of yours.'

Well, that made it easy to identify who she thought was visiting, Annie Broztri, her mother's friend, was also a well-known crime author.

She laid a hand on her mother's knee. 'Mum, it's me, Anna. Not Annie.'

Lyn frowned and her eyes glazed over momentarily before she seemed to shake herself and look directly at Anna. 'Of course, love, sorry. I was so caught up in the book, I forgot for a moment. And you do look a lot like Annie, don't forget. It's easy to confuse the two of you.'

Anna relaxed. Having to pretend she was Annie for the visit was never much fun. She was about to ask her mother about her day when Lyn jumped up and started pacing the small room.

'Mum?'

'I need to know who it was,' Lyn said. 'I need to know.'

'Mum?' Anna spoke gently, but her mother didn't seem to hear her.

Marty appeared at the door. 'Everything okay?'

'It was, but I think she's gone back to where you said she was earlier.'

'I need to know the truth,' Lyn said. 'Mal knew. He told Xavier. Xavier will know.'

Anna turned to meet Marty's eye. He raised his hands in question.

She shook her head; she had no idea who Xavier was. 'Mum?' Anna said again, this time getting her mother's attention.

'Oh, Anna, thank God you're here. We need to go. Right now. Find Xavier and ask him.'

'Ask him what?'

'Ask him who killed Jake. He knows.' She frowned. 'Something wasn't right about the accident. Your dad knew what it was and told Xavier. Asked him for advice. We need to find out so we can tell the police.'

'Oh, Mum,' Anna said. 'Jake's accident happened over twenty years ago.'

Lyn shook her head. 'No, don't be silly. It was last month. My poor boy died last month, and we need to find Xavier.' Her voice was steadily rising, soon to hit a point of hysteria.

Anna tried to put her arms around her mother to comfort her, but she shook them off. 'Find him, Anna. We need to do this for Jake.'

Anna looked to Marty for help. His clear blue eyes met hers, as her mother continued reliving the pain of twenty-two years ago as if it had happened that day. She had no idea what to do other than wait and let her ride it out.

'As much as I hate suggesting this,' Marty said, 'I think it might be worth sedating her. She's worked herself into a state that I can't see us getting her out of quickly. Are you happy if we give her something, Anna? It'll be a light sedative, but it will take the edge off her angst and help her sleep.'

Anna nodded, fatigue washing over her. She hated to think what must be going through her mother's mind. She kept flipping between references to Mal and Jake. At some stages, it was clear she knew Jake was dead, but she also seemed to think it had just happened, and Mal was still alive. But in the next breath, she needed to find out the truth of what Mal had said before he died. What was clear was that she was desperate to leave the facility and find someone called Xavier.

'You looked wiped,' Marty said as Anna, having kissed her now-sleeping mother on the forehead, made her way out of the room and towards the exit.

Anna smiled at him. 'Long day, that's all. And it's always draining when Mum's like this. Thank you for calling me and for looking after her.'

Marty frowned. 'She kept going on about this Xavier. Are you sure there wasn't someone by that name from your past? Or one of your dad's friends or hers?'

'I don't recall anyone by that name being a friend of either of them.' She cast her memory back, picturing the neighbours, friends of the family and even people her father worked with. It was an unusual name and one that she thought she would remember.

'It might be someone she met after your dad passed,' Marty suggested.

'I don't remember her meeting anyone new. She pretty much became a recluse. And she was saying that Dad would have told Xavier what happened, so that suggests Dad knew him.'

'You're right, I forgot about that bit.' Marty frowned. 'I guess it could have been anyone. His accountant, lawyer, barber, the guy down the road, or at the corner café. It's a bit like how long is a piece of string?'

Anna froze. 'That's it! You're a genius!'

'I am?'

Anna nodded. 'Xavier's was my dad's favourite restaurant! It was tucked away in an alley that runs off Little Collins Street. He always took Mum there for special occasions. I guess that could have been what she was talking about. Possibly the guy who owned it or someone who worked there.'

Marty pulled out his phone and keyed something into it. 'Xavier's, 8 Punt Lane, Melbourne.' He held his screen up for Anna to see. 'That photo's of the owner, Xavier Lowell, at the restaurant's fiftieth birthday celebrations.' He glanced at the screen. 'Taken last month. He's still alive.'

* * *

Zara stared at her phone. She'd found them!

Bruce and Samara Langford. They didn't look like the monsters her mother had made them out to be. She'd spent the past hour since her mother admitted the truth reading about them online. Her grandfather was a politician, or had been at least, and there was plenty of news items and articles about him. Her mum had been right that they'd moved to Canberra at one stage, but a recent article showed them living back in Melbourne and her grandfather had some sort of consultancy.

Surely he couldn't be that bad? When you read his policies, it sounded like he'd done all sorts of good things. Housing for the homeless. Additional funding for men's mental health. There was even a photo of him kissing a baby. Although that was completely cringe, but she assumed some publicist thought it was a good idea.

There wasn't as much on her grandmother, but it looked like she was active in the community, supporting charities and volunteering.

One benefit of having such a public-facing grandparent was that she would be able to contact him easily enough. She'd found an email address that would go to his office. She'd prefer to send a letter to their home, but she imagined that would be harder to find.

She pushed away a twinge of guilt when she thought of her mother and how she'd feel about this. Zara closed her eyes, imagining for a moment a big Christmas celebration filled with family. It'd be so nice. It'd almost make up for her dad not being there. As long as she could remember, it had been the four of them celebrating big events. Sometimes friends would come over, but it was never family. And now there would only be three of them. Since she was a little girl, she'd envied her friends who had large family gatherings.

She decided she couldn't wait. She was going to email her grandfather now, but she also knew she needed to give thought to what she was going to say first. She'd like to tell them all about herself and Hugo but knew better than launching into that detail and expecting them to be happy to hear from her. She had to play it cool. She picked up her laptop from her bed and started a new email.

Dear…

She stopped. What did she call them? It'd be weird to call them Grandma and Grandpa or anything like that, but equally weird to use their first names or even say Dear Mr Langford. She dismissed the thought and started again.

Hi. My name is Zara Sampson, and I believe we might be related. My mother is Rebecca Jane Langford. I'd like to make contact with you. Please reply via email or phone.

She added her phone number and stared at the message.

Very brief, told them everything they needed to know about her and gave them the option to contact her.

Nervous energy fluttered through her. What if they didn't contact her? What if they did? How would she react to either scenario? What if they turned up? What would her mother say? She shook her head. They weren't going to turn up, especially as she hadn't sent the message yet and hadn't included her address.

She reread the message. Maybe she'd remove her surname in case they did track her down. As much as she wanted to meet them, she wanted to make sure it was on her terms. She knew how her mother felt, and while she was going against her mother's wishes, she still wanted to do this as carefully as possible.

She changed the message to use her first name only and sent it. She closed the lid of her laptop and lay back on her bed. Well, she'd done it now; there was no turning back. As much as she knew her mum would kill her, her gut told her she was doing the right thing.

* * *

There were some nights that Anna wished she kept alcohol in the house, and tonight was one of them. But having watched her mother drink herself almost to death, alcohol was something she restricted to social occasions, and she never drank alone.

She picked up Smoko who'd been rubbing around her ankles since she'd arrived home, and smiled as he nestled into her neck. She often wondered if she should get him a friend. The days when she was out late for work always seemed unfair on him, and the fact that he was extra cuddly on her long workdays suggested he missed her more than usual.

She put him down when they reached the kitchen and switched on the kettle to make herself a cup of tea, her thoughts shifting to the next day. As she thought through ideas for an extension of the Echoes group her phone rang.

She slipped it from her bag and frowned at the unknown number. Her general rule was to let all unknown numbers go to voicemail, but for some reason she found herself answering the call.

'Anna?'

Anna's heart caught in her throat. Even after all these years she'd know that voice anywhere.

'Anna, it's Kieran.'

She remained silent.

He cleared his throat. 'Um, Kieran Bradley.'

Anna drew in a breath. 'I know who you are, I just can't imagine why you'd be contacting me.'

'I know and as inadequate as it is, I'm sorry.'

Anna had no idea what to say. Kieran, her boyfriend at the time, had disappeared the morning after Jake died and his parents made it very clear that he didn't want anyone knowing where he was. He'd gone to deal with his grief in his own way. At the time Anna assumed it would be for days, possibly weeks... not twenty-two years.

Kieran cleared his throat. 'I guess I owe you an explanation.'

Anna couldn't help the wry laugh that passed her lips. 'A bit late.'

'I know. There's no excuse. All I can say is I couldn't handle what happened.'

'And you thought I could?'

'I wasn't thinking. That was the problem. I lost my best friend. Jake was closer than a brother to me. I couldn't stay and watch everyone suffer. I knew I couldn't be there for you; I was such a mess. For the first few years, I tried my best to push anything connected with Jake away. And I know how lame that sounds. It's why, when I got my head together finally, I couldn't face you or your family.'

Anna was silent. She'd gone through this moment thousands of times in her head; if she ever heard from Kieran again, what she would say to him. That she'd rip through him, possibly even hit him, she'd been so hurt by him. But instead, she sighed. 'We both lost so much that night. We didn't just lose Jake, we lost our dream too.'

'I know. I don't think I've ever properly recovered. My late wife, Paige, she's the one who encouraged me to stop running from everything connected to Jake. Told me I had to face it and deal with my grief.'

'Your late wife?'

'Yes, Paige died twelve months ago.'

'I'm sorry, Kieran, I really am.'

'Thank you. But the one thing she did do was convince me that at some stage I needed to get back in touch and I needed to try and make things right. I'd planned to contact you over two years ago, but then she got sick and she passed away and life just felt too hard. I feel like I'm coming out of a fog finally and the anniversary of Jake's death a few weeks ago made it clear to me that this is what I should be doing.' He hesitated. 'I'd like to see you, Anna. To try and explain properly and to hear what you've done with your life. Would you have dinner with me on Thursday?'

Anna took a deep breath, surprising herself with her response. 'It'd be nice to see you. Hear about your life. So yes, Thursday sounds good. Text me the details.'

8

Bec could have kicked herself. She'd been lulled into a false sense of security the previous night, listening to Skye confide in all of them. It hadn't crossed her mind that the teenager would disappear in the middle of the night. She'd been more concerned about Zara when she'd gone to bed, and what she was going to do with the information she now had about her grandparents.

'What did you expect?' Zara said, rolling her eyes when Bec quizzed her the next morning to see if she knew anything about Skye's disappearance. 'You tell her you're going to contact her caseworker, which most likely means she'll end up back with the foster family she hates. It was hardly rocket science for anyone to work that out.'

'Do you know where she's gone?'

Zara shrugged. 'Not exactly. She mentioned a friend in Richmond, so maybe there.'

'She has to be at Reclaim this morning,' Bec said, 'or she'll be in breach of her conditions there, too.'

'Well, if she turns up,' Zara said, seemingly unfazed by the situation, 'tell her I said hi.' With that, she'd disappeared into her room to get ready for school.

Now, as Bec arrived at work and hurried from the car, she could only hope Skye would be there.

'Everything okay?' Damien asked as she dashed through the front door of the centre.

She stopped. 'Hoping Skye Miller's here, that's all.'

Damien glanced at his watch. 'The course doesn't start for almost an hour.'

Bec sighed. 'I know, but I've stuffed up.' She went on to tell him of the visit to Echoes the previous night and then her taking Skye home with her. 'I know I shouldn't have done that, and in hindsight I should have insisted on calling her caseworker last night, but that's all too late now.'

'Don't worry for now,' Damien said. 'If she doesn't turn up at nine, then we'll discuss next steps. We're supposed to notify the police administrators if she's a no-show, but we'll deal with that if it's relevant. Now, let's get you a coffee and you can tell me what you thought about Echoes and Anna Morrison.'

* * *

Anna's mind was all over the place the next day when she arrived at work. Hearing from Kieran had been so unexpected and she wasn't sure how she felt about it. She guessed she didn't have to overthink it. She'd see him the next night and quite likely never again after that. She had to admit, she was intrigued to learn where he'd gone and what he'd done with his life.

Her thoughts swirled and she found herself thinking of her mother. She was touched by Marty's kindness the previous night. Willowridge were certainly lucky to have him, as was her mother. He'd offered to come with her to

Xavier's if she decided to take her mother along. They learned from the restaurant's website that Xavier's ninety-year-old owner and namesake was still actively involved in running the business. Anna would call the restaurant and make sure Xavier would be there before making plans for an outing.

She was sitting at her desk, only an hour into the day, when her phone rang. She answered it, not recognising the number.

'Anna, it's Bec Sampson. We met last night at Echoes. I was there with Skye.'

'Of course, I remember you.' What she didn't remember was Bec's voice being so full of anxiety. 'Is everything okay?'

'No, not really, and I'm not quite sure why I'm calling you, but I'll fill you in anyway.'

'Go ahead,' Anna said, intrigued.

A few minutes later, she sat in silence, thinking. She'd thought Bec might want to speak about the synergy their two organisations might have, not be calling her for advice about Skye.

'Anna?'

'Sorry,' she said. 'I was thinking through the best approach. Unfortunately, you will need to let her caseworker know that she's not shown up to Reclaim today. If she doesn't have a good reason, and by that, I mean a doctor's certificate, it's going to cause problems with the police.'

'But if I do find her,' Bec said, 'is her situation one that Hopefield could help with? I'm not completely clear in what services you offer but thought I'd at least ask.'

'Definitely,' Anna said. 'We work with child services on foster placements and we can try and encourage her to have some counselling. We can also look at any financial benefits she might be entitled to and how we can help her generally.'

'That's great,' Bec said, 'I'm sure you can do a better job with the foster placement than they've done so far.'

'You'd hope so,' Anna said. 'We deal with quite a few of the foster support agencies, so hopefully she's being looked after by someone I know. Text me through the details of who the case-worker is when you find out.'

'Will do, and in the interim, I think I'll start searching for her. It's not going to hurt to drive the streets for a while.'

* * *

Bec's workday was mostly written off after driving around the streets of Camberwell and the surrounding suburbs for a good part of the day. She'd had to reschedule her creative therapy sessions, which she felt bad about but it couldn't be helped. She was hoping to find Skye and get her to Reclaim to sign in before they needed to report her as missing. She wasn't sure what it was about the girl that was making her care so much, but she did.

Bec even found herself driving past her own house mid-morning. She'd received a text from the school at nine saying Zara was absent. Calls to her daughter's phone had gone straight to voicemail. She sighed, glancing at the familiar frontage, noting the weeds taking over. As she went to move her eyes back to the road, a curtain moved in the room that faced the road.

Bec wasn't sure whether to be relieved or annoyed as she climbed out of the car. She knew her daughter well enough to know Zara had played a key role in Skye's decision to take off. The front door opened before she reached it, and Zara appeared.

'Hey, Mum.'

'Don't, hey Mum, me. What are you doing at home, and is Skye with you?'

Zara looked around her. 'Does it look like she's with me?'

'Zara,' Bec said, her voice trembling as she tried to control her anger. 'This is no joke. If we don't get Skye to the course at Reclaim, she's going to be in all sorts of trouble with the police. It's part of the agreement that's keeping her out of juvenile detention.'

Zara shrugged. 'I don't think she cares. She wants to be left alone. You know, like I asked you to leave me alone when Dad died but you insisted on checking on me every two minutes.'

Bec hesitated momentarily, realising she had work to do when it came to Zara. But right now, this was about Skye, and Zara was right, but it still wasn't helping the situation. She pushed past her daughter and into the house, hearing the back door fly open as she entered the hallway. She rushed to the back of the house and out of the door, catching sight of Skye as she went to scale the fence.

She ran over and grabbed her by the leg. 'Hey, come down, we need to talk.'

Skye looked Bec in the eye and for a split second she expected her to push her away and make a run for it, but she didn't. She sighed and dropped back down to the ground.

'Come inside,' Bec said, 'and we'll work out a plan.'

***

Anna was surprised to get another phone call from Bec so soon after the last, but hearing the desperation in her voice, she suggested she bring Skye to Hopefield for a conversation. She found out who Skye's support worker was, Ivy West, and called her while she waited for Bec to arrive.

An hour later, Bec and Skye sat across from her in her office.

'Thanks for seeing us without an appointment,' Bec said.

'Of course,' Anna said and smiled. 'So, from what I've heard so far, Skye, you're going through a rough time. Bec rang me earlier and gave me the details of your caseworker. I've known Ivy for a few years, and I'm pretty sure she'll be able to pull some strings for us to find you a better foster home and get you back to school and back with your friends.'

Skye's eyes were fixed firmly on her hands in her lap.

Bec raised an eyebrow at Anna. She wasn't sure if the teenager was even listening.

'Hey, Bec,' Anna said, 'can you give Skye and me a few minutes? If you head down the hallway towards reception, the kitchen's on the left. Make yourself a coffee.'

Bec looked to Skye, who didn't react, and stood and left the room.

'I know you're going through what I imagine is the worst time in your life,' Anna said, hoping to get through to Skye, 'but there are people who want to help you. It's not fair at your age to lose your mum and not have any family to fall back on, but it's also not fair for your life to be ruined because of things that were outside of your control. How do you think your mum would feel right now if she knew what had happened to you?'

A single tear rolled down Skye's cheek.

'I'm not trying to upset you,' Anna said, gently, 'but it's something to think about. You were close to your mum, weren't you?'

Skye nodded.

'And I imagine if she were alive, you'd want to make her proud.'

Skye nodded again.

'I'm sure she would be proud of you, but she'd want you to be making good choices now too.'

'I can't live with a foster family,' Skye said. 'My mum grew up in foster care, and it was awful. She was abused. I was supposed to live with Mum's friend. The plans were in place, but child services couldn't locate her. She's overseas for work. Mum would be so upset if she knew I was going into foster care too.'

Ah, thought Anna, now they were getting somewhere. The fact there was a family friend nominated to be Skye's guardian was a positive though.

'And you're assuming all foster carers are the same?'

'That first family *were* awful. They were mean and wanted a babysitter. They weren't abusive, though,' she was quick to clarify.

Anna nodded. 'I spoke with Ivy about them, and she said they're being investigated and may be taken off the foster register if their intentions aren't in line with the program. She thought you might be better with a smaller family. One where there are no kids. Even a single woman, perhaps. Someone who would be interested in you without a whole lot of other distractions. Would that appeal?'

More tears ran down Skye's cheeks, and Anna could see that it wouldn't matter what she suggested, Skye wasn't going to be convinced. Her heart contracted as she saw the pain in the teenager's eyes. She could only imagine what was going through her head. She was so young to be facing the world on her own.

She took a deep breath and decided to make an offer she'd promised herself she wouldn't, but had a feeling it might be what Skye needed for the short term.

'How about this?' she said. 'I'm a registered foster carer, but I only do emergency placements. That means I'll foster for a week, sometimes two or three, but usually no longer than that. It'd help you get into a routine and hopefully back to school, and during that time, we can work with Ivy to vet suitable foster families. We can arrange to visit them so you can see what they're like before committing to any. I can assure you, there are some decent people out there who'd love to have you as part of their family.'

Skye looked at her, her eyes lighting up ever so slightly. 'You'd do that? Let me stay with you, and then I'd have a choice about where I was placed?'

Anna nodded.

'Would your husband mind? And kids too?'

'No husband and no kids. Only stipulation is that Smoko would have to agree.'

'Smoko?'

Anna nodded. 'I have a feeling the two of you will get along.'

9

Anna had to smile as she thought of Bec's delighted face when she'd told her the news that she'd be the one looking after Skye temporarily. 'We're going to meet with Ivy, Skye's caseworker, tomorrow morning, so we'll let you know what the plans are. Whether she'll be back at Reclaim or returning to school.'

Now, having gone via the foster home Skye had ditched to collect her belongings, Anna was surprisingly nervous as she pushed her key in the lock. She'd done emergency fostering a few times, but not recently. She hoped this would work out and they'd find Skye a place she was happy in.

As per his usual routine, Smoko came bounding down the hallway and threw himself at Anna's legs. He quickly pulled himself up when Skye followed her inside and rubbed around the teenager. Skye reached down and picked him up.

'He's gorgeous,' she said, cuddling him to her.

'Meet Smoko,' said Anna. 'Now come on in and make yourself at home. I'll show you the guest room. It's made up with clean sheets, and I'll get you fresh towels.'

'You'll have to tell me the type of foods you like,' Anna said, later that evening when she served up a chicken pasta she'd been relieved to see she had the ingredients for. 'I'm used to cooking for one, and it's often very basic.'

'I'm happy to cook,' Skye said. 'I often did for Mum and me. And it could be part of my contribution to being here. I don't want you to think I don't appreciate what you're doing.'

Anna smiled, passing Skye the green salad. 'I think we'll get along fine. Unfortunately, we're going to have to explore all the legal options available to you and what the next couple of years are going to look like. You'll have a lot more choice once you turn eighteen, but for now, it will most likely be that you need a legal guardian appointed or go into foster care.' She studied Skye carefully. 'Is there no one at all from your mum's family or circle of friends? You mentioned the friend who couldn't be contacted.'

'Mum was in foster care because she didn't have any family,' Skye said. 'In her will she listed her best friend, Erin, as my guardian.'

Anna raised an eyebrow. 'What happened with Erin?'

Skye shrugged. 'No one knows. She works for the UN and went to Yemen last year. She was in touch up until a few weeks before Mum died, and I haven't heard from her since. She promised Mum she'd be back to look after me, but I guess she changed her mind.'

'Did you know her well?'

'Yes, she was around all the time. She was like a really cool aunt.'

'That doesn't sound right that she wouldn't honour her promise to your mum about looking after you. Yemen?'

Skye nodded.

'What's her surname?'

'Clarke. Why?'

'I'll see if I can find out anything about her. I'm not sure the centre has UN contacts but I'm sure someone will be able to help me out. Yemen's a very dangerous place to be. It's possible she's been detained. She might not even know your mum died, let alone what's happened to you.'

Skye's eyes lit up. 'You think we might find her and then she might look after me like she promised?'

'Honestly, I have no idea,' Anna said, 'but we should do our best to find her and at least find out.'

Disappointment flashed in Skye's eyes.

'Hey, try not to stress too much. Erin might be an option and if she's not, coming here has bought you time to get used to the idea of a foster family. There's not the same urgency or rush now to have you placed.'

'But you said you only do emergency placements and for a maximum of a few weeks,' Skye said. 'Don't get me wrong, I'm grateful, but that's not much time.'

Anna sipped her water. 'I'm flexible. If we can make this work, I'm open to you staying until we know if Erin's an option or we find you the right family. If that takes longer than a few weeks, we'll review the situation then.'

Her phone rang. 'Sorry,' she said, picking it up from the table when she saw Willowridge pop up. 'It's about my mum, so I'll have to take it.' She stood, indicating the food. 'Help yourself to more. I'll try and do this quickly.'

'Hey, Anna, it's Marty. Calling with an update on Lyn for you.'

'Thanks, Marty. How is she?'

'She's settled down a lot since last night. She was with it this afternoon, so I asked her about Xavier. She was a little confused but then seemed to remember something. She said that your dad told her something important after your brother died, but she can't remember what it was. She said they were at Xavier's when he told her, and she's convinced Xavier will remember what it is. I asked her why it was important now and why she hadn't brought it up before, but she couldn't answer that. Whether it's a memory that had been blocked and it's been re-awakened, I don't know.'

Anna frowned. 'It's strange. I don't get why she'd remember it now and not back at the time. I rang the restaurant and Xavier, while getting on, is there most nights. I guess I'll take her to see him.'

'I'll come with you,' Marty said, 'in case it sets her off. It'll be easier with two of us to calm her down.'

'Are you sure?' Anna asked. 'That's got to be outside of the scope of your job.'

'I've known Lyn for ten years,' Marty said. 'She moved into Willowridge the day I started working there. In some ways, I feel like she's family. You are too. I want to help, and if I'm honest, I'm kind of intrigued about what she's trying to remember.'

'I'm not sure it will be that intriguing or even relevant,' Anna said, 'but thank you. How about early next week?'

'You let me know,' Marty said. 'I'll make myself available.'

Anna found herself smiling when she ended the call. Everything about Marty's tone confirmed how kind and caring he was. She slipped her phone into her pocket and returned to the table.

'Everything okay?' Skye asked as she took her seat again.

Anna picked up her fork. 'My mum's been in aged care for about ten years. Suffering from dementia. She goes through different phases, but right now is agitated over a conversation she says took place over twenty years ago. Believes my dad had something important to tell her, and possibly the police, about an accident my brother was involved in.'

'Is this the brother you told us about at Echoes?' Skye asked.

Anna nodded. 'My mum never got over it. Ended up an alcoholic and eventually it affected her brain, which meant she had to go into the home she's at now.'

'Do you think what she's remembering is true?'

'That's the million-dollar question,' Anna said. 'It's most likely a wild goose chase, but we'll have to check it out or she'll remain agitated for months. Now, tell me more about you and school. What subjects are you doing, and do you enjoy them? And I guess more importantly, is the plan to continue with the course at Reclaim or go back to school?'

* * *

Bec was working at the kitchen island, doing her best to catch up on the lost day's work. Her thoughts drifted to Anna and Skye, and she hoped their first night was going well. She also hoped something suitable would be found for the teenager. She shuddered to think what it would be like for her kids if they'd been put in the same position. They'd have each other at least, but suddenly having to live with strangers after your whole life being wrapped in love from your parents, or parent in Skye's case, would be a huge adjustment.

She was surprised when Zara appeared in the kitchen a little before ten and started emptying the dishwasher without being asked. Her AirPods were nowhere to be seen, which immediately put Bec on alert. Being helpful and adopting a friendly demeanour suggested she was after something.

'Hey, hon,' Bec said. 'Homework done?'

'All up to date,' Zara said.

'Everything okay?' Bec braced herself, waiting for another barrage of reasons Zara should be permitted to contact her grandparents. Although if she was realistic, she knew Zara well enough to know she wasn't going to ask, she'd just do it.

'I'm worried about Skye,' she said.

Bec closed the lid of her laptop. This wasn't the line of conversation she'd been expecting. 'Oh?'

'She was telling me how her mum was abused in foster care and that there was no way she was going back to that family or any other random strangers. That she'd disappear before she let that happen. It'd be horrible to be her.'

'It would be,' Bec agreed. 'I think one of her big problems with disappearing, though, is that she doesn't have any money or anywhere to go.'

Zara didn't say anything but continued to unpack the dishwasher.

'Zar? Tell me you didn't give her money?'

'Not much. A couple of hundred. And I had to force that on her. She didn't want to take it. But it'll keep her going if she needs it. She needs to be able to take off if she chooses to. Imagine if it happened to me and Hugo, and we got put with psychos. You'd want us to be able to get away, wouldn't you?'

'Of course,' Bec said, and sighed. She couldn't fault Zara. She was pleased on one hand to think her daughter was kind enough to give Skye money. Zara hadn't found an after-school job since they'd arrived in Melbourne, so a couple of hundred would be a large chunk of her savings. 'I'm not sure what to suggest. Like you said, it's a horrible situation.'

'Can we ask her back for dinner tomorrow night?' Zara asked. 'It's nice that Anna's looking after her, but she's going to want to be around kids her age. She's hardly seen her friends since her mum died and she felt comfortable here because we didn't try and wrap her in cotton wool.'

'You didn't,' Bec said. 'If anything, you were pretty full on with your questioning.'

Zara shrugged. 'So, I was interested. I like her. I reckon we could be friends, and she needs a friend now. Also, if we keep an eye on her, I'll know if she's going to run away, and I can decide whether to tell you so you can tell Anna and stop her.'

'Would you do that?'

'Not sure. Maybe. But we'll need to keep a check on her and like I said, she needs a friend right now.'

And so do you, Bec thought. Zara had been quick to find a friend group at her new school, but she wasn't hanging out with one or two good friends in the same way she had in Sydney. She wasn't sure if her daughter hadn't met the right people or if she was deliberately distancing herself. Getting close when people might want to know about Owen's death could be hard.

'I'm happy to have her over for dinner. Did you want to text her? And I'll contact Anna tomorrow too, check if it suits her. They'll be settling into a new routine, so we don't want to interfere with that.'

Zara took the last of the glasses from the dishwasher and put them away before closing it. 'Okay, I'll message her now.'

'Before you go,' Bec said, 'is there anything more you want to know about my parents. Now that I've told you the truth I'm happy to share anything you want to hear about. I'd like you to know what they're like before you think about reaching out to them, if that's your plan.'

Red splotches appeared on Zara's cheeks.

Bec shook her head. 'You've already contacted them?'

'Kind of,' Zara said. 'I found them and sent an email to my grandfather's work. They live in Melbourne by the way, not Canberra.'

A lump rose in Bec's throat. For all of the years she'd tried to keep them out of her life, and just like that, not only was Zara making contact but they also lived in Melbourne.

'You don't have to see them,' Zara said. 'I just want them to know I exist. I want more family. I miss Dad so much and can't even visit him.'

'What do you mean, you can't visit him?'

'You didn't bury him. He's in that urn still. At least if you scattered his ashes, I could go and sit wherever that was and chat to him.'

The lump seemed to be growing in Bec's throat. She tapped her chest. 'He's in here, Zars. You don't need a place to go and talk to him. He's with you all the time.'

'Maybe,' Zara said. 'But he's not physically here and my grandparents are. I want to meet them.'

Bec wasn't sure how to respond. She wasn't ready to let go of Owen's ashes, but she did need to consider Hugo and Zara in this decision. She imagined that in Zara's shoes she'd want to know her grandparents too. 'All I'll say is be careful. I've made it very clear that I don't want them in my life and there are very good reasons for that.'

* * *

The next day, Anna debated whether to cancel going out with Kieran now that she had Skye staying with her, but Bec had called her to check how it was going and to invite Skye and Anna, if she was free, to dinner that night. Anna had declined for herself but tentatively accepted for Skye. When she'd asked Skye, the teenager had said yes immediately.

'Zara messaged me last night, which was nice of her. I'd love to go, thanks.'

'No need to thank me; you can thank Bec. Or from what Bec said, I think it was Zara who wanted you to go. Sounds like you're quite a hit with both her and Hugo. I guess you've all got quite a bit in common with them losing their dad recently.'

'Yeah, that was awful for them. They're lucky they've got each other though, and Bec of course. I haven't spent that much time with them, but Hugo seems to be doing okay. I think Zara's having a harder time. It's why she's trying to find her grandparents. Did Bec tell you how she lied to them their entire lives, telling them they were dead, and they actually live here in Melbourne?'

'Really?' Anna wondered what was behind that decision. It was a pretty extreme thing to do.

Skye nodded. 'Pretty messed up, isn't it? I think their dad dying is partly why Zara wants to find them. She said something about it the night I met them. That if something happened to Bec she'd have grandparents at least.'

Anna dropped Skye off at Bec's on her way to meet Kieran at the Oak Cellar in South Yarra. He'd suggested in his text that he could pick her up, but she preferred the idea of meeting him somewhere neutral.

Having come straight from dropping off Skye, she arrived fifteen minutes early and with nerves fluttering in the pit of her stomach she decided to wait at the bar. She wondered if she'd even recognise Kieran; after all, a lot of years had passed.

Anna sat down on one of the bar stools at the counter. She hadn't been to the Oak Cellar before but had heard about it from some of the team she worked with, who had raved about it, and Anna could quickly see why. The walls were warm, earthy brick, adorned with black and white photos of old Melbourne. A polished bar stretched across one side, its glass shelves lined with glasses, and the bench was filled with bottles of spirits. Down either side of the bar, from roof to floor, dark wooden racks displayed an extensive collection of wine bottles.

The bartender grinned at Anna as she took in the striking scene before her. The soft jazz music adding to the atmosphere.

'Drink?'

Anna nodded and sat herself down on one of the bar stools. 'Cab sav please.' It didn't count as drinking alone, as Kieran would be there any minute, and she needed something to settle her nerves.

The bartender nodded. 'Happy for me to choose? There's a nice New Zealand one I'd recommend from Hawke's Bay.'

'Perfect.'

She continued to take in the ambience of the Oak Cellar while her drink was being prepared. Her mind flitted back to Tuesday night and the call from Marty to go and see her mother. So much had happened since that call that it felt like it was weeks ago, not only two nights. She'd been agitated. More so than Anna ever remembered seeing her.

She assumed it wouldn't hurt to take her to Xavier's, the restaurant she'd been mentioning. She would wait until she saw how her mother was on Saturday and talk to Marty about it as well.

Her thoughts were interrupted as Kieran, tall and broad-shouldered, walked in. She'd expected him of course but seeing him made her heart skip a beat. She told herself she should be angry – twenty-two years of silence – but the truth was, it probably wouldn't have worked out back then anyway. He moved with the same easy confidence she remembered. Sun-kissed blond hair, a little thinner at the temples, and those familiar blue-grey eyes, lined with faint laugh lines, met hers.

His lips turned up in a tentative smile and she couldn't help but smile back. She stood as he reached her and stepped forward and put her arms around him.

He visibly relaxed as his arms slid around her.

Eventually they pulled apart.

'Come and sit down,' Anna said. 'Tell me where you went and what you did. I want to hear everything.'

The bartender took Kieran's drink order and he started to tell her about his life. About moving away from Melbourne and training to become a pilot.

'Really? But you never liked flying. That was Jake's dream, not yours.'

Kieran shrugged. 'I guess things changed for me after the accident. I moved to Adelaide and did my flight training there. I wanted to do something to feel close to Jake. It was his dream so I wanted it to happen, even if it was me and not him.'

'And what about you?' Kieran asked. 'Husband, two-point-four kids?'

Anna shook her head. 'No. Divorced. Ironically, over the two-point-four kids. Ex wanted kids, I didn't, and it ended up being a deal breaker.'

Kieran frowned. 'But you *always* wanted kids. You had them all named. Mallory, Michael, Mitchell and Marilyn. All the M names.'

Anna's mouth dropped open, surprised that he remembered. 'Well, yes, at one stage I wanted my M kids. But losing Jake changed everything. I couldn't imagine having kids and then losing one of them like my parents did. Like we did.' She shook her head. 'It killed them. Dad, literally. He was heartbroken. He died a few months after Jake. Hit by a bus.'

Kieran's eyes widened in shock. 'No.'

Anna nodded. 'Witnesses said he stepped straight in front of it. Deliberately, they assumed.'

'No way. He'd never do that.'

Anna smiled. 'Thank you. You're probably one of the few people who knew him well enough to know he would never have done that to Mum and me.' She sighed. 'He walked around in a daze after Jake's death, couldn't pull himself out of it. My guess is it was as simple as him being caught up in his head, not paying attention, and he stepped into the road.' She shrugged. 'Doesn't matter. Same result.'

Kieran shook his head slowly. 'It does matter, and I would say with absolute certainty that it wasn't intentional. He was one of the kindest men I've ever met. I can't believe my parents didn't tell me. There's no way he'd subject you and your mum to that, but also the bus driver, passengers and witnesses. How is your mum?'

'Not great. She's in care.'

'Care? Really. But she's the same age as my parents. She can only be in her late sixties.'

'She befriended gin and vodka after Dad died. Spent her days drinking herself into a coma. She never really drank before Jake died, but started having a few then, and once Dad was gone, it got out of control. Fried her brain. She's now suffering alcoholic dementia.'

'Is it reversible?'

'Not really, the damage to her brain is too severe. She's a little better since she went into care and stopped drinking, but not great. It was over a decade of intense drinking before I could get her to agree to go into a facility ten years ago.'

Kieran reached for her hand and squeezed it. 'I'm sorry you've had to go through all of that.'

'Thank you.' Anna sighed. 'Who would have thought that all these years would have passed already. I still wake up most days with this feeling of dread, as if it were yesterday.'

'Me too,' Kieran said. 'I still miss him, An.'

Anna sighed. 'I often wonder what he would have done with his life.'

'What else have you done with yours?'

It was after nine by the time they'd finished their meals and were ready to leave. Anna texted Skye to say she was on her way and received a thumbs up.

'It was so nice catching up,' Kieran said as they pulled their jackets around themselves and stepped out into the cold air of Chapel Street. It was busy with people, as was the norm any night in South Yarra, but particularly on Thursday and through the weekend. 'Can we do it again sometime? I know from what you've told me tonight that you've got Skye staying, but if you've got any time over the weekend, it would be lovely to do something. Go for a hike or up to the Dandenongs for lunch. Skye's welcome to come if she'd like.'

Anna hadn't had to think about her reply; she'd enjoyed every minute with Kieran. She felt like she'd been transported back twenty-two years, and they were two teenagers out on a date. 'I'd love to,' she said without hesitation. 'Not sure about Skye, but I'll have a chat with her and let you know. I usually visit Mum on a Saturday, so perhaps we could plan for Sunday?'

* * *

As Bec cleared away the dishes from dinner, she smiled as she heard laughter coming from Zara's room. Hugo was in there with the girls, which was nice, as her twins – while friendly and protective of each other – didn't usually spend much time together.

It was after nine thirty when Anna arrived to collect Skye.

'Sorry, it's so late,' she said as Bec met her at the front door.

Bec laughed. 'You either get up very early or you don't usually live with teenagers. This is not late. Come in for a drink or a cup of tea if you've got time? The kids are playing a game of something in Zara's room.'

'Sounds good,' Anna said, following Bec into the house. 'I should probably let Skye know I'm here. Is that okay?'

'Sure. Second door down on the left.' Bec pointed down the hallway. 'Although the noise should have made that pretty apparent.'

Anna grinned and headed in the direction of the shrieks of laughter coming from Zara's room. She knocked and pushed open the door.

'Just letting you know I'm here,' Bec heard Anna say to Skye. 'No rush though, I'm going to catch up with Bec for a little while.'

She couldn't make out what Skye said, but from the laughter that followed, it seemed that the game was continuing.

Anna came back to the kitchen and took a seat at the bench. 'They've hit it off quickly for kids who've only just met.'

'I know,' Bec said, holding up an open bottle of wine. 'Wine or tea?'

'Tea, please,' Anna said. 'Would love something herbal, if you have it?'

Bec busied herself making the tea, at one stage eyeing Anna with a cheeky grin. She took in the fitted navy dress and neat heels, the kind of outfit that was polished yet conservative, exactly how she'd sum Anna up too. 'You look very nice, by the way. Was it a date tonight?' Anna's cheeks flushed red, and Bec laughed. 'Well, that answers that question.'

'I don't know if it counts as a date or not.' Anna took a deep breath. 'Kieran was my first boyfriend and he was also my brother's best friend. He disappeared the day after Jake died.'

'Disappeared?'

Anna nodded. 'We'd dated for two years.' She blushed. 'He was my first in every way. I was completely in love with him. Even though we were young, I couldn't imagine my life without him. And then he was gone. Left town and only resurfaced last week.'

'What?' Bec imagined her eyes getting bigger as she learned the background of their relationship. 'So, he left after Jake died, and last week was the first time you heard from him?'

Anna nodded. 'And tonight was the first time I've seen him. He's the same. Older, I guess, with a sadness that wasn't there before, but his wife died a year ago, so he's had his fair share of loss and pain, so that's understandable.'

Bec shook her head. 'I think I would have killed him.'

Anna laughed. 'For years I assumed that's exactly what I'd do if he ever made contact.'

'Well, as you didn't kill him, are the old sparks still there?'

'Kind of. I always imagined if I saw him again, I'd still be mad at him for leaving when he did. But I wasn't. I suppose I've worked with enough teenagers now to know that it was unrealistic to expect a teenage boy to be able to cope with the death of his friend and be there for me and our family. Luckily, he didn't go off the rails. As an adult, it's much easier to look back and see it for what it was. If Jake hadn't died, I can't imagine Kieran and I would have even stayed together, once we went our separate ways to university.'

'You might have,' Bec said. 'I met Owen when I first got to Sydney when I was twenty. We were very young and were madly in love...' Her words petered off.

Anna reached across and squeezed her hand. 'How are you coping with everything? It can't be easy.'

Bec blinked away tears. She'd been doing much better lately, not bursting into tears at random moments, but sometimes it only took something little like the tone of a kind voice. 'I have my days,' she said. 'I think I'm lucky with the business and that I have the kids to keep me busy. Although Zara's a master at pushing my buttons and giving me grey hairs. Which reminds me, I need to tell you that she's given Skye money. Skye's made it clear that under no circumstances is she going into a foster home, so I get the impression that she'll use the money to escape the moment she thinks she's being shipped somewhere new.'

Anna sighed. 'I was worried about taking her on, to be honest. Mainly because it's only temporary. I'd hoped that doing it this way, we could meet some families and she could get to know them before she moves in.'

'Have you ever thought of fostering more long-term?'

Anna sipped her tea before nodding. 'I was married for eight years. My ex wanted kids, but I didn't, so I agreed to foster as – I don't know – a bit of a compromise. We were given a three-year-old for short-term care. It was supposed to be for a maximum of three months. We ended up having Maisie until she was six. Giving her back was one of the most heartbreaking experiences of my life. Don't get me wrong, it doesn't compare to losing my brother or my dad, but it was a different type of heartbreak.'

'I can only imagine,' Bec said. 'Were you able to stay in touch with her?'

Anna nodded. 'We could, but after a few months, when we could see she'd settled back in with her mum, we stopped visiting. It was too hard to leave. Her mum sends an update and Christmas card each year, but that's all. She's twelve now and she's great from what I can see.'

'That must have been so hard. You'd raised her for half of her life by then.'

'And she was calling me Mama. As much as I wanted her mum to get better, I also didn't.' Anna clasped her hand over her mouth as the words escaped. 'Sorry, I've never said that out loud.'

'No need to apologise. I would have been the same. I get it. You're too scared to foster again in case you get attached and then the kid leaves?'

'I guess,' Anna said. 'Or something would happen, like it did to my brother, and I'd lose them that way.'

Bec nodded, now understanding what Anna feared. She'd been about to point out that Skye was older and had no mother, but that didn't solve the problem of something happening to her.

'What about you?' Anna asked.

'Me. Foster?' Bec almost laughed out loud. She'd just lost her husband, moved states and if Zara had any say in it, was quite likely going to have to deal with her parents re-entering her life. She had no capacity for anyone or anything else.

Anna nodded. 'You've got two great kids, which is a reflection of your parenting.'

'Probably more Owen's, but regardless, I'm not in the right place to even consider looking after someone else right now. As much as I look for distractions from my own problems that's a huge stretch.' Bigger than huge, Bec thought. She had room in her heart for her kids, and that was all. 'What will happen to Skye, do you think?'

'She mentioned that her mum had a very close friend who was supposed to step into the guardian role, but she works for the United Nations and ended up in Yemen a few months before Jodi, Skye's mum, died, and as far as Skye knows, she lost contact with them.'

'Oh wow, do you think something's happened to her?'

'Quite likely. If she'd been killed you'd assume Jodi and Skye would have been notified. She could have been captured or anything. I'm going to see if I can find out any information tomorrow. Don't suppose you know anyone at the UN?'

Bec shook her head.

'I'll also speak to her caseworker and see what the options are, based on the fact she's likely to flee.' Anna sighed. 'I feel very sorry for her.'

'For who? Me?' Zara came into the kitchen with Skye and Hugo following her. 'You should. Having to live with Hugo and Mum. It's tragic.'

They all laughed, and for once, Bec was glad her daughter had the foresight to change the subject.

Anna slipped off the stool and smiled at Skye. 'Ready to go?'

Skye nodded and laughed as Zara hugged her goodbye.

Bec couldn't help but notice the look on Hugo's face as his twin did this. She wasn't sure if she was reading it right, but it looked very much like envy. Did he have a crush on Skye?

'You'll never believe this,' Zara said, letting Skye go. 'Guess when Skye's birthday is, Mum?'

Bec shook her head. 'No idea.'

'July twelfth.'

All three teenagers looked at her expectantly.

'No way.'

'What's the significance?' Anna asked, clearly the only one not in on the answer.

'And,' Zara added, 'she was born at eleven past eleven in the morning.'

Bec's mouth dropped open as the teenagers all laughed.

'Hugo was born at ten fifty-five on the twelfth, and I was born twenty minutes later at eleven-fifteen. Skye makes us triplets, and she's the middle child.'

Anna looked to Bec, who nodded in confirmation that these times were correct. 'That's crazy,' she said.

'Not crazy,' Zara said. 'It was meant to be. Skye is meant to be in our lives, or we're meant to be in hers. Who knows which way it goes, but the main thing is, our sister is here.' She flung her arms around Skye, who laughed even harder than previously.

'There might be a bit of the biological stuff missing to make that a reality,' Bec said, 'but it's a lovely idea and a huge coincidence.'

'I don't know,' Zara said, 'Skye has no idea who her father was. Maybe it was Dad. We don't know what he got up to on his business trips.'

'Zar,' Hugo reprimanded. 'Shut up.'

Bec shook her head, a smile playing on her lips. 'Don't worry, I'm not sure there's anything that could come out of Zara's mouth that will shock me these days.'

Zara grinned. 'I'm kidding. Dad and you were sickening with how much you loved each other. He'd never do that, but I love that we have a birth connection with Skye. It's got to mean something.'

'Come on, you,' Anna said, throwing her arm around Skye's shoulders. 'Let's get home and see what mischief Smoko's been up to and leave Zara to come up with some other crazy theories.' She turned to Bec. 'And thank you for tonight. We'll have you all over soon.'

Bec, Zara and Hugo waved, as Anna and Skye got into Anna's Mazda and reversed out of the driveway.

Zara's phone pinged immediately.

'Who's that?' Bec asked. 'It's getting late.'

Zara glanced at her phone. 'Skye.' She smiled and walked back inside.

Bec slipped her arm around Hugo and walked back in with him. 'It sounds like all three of you were having fun tonight.'

'Yeah, she's nice. I hope Zara doesn't mess her up too much.'

'You think that's likely?'

He shrugged. 'Who knows. Zara's predictably unpredictable.'

10

Skye had only spent three nights at Anna's, but it felt natural to have her to stay. She was quiet and gentle with Smoko and in her general demeanour, not unlike Anna herself.

'Your mum must have been pretty special,' she said to her on Saturday morning, when she found Skye cleaning the kitchen. 'She certainly raised you well. Or are you doing this for my benefit, hoping you can stay longer?' A flush of colour crept up Skye's cheeks, and Anna wished she'd thought before she'd spoken. 'Hey, I was joking. It's lovely having you here. I'm not used to anyone helping. I've been on my own for years now, and when I was married, my ex didn't do a lot to help.'

'Well, you were right about Mum,' Skye said. 'She was the best mum in the world. She worked so hard to keep everything nice. She didn't earn a lot, so the place we were living in was a rental, but she made it feel like home. She would do things like volunteer on community projects where they were doing painting or sewing or something like that, and instead of being paid, would agree with them that she could take the excess paint home and borrow the brushes and rollers for the weekend so she could paint our place. She did the same with making cushions and curtains, too. Would use leftover materials and trade her time for using the machines.'

'She sounds like a real entrepreneur,' Anna said. 'What did she do for her paid job?'

'She was a kindergarten teacher, but she was only employed on a contract basis, so when she got sick, she didn't have health insurance or income protection. She had to go onto benefits when she was too unwell to work.'

'That would have been hard.'

'It was,' Skye said. 'The worst thing was, she didn't tell me she was sick until a few weeks before she died. I knew she wasn't well, but not that it was cancer and too late to do anything about it. She hid how bad it really was.' Skye's eyes filled with tears. 'She said she couldn't tell me. That she didn't want me to be different towards her in those last months and that she couldn't bear to see me sad at the thought of losing her.'

Anna drew in a breath. She wasn't sure who that situation was worse for, Skye or her mum.

'And then she was stressed because she couldn't get in touch with Erin. The plan was that I was going to live with her once Mum...' Skye hesitated. 'Well, once she was gone.'

Anna reached out and covered Skye's hand with her own. 'That's a horrible situation for both you and your mum to be in. I can't even begin to imagine what either of you went through.'

'I was mad with her to start with that she didn't tell me and that she didn't have treatment.'

'Would the treatment have made any difference?' Anna asked gently.

Skye shrugged. 'It would have bought us more time, I guess. She said she didn't want the time she had left to be really painful and horrible. She knew she was going to die and that there wouldn't be a miracle cure to hang around and wait for.'

'How did you end up in foster care?' Anna asked.

'Mum was really unwell at the end and we had a home nurse coming in. I'd told Mum that Erin had called and was on her way home, which wasn't true, but it helped Mum relax. But the nurse realised there were no plans for me and contacted social services. Mum was drugged up enough by then to have no idea what was going on.'

Anna impulsively reached out and drew Skye to her. 'That's an amazing thing you did for your mum, especially when it left you on your own and suddenly in the system she was doing her best to keep you out of.' She felt Skye melt into her and gently rubbed the teenager's back.

Anna closed her eyes as she felt Skye doing her best to keep it together and then finally succumbing to the tears that she'd probably been holding in for weeks.

Minutes passed before an impatient mew had Skye pull away from her.

'I think Smoko needs you,' Skye said, wiping her eyes.

'He can wait,' Anna said. 'You're more important right now.'

Smoko mewed even louder, causing Skye to laugh. 'Nope. Mr Smoko is definitely more important. I think you need to feed him or brush him or something.'

Anna smiled and leaned down and scooped up Smoko, who purred and snuggled into her neck. 'He's been fed and brushed; he just wants attention.' She stroked the cat who continued to purr, and her heart contracted at the thought of what Skye had been through and what was still to come. Adjusting to a foster family wasn't going to be easy. It was a shame Bec wasn't in a better place emotionally. They would offer Skye a ready-made family, which Anna believed she'd thrive in.

Eventually Smoko pushed away and demanded to be put down. Anna deposited him on the kitchen floor and glanced at Skye, relieved to see her smiling at Smoko and looking happier than she had moments ago.

'Now,' she said, 'I must go and visit my mum. I do that every Saturday and usually once during the week too. As I mentioned, she's in a care facility and has dementia. She varies every day, sometimes changes hourly. You're more than welcome to come with me unless you have other plans?'

Skye blushed. 'Hugo asked if I'd like to go to the movies with him this afternoon.'

Interesting. 'That sounds nice,' Anna said. 'And Zara too?'

Skye blushed even deeper. 'No, just the two of us.'

'Like a date?' Anna couldn't imagine Zara being happy with that development. Skye was her friend.

Skye nodded and then shook her head. 'Yes and no. I think he'd like it to be a date, but I'd like him to be a friend. More like a brother. I'm going to tell him that today. I hope it doesn't upset him, because I want to be able to hang out with him *and* Zara.'

'I think you can assume Zara will insist you still come and hang out.' Anna thought about it for a minute. 'Bit of advice though, if you're wanting to be friends with Zara, let her know you're going to the movies with Hugo. She might be upset if she finds out later. She'll feel excluded and, my guess, jealous, as I imagine in her mind you're her friend more than Hugo's.'

'Okay,' Skye said. 'Thanks, I was a bit worried about that. Hugo didn't want her to come, which is why he didn't tell her, but I'd hate to upset her. I'll let her know.'

'I should be home mid-afternoon,' Anna said, 'and I'll be in tonight if you feel like getting some takeaway and watching a movie. Zara and Hugo would be welcome to join us.' She glanced at her watch. 'I'd better go. But first, are you okay?'

Skye nodded and Anna pulled her into another hug. 'Good. But remember, it's okay not to be okay. What you're going through is a lot. You don't have to work out everything now either. You need to process what's happened and sometimes that's by not doing anything. Just let the feelings come up and let them come out if they need to. But, if you need anything at all, ask, won't you.'

The gentle squeeze Skye gave her was good enough as a yes.

* * *

'What is wrong with you?' Bec asked as Zara snapped at her for the fifth time in about ten minutes. 'Is it that time of the month?'

'No, it's not!'

'Are you sure? Cause you're snippy.'

Of course I'm snippy, Zara wanted to say. Although who used the word snippy? People born in the Dark Ages she guessed. And, yes, she was being bitchy, which she knew was completely unreasonable and unfair to her mother of all people, but it didn't stop her. It wasn't her fault that her grandparents hadn't replied to her message, or messages.

She'd sent the first message on Tuesday and had assumed she would have heard back the very next day. When, by late Thursday, there was no reply, she sent another email and messaged through Facebook and sent a letter to an address she found for their house. Like a regular snail mail letter. She knew that one wouldn't be there yet, but the email and Facebook message would have been delivered. It had never crossed her mind that they might not respond.

'You know when you left Melbourne?'

'Yes.' Her mother's tone was wary.

'Did you miss your parents?'

'Oh.' Her mother sat down on one of the kitchen stools. 'I wasn't expecting you to ask that.'

'I wondered,' Zara said. ''Cause if you and I had a massive falling-out and I ran away, I think I'd still miss you, even if I hated you for whatever happened.'

Bec nodded. 'You know, you're right, and there was part of me that did. But then I'd think of what they did to Chris, and I saw red. It was like Dad was covering up everything, so it didn't impact his career. I just couldn't forgive him or be around him.'

'Do you think he believed people would think it was his fault that Chris...' she hesitated '...that Chris ended his life?'

Bec nodded again. 'Definitely, and to a large degree it was. Something happened around two years before Chris died. He came home one night upset, and I don't mean a bit upset, he was hysterical.'

* * *

Bec was up in her room when she heard someone sobbing uncontrollably outside the house. Her heart thumped as she'd raced down the stairs, grateful to see both Spaniel, their cocker spaniel, and Cleo, their Siamese cat, curled up in the lounge. It sounded like Chris crying, and her immediate thought was that something had happened to one of the animals, but it hadn't. Fear ran down her spine. Was it their parents?

She rushed outside and found him doubled over in the driveway, unable to control himself. She hurried to him and put her hand on his back, the smell of alcohol immediately hitting her.

'What's happened? Has there been an accident? Is it Mum or Dad?' A wave of nausea washed over her. He'd gone out to a party that night. He'd been excited because he had a date.

'Everyone's okay,' her father's booming voice called, causing her to jump. 'Your brother's drunk and emotional, nothing more.'

Bec stared at Chris. 'But, what happened?' Surely this level of distress wasn't normal just from being drunk?

Her father rolled his eyes. 'He drank too much, simple as that. Now, you'd better get back to bed. I'm hoping my good child, the one without the hangover, will come out campaigning with me tomorrow. Don't worry about Chris, your mum's just gone in to get a bucket. She'll fuss over him.'

Moments later, Bec's mum appeared with a bucket and towels. She glanced at Bec. 'Head back to bed, Rebecca, we'll get Chris sorted.'

Bec glanced at her brother one last time, and retreated indoors.

* * *

'So he got drunk, what's the big deal?' Zara asked.

Bec shook her head. 'The way he was crying wasn't like I'd ever seen before and it was the night that everything seemed to change. I asked him about it the next day, and he wouldn't tell me. A few weeks later it was obvious that he was taking drugs which over the next few months turned into a problem. And he'd never touched drugs, well, I don't think he had, before that night. He was outgoing before that, and we were good friends as well as being brother and sister, but it all changed. He withdrew and wouldn't talk to me about anything. Mum was worried too, but Dad kept saying everything was fine and that Chris was going through a phase.'

'But it wasn't a phase?'

Bec shook her head. 'No, his phase continued for close to two years until the night he'd had enough and checked out permanently.'

Zara shuddered. 'I can't imagine how I'd survive if Hugo did that.'

'Did what?' Hugo said, entering the kitchen.

'I was telling Zara about my brother,' Bec said, noticing with interest how nice Hugo looked and how lovely he smelled. 'New cologne?'

Hugo didn't meet her eyes, but couldn't hide the red that crept up the back of his neck. 'Not new,' he said, 'just one I don't usually wear. I'm going out. I'll be back by dinner, I think. I'll text you if that changes.'

'Going anywhere nice?'

'Movies. See you.' He didn't look either of them in the eye and hurried out of the kitchen.

Bec called after him. 'Hold on a sec.'

Hugo stopped and turned to face them. 'What? I'm in a hurry.'

Bec could see how much he didn't want to have to explain where he was going.

She got up from the stool, took the scissors from the kitchen drawer and went over to him. She cut off the clothing label that was dangling from the shirt she'd never seen but was ironed perfectly. She leaned forward and kissed him on the cheek. 'Have fun.'

Like an unspoken pact, she and Zara waited until the front door was not only shut, but his footsteps had disappeared down the pathway and out onto the street. Then they both started laughing.

'Wow,' Bec said, 'he's made such an effort. I wonder who he's meeting.'

'Skye,' Zara said. 'They're going to the movies.'

'Oh?' Bec was surprised Zara seemed so unfazed. She studied

her daughter. 'But I thought she was your friend, or that all three of you were friends?'

'She is, but she's also being nice to him. She rang me earlier to tell me that he'd asked her out and that he didn't want me to know because, I guess, he thought it was a date. She wanted to check that I was okay with her going, but also to tell me that she liked him, but like a brother, which makes sense based on our birth times, and not anything else.'

Bec's emotions were immediately torn. On the one hand, she was gutted for Hugo, but on the other, happy for Zara that Skye knew where her loyalties lay. 'Poor Hugo.'

'Nah,' Zara said, 'she'll let him down gently and then set him up with one of her school friends. They're very hot, from what she's said. It's not going to work long term if she and Hugo date.'

'What do you mean, long term?'

'She's one of those people you know you'll be friends with forever,' Zara said. 'We can't have that messed up because Hugo likes her. I've got an idea that will help him get over her too.'

Bec shook her head. The last time Zara had *an idea,* the whole family had found themselves in Broome in Western Australia, riding camels at sunset. An idea and memory she would hate not to have now. She could still picture Owen's laughter and him almost falling off the camel; he'd laughed so hard when the one Bec was supposed to be riding not only refused to stand up but had also done its best to spit on her no matter where she walked to get away from it.

'Don't be like that,' Zara said. 'I have good ideas. Remember the camels?'

It was as if Zara could read her mind, and Bec had to respect the fact that, overall, her daughter had a kind heart and often did come up with good ideas.

'Okay, lay it on me,' Bec said. 'But promise me nothing's going to spit at me this time.'

* * *

Anna was pleased to see Marty at the reception area talking to Rosalie, one of the other carers, as she walked through the entrance doors of Willowridge.

'Do you ever have a day off?'

Marty shook his head, his blue eyes twinkling. 'Nope. I'm rostered on twenty-four seven. No breaks, they don't even give me meals. I'm a slave to the system.' He grinned, widening his hands to indicate the centre. 'They don't even pay me. I do all of this for love.'

Rosalie rolled her eyes. 'Don't listen to him, Anna, he's full of himself. You'd think he ran the place single-handed the way he goes on, whereas the reality is we have to go hunting for him half the time. He's busy having cups of tea and biscuits with the residents.'

Marty laughed, patting his toned stomach. 'You have no proof of that. Now, Anna,' he said, becoming serious, 'your mum's been good since the other night, but she has brought up this Xavier a few more times. She's pretty alert this morning, so I expect it'll be the main topic for the day.'

'I was expecting that. Although I'm worried it might make Mum worse if it brings up a lot of memories. I'm just not sure though – if she'd be worse if she learns new information about Jake, or if she'd be worse if I don't take her to visit this Xavier.'

'I think you need to take her to visit him,' Marty said. 'It might come to nothing, but at least she'll have the chance to speak to him. See how she is and give it some thought.'

There was no need to think, Anna realised as soon as she

walked into her mother's room. Lyn jumped up from one of the two armchairs by the window, dressed to go out with a handbag slung over her arm.

She smiled at Anna. 'Let's go.'

'Go?'

'To Xavier. I need to speak to him.'

'We can't go now.'

'Why not? Give me one good reason.'

Anna thought about it for a moment. There was no real reason not to go, other than there was no guarantee Xavier would be there, and they didn't have a reservation.

'Let me give the restaurant a call, Mum,' Anna said. 'If Xavier's there, then we'll go now. But if he's not, we'll find out when he'll next be in and then go and see him.' She was relieved to see her mother visibly relax. Lyn sat back down on one of the chairs, and Anna joined her on the other. She slipped her phone from her bag and looked up the restaurant. Finding the number, she pressed the call button.

It was only just after three, so there was no guarantee the restaurant would be answering this early in the day, but they did.

Anna ended the call a few minutes later and turned to her mother. 'Not today, Mum.'

Lyn's face crumpled with disappointment, and Anna reached for her hand and squeezed it. 'We'll go tomorrow, okay. He'll be there tomorrow night. I've booked us for an early dinner. I'll come and collect you around five.'

Lyn closed her eyes briefly. She opened them and smiled at Anna, her eyes full of warmth and appearing as her old self.

A lump rose in Anna's throat, knowing it was her mum she was talking to in this moment, not her dementia mum, as she would rather inappropriately think of Lyn at times.

'Thank you, Anna. I'll be ready at five.'

* * *

Bec took herself out into the garden after her conversation with Zara. Her idea wasn't something she was going to contemplate. She hadn't shut her down immediately, but found herself changing the subject, to – of all things – her parents.

'Have you heard from your grandparents?'

Zara's eyes had widened in surprise at the question. 'I thought you didn't want to know anything about it.'

'So did I,' Bec said. 'But it's playing on my mind. I don't want them just turning up here suddenly. I don't know how I'd feel if I did have to speak to them.' And that was the truth; she really didn't. Her anger towards them didn't feel as raw or as big as it had over the years. As much as she didn't want anything to do with them, after Owen's death she'd wondered how she'd feel if she'd learned they'd died. She was beginning to realise she'd be very upset if she never saw her mother again. But then her emotions swung back the other way, reminding her that they'd abandoned Chris and in her mind were the cause of his death. Could she have anything to do with them again?

'Well, you don't need to worry,' Zara said. 'They haven't responded and I've emailed them and even sent a letter to their house.'

'You found their house?'

Zara nodded. 'It's in Canterbury.'

'Not Wentworth Street?'

'Yes, that's it. Is that where you grew up?'

Bec pulled out a weed from the garden bed, still thinking about her parents and being surprised to learn they were back in the family home. She'd assumed they would have sold it when they moved to Canberra but this suggested they'd rented it out. She gave herself a shake, annoyed at how much energy she was spending on thinking about them and Zara's idea. She sighed. Would her daughter ever listen to her and do what she wanted? Owen's voice was in her head. *Don't let her push you around, Becks, you're still in charge, don't forget.*

She smiled. They'd both worked out very early on with Zara, probably when she was around two and a half and going through the terrible twos, that neither of them had a chance.

'She outnumbers us,' Owen had said one day, lying on the lounge room floor after they'd put Zara and Hugo to bed, *'and there's only one of her.'* He'd groaned. *'I hope she doesn't train Hugo up to be like her. Then it'll be like ten of them against us. The whole point of only having two kids was that it's supposed to be even. Two of us against two of them.'*

Bec had snuggled against him and laughed at the time, but she had to admit, overall, he was right. They'd had to do their very best to ensure she wasn't running the show.

She wiped her cheeks, as the tears fell. She was lucky; she knew that. She'd had an amazing husband.

As she continued to pull weeds her thoughts shifted to Chris and she wondered what had caused him to go so out of control with drugs.

After their father had won the local council election, he'd gone on to run for mayor, which he'd won, but that was certainly no help to Chris.

* * *

'What are you doing?' Bec's eyes flitted around the garage, taking in the scene before her. Chris with a marker pen in hand and what looked like her father's election signs.

'I thought he was paying you to put those out tonight,' Bec said.

'He is. I'm making sure they're accurate.'

Bec looked at the signs. 'Are you stoned? You can't do that!'

The signs previously said, 'It's not who you know, it's who you serve.' Now they said, 'It's not who you know, it's who you bribe.'

'Why do you hate him so much?' Bec asked.

'Because everything he does is for his career. He doesn't give a shit about us. He just wanted a family to make him look good.'

She shook her head and went to leave the garage. Before she did, she turned to him. 'If you really believe that then he's probably wishing he didn't have a family with the way you're acting. Maybe you should look at yourself and your drug use instead of using Dad as an excuse for what's wrong in your life.'

* * *

But of course, she'd regretted her words later when he'd distanced himself from her, got heavier into drugs and had eventually taken an overdose.

She sighed as she pulled more weeds. She looked up at the sky, her mind returning to Owen. *'Sorry, hon, I should be thinking of you, not Chris. It's bloody Zara, of course.'* She smiled as she had this thought. *'Threatening to contact my parents has brought this all up again. But if it's any consolation, I'm pretty sure I'm using it as a distraction, so I don't have to think about how much I'm missing you.'*

11

When Anna left Willowridge, she found herself driving in the direction of the cemetery. She hadn't visited Jake and her father for a few weeks and felt like she needed to be close to them. And she knew it wasn't the cemetery or the gravestones that made her feel that way, it was taking time out to think about them and talk to them, which was easier to do in a specific location.

She shook her head as she weaved her way across the grassed section of the cemetery. So many lives ended here, each one leaving behind grief that altered the course of others. She knew that all too well – losing her brother, then her father, had shaped her life in ways she still felt every day. She sometimes felt guilty that her thoughts and grief tended to lie with Jake rather than her dad. She wasn't sure why that was. Her father's death had been a huge shock, and yet, it was Jake she fixated on.

Anna brushed away the leaves, first on her father's, then Jake's gravestone, wishing she'd thought to bring flowers. Although she knew what Jake's reaction would have been.

Flowers, what do I want with stupid flowers?

Nothing, Jake, they're really for me, was the reply playing over in her head. She sat on the grass between the two gravestones and closed her eyes. She didn't want to think. She just wanted to be in their presence. To feel close to them.

Hours later, she'd been surprised when she'd opened the front door to a delicious smell of garlic and herbs, and to find Skye and Smoko curled up together on the couch, Skye reading a book. Anna's heart had contracted a little, seeing the two of them so comfortable and Skye looking so relaxed. Considering only days earlier she'd been hiding from her foster family and doing her best to avoid the police, things had turned around quickly. Maybe Anna should consider a longer-term fostering arrangement? She gave herself a mental shake. No, after Maisie it wasn't something she'd ever be able to bring herself to do again, and this was early days with Skye, who was no doubt on her best behaviour.

'Something smells delicious,' she said, smiling as she walked into the family room.

Skye looked up from her book, and Smoko stretched his legs before curling back up with Skye.

Anna laughed. 'I think you've found a friend. Before you came to stay, Smoko hardly went to anyone but me.'

Skye stroked his grey head. 'He's beautiful. He makes me feel calm and cosy.'

Anna had to agree with that. When Smoko cuddled up to her, she was guilty of relaxing so much with his warmth that she'd fall asleep. 'What are you reading?'

Skye blushed, holding up the book so Anna could see the cover. 'Hope it's okay. I got it from your bookshelf.'

'Of course,' Anna said, surprised at the teenager's choice. '*Catcher in the Rye* can be quite heavy, though.'

Skye shrugged. 'I can relate to some of what Holden's going through.'

Anna nodded. 'If you ever feel like talking about any of it, I'm here. It's a lot to carry on your own.'

'Thanks. It's been good to be able to speak with Zara and Hugo too. They get what it's like.'

'And how was the date?'

'I told him straight away that I want to be friends, so it was a bit awkward to start with, but once he relaxed, we had a nice time. He's lovely; so is Zara. I hope if I end up with a foster family, it's not too far away and I'll still be able to see them.'

Anna could hear the concern creep into Skye's words. 'We'll make sure it's a family that works for you in terms of location and everything else. Don't stress about it for now.' She smiled. 'More importantly, I'm starving and can smell something delicious. Please tell me there's some left over.'

Skye moved Smoko, much to his disgust, from her lap and stood. 'It's not leftovers. I was waiting for you to get home so we could eat together. I used the mince to make a bolognaise sauce. I'll cook the pasta and there's a salad in the fridge. I hope that's okay?'

'Better than okay,' Anna said fifteen minutes later when the pasta had cooked and they sat across from each other. 'This is delicious, but different.' She frowned. 'There's a flavour I can't place.'

'Sage,' Skye said. 'Mum loved Italian food and always said sage added depth to tomato flavours. This is her recipe.'

'Well, thank you again, it's delicious. Any other news from your day?'

Skye shook her head. 'Actually that's not true, Zara called before and asked if I wanted to go over there tomorrow night for dinner. Would that be okay?'

'That'd work well,' Anna said, and then went on to explain

the situation with her mother and the dinner that was planned at Xavier's.

Her phone pinged as she was talking, and she glanced at the screen. Kieran! She'd completely forgotten.

'Everything okay?' Skye asked, studying her face as she read Kieran's message.

Anna could feel her cheeks warming and imagined she'd turned bright red. 'I'd forgotten I had plans with a friend in the daytime tomorrow too; that's all. But I'll just let him know I'm busy. You and I should get out and do something together.'

Skye shook her head. 'God, no, don't do that. I can stay here with Smoko; it's not a big deal. You don't have to babysit me.'

'I know, but you've only been here a few days and I've hardly seen you.' She reread Kieran's message and sent a quick reply, giving him a summary of the situation and letting him know she had Skye with her. A message came straight back. She smiled and looked up at Skye.

'Feel like getting out of here tomorrow?'

'Maybe.' Skye's hesitation was obvious.

'Kieran's an old friend of mine,' Anna explained. 'I had dinner with him on Thursday night when you were with the Sampsons. It was the first time I've seen him in twenty-two years. He was my brother's best friend before he died. He's suggested a walk up in the Dandenongs tomorrow, followed by lunch at Olinda. He'd love you to come. We both would.'

Skye considered the invitation. 'He's a friend?'

Anna nodded, slightly uneasily as her stomach flip-flopped thinking of him.

Skye grinned. 'Okay, that'd be great.'

* * *

'How about we get some pizzas tonight?' Kieran said as he manoeuvred his silver Prado around the windy roads through Sassafras on the way back down from Olinda in the Dandenong Ranges.

The three of them had had a lovely day. Anna had introduced Skye and Kieran, and they'd had a long discussion on the drive from Prahran to Ferntree Gully about Kieran's flying career and the steps Skye could take if she was interested in following a similar pathway.

'There are lots of opportunities and grants for women in aviation,' Kieran had said. 'I can send you some information if you like.'

'He's nice,' Skye had whispered to her later as he'd excused himself during lunch to use the bathrooms. 'Are you sure you're only friends?'

Anna had found herself blushing. 'Right now, we are, yes. We did date back in high school, though, which was a million years ago.'

Skye then raised her eyebrows much more suggestively than a sixteen-year-old should, and Anna had chosen to look away and do her best to ignore her. She did have to admit to enjoying spending time with Kieran. At one stage on their walk to Olinda Falls and then on to the Botanic Gardens, Skye had walked ahead, leaving them an opportunity to talk.

'We were only a bit older than Skye when we got together,' Kieran had said. 'It's hard to believe that now, isn't it?'

'It is when you look back at everything that's happened in between,' Anna had said smiling. 'I feel positively old.'

'Any takers on that pizza?' Kieran said, breaking into Anna's thoughts.

'I can't,' Skye said, reminding Anna that she was going over to Bec's for dinner, 'but thank you.'

'Me either,' Anna said. 'Another time definitely.'

Kieran glanced at her sideways, and she knew he wanted a better explanation than that.

She sighed. 'It's Mum. I promised to take her out for dinner tonight. She's been a bit agitated about that old acquaintance of Dad and hers. She thinks Dad told him something about Jake's death that would prove it wasn't an accident. Dad would have gone to the police back then if that was the case. She's confused, but hopefully this guy, Xavier, will talk to her and reassure her it was nothing like that.'

Kieran frowned. 'You're not worried that seeing him might upset her even more?'

'I don't think it could make her any worse. She's currently fixated on talking to him Thinks he'll know something about Jake's accident. Mum's suggesting that Dad knew something and that maybe it wasn't the straight-out accident that we've always been led to believe.'

Kieran said nothing, but his hands tightened around the steering wheel, knuckles turning white as the road curved sharply ahead.

She felt the urge to reach across and squeeze his knee. She knew how difficult it was to discuss Jake without having some kind of physical or emotional reaction. But she loved that it wasn't just her who had loved her brother so much.

Kieran cleared his throat. 'What do you mean by not a straight-out accident?'

'I'm not completely sure. Mum's always struggled with it. Jake was a good driver, and she never understood how he drove off the road like that. I think she wants, or perhaps needs to believe, something else happened.'

Kieran glanced at her. 'It was an accident. He didn't deliberately drive off the road if that's what she's thinking. He would never have done that, any more than your dad would have stepped out in front of that bus on purpose.'

'I don't think she knows what she's thinking, but she won't have closure until she's spoken to this guy.'

Anna glanced at Kieran. 'Would you like to come with me? One of the carers from Willowridge was going to join us, but if you're at all curious, I can cancel the carer, and we can go.'

Kieran lapsed into silence.

'But you don't have to,' Anna added, noting his knuckles were whiter than before. 'I know how hard, even all these years later, anything involving Jake can be, and Mum's not at all like you'd remember her.'

Kieran flashed her a grateful smile. 'It surprises me how much I still struggle. I'll let you and the carer take your mum, if you don't mind. I know you haven't seen this side of me, but I've spent the last few years trying to get myself to a better place over what happened with Jake and the way I behaved, and I'm not completely there yet. I hope to be one day, but I know it's not today.'

'Of course,' Anna said, registering the flicker of disappointment that ran through her. She shook it away, knowing that if the situation were reversed, she'd decline the invitation too.

'I'll leave you to say goodbye,' Skye said, when Kieran pulled into the shared driveway of the Prahran apartment block, and they all climbed out of the four-wheel-drive. 'Thanks for a great day, Kieran.'

'No problem,' Kieran said, flashing her a smile. 'And I'll send you that pilot training information. I did my training in Adelaide, which I'd recommend, but you can have a look at other options. I think Qantas have a facility in Toowoomba now too.'

Skye thanked him again before disappearing into the apartment block.

'Nice kid,' Kieran said. 'She's pretty amazing when you consider what she's been through.'

'She is,' Anna agreed. 'I expect she'll have her ups and downs.'

'God, I wasn't that together a few months after Jake's death, let alone after Paige's. And Skye's lost her mum.' He shook his head. 'I think I was born with incredibly low resilience.'

'I wouldn't sell yourself short, or overanalyse,' Anna said. 'We all handle things differently.' She glanced at her watch. She needed to leave soon to pick her mother up. 'Thanks for today, I enjoyed it too.' She hesitated momentarily before relaxing again. It was only Kieran; she didn't know why she was so nervous. 'Would you like to come over for dinner one night during the week? Skye will probably be here too.'

Kieran hesitated long enough for it to feel awkward. 'Can I let you know?' he finally said.

'Sure.' Anna smiled, doing her best to hide her mortification. Maybe he hadn't enjoyed the day? Although why had he then suggested pizzas for tonight?

'Crazy week coming up,' Kieran said. 'But we'll work something out. And give me a call after you speak to this Xavier. As much as I'd prefer not to revisit that time, I must say I'm intrigued.' He leaned forward and gave her a brief peck on the cheek, before grinning and opening the door of his car.

Anna waved as he reversed out of the drive, wondering if she'd imagined the abrupt ending to their day. She pushed the thought from her head. It was the early days of reconnecting with Kieran. He wasn't the same teenage boy she'd been in love with all those years ago. She needed to get to know him as an adult and not read anything into it.

* * *

Bec did her best to smile as she took a lemon from the fruit bowl, pretending she was listening to the conversation between the three teenagers who were sitting on the couches in the open-plan area that ran off the kitchen. She loved that Skye had fitted in with her two so effortlessly but she wasn't sure whether to feel guilty that her mind was elsewhere or grateful to Skye for giving her two a distraction so that they didn't notice.

'Did you hear that?'

'Mum?' Zara raised her voice, causing Bec to snap to attention.

She looked up. 'Sorry, what did you say?'

'Skye said the guy she and Anna went out with today is Anna's ex-boyfriend from when she was our age.'

Bec nodded. 'She mentioned him on Thursday night. They had dinner. She hadn't seen him for over twenty years.'

'He's pretty hot,' Zara said.

'I didn't say that,' Skye said. 'I just said he was nice-looking for an old guy.'

Bec smiled. *Old guy.* If he was the same age as Anna he'd only just be forty. How nice to be sixteen and think anyone over twenty-five was old. And she had to admit to feeling a little curious as to what he was like.

'Skye got photos,' Zara said, clapping her hands together as Bec squeezed the lemon on the guacamole, which would accompany Hugo's favourite taco dinner.

'Photos of Kieran?' Bec asked, doing her best to tone down her excitement. She wasn't sure why she felt excited for Anna; she hardly knew her, but she was such a nice person, you wanted good things for her.

'He's nice,' Skye said. 'Smart, nice-looking. He's a pilot, so probably has flight attendants throwing themselves at him.'

'Can you see them together?' Zara asked.

Skye narrowed her eyes as she thought about this. 'Maybe, although I kind of imagine Anna with someone a bit more down to earth. Don't get me wrong, he's lovely, but there was something a bit weird when he dropped us off.' She went on to tell them what Anna had relayed about Kieran saying no to the dinner at Xavier's. 'You'd think after all these years he'd want to go, even just to make up to Anna for how he behaved when they were younger. He made it all about him, which seems a bit off.'

'How did Anna take that?' Bec asked.

Skye shrugged. 'She acted like it was fine. Anna's too nice, though. She'll be looking at what a hard time Kieran had when her brother died, because he was his best friend, rather than what Kieran's disappearance afterwards did to her. Don't get me wrong, I liked him, but that was awful if you ask me.'

* * *

Anna did her best to push all thoughts of Kieran and the abrupt ending to their day away as she'd arrived at Willowridge to collect her mother and Marty. She knew it wasn't reasonable of her to expect him to reopen old wounds of the past, and she'd need to be careful moving forward with what he felt comfortable discussing when it came to Jake.

As they made their way into the city, Marty kept them entertained with stories about his terrible golf game and the number of balls he'd managed to lose that afternoon.

'I thought you lived at Willowridge,' Anna said. 'You know, how you kind of run it and are there twenty-four seven.'

Marty laughed. 'Not on a Sunday. On a Sunday, I do my best to murder the golf ball and not use up all my swear words for the week. I need plenty of those ready for dealing with the likes of you, don't I, Lyn?'

Her mother managed a small laugh, but she was very much caught up in her own thoughts. She was, at least, having a good day and knew where they were going and why.

'I'm going to suggest we record the conversation with Xavier on one of our phones,' Marty had said when he'd met her outside her mother's room that afternoon. 'That way, if Lyn doesn't remember seeing him, we can replay it to her rather than having to go back and visit again and again.'

'It's only another hundred metres or so,' he said now, glancing up from his phone where he was getting directions.

Anna realised how grateful she was to Marty for his advice about the visit to the restaurant as she linked her arm through her mother's and guided her along Little Collins Street in search of Punt Lane.

The previous day, he'd come into her mother's room after she'd spoken with the restaurant and found out Xavier's movements.

'I'm sure you'll be fine, but if this restaurant triggers anything like it did for Lyn the other night, it might be good to have some backup.'

'Only if you'll let me pay for your time,' Anna had said.

Marty shook his head. 'Absolutely not. You can buy me a drink if you and your mum decide to stay for a meal, but I'll be discreet and leave you to your night. And I'll hover nearby somewhere in case something goes wrong.'

'Absolutely not,' Anna retorted. 'I've booked for three and I'd like you to join us.'

Marty opened his mouth as if about to object but instead smiled and closed it again.

Now, as they walked from the parking garage along Little Collins Street in the direction of Xavier's, Anna wasn't sure what she was trying to achieve with the visit to the restaurant, other than knowing it was where her mother had insisted on going.

She glanced sideways at her mother, who had a small smile playing on her lips as she took in the city streets.

'You okay, Mum?'

Lyn nodded. 'It's exactly as I remember it.'

They turned into the laneway marked Punt Lane, and Anna saw the signage to Xavier's. Her mother seemed to know where they were and what they were doing, but Anna wasn't going to assume it would stay that way.

She guided her through the front door of the restaurant and gave their name for the reservation and a few minutes later, they were seated at a table near an open fire, which was cosy and inviting. Anna could see why her parents had enjoyed it here.

'Ask if Xavier's here,' Lyn said. 'I need to speak to him.'

Anna got to her feet and went back over to the front door where they'd been greeted. 'Can you tell me, is Xavier here tonight?'

The maître d smiled. 'As in, the owner?'

Anna nodded. 'My mother's hoping to talk to him. She and my father used to come here a lot. The last time they came would have been over twenty years ago.'

He looked at his watch. 'He'll be in around seven, but I should warn you, he might not remember your mother. He's well into his nineties now and his memory isn't always great.'

'Could you send him over to us when he does get here?' Anna asked. 'Tell him Lyn Morrison is here. I'm not expecting him to remember my parents, but it'd be lovely if he had a few minutes. It'd mean a lot to my mum.'

'Sure, I'll let him know she's here when he arrives.'

They'd ordered their meals, and the mains had been delivered to the table when an elderly man approached them. He smiled and reached for Lyn's hand. 'Lyn Morrison, what a pleasure to see you after all this time. I've missed seeing you and Mal.'

'I'm Anna, their daughter,' Anna said, introducing herself, a small thrill running through her that he'd remembered her father's name. 'And this is Marty. Would you be able to join us for a few minutes?'

Xavier nodded and pulled out the chair next to Marty. He shook his head, smiling at Lyn. 'It's been a very long time. And how is Mal going?'

'My father died over twenty years ago,' Anna said before her mother had a chance to respond.

Xavier frowned. 'Sorry, yes, I think I did know that. I'm very sorry, Lyn. You must miss him.'

'And Jake,' Lyn said. 'My son.'

Xavier nodded again, and Anna could see him doing his best to try to remember the details from the past. She had to remind herself that he'd only been an acquaintance of her dad's, and with the hundreds, if not thousands, of people who would have passed through the restaurant, there was no reason he would remember the details of their family's story. He cleared his throat. 'I'm sorry,' he said. 'My grandson—' he nodded towards the young guy who Anna had spoken to earlier '—might have mentioned I struggle with my memory a little these days. I used to remember every detail of my customers' lives, but now it's all a bit foggy.' He gave a little laugh. 'Don't get old.'

'We don't expect you to remember anything,' Anna said. 'Although I know Mum's hoping you might remember the last time you saw her and my dad.'

Xavier frowned, seeming to rack his memory.

'It was a few months ago,' Lyn suddenly said. 'Jake died. I think you knew that already, and Mal wanted to ask your advice on something or tell you something. I was never quite sure which. He wouldn't tell me what but said he would share the details once he'd spoken to you.'

'A few months ago?'

Anna reached out and took her mother's hand. 'No, about twenty-two years ago. I'm afraid Mum's memory is playing tricks on her these days. Marty—' she nodded towards him '—works at Willowridge, the care facility where Mum lives.'

Xavier nodded, seeming to understand what Anna was telling him.

'I vaguely remember Mal being upset,' Xavier said. 'It was something about his son's accident.' He closed his eyes briefly, trying to remember the detail, eventually opening them and shaking his head. 'I'm so sorry, I can't remember.'

'He told you who killed Jake,' Lyn said. 'I know he did, and we need to know.'

Xavier's eyes met Anna's, alarm flaring in his. 'No, that wouldn't be the case. If he had I would have my friends on the force look into it. I'm an ex-cop.'

'That's right,' Lyn said. 'That's why Mal chose you to talk to. He was sure you'd be able to give him good advice.'

Anna glanced at Marty and could see he was thinking the same. At least they now had their answer to why Mal sought out Xavier to confide in.

'Hold on, it's coming back to me a little,' Xavier said. 'Jake died in a car accident, didn't he?'

'He was murdered,' Lyn said, reminding Anna of Clare Fleming and how she viewed her husband's death.

'Jake hit a tree with his car,' Anna said. 'He was the only occupant, and there were no witnesses. I think Mum's a bit confused.'

Lyn shook her head. 'No, that's not right. That's what we thought, but then Mal heard something else. He wouldn't tell me what. He said he'd bumped into Xavier at the pub and asked his advice. That's all he said.'

They all focused their eyes on Xavier, waiting for his response.

'I'm sorry, my memory isn't what it used to be, and I did get to know so many people.' He frowned. 'I don't recall seeing Mal at a pub. Perhaps leave it with me for a few days, and I'll do my best to remember.'

'But we need to know what he told you,' Lyn said, her agitation suddenly apparent. 'Jake was a good driver, and Mal found something out. It might have been about the car. That someone did something to the car?'

Xavier looked at Anna, a helpless expression on his face. 'I'm sorry that I can't remember. But like I said, leave it with me for a few days. It'll come back. I'm sure if it was important he would have spoken to me about it further on other occasions. I'm sure I'd remember if I was seeing him regularly.'

'He died a few weeks after Jake's death,' Anna said. 'So it may be that he spoke to you the once and then died. And please don't apologise – you've been lovely.' She took a card from her purse and handed it to him. 'If you remember anything later, please give me a call.'

Anna did her best to calm her mother down and suggested they order dessert, but Lyn was no longer in the right mindset. Anna paid the bill, and with Marty's help, they guided Lyn back along Little Collins Street to the parking garage.

'I'm sorry, Mum,' Anna said. 'That didn't go as planned.'

Lyn looked at Anna, her eyes glazed over. 'Where are we, Annie? Is this one of your book launches?'

Anna blinked back tears, wondering if she'd ever get used to this sudden departure of her mother.

'Hey,' Marty said after carefully depositing Lyn into the back seat of Anna's car. 'You're doing an amazing job with her. It's not easy.'

Anna managed a smile, grateful for his support, but at the same time, her mind shifted back to her father. She had a strong feeling her mother was confused. Her father would have taken his query to the police station, not an ex-cop, if he'd thought there was something suspicious surrounding Jake's death.

12

Anna pulled her jacket around her as she made her way up Bec's driveway after dropping her mother and Marty back at Willowridge. It was a beautiful, clear night, but the temperature had dropped significantly while they'd been at dinner.

She rang the doorbell and grinned when Bec opened the door. 'This is becoming a habit,' she said, ducking into the warmth of Bec's cosy home. 'Thanks so much for having Skye again. She was looking forward to coming over.'

Bec leaned forward and hugged Anna. 'Come in. They're all having a great time, and it's still early enough. Cup of tea? Wine?'

'I'd love a cuppa,' Anna said, following Bec through to the kitchen. She plonked herself on one of the stools. 'What a night.'

Bec looked up. 'Everything okay?'

Anna shook her head and quickly summarised the evening.

'So, your mum's convinced something else happened to your brother.'

Anna nodded. 'Yes, but I'm not sure what it could be. Jake was killed in a car accident. Single vehicle, coming back from a party alone. The way Mum's behaving, you'd think it was something quite sinister.'

'Peppermint?' Bec asked, holding up the box of teabags.

'Yes, please.'

'And it was a few weeks later that your dad mentioned something not being quite right?'

'According to Mum, yes. He told her and confided in their friend, this restaurateur guy, Xavier. Turns out he's an ex-cop and Dad happened to run into him at the pub, so Mum said, anyway. My guess is he just wanted advice from someone who'd know, not that he was convinced foul play was involved. If there had been, he would've gone straight to the police back then – Xavier would have had to, as well. Jake's death destroyed Dad. Literally killed him.'

She went on to tell Bec about her father's death.

Bec dropped the teabags into the cups, poured steaming water over them and pushed one across to Anna. 'You've had a rough time, haven't you?'

Anna shrugged. 'I'm not sure any of us have it easy. I wish I was one of those people who believed everything happened for a reason. I can't see any reason why both Dad and Jake dying would have a positive side to it.'

'It's not easy, is it, having lost a brother?'

Anna shook her head. 'No, it's not. I know you said you'd lost your brother at a similar age. That he took his life?'

Bec sighed and nodded. 'Chris had mental health issues and his depression led to drugs. He wasn't given any help and he decided to check out.'

'I'm sorry,' Anna said 'That must have been so hard. No doubt, still is.'

'It is,' Bec admitted. 'Hard. It's hard not to think about what I could have done differently back then. How I could have reached out and helped him before it was too late, and what my parents should have done.'

Anna nodded. She'd heard stories like this many times in her counselling work, but each one still struck deep. She knew how suicide could leave behind a maze of guilt and unanswered questions. 'Losing someone to suicide is unlike any other kind of grief,' she said softly. 'It's not just the loss, it's the shock, the confusion, and the "what ifs" that can haunt you. I'm so sorry you've had to go through that.'

'Thank you. And yes, it's not an easy one.' Bec cleared her throat, and Anna expected a change of subject, which she got. 'How's the man? Skye mentioned that the three of you went up to the Dandenongs today and had a great time. She said he was good-looking too.'

Anna laughed. 'Yes, he is.' Her laughter drifted off. 'But he was also a bit strange when we got home. Couldn't get out of there quick enough. Didn't want to come with me tonight with Mum to Xavier's.'

'Do you think he knows something and he's not letting on about it? Perhaps whatever it is that your dad told this restaurant guy? And that's why he didn't want to go with you?'

Anna considered this suggestion but ended up shaking her head. 'No, that wouldn't make sense. He was devastated at the time and left Melbourne shortly after. He wasn't hiding anything and certainly didn't know anything. He wasn't with Jake that night. I'll never forget the next morning, though, when he came around. He'd already been told.'

* * *

Anna wasn't sure what to do. She'd woken to the sound of sobbing and had come down to the kitchen to find her father holding her mother, both of them crying.

'What's happened?'

Her father deposited his wife into a seat and put his arms around Anna. 'We've had some bad news, sweetheart.'

Anna's heart raced. The last time her father had used these words, she'd learned that his mother, her grandmother, had passed. 'It's not Granddad, is it?'

Her father took a deep breath. 'It's Jake, honey. He's had a car accident.'

Anna pulled away from her father, her mother's sobs intensifying. 'Where is he? I need to see him. Is he at the hospital?'

Her father pulled her to him again. 'I'm sorry, sweetheart, but he was injured badly. They couldn't—' His voice caught. 'They couldn't save him.'

She shivered at the memory.

Around an hour later, Kieran appeared in her bedroom doorway. His eyes were red from crying, his clothes rumpled as if he'd slept in them.

'Charlie told me,' he said, before stepping into the room and hugging her tightly. 'His dad was one of the first responders.'

They stayed sitting on her bed, hugging for a long time. Both were crying, unsure of what to do. Eventually, Kieran stood, kissed her on the forehead and left the room.

Anna had assumed he was going to get them some drinks or going to the bathroom. Something normal. But he'd never returned. It was the last time she'd seen him until now.

* * *

Her phone dinged with a text message breaking into her thoughts.

'Sorry,' she said to Bec, glancing at her phone. 'That's him now.'

'Read it,' Bec said. 'I'm intrigued.'

KIERAN

Hope it all went well with your mum and the visit. Did Xavier have anything interesting to say?

ANNA

No, he remembered Mum and Dad, and a bit about Jake having an accident but that was all. Possibly has some dementia or old age memory loss.

KIERAN

Did it help your mum?

ANNA

Not really. But then she's not with it half the time, so who knows? She did say she'd love to see you again if you ever got the time.

KIERAN

Of course. Let me know when. Perhaps we could see her after work one night and then have some dinner?

ANNA

Sounds good.

Wednesday?

Anna smiled at the messages, realising she had misread Kieran's abrupt end to their outing. She was looking forward to seeing him again.

'Looks like he's made up for today,' Bec said, raising an eyebrow. 'Nice messages?'

Anna could feel her cheeks burning. It had been years since

she dated or even thought about dating, and this felt very strange, particularly that it was Kieran.

'Yes, I think I overanalysed earlier. He's agreed to come and see Mum, which hopefully, if she's with it, will be nice for her. Remind her of some of the good times when we were kids.'

'That's great,' Bec said. 'I'm happy for you. Those early days of dating are exciting.'

'They are,' Anna said. 'I don't think I ever got over him, so who knows, perhaps I wasn't supposed to, as he was destined to come back.'

'Maybe. Or he's very lucky that you're willing to forgive him for the past and start afresh. Speaking of fresh starts, I was thinking more about Skye's situation. Are you sure you're not able to foster her? It'd only be for two years until she was eighteen. It's not the same as the little girl you had. Not at all.'

Anna shook her head without hesitating. 'No, and don't get me wrong, I've given it a lot of thought, but it's not something I'm willing to do.'

'I get that you need to protect yourself,' Bec said, 'but can't you look past that? The other woman might reappear, the one who works for the UN, so it might only be for a matter of months.'

Anna sighed and stood. 'If I knew for sure it was only for a few months then I might say yes, but we might never find out what's happened to her, she could very easily be dead for all we know. Getting Skye settled in with a family will help her get back into a routine.'

'That's a shame, you'd be good for each other.'

'Not as good as you would be for her,' Anna said. 'Rather than look at me as being the perfect option, why don't you give more thought as to what you, Hugo and Zara could give Skye. You're a ready-made family.' She didn't give Bec a chance to respond. 'I'm going to get Skye. It's been a long day. Thanks again for having her tonight.'

* * *

Bec had to restrain herself from shaking Anna. Couldn't she see how much she had to offer Skye and what a perfect solution it would be for both of them? Surely Anna got lonely coming home to an empty house each night? And in her line of work she saw so many troubled people who she tried to help. Now she had a chance to take this one step further. As for Bec taking on Skye, she almost laughed at the thought. Imagine it, her, in her current state, still grieving Owen, barely managing to get out of bed some mornings, somehow taking responsibility for another teenager. She was pretty sure she was messing up the two she already had. She wasn't willing to inflict herself or her situation on another. If Owen were still alive, that would be different. But he wasn't.

Now, as she and Zara waved goodbye to Anna and Skye, she turned and hugged her daughter.

'What's that for?' Zara asked, pulling out of her mother's embrace.

'No reason,' Bec said. 'But I'm proud of you for being so good to Skye.'

Zara shrugged. 'It's not like I have to try. She's cool. Both Hugo and I like her, so that's perfect. We have a mutual friend for once and can all do stuff together.'

Bec slung an arm around Zara's shoulders as they walked back into the house and down the hallway towards the kitchen.

'Any contact since yesterday from my parents?'

'Nope, still no response?'

Bec was filled with a mixture of relief for herself and mild disappointment on Zara's behalf. Although, as much as she wanted nothing to do with them, the fact that it was highly possible they would reappear in her life had made her a little curious. She knew her dad could shut himself off and you could be dead to him, which he'd done to Chris and no doubt her when she left, but her mother had loved her and Chris with a fierce passion. A passion Bec herself understood when she'd had her twins. What she'd never been able to understand, though, was how her mother could have let her walk away and then never tried to track her down. She felt an inkling of guilt when she considered this. She hadn't exactly made it easy for anyone to find her. She imagined if Zara did the same to her, how she'd feel. To be excluded from her daughter's life and her grandchildren's. She pushed the thought away quickly.

The difference between her and her mother is that she would never have gone along with Owen if he'd done something like her father had. They were ashamed of their son and had been happy to cover up the circumstances of his death. She shook her head.

'What?' Zara said. 'You're a million miles away.'

'Thinking about my mum,' Bec admitted. 'About how I still can't believe she never tried to track me down. If you went missing, or ran off like I did, I would have found you.'

'Does that mean you want to see her?' Zara's tone wasn't accusatory, just curious.

Bec stared at her daughter. She'd spent so many years channelling hate at her parents, but since Owen's death something had changed. As much as she'd been frustrated by Zara's detective work, there was a small part of her that missed her mother and wondered how her life had played out with no kids around. Samara had been a stay-at-home mum for her and Chris's entire childhood, and then both children were suddenly taken from her. It must have been a huge adjustment.

'I guess there's part of me that's interested,' Bec finally said. 'Perhaps it's been easier to pretend they don't exist rather than deal with what happened. I don't know really.'

'Maybe she *has* been looking for you,' Zara said. 'If she ever responds to my message, I guess you or I can ask her.'

* * *

Samara Langford stood in front of the bookshelf in her study, as she did every evening before she went to bed, and reached out and ran her finger down the edge of the photo frame. It had been twenty years, yet she found she couldn't start or end the day without acknowledging her son. Those who'd told her that her grief would lessen as time moved on had never experienced the death of a child. Sure, there'd be times through the day when she'd be doing something and realise she hadn't thought of Chris for a few hours, but then it would hit her just as hard again.

She'd learned within weeks of Chris's death that she needed to deal with her grief alone. Bruce seemed to have closed the door on any emotion the death of his son might have, or should have, brought up. He'd hugged her tight each night when they were in bed and wiped her tears more than once, but he refused to speak about it. Samara's resentment built every time she thought about that.

She'd done her best to be there for Rebecca, but her daughter had pushed her away. She'd been angry, furious even, at both her and Bruce. She'd blamed them for Chris's death and was enraged with them for covering up the details of Chris's suicide. Rebecca had been young, and Samara knew she couldn't see it from her parents' point of view. She saw them covering up the suicide as something to hide their embarrassment and shame, rather than it being to protect Chris's reputation. To bury him with respect and love, rather than have people poking into his death and the difficult last two years of his life. *Difficult*. That was an understatement.

Samara found it surprising that she'd been able to get out of bed each day after Chris's death and then Rebecca's leaving. She was often transported back to the last time she saw or spoke to her daughter, although *spoke* was a rather wishful description. Received a barrage of abuse might be more fitting.

* * *

'Stop pretending you care,' Rebecca shouted.

They'd returned from Chris's funeral, and Rebecca was brimming with anger and emotion. It had been incredibly difficult seeing her son's friends in tears as they comforted each other and listening to the speeches several of them made. Her parents and Bruce's had been there by their sides, but nothing helped. It was so awful.

'No one should ever have to bury a child,' was a mantra that played constantly through her mind. Bruce had spoken beautifully about Chris, and she was grateful that he'd taken on the role, and she hadn't had to. He spoke of how proud he was of his son and what a fine man he'd become. How their lives would never be the same, and how much he loved him. To have returned home to have Rebecca confront them and do her best to tear them apart was more than she could handle.

'Why couldn't you tell people the truth?' she demanded. 'Let them know that Chris was struggling? All you and Dad ever worry about is Dad's reputation. His precious image. God forbid anyone know what Chris went through!'

Samara flinched. 'That's not fair or true. We were protecting Chris.'

'From what? From anyone understanding his mental health problems?'

'Is that how you want people to remember him?' Bruce asked her. 'As a junkie who couldn't handle his life? Who didn't have the strength to pull himself out of the hole he'd got himself into?'

'The hole you put him in,' Rebecca shouted. 'He turned to drugs because of you. Because your career was more important than any of us were to you. Why couldn't you see that? Why didn't you help him?'

Bruce walked away at that point, and Samara asked Rebecca to leave her alone, too. 'I can't do this today, Rebecca. Not today of all days. All I wanted was to protect Chris. To let him be remembered with dignity.' Her head was pounding. She knew Rebecca was hurting. Chris was her twin. But right at this moment, she needed to look after herself. She'd just buried her son.

* * *

A tear rolled down her cheek, bringing Samara back to the present. She moved across the room in front of the only family portrait of the four of them that wasn't boxed up and hidden at the top of a cupboard. When Rebecca had disappeared, Bruce had initially been worried and, like her, reached out to everyone he knew, trying to locate his daughter. But when they received a note from her that clearly said she'd left of her own accord, and would never forgive them for their treatment of Chris or the cover-up of his death to protect Bruce's political career, his concern had turned to anger.

Samara had come home from a charity event one afternoon to find that Bruce had instructed the cleaner to remove all photos of Rebecca from around the house, as he had done of Chris following his death. They'd been boxed up and were sitting by the front door to be thrown out. Samara hadn't said anything. She'd taken the box and put it at the top of a cupboard in what had been Chris's bedroom.

The box had travelled with her ten years earlier when they'd moved to Canberra. It was a large house, and Bruce had insisted she turn one of the rooms into a space for herself. *A lady cave*, Bruce had said, insisting she'd like having somewhere to retreat to from time to time. When they moved back to Melbourne, she'd chosen one of the bedrooms as her *cave*, and she couldn't imagine life without it. She spent most of the time when she was at home in this room, and it allowed her to have some of the photos Bruce had removed on display. He never came into this room.

One of the things she found the hardest was that Bruce wouldn't speak about Chris or Rebecca. It was as if their children had never existed.

But they had, and as far as she knew, her daughter still did.

She wondered where Rebecca was and what her life looked like now. Was she married? Did she have children? Where did she live, and what did she do for work? There were so many questions and so much she was sure she'd missed out on. Questions she now needed answers to.

It was getting late, but it didn't stop her from picking up the phone she'd left on the desk. It had been weeks since she'd engaged the private investigator's services and still nothing. She found his number and pressed the call button.

13

On Monday afternoon, Hugo grinned and waved to the girls as he took off in the direction of the gym. Skye had caught a bus from her school in Richmond to Camberwell and surprised the twins with an afternoon visit.

'It's so weird,' Zara said, lying back on the chairs they'd positioned in the front garden to catch the late afternoon sun. 'We only met you last week, yet it feels like we've known you for ages. Hugo was saying the same to me this morning. He reckons it's our birth connection and that you lost your mum and we lost Dad. We all get each other. He's probably right.' She grinned at Skye. 'Whatever it is I'm so glad you were hiding from the cops and everyone else and we got to meet you. How's that going by the way?'

'What – the cops?'

Zara nodded. 'And the foster situation.'

'Cops are fine,' Skye said, sipping the tea Zara had made for her. 'Anna had a good chat to my caseworker and she smoothed things over with the police. She got me off having to do the stuff at your mum's work on the condition I was in school and staying with Anna.'

'How's it going living with Anna?'

'Good so far. It's a shame she won't do long-term fostering. It'd be great to stay there.' She sighed. 'But she's promised me she won't kick me out or anything.' Her eyes followed a white Mercedes as it slowed down in front of the house and then sped off again. 'Strange. Someone you know?'

Zara shook her head. 'This might sound like a weird question, but how do you keep it so together all the time? You've lost your mum, you've been farmed out to live with a stranger, but you seem totally chill. I don't get it. I'd be a mess.'

Skye shrugged. 'I'm not always so relaxed. I have my moments. I really miss Mum. I still don't really believe she's gone. I expect her to turn up and say it's all been some stupid joke or something.'

Zara nodded. 'I get that. My dad was this fantastic guy. It seems so surreal he's gone.'

'You seem to be handling it pretty well,' Skye said.

Zara rolled her eyes. 'You reckon? I'm tracking down grandparents and going against everything my mum's asked. She wants to kill me.'

'She knows why you need more family,' Skye said. 'She gets it. Even if she might not like it, it must be hard on her too, losing your dad.'

'She cries a lot,' Zara said. 'She thinks Hugo and I don't hear her, but we do. It's usually late at night. It's normal, I guess, but it's hard hearing how much she misses him.' She sighed. 'At least we know she loved him. We were embarrassed by how much they loved each other. Always kissing and hugging and telling us to look the other way if we had a problem with it.'

'Did you?'

Zara shook her head. 'I pretended to. You know, making retching noises and get-a-room kind of comments, but no, I loved seeing it. One of my friends in Sydney had parents who never kissed or showed any kind of intimacy in front of her or her sisters. Mind you, they then got divorced, so I guess that makes sense.'

'There it is again,' Skye said as the white Mercedes passed. 'Some rich woman, by the looks of her. I wonder if she's lost?'

* * *

If it hadn't meant she'd probably crash her car, Samara would have ducked. What was she thinking? She'd been awake most of the night following her conversation with the private investigator and was now acting impulsively, having not been able to think of the best way to approach her daughter. She probably should have asked the investigator for tips during their conversation the previous evening.

* * *

'Your daughter wasn't easy to find.'

'You found her?' Samara's heart raced.

'Yes, hold on.'

She waited a moment and then her phone pinged with a text. She opened it to find herself staring at Rebecca. Her heart contracted as she stared at the older version of the daughter she'd known.

'She's been living in Sydney with her husband and two teenage children. Twins. Boy and girl, aged sixteen.'

Twins! She was a grandmother of twins! 'Sydney?'

'Until recently. Her husband died a few months ago and they moved back to Melbourne. They had a business in Sydney with an

office in Melbourne too, and evidently she decided to close the Sydney branch and come and work in the Melbourne one.'

* * *

Samara found herself awake all night looking at the documents he'd forwarded and replaying everything he'd told her. She had grandchildren. Twins now only a few years younger than Chris and Rebecca were when she'd lost them. The information included Rebecca's home address. She lived in Camberwell, only about ten minutes away.

She hadn't been able to help herself and fuelled on adrenalin and coffee, that afternoon she'd driven to Camberwell. After sitting in a side street for twenty minutes she had conjured up the nerve to drive past her daughter's house. To do it once was perhaps understandable, but twice, she was asking for trouble. She'd assumed Rebecca would be at work, and she most likely was, but one of the girls in the front garden was the spitting image of her at the same age. Her heart had almost stopped when she saw her. The other girl, a pretty blonde, had looked straight at her. Luckily, there was no reason that either of them would have any idea of who she was.

She stopped around the corner from the house, willing her heart rate to calm. She could imagine the news headline, *Ex-politician's wife has heart attack while stalking estranged daughter.* She would almost laugh, except it wasn't funny. God, what would Bruce say? She didn't know, and it hadn't been enough to stop her from driving by again. She wanted one more glimpse of the girl who was certainly her granddaughter.

The question of what Bruce would say was playing over in her mind when she arrived home. He was climbing out of his car as she pulled the Mercedes into the driveway. He smiled and waved. She smiled back. With all his faults, she was the first to admit that he was still a very handsome man.

She wondered, as she'd done many times over the years, why she'd stayed with him. She knew he was passionate about his job and serving the community and country, but it had been at a huge price.

'Hey, darling, good day?' he asked as he opened her door.

She stepped out and gave him a perfunctory kiss on the cheek. She could hardly tell him what she'd been doing or that she'd seen her granddaughter, a granddaughter he had no idea they had.

'Just some shopping,' she replied.

He nodded and automatically went to open the boot.

'Don't open that,' she snapped, not wanting the empty boot to catch her in a lie. 'Sorry,' she said, registering the hurt that flashed in his eyes. 'I've got your birthday presents in there. I don't want you seeing anything.'

Bruce stepped back, lifting his hands in the air and laughing. 'You're getting in early this year. It's still a month away.'

She forced a smile. 'It's not only your birthday coming up.' She knew she was treading on dangerous ground bringing this up. It had been an unspoken rule for years now that they didn't talk about Chris or Rebecca or acknowledge their birthday or any other significant dates. A flash of pain crossed his face, but she reached for his hand and continued, 'I need to see her.'

He stared at her. 'Why now? It's been years.'

'She's my daughter. I think about her every day,' she said. 'I'd like to try and reach out to her.'

He dropped her hand. 'No. She walked away. She can't walk back into our lives now.'

'She's not asking to walk back into our lives. I'm saying I want to be part of hers or at least see her once. Talk to her.'

He snorted. 'I think you'll find she'll appear soon enough without you going in search of her.'

Samara took a step backward. 'What do you mean "she'll appear"?'

He stared at her for a long moment and then extracted something from his back pocket. 'This arrived last week. My guess is our daughter's behind this and is probably after money.'

He handed her the piece of paper he'd taken from his pocket and turned to leave. He stopped and turned back. 'For the record, I want nothing to do with her or her family.'

Samara put a hand on his arm. 'Why not? It's been a long time, Bruce.'

He closed his eyes, and Samara saw the pain flash across his face. Sometimes she had to remind herself that he'd lost his children too. He'd seemed to be able to throw himself into his work straight after Chris's death and Rebecca's departure and act as if nothing had happened and he'd never had any children, but occasionally she'd see a glimpse of something else.

'She'll bring nothing but pain into our lives.' With that, he turned and walked into the house, leaving her holding the envelope he'd handed her.

She unfolded the paper. It was a printout of an email.

> Hi. My name is Zara, and I believe we might be related. My mother is Rebecca Jane Langford. I'd like to make contact with you. Please reply via email or phone.

An email and phone number stared at her.

Her heart raced. Her granddaughter was reaching out. She shook her head at the irony. The amount of time and money she'd invested in the investigator trying to find Rebecca and her family. She could have sat back and waited for Zara to contact her.

Zara. She had to smile. She'd always assumed Rebecca hated her. She'd left and never made contact, changing her name and making it virtually impossible to track her down. But she'd had a daughter she'd named Zara. When she was little, she'd struggled to pronounce her mother's name, and when she'd hit her teenage years, she decided her mother needed a cooler name.

'You should call yourself something else,' she'd said. *'Samara's a weird name. You're going to be famous with Dad's stuff, so you should have something more glamorous.'*

Samara had laughed. *'You only need to call me Mum, so it doesn't really matter.'*

Rebecca had shaken her head. *'No, you need a better name. Something more exotic. I'm going to tell my friends' parents your name is Zara from now on.'*

And now she'd named her daughter Zara. Samara hugged herself. Maybe there was some hope in reconnecting with Rebecca after all.

14

Anna had spent time the previous day trying to find out more information from a contact Isabella had at the UN as to Erin's whereabouts. She'd hit dead end after dead end but wanted to try every avenue to contact her. Erin had agreed to be Skye's guardian and Anna's gut told her that this woman didn't even know her friend had died, let alone that Skye was in the situation she was in.

It had plagued her through the Echoes session the previous night and for once she found herself quite distracted and very grateful to the guest speaker she'd organised for the evening as it took the focus off her.

Now, late on Wednesday afternoon as they walked through the front entrance of the care facility, she found she was a little nervous. She was pleased that Kieran had agreed to visit her mother. She'd half expected him to cancel, saying it was too much and would bring his memories of Jake back, but he hadn't.

Marty waved from the front desk where he was working on the computer and stood as she and Kieran moved closer.

'This is Marty,' Anna said, introducing the two men who

shook hands. 'Marty's been amazing to Mum for the entire time she's lived here.'

Anna had filled Kieran in on her mother's living situation on the car ride over to Willowridge and had told him about the incredible care and support she'd received from the centre and Marty and some of the other carers.

'Hold on a minute, the carer who went to the restaurant with you was this guy, Marty?'

She'd nodded and then launched into more anecdotal stories about the various things Marty had done for both her mum and herself over the years, finding herself laughing as she relayed many of the funny things he'd done and then reinforcing how good he'd been to her mum.

'And that's normal?' Kieran had said. 'That he'd do so much for your mum? Or is he doing it for you?'

'For Marty it's normal and definitely for Mum,' Anna had replied. 'He's not interested in me.' But even as she'd said the words, Anna had wondered if they were true. She'd never thought of Marty like that. He was always over-the-top lovely to her, but she'd assumed he was like that with all the families of patients and that it was his way of easing the situation for them.

But now, as she introduced the two men, she couldn't help noticing the wary look on both of their faces as they shook hands.

'Good to meet you, mate,' Kieran said.

'Haven't seen you here before,' Marty said. 'Do you know Lyn?'

Kieran nodded. 'Grew up with Anna and her brother. Lyn and Mal were like my second parents.'

Marty frowned. 'But you haven't visited before?'

'Long story,' Anna said. 'Kieran and I only reconnected last week. We went our separate ways after Jake died.'

Kieran surprised Anna by putting an arm around her shoulders. 'And now we're getting to know each other again.'

'Nice,' Marty said. 'I'm sure Lyn will be pleased to see you. Although she's not really with it today, so see how you go. Now, I'll leave you to it. I need to get on with my work.' Marty flashed Anna a quick smile before sitting back down and refocusing on the computer screen.

'Interesting,' Kieran said, removing his arm. 'I think you've got an admirer.'

Anna gave an awkward laugh, conscious of Kieran's possessive move with the arm drape. 'I'm sure he's not and I'm sure he's taken. He's one of those guys who'd have his pick of women, or men, for that matter.'

'He's gay?'

'I have no idea,' Anna said, realising with embarrassment that she hardly knew anything about Marty. He knew so much about her and her family and yet the conversations had been very one-sided. 'Now, come and say hi to Mum. And remember what I said about how she might be.'

Anna was pleased she'd forewarned him. Even then, she could only imagine what was going through Kieran's head as he did his best to have a conversation with her mother. Lyn was miles away. She had no idea who Kieran was and kept asking him to get her a bowl of soup.

'Sorry,' Anna said. 'She must think you're one of the carers or that you work in a restaurant. She's not here right now.'

'It's no problem,' Kieran said.

'Anna Rachel Morrison,' her mother suddenly said, 'how dare you say I'm not here. I'm right here.' She looked from Anna to Kieran and back again. 'Wow, Kieran Bradley, you're a sight for sore eyes. It is you and not your dad, isn't it?'

Kieran laughed and leaned down and hugged her. 'It's good to see you again, Mrs Morrison. It's been a lot of years, and yes, it's me and not my dad.'

'Your father was in his early forties the last time I saw him,' Lyn said. 'How is he?'

'Good. No complaints. He and Mum moved to Queensland when my sister married and moved away. She had three kids, so my parents like being closer to help and spend time with them.'

'I thought you and Anna would have kids,' her mother said. 'You were too young back then, but we, your father and I, thought you would.' She narrowed her eyes. 'But then you disappeared.'

Kieran's face turned red. 'I did, and while I've apologised to Anna, I wanted to come and apologise to you too. I should have stayed.'

Lyn fell silent, and Anna could see her searching her memories. 'Mal didn't like you after that. You did something to upset him.' She sighed. 'I can't remember what it was.' She looked at Anna. 'Why can't I remember anything?'

'I think you might have that confused, Mum,' Anna said. 'We never heard from Kieran after he left.' She turned to Kieran. 'You know, even your mum and dad didn't want to share any information about where you were. Did they know? Because they made out like they had no idea. They said you'd disappeared from their lives, too.'

Kieran blushed. 'No, they did know where I was. I didn't want anyone from home finding me, so I asked them to say that, even to you.'

Anna jumped as Lyn clapped her hands together. 'That's it. I remember now, your mum did eventually tell me you'd gone to live in South Australia with her sister and you were hoping to get into a pilot training course.' She frowned. 'But that was too expensive so she wasn't sure what you were going to do.' She looked at Anna. 'Didn't you say Kieran became a pilot?'

Anna nodded and looked at Kieran, whose cheeks had coloured.

'It was very expensive, but I was lucky and got a partial scholarship and was able to work part-time to fund the rest. I wanted to do something for Jake, and being a pilot was what I knew he wanted.'

Lyn's frown remained. 'Jake's plan was to join the Air Force. He couldn't afford the flight training courses either, and that was a way to get into flying. Why didn't you do that if you wanted to do something for him?'

Kieran hesitated before responding. 'His ultimate dream was to get a spot with Qantas; it wasn't to join the Air Force. He just thought that was his only option to get his Commercial Pilot Licence. I decided to look at other options and hopefully get the job he'd dreamed of.'

'And did you?'

Kieran nodded. 'Yes, I've been with the airline for close to twenty years.'

Anna was shaking her head throughout this exchange. Part of her would like to kill her mother right now. It had been bad enough losing Jake all those years ago, but to lose Kieran at the same time had added another layer of awfulness to the situation. 'I can't believe you knew where Kieran was and you never told me.'

'I discussed it with your father, and we decided if Kieran didn't want you to know where he was, and didn't have the decency to treat you with the respect you deserved, you were better off without him.' She smiled, looking at Kieran. 'I'm sure that was it. Why Mal was upset with you.' She turned back to Anna. 'And, it's Kieran you should be mad with. Not your father or me.'

Anna almost laughed at the awkwardness of the situation,

and did acknowledge that her mother was right. Kieran's cheeks had drained of the previous embarrassed colour, the more her mother spoke. Even though Lyn's delight at remembering had nothing to do with *what* she'd remembered, but rather the fact that she'd been able to remember at all.

'Well, regardless of anything,' Kieran said, 'I hope you'll forgive me now. I was young and had no idea how to handle the situation, and obviously didn't handle it very well.'

Lyn sighed. 'None of us did.' She looked out of the window, silence falling over the room as they sat with their own thoughts. A few minutes later, when she turned back to them, Anna could see the change in her eyes.

'Annie! Have you come to take me to the book launch?'

* * *

'I'm so sorry,' Anna said, as she and Kieran climbed back into her Mazda.

Kieran slipped into the passenger seat beside her and reached for his seat belt. 'Why are you sorry?'

'For what Mum said about Dad being upset with you.'

Kieran shifted in his seat. 'That's hardly something to apologise for. He had good reason to be. Not just because I left but the way I did it. I was eighteen and didn't know how to handle the situation. The one thing I was happy about was getting a place at the flight training school. Yes, Jake would have gone via the Air Force, but this gave me a much faster road into working on a commercial airline, which is what I think he really would have preferred to do.'

It was on the tip of Anna's tongue to ask how Kieran had afforded the flight training, as his family weren't wealthy, but she remembered he'd said he had received a partial scholarship and worked to meet the shortfall.

Anna started the car and manoeuvred out of the centre's car park and onto the main road. She glanced at Kieran to find him rubbing his collarbone, exactly the way he'd done when he was younger and was lying or hiding something.

* * *

It was hard to believe a whole week had passed since Samara had seen Zara and Bruce had handed over Zara's message to her. As much as she'd been dying to contact her granddaughter, Samara also hadn't wanted to rush into anything. Any contact she made with Rebecca or her family was likely to cause issues between her and Bruce, and she wasn't sure how to deal with this. When he'd been in public life, she'd been conscious of them presenting a united front, and while he was now in private business, she still felt it was important.

Her husband had hardly spoken to her since he'd given her Zara's email. She knew him well enough to know that he was waiting to see what she was going to do. He would make his feelings even clearer if she did suggest she was going to contact Zara, but she wasn't sure that he would stop her.

She bent to pull out a handful of stubborn winter weeds from the edge of the lavender bed, the cold air biting at her fingers despite her gloves. Gardening had always helped her think, and lately, she'd spent more time out here than usual, pruning back overgrown shrubs and preparing the soil for the quiet months ahead.

In the past week, she'd found herself driving past Bec's house on more than one occasion, but other than the initial sighting of Zara, she hadn't seen Bec or either of the children. She wasn't sure what she would do if she saw her daughter. Part of her would like to pull over and get out of the car and go and talk to her, but the realist in her knew this wasn't likely to have a happy ending. While her granddaughter might be reaching out, over twenty years had passed since Bec had made her choice to leave her family and, assuming she was as stubborn as she had been as a little girl, Samara doubted anything would have changed.

Her thoughts were interrupted, and she was surprised to hear Bruce's car in the driveway as she pulled another weed. She stood and brushed her hands off on her trousers as he pulled to a stop next to her, and the window of his Tesla came down. He gave her a tentative smile. 'Having a good day?'

She nodded, debating whether to broach the issue of Bec now or later. 'You?'

'Meetings as usual. Lots has been happening since the budget was passed down last week. Usual stuff with the end of the financial year approaching. Lots of investors to hit up for donations. I do have a few dinners coming up that I'd appreciate you attending with me.'

She nodded again. 'Bruce?'

He sighed. 'The Rebecca situation isn't going to go away, is it?'

'I need to see her. I need to meet my... our grandchildren.'

'You do what you must. Just leave me out of it.'

The window of the Tesla went up, and he drove down to the garage, leaving her staring after him.

15

Almost two weeks had passed since Anna agreed that Skye could live with her temporarily. The previous week, she'd visited two potential foster families but couldn't imagine Skye living with either of them. One home felt too rigid, with polite smiles and stiff rules taped to the fridge. The other, though warm and tidy, had an overwhelming sense of loneliness – its well-meaning carer seemed eager to fill a void rather than offer space for Skye to heal. Neither place felt like it would give her the quiet understanding or stability she needed. As a result, Anna hadn't brought up the visits with the teenager and had continued her phone calls to try and find out information about Erin.

Overall, Skye had adjusted to living with Anna, but Anna was very conscious that she was still struggling. What teenager, or child of any age, wouldn't be, having lost their mum recently? Unfortunately, there was nothing, other than time, that would help Skye adjust. Actually, that wasn't true. Time was a key component, but having a good support system around her would also help.

Now, as Anna logged into her computer at work early on

Monday morning, she thought back to a conversation she'd had with Skye the previous night. It had surprised her that Skye felt she needed to ask if it would be okay to return to the Echoes group the next evening.

'Of course,' Anna said when Skye raised it. 'Having you there the other week made me think that perhaps we need to consider a group for younger people.'

Skye considered the suggestion. 'I don't know if you need a separate group,' she said. 'But if you do want some younger people there, I thought, if it's okay, I might see if Zara and Hugo want to come with me. They had some counselling when their dad first died, but nothing since they moved to Melbourne. It sounded like the person they saw in Sydney was a bit useless. I think they could maybe use something like Echoes. Zara pretends to be okay, but she's not. She's really missing her dad.'

Anna had, of course, encouraged Skye to invite the twins along and had made a note to give Bec a call later that morning to not only give her the heads-up about Echoes, but also to relay what Skye had mentioned about Zara.

She shot off an email, conscious that her first client of the week would be arriving in ten minutes. Clare Fleming. A shiver ran down her spine as the full force of Clare's situation hit her. She picked up her phone to call Detective Masters to ensure she was up to date with what was happening before Clare arrived.

* * *

Anna had only just finished her call with Detective Masters when a message popped up on her screen to let her know Clare was in the reception area.

A few minutes later, she guided the woman back into her office, gesturing towards the small lounge area she'd arranged with clients in mind. Clare sank into the armchair. Her cheeks were pale and drawn, her eyes shadowed and hollow. Anna decided to launch into what she'd found out, before getting to how Clare was.

'I've just spoken with Detective Masters,' Anna said. 'It appears there's no further information at this stage about the accident. I'm sure you know this already.'

Clare nodded, and Anna continued. 'I've also spoken to Regina Murgon, a contact of mine at Channel Ten. She's involved with the production side of *The Briefing Room*, you know the nightly news show that follows the national news.'

Clare moved to the edge of her seat, suddenly interested.

'She'd be willing to talk to you and consider running a story on your situation. See if it brings forward any new information.'

'Really?'

Anna nodded. 'She can't guarantee it will air. They research several stories before they make the executive decision whether to run them or not, but she'll put it as a priority to consider. Are you happy for me to give her your contact details?'

Clare nodded, her eyes filling with tears. 'Thank you.'

Anna pushed a box of tissues across the small coffee table towards Clare. 'So, tell me how things are going this week. And by that, I don't mean what's happening with the police or the investigation. I mean, what's happening in here?' She tapped her chest and wasn't surprised when more tears rushed down the other woman's cheeks.

Clare gripped a tissue, her fingers trembling as she took a deep breath. 'Some days I forget he's gone. I reach for my phone to tell him something, and then it hits me all over again. I can't eat. I can't sleep. I keep thinking if I'd done something differently – if I'd noticed the other car earlier – maybe he'd still be here.'

Her voice broke, and Anna let the silence stretch, giving the woman room to breathe in her pain.

By the end of the hour, Anna felt like they were getting somewhere. Clare had opened up more about her grief than she had in previous sessions.

'I think I'll come to the Echoes group tomorrow night,' Clare said as she stood to leave. 'I'm not sure I'll talk, but I'll be there. And I promise not to get angry with anyone this time. If that woman's there again, I'll stay away from her.'

Anna offered a gentle smile. 'I think you have a lot to offer the group. You don't have to talk, but if you did, even addressing the situation from the other week with Bec would be interesting for the group. There are so many outside factors that upset us when we lose someone. Factors we wouldn't have given a second thought to previously.' She gave Clare's elbow a gentle squeeze as she turned to leave the room. 'See you tomorrow night.'

* * *

Bec was surprised to see Anna on her caller ID when her phone rang mid-morning. She usually had it switched to silent when working with a client but had forgotten. There'd been a bit of tension when she'd last seen her over the Skye situation, which part of her regretted, but another part of her still felt Anna should move on from the past and consider fostering.

She glanced at Gail, a sixty-year-old reformed prisoner who was concentrating on her watercolour with a fierce intensity, and moved towards the back of the room so as not to interrupt her flow.

'Hey, Anna. Everything okay? How's Skye?'

Anna's gentle laugh filtered down the phone line. 'Skye's fine, and yes, everything's okay. I wanted to give you a heads-up.' She went on to relay what Skye had told her earlier about inviting Zara and Hugo to Echoes, and that Skye had felt Zara needed help.

Bec sighed. 'I've let the kids down. Too caught up in my own grief to give them the time and attention they really needed.'

'Hey, don't be so hard on yourself. From what I've seen, they're both great kids. Hugo seems to be doing well, and I think Skye's only aware of Zara's struggles because they're getting closer, and she's spoken a lot about finding your parents.'

'She's already *found* them. It's when she decides to bring them into my life that worries me.'

They ended the call with Bec also promising to be at Echoes the next night.

When she arrived home later that evening, Zara was waiting for her, or at least that was what Bec assumed as she watched her daughter pacing up and down in the kitchen.

'You okay?' she asked as she put her bag on one of the stools at the island bench.

Zara stopped pacing. 'I've done something.'

Bec went to the fridge and took out the bottle of Sav Blanc she'd opened on Saturday night. She usually didn't drink on Monday nights, but she knew tonight, with whatever bombshell Zara was about to drop, would need to be an exception. She hesitated. When Owen was alive they'd only ever drunk on a Friday or Saturday night. It just wasn't something they did mid-week, yet suddenly she was drinking most nights. Only a glass, sometimes two, but it wasn't a good habit. She put the bottle back in the fridge and exchanged it for a bottle of mineral water before turning back to Zara. 'What have you done?' She braced herself, waiting to hear that her parents were arriving for dinner or something just as unwelcome.

Zara took a deep breath. 'I've agreed to go to Echoes tomorrow night with Skye. You know, the group Anna runs.'

Bec put her glass down. That was the last thing she expected Zara to say.

'Is that okay?'

'Of course it is. It's an excellent group, from what I've experienced so far myself.'

'So you'll be there tomorrow night too?'

'I had actually planned to go, but if you think it's something you'd like to do without me around, then that's no problem. I can easily miss a week.'

'No.' Zara forced a smile. 'I want you there. You know, in case it's too much and I need you.'

Bec studied her daughter. 'Zar, you're acting strange. Are you sure everything's okay? You know, you can talk to me if it's not. We're all going through a really difficult time right now.'

'I'm fine,' Zara said. 'Although it'd be good if you could help me convince Hugo to come tomorrow night too. I think the group sounds like it's something we should all be going to.'

'I'm going,' Hugo said, entering the kitchen. 'I already told Skye I'd go. But it might be a one-off. I'm not sure I want to hang around a bunch of people who are going through a hard time. It doesn't sound like much fun. I'd rather go to the gym and concentrate on something else other than getting caught up in other people's grief.'

'But you're definitely going tomorrow?' Zara questioned him.

He nodded as he took an apple from the fruit bowl.

'I was going to go straight from work,' Bec said, 'but I can come and pick you both up first if you like?'

Zara shook her head. 'Nah, I said we'd meet Skye first. It's not far. We can walk.' She forced another smile and left the room.

'End of subject,' Bec said. 'Hey, Hugo, do you think Zara's okay? That was weird.'

Her son shrugged. 'She's going through stuff, I guess. This group might be what she needs. Skye said it was pretty good and that Anna's talking about starting a group for younger people, so that might be even better.'

'It's unlike Zara to insist we accompany her,' Bec said, thinking over her daughter's words and especially the possibility of needing her. It was unusual, but it also meant that Bec could keep an eye on her. She could watch Zara's reactions to the group and to Anna and get Anna's thoughts on whether further counselling would be a good idea.

'Zara's doing all sorts of strange stuff,' Hugo said. 'Her way of coping is basically weird.'

Hugo's words played over in her mind as she left the kitchen, and while to a degree she had to agree with him, she hoped Zara wasn't going to do anything too unusual. At least in the group, nothing she did would be considered out of the ordinary.

16

Anna was pleased to see a decent turnout at the Echoes group. She knew Skye had convinced Hugo and Zara to come along as well, which was good as she did like the idea of having younger people in the mix with the potential to split them out into their own group session as time moved on.

Now, as she looked around the room a few minutes before the six o'clock start time, she smiled as she saw Bec in the third row.

Clare Fleming gave her a tentative smile as she slipped into a seat at the back of the room near where Skye and Hugo were sitting. Zara wasn't with them, which was disappointing as from what Skye had said she was the one who would really benefit from the group. She hoped she would make the session as planned.

* * *

Half an hour passed of the Echoes group, and even though part of her didn't want to take on board other people's grief, Bec found the stories they shared were interesting, and in fact, often heart-breaking.

'Would anyone else like to speak tonight?' Anna asked, looking around the room. Her gaze stopped on Bec momentarily, and Bec was quick to give a gentle shake of her head. There was no way she was sharing anything. She wasn't ready and might never be.

'I will.' The voice came from towards the back of the room. The woman cleared her throat. 'I hadn't intended to talk tonight, but hearing everyone else's stories has given me the courage.'

Bec froze. She almost turned around to check that she was right, but there was no need to. Tears burned her eyes as the sound washed over her, sharp with familiarity. A voice she hadn't heard in twenty years and never thought she would again. Never thought she wanted to.

'My son took his life several years ago and I've never recovered. It's ruined my marriage and my relationship with my daughter.'

Bec had difficulty controlling her breathing. She was going to kill Zara. Now her daughter's strange behaviour in ensuring she and Hugo would be here tonight made sense. She'd been set up. Part of her wanted to get up and leave, another part wanted to put her hands over her ears and refuse to listen, and then another part of her craved hearing her mother's words. She closed her eyes, doing her best to hold her emotions together as her mother continued to speak.

* * *

The sense of relief Anna felt when she saw Zara slip into the seat beside Hugo was quickly replaced by a prickle of unease that crept across her skin as the new woman began to speak.

'I'm Samara,' she said, 'and my son took his life twenty years ago.'

Like Anna's own situation, Samara's loss was over twenty years ago, but you could hear in her voice how raw it still was. How much she'd lost. Anna glanced at Bec, knowing this story would affect her too, and sure enough, her eyes were closed and her face filled with pain. While other people's stories often helped deal with loss, at times, they were far too close to home.

'When my son died, I thought I'd never breathe properly again. And in all honesty, I'm not sure I have. For two years before he died, we watched him disappear in front of us. He was withdrawn, angry, and using drugs. Something changed during his last year of high school. Until then, he'd had everything going for him. Athletic, academic, popular. But he suddenly gave up his sport, he did badly in his final exams, and kept most of his friends away from him. He wouldn't let any of us get close to him, not even his sister, whom he loved to bits. I told myself it was a phase. My husband—' her voice caught '—he kept saying it was normal teenage stuff. That he'd grow out of it, snap out of it. I wanted to believe him. I needed to.'

She paused, her eyes glistening. 'But he didn't snap out of it. He was twenty when he took his life. And I have to live with the fact that I didn't stop him. I was his mother, and I didn't see how much pain he was in until it was too late.'

Her breath caught again. The room was silent.

'After we buried him, a few months later, we lost our daughter. Not in the same way,' she was quick to add. 'She left. Walked out. Never came back. We never heard from her again. And I've spent every day since knowing she left because of me. Because of what I didn't do. What we didn't do. Because I failed them both.'

Anna's heart pounded. Surely this wasn't Bec's mother? She glanced at her friend whose eyes were still tightly shut, her face drained of colour. Her eyes darted to Zara who was on the edge of her seat. Had she orchestrated this?

The woman finished speaking and Anna was unsure what to do. The words left her lips before she had a chance to stop them. 'Have you ever reached out to your daughter?'

Samara shook her head. 'Not directly. For years, I thought she was better off without me, and my husband didn't want me trying to find her. I'm still not sure if he was angry with her for leaving or whether it was easier for him to manage his guilt by not having to confront her or the situation. As time goes on, I think that it's most likely his guilt, whether he's going to admit it or not.'

'That was like my husband,' Leah, one of the regulars in the group, said. 'As some of the group know, my niece died in a boating accident the first and only time she went out with Frank fishing. My husband had forgotten to replace the life jackets in the storage area of the boat and hadn't checked before they went out. They hit rocks and the boat sank. Frank was a strong swimmer, but my niece wasn't. Frank won't talk about the accident. He won't see any of my family either. I'm surprised he's stayed married to me.'

'Do you blame him for your niece's death?' Samara asked.

Tears ran down Leah's cheeks as she slowly nodded. 'At some level, I do.'

'I don't blame my husband,' Samara said. 'Well, I don't only blame him. I blame us both. We could have stopped it; I know we could have.'

'And it's had a huge impact on you,' Anna said.

'It has. It happened twenty years ago and it's only now that I feel like I'm coming out of a fog,' Samara said. 'A fog or daze I've been in for the past twenty years. I don't know how to describe it. It's like I've been a walking ghost, watching life happen around me in a complete void. I want to fill that void again. Get back to living and having something to live for. I want to reconnect with my daughter and her family.'

Anna could see that the group were mesmerised by both Samara's story and Leah's contribution. Many could relate and, for some like Clare, it gave them a slight breather from their own situation as they empathised with someone else's.

She glanced across at Bec and felt her stomach twist. In her place she'd feel humiliated and mortified that this was the first time she was hearing from her mother in all these years. She imagined Zara was going to be in big trouble.

* * *

Bec made a beeline for the exit door the moment Anna called the tea break. She couldn't think straight, other than to feel absolute fury at her daughter. She hadn't even been able to look at her mother. While she expected Zara to reach out to her parents, she certainly didn't expect to be ambushed like this.

She had to blink back tears as she pulled her jacket around her.

'Mum, wait—'

She ignored Zara's call, pushing open the door and stepping into the cold night air. A hand grabbed her shoulder.

'Wait.'

She stopped and turned to face Zara, anger overcoming her. 'How could you?'

'She wanted you to hear her story,' Zara said. 'Actually, that's not quite true. She wanted to see you. I suggested she come tonight and talk. I didn't think she would. She even said she wasn't going to before she came, but she did.'

'You've met her before tonight?'

Zara nodded. 'She responded to my email yesterday and I met her yesterday afternoon. We talked for almost two hours. She's lovely, Mum, and she misses you so much. I want you to talk to her, to meet her again.'

'But, like this?' Bec said, gesturing to the building. 'You thought this would be a good place to air our dirty laundry, rather than meeting somewhere just the three of us, or four, if Hugo wanted to come?'

'You wouldn't have done that,' Zara said. 'And don't lie and say you would. She's your mum. Imagine if I left tomorrow and refused to see you or speak to you! How would you feel?'

'Devastated,' Bec said, 'but I wasn't responsible for the death of your brother, was I? If I were, then I'd probably realise you needed to leave, and I needed to let you go.'

'That's exactly what I realised and why I haven't reached out until now.'

Bec's stomach churned as, for the first time in over twenty years, she turned to face her mother. There were more lines around her eyes now, her hair was greyer and there was more heartache etched into her face – but beneath all of that, Bec saw something achingly familiar. She shook her head. 'I can't do this. Not here. Not now. You shouldn't have come.' She looked between her mother and Zara. 'You both should have known better.'

Her mother reached out and placed a hand on her shoulder, exactly like she'd done to calm Bec when she was younger.

'Please. It doesn't need to be tonight, but I need to see you, to explain.'

'Explain what?' Bec's emotion turned to anger. 'That your weakness killed Chris?'

Even though the words made her flinch, her mother's gaze remained set on Bec. 'Yes, that's exactly what I want to explain and I guess, apologise for, not that that word is in any way adequate.'

Bec stared at her mother. For years, she'd imagined her parents caught up in their world of politics, not giving thought to her or to Chris. Looking at the broken woman standing in front of her, she realised that this hadn't been the case, not for her mother at least.

'Just you?' she asked now.

Samara nodded. 'Yes, just me. Could we meet for coffee?'

Bec considered her answer. Meeting in public was a risk. The risk was that she was likely to break down.

'No, come to me. What's your number? I'll text you my address.'

'No need,' Samara said and then blushed. 'Sorry, I had a private investigator find you. I know where you live.'

Bec continued to stare at her. 'You know where I live?'

Samara nodded.

'Have you been there?'

'I drove past, that's all. Last week, before I knew Zara had already sent an email to your father. I couldn't work out how, or even if, to approach you, but then Zara's email changed everything.'

Bec looked at her daughter, whose usually defiant expression had been replaced by one of worry and vulnerability. She thought back to the conversation she'd had with Anna the previous day. Skye had mentioned how much Zara was struggling. She needed to listen. She didn't want the kids having anything to do with her father, and most likely not her mother. But perhaps she owed it to her mother to hear her out.

'Fine. Come at five tomorrow and don't bring Dad.'

* * *

Anna wasn't surprised to find Bec and her family's seats empty when the group returned from the tea break. Skye's was empty too and thirty minutes later she was pleased to find her waiting for her when she'd said goodbye to the last of the participants. She smiled her thanks as Skye put the chairs back in their place.

'How did you find tonight?'

'Not sure,' Skye said. 'I didn't realise who that woman, Samara, was until later. You might need to check on Bec. She's upset.'

'I'm not surprised,' Anna said. 'I imagine Zara's going to cop it, assuming she was behind tonight.'

Skye nodded. 'She was, but it turned out okay. Bec's agreed for her mother to visit her tomorrow night. That's all Zara was trying to achieve.'

Anna shook her head. 'But it was such a public way of doing it!'

'She knew Bec would say no if she didn't put her on the spot. She's been trying to get her involved in finding her grandparents. Bec keeps saying no. Zara wants them in her life. She does have rights around that.'

'She does,' Anna said. 'But I'm not sure that was the best way to go about things for her relationship with Bec.'

***

Bec refused to speak on the way home from Echoes. So much for the support group being good for the family and giving them an outlet. Zara had certainly ruined that idea.

'I'm sorry,' Zara said for what felt like the hundredth time. 'I should have gone about it a different way. I wasn't sure how I could have got you to speak to her.'

'You should have kept out of it,' Hugo said, his anger on a par with Bec's. 'We've been through enough this year; we don't need this too.'

'I do,' Zara said. 'I need to know where I come from, and I want more family in my life. That's not such a terrible thing to ask for. And they're good people. They're not awful people. Yes, they did a bad job as parents, but that doesn't mean they'll be terrible grandparents.'

A bad job as parents. Is that how Zara saw their total lack of assistance to Chris? It was more than a bad job. They'd killed their son.

A cold shiver ran through her as images of Chris in his depressed state flooded her mind. While she thought of her brother regularly, it was in manageable doses, not with this kind of onslaught.

'Mum,' Zara said, her voice gentle.

'Not now,' Bec said as she turned into the driveway. 'I'll see your grandmother tomorrow night and we'll go from there. Right now, I need to process this and I need to do that alone.'

She caught a glimpse of Zara's stricken face in the rear-vision mirror, but didn't have it in her to comfort her daughter. Zara was getting what she wanted, but at a huge cost to Bec.

She made her way into the kitchen for a glass of water and then headed straight to her bedroom. Her phone pinged with a text as she placed the glass on the bedside table, kicked off her shoes and threw herself down on the bed. Anna.

> Skye's filled me in. Let me know if you'd like to talk tonight or tomorrow. Hugs.

Bec clicked the heart emoji so Anna would see that she'd received the message and appreciated it and then turned her phone off. The only person she wanted by her side tonight to hold her and to know he'd be there to support her was Owen.

She pulled back the covers of the bed and slipped in, still fully dressed. She'd give anything to have his strong arms around her. She closed her eyes, not even registering the tears that rolled down her cheeks.

* * *

'You did what?'

Samara watched her husband's nostrils flare and temper rise as she relayed her evening to him. She continued to speak, in a calm voice that was foreign even to her. 'I spoke to Rebecca, and I'll be visiting her and our grandchildren tomorrow night.'

Bruce shook his head, continuing to pace the kitchen as Samara made herself a cup of tea. The shake in her hand belied her calm tone as she picked up the kettle and poured the boiling water into the cup.

'It's time, Bruce,' she said, watching as her husband stopped at the drinks cabinet and poured himself a large whisky. 'I honestly don't know why you're so upset. She's our daughter, and these are our grandchildren. Surely you're interested in getting to know them?'

Bruce threw his drink back and shook his head. 'No, I don't want to get to know them. She walked away from us at the hardest time in our lives. I'm not welcoming her back.'

'We pushed her away,' Samara said. 'She blames us for Chris's death – don't you see that? He was struggling, and none of us did anything.'

'Maybe she should point her finger at herself,' Bruce said. 'What did *she* do to help Chris? Nothing.'

'Which is another reason I'm sure she left us,' Samara said, 'and another reason she'll find it as hard to face us as I found it to face her tonight. We're all guilty of letting Chris down.'

Bruce shook his head. 'That's not true. We did everything for both of our kids. We're not responsible for what he did.'

'Do you really believe that? You really believe that if we hadn't done more to help him when he was so depressed, he might still be alive?'

Bruce poured himself another drink and threw it back. 'I did everything possible to save that boy. You don't know the half of it.'

Samara stared at her husband. It was the most he'd spoken about Chris since their son's death. 'Then why don't you *tell me*? You've shut me out for twenty years. It's destroyed the relationship with our daughter, and if we're honest, our relationship with each other too. Tell me what this "other half" is.'

Bruce's eyes flashed with anger. 'All you need to know is that I protected Chris as much, if not more, than any father could. His way of repaying that was to kill himself. He was a coward, Samara. A little coward.' He slammed his empty glass onto the kitchen counter with such force that Samara was surprised it didn't shatter. 'I don't want to hear anything more about Rebecca or her children. If you choose to visit her, that's up to you. But I don't want her back in our lives, and I don't want her or either of her children here at my house.'

'Your house?'

'Yes, my house. Our house, whatever you want to call it. But it's not her house any more, and I don't want her here. Do you understand?'

Samara didn't respond. She'd spent her entire married life supporting her husband. His career had come first in every decision they'd made. From where to live, even down to what cars to drive. *Nothing too flashy. Nothing that greenies would find offensive.* It'd only been after he'd left public office that she'd been able to drive a car of her choice.

'I said, do you hear me?'

She stared at her husband, as if seeing him for the first time. She'd gone along with everything following Chris's death. In all honesty, she'd been in a trance for a good many years after losing Chris and Rebecca's departure, and it appeared she was finally beginning to wake up.

She picked up her teacup, deciding she would sleep in the spare room. The last thing she wanted was to be anywhere near Bruce Langford. 'I hear you.'

17

Anna was typing up a client report the next morning, her thoughts jumping from where they should be back to the previous night. She hoped Bec was okay. She was tempted to send her another text but also knew that respecting her new friend's boundaries was important right now. Zara had overstepped the boundaries big time, and she could only imagine that Bec was feeling quite fragile and might want to be left alone.

Her mobile rang, and her heart quickened as she saw Willowridge pop up on the caller display. She accepted the call.

'It's Marty, Anna. Sorry to interrupt you, but Lyn's had a particularly bad night and is very agitated again today. It's about Jake. She wants us to go and see Xavier again.'

Anna sighed. 'What do you think, Marty? Are these real memories or is she confused?'

'Honestly, I have no idea. I'm assuming it's confusion because otherwise she would have addressed this all those years ago. She's talking about events that happened before she started drinking and before she was diagnosed with any form of dementia. If she'd believed something wasn't right, surely she would have done something about it then?'

'You'd think so,' Anna said. 'It's strange that it's come up now; all of a sudden, too.'

'She was talking about the anniversary of your brother's death a few weeks ago,' Marty said. 'She has it marked on her calendar and special dates and events can trigger episodes.'

'What do you think I should do?'

'I think it would be worth reaching out to Xavier, to check if he's remembered anything. Otherwise, it's probably a case of visiting if you can. Perhaps bring your boyfriend if she enjoys seeing him.'

'Boyfriend?' Anna's cheeks heated as she realised who Marty was talking about.

'That guy you were with last week. Sorry, I assumed he was your boyfriend.'

'He's just a friend,' Anna said. 'I'll drop in after work today, and Marty, thanks. You do far more than you should for Mum and for me.'

'Pleasure,' Marty said. 'I'll see you a little later.'

Anna ended the call, and her phone rang again. This time, it was Kieran. A slight sense of unease came over her from Marty's comment. She wasn't sure why, as she liked Kieran and thought this might be their second chance.

'Hey,' Anna said, accepting the call.

'Hey, yourself,' Kieran said, causing them both to laugh. It had been their standard greeting when they were teenagers.

'Just wanted to check in,' Kieran said. 'See how things were going with Skye and whether you might want to go to dinner again one night? Tonight even, if you're free?'

'I can't tonight,' Anna said, and went on to explain the phone call she'd received from Marty.

'Well,' Kieran said, 'why don't we kill two birds with one stone? I'll come and pick you up, and we can have dinner at Xavier's. If Skye's around, she's welcome to come too.'

'Are you sure? Last time, you didn't want to be involved. You said it was too hard with trying to deal with losing Jake.'

'I'm realising I didn't handle that very well. I'd like to make it up to you and be there for you. What do you say?'

Anna thought about it. As Kieran said, it would kill two birds, and she was looking forward to seeing him.

'Sounds good,' she said. 'I'll check with Skye after school and then make a booking. I might need to drop in and see Mum after, so could we go a bit early?'

'Of course. How about I pick you up at five-thirty?'

'Perfect.'

'And Anna,' Kieran said, 'I'm really looking forward to seeing you.'

Anna ended the call, butterflies flitting in her stomach. She wasn't sure where this was going, but she was looking forward to seeing Kieran, too.

* * *

Samara pulled up outside her daughter's house, her heart pounding at the thought of seeing her again. She'd half expected to hear from Zara to say that Rebecca was cancelling, but instead she'd had a brief text from her granddaughter saying that they were looking forward to seeing her that evening.

Now, standing at the front door, she clasped a bottle of wine tight in one hand and pressed the doorbell with the other before she could change her mind.

The door opened after a few seconds. It was her grandson, Hugo.

She'd seen him the night before, sitting stiffly beside his sister, anger written all over his face. But they hadn't spoken; they hadn't even made eye contact. Now, up close, she could see traces of her daughter in him in the set of his jaw, the sharpness in his eyes. There was quite a lot of Chris in him, too. She wondered if Rebecca saw that.

'Hi,' she said. 'We didn't get to meet properly last night.'

He gave a small nod, shoulders tense, making Samara wonder what had been said after they'd all gone their own ways the previous night. He certainly wasn't as friendly or welcoming as Zara had been when they first met.

'Mum's coming.'

'Thank you.'

An awkward pause settled between them. Samara shifted her weight. He didn't move aside or invite her in. Was it possible that her conversation with her daughter was going to take place on the doorstep? She certainly hoped not.

* * *

Anna was torn as to whether to cancel on Kieran, when she checked with Skye, who said she didn't want to go out.

'I've got a tonne of homework, and anyway, it's a date; that would be weird and kind of creepy for me to come along.'

'It's not a date,' Anna said. 'We're friends.'

Skye rolled her eyes, making her thoughts very clear.

'How about I make you a meal before I go?'

'No, I'll be fine. You seem to forget that I cooked for myself and Mum a few nights a week to give her a break. It's nothing new. The only new, and really nice thing, is I have Smoko to keep me company. He'll curl up next to me while I write my English essay.'

'If you're sure?'

Skye smiled. 'It's like I'm the grown-up and you're the kid asking for permission.' The smile slipped from her lips and a wary, hurt look crossed her face.

'You okay?' Anna's words were gentle. She wasn't sure if Skye's reaction was related to her mum or something else.

Skye sighed. 'I'm going to miss it here, that's all. I like you and Smoko. It's easy-going and I feel like I know you, even though I don't really.'

Anna moved forward and pulled Skye into a hug. 'I'm not going to dump you on some family and never see you again. I really like you, too and would like us to be friends moving forward. I'll have you over for dinner and we can get out and about and do things when you're free.'

Skye forced a smile. 'That'd be nice, and I might see you if we're both at Bec's. I wonder how she's going?'

Anna had wondered the same. She knew Bec's mother would be visiting that evening; she might even be there now. She couldn't imagine a situation where she didn't see her mother for twenty years.

'I'll give her a call tomorrow,' Anna said, 'although I guess you might get an update from Zara tonight.'

'Zara's pretty worried,' Skye said.

'Worried?'

The teenager nodded. 'She's worried Bec will lose it at her mother, and that's the last time they'll ever see her.'

'Zara's old enough to see her grandparents if she chooses,' Anna said. 'And considering she's responsible for their reappearance, I'm surprised she's worried about that.'

'I think she's more worried that her mum will hate her,' Skye said.

Anna frowned. 'Hate her? Bec would never hate her. She

might be upset with her, but that's normal and reasonable under the circumstances.'

'I think Zara needs counselling or something,' Skye said. 'She's pretty messed up when you get to know her, but she puts on this front of being cool and like she doesn't care. I think she's terrified that something might happen to her mum, and then she'd end up like me. Well, not quite like me as she's got Hugo, but you know what I mean.'

Anna's heart contracted as she thought of the feisty teenager and how much her father's death had impacted her. She herself had been eighteen when she'd lost her dad, and she knew exactly how hard that had hit her, doubly hard after having only just lost Jake. 'Thank you,' she said to Skye, glad that the teenager felt comfortable sharing this with her. 'I'll talk to Bec tomorrow and suggest Zara comes into the centre for some counselling. Not with me, obviously, as we're friends, but with one of the others. We do offer some good services there. Now, I'd better feed Smoko and get changed if I'm going out.'

Skye raised an eyebrow. 'Into something sexy?'

Anna blushed and swatted Skye's arm. 'No, something more comfortable than my work clothes.'

* * *

Bec took a deep breath when she heard her mother's car pull up and braced herself. For what exactly, she wasn't sure, but she was nervous. She'd asked Zara to stay in her room. To let her talk to her mother first before she appeared. Hugo, however, was allowed to open the door.

She'd been tempted to pour herself a large vodka when she'd got home from work and down it in one gulp, but instead had opted for a glass of wine, which she'd been sipping slowly. She wanted to take the edge off her nerves but not completely numb herself to the point that she might say the first thing that came into her mind, which, in relation to her mother, was unlikely to be flattering or friendly.

Now, she listened as the doorbell rang and Hugo hurried to open it. She heard a brief exchange and then nothing. She could imagine him blocking the doorway protectively, not willing to let her in if he didn't have to.

She moved from the kitchen into the hallway and could see that her assumption was correct. Hugo's back was facing her, but he certainly hadn't invited his grandmother into the house.

She reached her son and placed her hands on his shoulders, grateful for his care, and moved him gently to one side, leaving her face to face with her mother. Her heart pounded.

She cleared her throat. 'Come in.'

Samara stepped into the house, relief filling her eyes. 'I was worried it might be a quick hello and goodbye on the doorstep.' She handed Bec a bottle of wine.

Bec took the wine, unsure how to respond as she had no idea what she wanted from her mother, if anything. She led her through to the kitchen and open-plan living area and pointed in the direction of the couches. 'Take a seat, and I'll pour the wine.'

Samara made her way over to the couches and sat down. 'You've got a lovely home. Did you bring everything back from Sydney with you?'

Bec looked up from pouring her mother a glass of wine. 'How did you know we're from Sydney?' She certainly hadn't told her anything the previous day.

Samara coloured. 'Zara told me a little bit when I met her, but the private detective I hired found out that you'd left Sydney earlier this year. I was very sorry to learn about your husband. Your father,' she added, looking to Hugo.

He nodded. 'I'm going to my room. I'll leave you to chat.'

'He's a lovely boy,' Samara said, waiting until Hugo had closed his bedroom door and was out of hearing. 'Both of your children are a credit to you.'

Bec brought the glass of wine over to her mother, handed it to her and then took a seat across from her.

'You can thank Zara for being here,' Bec said. 'If it were up to me, I wouldn't have made contact with you.' She felt partly pleased and partly guilty to see a flash of pain in her mother's eyes.

Samara sipped her wine, appearing as unsure as Bec of what to say. Eventually, she spoke. 'Well, I'm glad Zara has pushed for the contact. As I said briefly last night, I had been going to reach out myself.'

'Why now?' Bec asked. 'Why not years ago, when I left or any time more recently. It's a bit convenient to say now that Zara's found you that you were planning to find us.'

'I've thought about reaching out to you many times,' Samara said, 'but each time I'd come back to thinking that you were better off without me, without us. That we'd done enough damage when you were younger, and I should leave you alone.'

'What changed?'

'Ever since Chris's death and you left, I've seen a multitude of psychologists to try and help come to terms with what happened; to explain why I didn't do more to help Chris when he was obviously needing me and also to come to terms with you leaving. It was only when we moved back from Canberra a couple of years ago that I found someone who helped. She made me see that as much as I was blaming myself, I wasn't actually to blame for what happened.'

Bec had to keep her mouth forced shut, so as not to laugh out loud at this.

'I can see from your face that you don't believe that, but I do. I did what I thought was right for Chris at the time.'

'You didn't do *anything*!' The words exploded from Bec's mouth before she had a chance to control them. 'Sorry,' she added, seeing the shock on her mother's face. 'But—' her voice was a little calmer now '—you didn't.'

Samara stared at her. 'I dragged four different psychologists into the house to see Chris. None of them could get through to him. He refused to talk to them. And then, when I was worried he might harm himself, I called the police. You probably don't remember the night they came over. The fuss I made trying to get them to put him on suicide watch?'

Bec frowned. She hadn't been aware of any of this. 'I was living in the house. How didn't I know this?'

'You were at university,' Samara said, 'and I made sure the psychologists came during your lecture times. The last thing Chris needed at that time was us all talking about him and knowing his business.'

'And the police? Was I out the night they...' Bec's words petered off. She vaguely recalled coming home from her lectures to a heated argument between her parents and the police being in the house. 'You and Dad were arguing.'

Samara nodded. 'He didn't agree with me that suicide watch was the right approach. Thought I was being overly dramatic, and that night, maybe I was. Chris didn't take his life for another year after that, ironically at a time when he'd seemed so much better. He'd started that job, remember?'

Bec nodded, realising her memories, up until this conversation, were rather distorted. She'd been so fixated on blaming her parents that she'd never considered they'd done anything to help. 'Why didn't you tell me about the psychologists after Chris died?

When I was blaming you and saying you hadn't done anything to help him?'

'At the time, I agreed with everything you said. I didn't think I had done nearly enough to help him. Everything I'd tried had failed, and all the experts I approached looked at me like I was exaggerating the situation and being overly dramatic.'

The two women sat in silence for a few minutes, each with their own thoughts.

'I'm sorry,' Bec finally said. 'I had no idea you'd done all of that. I wish you'd told me at the time though, because I *did* ask.'

Samara gave a wry smile. 'Not sure if screaming at me is really defined as "asking" me.'

Bec blushed. Her mother was right: she'd been quick to fly off the handle when she was that age.

'I take it Zara gets some of her more outspoken moments from you, then?'

Bec smiled. 'I guess so. Owen and I always joked that she was an alien, delivered to us, and not genetically linked, but now that you're reminding me of what I was like, perhaps that's not the case.'

'Who's an alien?'

Bec looked up as Zara entered the room. She could see the hesitant look on her daughter's face, which was expected as Bec had asked her to leave her to talk to her mother until she called her to come and join them.

'You,' Bec said.

Zara pouted. 'That's hardly a nice thing to say.'

Bec shrugged. 'Well, you did always have a suspiciously advanced eye-roll for a toddler.'

'As did your mother,' Samara added, smiling tentatively at Bec.

'Really?' Zara asked. 'What was Mum like as a kid?' She sat down on the couch next to Bec, and Bec put an arm around her, finding herself relaxing a little as her mother started talking about her.

'When the twins were little, about five, there was that time they convinced the elderly neighbour that their dog could talk. Chris would stand behind the hedge, whispering the answers while Bec made the dog's mouth move. To this day, I'd say poor Mr Pearson still swears that spaniel told him to paint his roof orange.'

Zara clasped her hand over her mouth. 'You didn't?'

Bec smiled. 'It was Chris's idea.'

'Rebecca Jane!' Her mother adopted the stern voice she'd used to reprimand her as a child.

Bec couldn't help but laugh. 'Okay, fine, it was my idea. I got Chris into lots of trouble, similarly to how you used to get Hugo into trouble.'

Hugo, most likely hearing the change in mood, came and joined them. Bec could only imagine how curious he was to properly meet his grandmother, too.

'More wine?' she said, standing to refill her glass.

'Yes, please,' Samara said, smiling gratefully at Bec. Bec knew the smile was for a lot more than the wine. It was for listening.

18

Samara looked at her grandchildren with fascinated curiosity. It was hard to believe that these two teenagers had lived for sixteen years, and she knew nothing about them, other than a tiny smidge of what Zara had shared with her and first impressions of what she'd seen of Hugo. She so hoped that this wasn't going to be the only time she saw them.

She found herself asking them questions, and an hour passed quickly before Hugo stood, apologising that he had homework to finish.

'I do too,' Zara said, 'but I don't want to miss out on this conversation.'

Samara took that as her cue to leave. 'How about I go and not distract you any further? Hopefully, we can do this again soon.'

Bec wasn't sure why she hesitated to respond. She had to admit she'd enjoyed being in her mother's presence again. 'I'll think about it,' she finally said.

Much to Samara's delight, Zara hugged her goodbye before retreating to her room.

'They're gorgeous kids, Bec,' she said. 'I do hope you'll let me see more of them. Become part of your lives.'

Bec didn't respond immediately. 'We'll see, okay. Tonight's been nice, and I'm glad that I had it wrong and that you did try to help Chris. I'm not sure that I'm ready to rush back into playing happy families. Not with Dad, anyway.'

'That's fine. You don't have to see him if you don't want to.'

Bec smiled. 'I think the kids are old enough to make their own minds up now that they know who you are.'

'They are. But I'd like to see you too. Get to know you as an adult. I know it's early days, but would you be open to considering that?'

Samara could practically see the cogs turning over in Rebecca's mind. It would no doubt be easier to shut the door on her parents, to close out the painful memories that reconnecting with them might bring up about Chris.

It was a surprise when Bec nodded slowly. 'I'm open to it. I know Zara, and possibly Hugo too, would like to get to know you.'

'I'd like to learn more about them,' Samara said. 'See their baby photos and hear about their childhoods. It's such a lot to have missed.'

Guilt settled on Bec's shoulders. When the twins were born, she'd immediately thought of her mother and how much she'd love to be involved but found it easier to dismiss the thought than deal with it. Owen had encouraged her to consider reaching out, but she'd been steadfast in her decision to stay away. Now, sixteen years later, it was time to deal with it.

'Why don't we catch up for coffee, the two of us?' Bec said. 'Zara ambushed us tonight, which is understandable, but there's a lot to discuss.'

* * *

Anna lingered at her wardrobe longer than she cared to admit, nerves tying her in knots at the thought of seeing Kieran again. Yet even as she weighed up what to wear, her thoughts kept drifting to Marty. Surely Kieran was wrong and Marty wasn't interested in her? But the tone in which he'd referred to Kieran as her boyfriend had had an edge to it.

She did her best to push thoughts of Marty away when Kieran picked her up and drove her into the central business district.

'I didn't want to say it in front of Skye earlier when I collected you,' Kieran said, after they'd been seated at one of the corner tables at Xavier's, 'but you look incredibly beautiful tonight. Sexy actually.'

Anna's cheeks heated for the second time that night, and she found herself smiling at the gorgeous man sitting across from her. She wore a tailored navy dress and simple heels, elegant and understated, and certainly not what she considered sexy, but she was glad he did. It was the first time he'd said anything like that to her since they'd reconnected, and it made her wonder where they'd be now if they hadn't broken up. Would they have stayed together? Had kids?

Kieran reached across the table and interlaced his fingers with hers. 'I'm thinking we should rewind twenty-two years and pretend life didn't play out as it did, that we're still a couple and still have lots to learn about each other. What do you think?'

'I think that could be—' Anna didn't get to finish her sentence as their drinks arrived at the table, with Xavier following close behind.

'Anna,' the older Italian man said, greeting her like he'd

known her forever and not met her just the one time. 'How are you and how is your mother?'

Anna exchanged pleasantries with Xavier and introduced Kieran.

'Kieran?' Xavier said, frowning as the two men shook hands. 'Why does that name ring a bell?'

Kieran shrugged. 'No idea. It's not all that common. Perhaps Anna mentioned me when she was here recently?'

Xavier shook his head and gazed into the distance for some time, appearing to be deep in concentration.

'No, it wasn't Anna,' the older man eventually said, 'It was Anna's father.' He smiled. 'Finally, I remember something – not a lot, I'm afraid, but more than I remembered earlier.'

'What do you remember?' Anna asked, moving to the edge of her seat.

Xavier pulled out a chair from the empty table next to them and sat down. He looked from Anna to Kieran. 'You were a couple all those years ago, yes?'

'Yes,' Anna said.

'The last time I saw Mal, he seemed confused. Said he'd been told that someone else was at the scene of the accident that night. Maybe more than one person. That Jake wasn't alone when it happened, but he was alone when the paramedics arrived. He said the person or people had fled the scene and he wasn't sure why.'

'But that doesn't make any sense,' Anna said. 'Why wouldn't he have told Mum or me that?'

'I think he wanted to be sure of his facts,' Xavier said. 'He'd received an anonymous letter, so he didn't know what was true and what wasn't. He mentioned your name.' He looked at Kieran. 'I remember now, as you have the same name as my cousin.'

Anna looked at Kieran, whose face had noticeably paled. 'He thought you were in the car with Jake?'

Kieran shrugged, his shoulders tight with tension. 'I have no idea why he would think that. I wasn't in the car with Jake. I found out the next morning what had happened.'

Anna realised she'd jumped to this conclusion without checking with Xavier. 'Did Dad say he thought Kieran was in the car?' she asked.

Xavier shook his head slowly. 'No, it wasn't that. He was worried about where Kieran was. The letter said something like Kieran might know more details, but he'd disappeared, and whoever wrote the letter hoped nothing bad had happened to him.'

He turned his attention back to Kieran. 'He said he didn't know how to contact you. That you'd left when his son died. He was asking me if I knew someone who could help track you down. I think he was more worried that something had happened to you rather than you being involved in Jake's accident. He hoped I could lean on some of my mates in the force to help.'

'How long after Jake's death was this?' Kieran asked, his face now drained of all colour.

Xavier ran a hand through his thinning hair. 'I don't know. Maybe weeks. I'm told Mal died a couple of weeks after the last time I saw him, so I don't know if he got any answers about the letter.'

Anna sat in silence for a moment, processing this information. 'So, Dad was led to believe you might have known something about the accident or you might have been in trouble yourself.' She looked directly into Kieran's eyes. 'Did you know anything about that night?'

Kieran shook his head. 'No more than you did. I was told Jake left the party on his own. I never heard anything different to that. I didn't start my flight training for about six months after I left Melbourne either, so that might be why your dad couldn't find me. Mum and Dad knew I was travelling initially, but I didn't keep in touch those first few months. I needed to be on my own. Deal with my grief and sort my head out. It was only once I got to Adelaide and was enrolled in the training that they knew where I was.'

'Did Dad say anything else?' Anna asked Xavier.

'No, nothing important like that,' Xavier said. 'And I apologise that I didn't remember the other night. My memory isn't as good as it used to be. Please tell your mum I'm sorry I didn't have more news for her then or now. Mal was very wound up that night at the pub when he spoke about it to me.'

'It's strange he didn't talk to Mum about it,' Anna said. 'Or maybe he did, and she can't remember. I'd like to see the letter, although I'm not sure what we can do with it all these years later.' She thought for a moment. 'All of Mum and Dad's stuff is in a storage unit not far from my house. I wonder if the letter is amongst it?'

'It doesn't sound like it gave much information,' Kieran said, 'if neither your dad nor Xavier could make anything of it.'

'I think I'd still like to find it,' Anna said. 'It might not come to anything, but if there was something covered up at the time of Jake's death, even something as simple as someone witnessing what happened, then I'd like to know. They found alcohol in his car that night and in his bloodstream.' She looked at Kieran. 'We never told anyone because we didn't want them to think he'd been driving drunk. Not a lot of alcohol, but he'd only had his licence a few months, so he should have had zero. If there's more to the story, I'd like to know.'

That thought played over in Anna's mind on the drive home

from the restaurant. Neither she nor Kieran had much appetite by the time Xavier left them to their meals, and they ended up leaving early. Early enough for Anna to visit her mother if she chose.

'I can't face her tonight,' Anna said. 'She won't know any different anyway. I'd like to find that letter if I can before I visit her. It might be something she remembers too, once I show it to her, and if she doesn't, at least she'll know that we've found out as much as we can about Xavier.'

'Good idea,' Kieran said, reaching for her hand and interlacing his fingers through hers.

She smiled, enjoying the sensation of his touch. As confusing as the meeting with Xavier had been, she had to admit that getting to know Kieran again was very nice.

19

Anna couldn't help but eavesdrop when she'd returned home from dinner with Kieran the previous night and heard Skye on the phone to Zara. She was only hearing one side of the conversation, but from the tone of Skye's voice and the questions she was asking, it sounded like the catch-up with Bec's mother had gone well.

She did her best to sound casual when Skye ended the call. 'How's Zara doing?'

'Good,' Skye said. 'Her grandmother's really nice and Bec didn't throw her out or kill her, so it was a success.'

Anna laughed. 'If that's the definition of success, then yes, sounds good. I'll give Bec a call tomorrow and see how she is. It would be strange after all these years to be in touch again. And how are you doing with everything?'

Anna had been careful not to push Skye about her feelings or her mother but tried to check in every now and then.

Skye sighed. 'It's hard. I look at Bec's situation and think how crazy it was that she walked away from a mum, who, from what

Zara's said, is lovely. My mum's gone, and I wasn't given the choice, and if I had been there, there's no way I would have left her, no matter what she or I did. We were family. You can't get closer or better than that.'

A lump formed in Anna's throat as she heard the sincerity in Skye's voice. She was lucky to have had such a good relationship with her mother. 'Not everyone's as lucky as you were, as far as being close to their parents or family. For some people, the only way to get on is to do it alone. I agree, though, it is sad that Bec felt she had to walk away. Maybe now there'll be some sort of reconciliation and chance for them to have a relationship again.'

'Maybe.'

'And as for not getting close to people, I think you're wrong there, too. It doesn't have to be blood ties to feel like family.'

Skye gave her a sideways look. 'Are you saying that to try and convince me to like whichever family I end up being dumped on?'

Anna sighed. 'You're not going to be dumped on anyone. We'll find someone you like...' she gave a wry smile '...or can tolerate at least.'

* * *

Bec was pleased to wake up on Saturday morning to a quiet house and no alarm. With the reappearance of her mother, it had been a big week. She was still trying to digest exactly what it would mean to have her back in their lives and how she felt about it.

She reached for her phone from the bedside table, smiling as a message from Anna appeared.

Wondered if you had time to catch up today? Hope all went well with your mum's visit. If you're free for lunch, coffee, or a late afternoon wine, let me know.

Bec didn't have to think too hard. Having plans on a Saturday would be nice. Hugo and Zara would be heading out with their friends, and she and Owen would normally fill the day with gardening, or going out for lunch or a walk. The weekends had dragged since he'd died.

BEC

Afternoon wine sounds perfect. Would you like to come here or meet somewhere?

ANNA

How about the Botanical Gardens at four? Jardin Tan does delicious cocktails, and I feel like getting out amongst the trees.

BEC

Lovely. See you there.

Bec lay back against her pillows. It was nice to hear from Anna. She would be interested to hear if she'd had any luck finding a family for Skye. A shiver ran down her spine as once again she put her twins in Skye's position. At sixteen, they were all so close to adulthood, but still didn't have the independence to be treated as adults by the law.

'Mum?' A knock followed Zara's voice.

'Come in.' Bec moved to one side of the bed, patting the bedding as Zara entered the room. She was still in her pyjamas, her hair tousled from sleep. Zara slipped onto the bed next to her, lying on her back and pulling a pillow under her head.

'Everything okay?' Bec asked.

'I wanted to check it was with you,' Zara said. 'You haven't said anything much since your mum was here, and that was a few days ago.'

Bec sighed. 'I haven't worked out what I want to do about her. It was such a big decision to walk away from my parents, and I'm not sure how keen I am to bring them back into my life.' She glanced at Zara. 'What are you going to call her? You can't keep calling her "your mum".'

'I need to ask her,' Zara said. 'Gran maybe? She doesn't look like a Grandma or a Nana. She doesn't look that old.'

'She looks a lot older to me,' Bec said. 'You can really see how Chris's death aged her. She looks good, but she looks her age. She always used to look a lot younger than she was.'

'I'd like to meet your dad too,' Zara said. 'Even if it's only once.'

Bec nodded. 'It might be a case of making sure he wants to meet you. I'm sure he won't want to see me.'

'Why?'

'He would have been angry when I left. I don't imagine he'll welcome me back.'

'But you were only twenty. He's probably changed his mind by now.'

'Even if he has, I'm not sure I want to see him. I'll catch up with Mum for a chat, maybe tomorrow if she's around, and then we can go from there. I know you want to get to know them, Zar, but have a bit of patience, can you? There's plenty of time.'

Panic flashed briefly in Zara's eyes, causing Bec to sit up and study her daughter.

'What's going on, Zars? Is this about Dad?'

'What do you mean?'

'Well, it's quite normal to be scared after something like that happens, to think that maybe there isn't all that much time for any of us. Is that why you're keen to meet your grandfather?'

Zara thought about it for a moment. 'I guess. I was worried before we met Skye about what would happen to us if something happened to you. But now, seeing her situation, it's started really freaking me out. At least if something did happen, Hugo and I could live with our grandparents, maybe.' She shuddered. 'I don't like the thought of foster care, and what if they split Hugo and me up?'

'I'm not planning on going anywhere any time soon,' Bec said gently. 'But you're right, it does give you a backup plan if you ever needed it.' She had to be careful saying anything like she wasn't going to die, as they'd had no warning about Owen's death, so she knew better than to make a promise like that.

'And more family, even if we don't need it,' Zara said. 'I like the idea of grandparents. They're supposed to spoil you.'

Bec laughed. 'That might be more when you're a little kid. Sorry, you might have missed out on that bit.'

Zara pretended to pout.

'What are your plans for today?'

Zara stretched. 'Said I'd meet up with Skye later. She wants to visit a park her mum loved. It's the one place that she feels really close to her, but doesn't want to go on her own. We'll do that, and then I don't know, maybe come back here and watch a movie or something. Can she stay over if she wants to?'

'Sure,' Bec said. 'I'm having a drink with Anna later, so maybe we'll come back here too. Get some Thai or Vietnamese takeaway.' She glanced at the clock on the bedside table. 'The day's disappearing. I guess I should get up.'

She stood and was about to head into the en suite when a thought crossed her mind. 'Will you be okay going to the park with Skye?'

'Why wouldn't I be?'

'Just with Dad and everything.'

'It's not like there's a park that reminds me of Dad. There's nowhere in Melbourne that I can feel close to him.' Zara shivered. 'He's in that pot you refuse to do anything with, which is quite freaky really. When are you going to scatter his ashes?'

It was the second time Zara had brought this up recently. 'I haven't worked out where to scatter them.'

'Really? It's obvious, isn't it?'

'Is it? And don't say where those camels were. He would not want the smell of dirty camels with him for eternity.'

Bec was pleased to see her comment elicit a smile from Zara.

'No camels involved. I was thinking of that part of the Murray River you and he always went on about. Where you used to love going as a kid, and he did too, and even though you didn't know each other then, you worked out you would have been there at the same time during lots of school holidays. And then didn't you go back there together and say it was your favourite part of Australia?'

Bec swallowed down the lump at the base of her throat. Neither she nor Owen thought Zara ever listened to anything they said. To have remembered all of this, which was something they'd discussed a few years earlier, was quite out of character, but it was also perfect. They'd planned to hire a houseboat one day and travel down the Murray River from Echuca, the port Zara was talking about. It had been on the bucket list, but not been something they'd ever ticked off.

Zara reached across and hugged her. 'Sorry, didn't mean to upset you.'

Bec realised tears were running down her cheeks. 'Happy tears,' she said. 'I can't believe you remembered Echuca, and yes, it's perfect. Maybe you, me and Hugo can plan a trip and scatter

Dad's ashes.' She squeezed her daughter to her. The only problem with this suggestion was that she still wasn't sure when she'd be ready to let Owen go.

* * *

Anna had hoped Kieran would be available to help her go through her dad's belongings on Saturday morning, but he'd reminded her the previous night that he was returning to work from today with close to a week of flying before he'd be back in Australia. She wasn't sure if she'd get used to his schedule, but she did know that she wasn't going to wait for him to look for the letter.

Finding the letter Xavier mentioned might not provide any more information than they already had, but it would be good to show her mother and for her mother to know that she'd been right about her father being agitated only weeks before his death.

'You going out today?' she asked Skye as the teenager walked into the kitchen, already showered and dressed. 'Tea?' She held up the pot she'd brewed.

'Later and yes,' Skye said. 'As in, going out later, and yes to the tea. Zara's coming with me to visit Mum's favourite park, and then she asked if I want to go back to hers for a movie and maybe stay the night. Would that be okay?'

'Of course,' Anna said. 'Bec and I are catching up this afternoon, so I might see you at Bec's if we end up back there. But I can also suggest she comes back here if you'd prefer to have a bit of space from us old people.'

Skye laughed. 'It doesn't worry me. I like both of you, and as neither of you is my mum, it's not the same as having a mum hanging around, if you know what I mean.'

Anna laughed. 'I do. Now, after I finish my tea, I'm heading off to the storage unit to see if I can find the letter the guy from the restaurant mentioned.'

'Can I come?'

Anna was surprised at the offer. 'I'd love you to. It's only in Malvern and I can drop you at Zara's after if you like.'

Thirty minutes later, Anna unlocked the padlock of her parents' storage unit and paused, her hand resting on the handle. The roller door groaned as she pulled it up. Boxes were stacked to the ceiling. Furniture wrapped in blankets. Her parents' lives were packed away. How much nicer it would be to walk through their front door instead of this.

'Why are you holding on to all of this?' Skye asked. 'Does your mum even know it's here?'

'She does, but she's never asked for any of it. I don't know really, it felt too awful to throw it all away after Mum ended up at Willowridge. I should probably get rid of it all.'

'Good thing you didn't, though,' Skye said. 'Then you'd have no hope of finding this letter. Who knows what else is hiding in here.'

'True,' Anna said, 'and another good thing is Dad was very tidy when it came to personal correspondence and paperwork. There are a couple of drop files to go through, and that's probably the only place it's likely to be. They're over here,' she said, leading Skye to the back of the storage unit. She pulled off a sheet that was draped over two grey filing cabinets. 'Let's take one each. Look for any letters and feel free to open them if they're in envelopes.'

The two worked side by side for ten minutes before Skye spoke. 'There's a lot of interesting stuff here.'

Anna had been thinking the same as she leafed through historical news clippings her dad had filed away.

'I didn't know your dad was a school principal!'

Anna looked up as Skye held up a folded newspaper, its headline visible: *LOCAL SCHOOL PRINCIPAL GOES EXTRA MILE TO KEEP STUDENTS FED.*

Anna reached for it.

'Apparently, he started a breakfast program out of his own pocket,' Skye said. 'And got local cafés and bakeries involved. He did a ten kilometre run to raise awareness and money to help support it as it grew bigger. There's even a photo of him cooking eggs on a camping stove out the back of the school library.'

'I remember that.' Anna sighed. 'He was always trying to make things better for people.'

Her thoughts drifted to her father, and she realised how much she missed him.

She pushed the thought away and pulled out another file and started leafing through it.

A few minutes passed before Anna sucked in a breath.

Skye stopped going through her file and looked over to what Anna was reading. 'Are they news stories about your brother?'

Anna nodded, flicking through the cut-out articles. She hadn't realised her dad had kept them all. It was a file full of pain. She closed her eyes, feeling the file being taken out of her hands.

'I'll look through this one,' Skye said. 'If it's a file on Jake, then it would make sense he put it in here.'

Anna nodded again, doing her best to control her emotions. She took slow, deep breaths, keeping her eyes shut. The pictures in the news articles still triggered her. The car, the tree. A photo from the funeral.

'This is it,' Skye said, causing Anna's eyes to flick open.

'What does it say?' Anna asked, looking at the piece of paper Skye was holding.

Dear Mr and Mrs Morrison,

I was someone who knew Jake, and I'm so sorry about the accident and you losing him. He was a great guy. I wanted you to know that something else happened that night – something different to what you've been told. Jake wasn't drunk, and he wasn't drinking at the party either. The accident wasn't his fault. Someone ran him off the road.

The driver of the other car fled the scene, and it was made to look like Jake hit a tree and was alone at the time.

Someone's trying to cover up what happened. Threatening people and paying people off. I know, cause I was one of them. They're not cops. They seem dodgy. I thought Kieran Bradley might know something, but he's disappeared. I don't know if he's left by choice or if someone's done something to him.

I hope you can find some answers.

She looked up at Anna. 'That's it. It's not signed or anything.'

Anna took the piece of paper Skye was reading from and turned it over. The back was blank.

'Imagine if this were true,' Anna said. 'Dad would have taken this to the police, though, I'm sure he would have. Then they would have been asking around, trying to find out who the guys were. It doesn't make any sense.'

'What are you going to do?' Skye asked.

'I don't know. I guess we go through the rest of the file on Jake and see if there's anything else in it, but otherwise, I'm not sure there's anything I can do for something that happened so long ago.'

'The letter says Kieran might know something.'

'He doesn't. We already discussed it last night, when Xavier remembered my dad mentioning his name. He said he never heard anything different from the story we were told, and then he left town.'

Skye looked back at the letter. 'We need to know who wrote this. Has your old school got a Facebook group or something like that for your class?'

'They have,' Anna said. 'Why?'

'You could ask there if anyone remembers anything. Even ask about this letter. It's handwritten. Someone might recognise the handwriting. But if these guys were asking around, it makes you think someone would know something. If it was covered up, people might have been told to keep their mouths shut. Who knows?'

Anna thought about Skye's suggestion. 'It'd be worth a shot,' she said.

Forty minutes later, Anna pulled her Mazda to a stop outside Bec's house. She reached for her bag and took a fifty-dollar note from her purse. She handed it to Skye, whose eyes instantly widened. 'What's this for?'

'To buy lunch for you and Zara.'

Skye shook her head. 'I can't accept this.' She held it out to Anna, who put her hand over Skye's and closed the money into her fist.

'Yes, you can. I'd like you to do something nice after you go to the park. It's hard on you not having much money. Not being able to access your mum's estate until you're eighteen makes sense on one hand but isn't exactly practical. And I know you're going to try to get your old job back or a new one, but for now, let me help you. Okay?'

Skye nodded, and Anna could see she was doing her best to blink away tears. She squeezed her hand. 'Have a good visit with your mum, which I know sounds like a weird thing to say, but it's a chance to sit and tell her what's going on. That's what I do when I visit Jake.' She smiled. 'And the best bit is they don't argue or talk back with anything you say.'

'I'd give anything to argue with Mum,' Skye said wistfully, and then smiled at Anna. 'Thank you for the money. I think Zara will love a treat too.'

'You're welcome.' Seeing the look on Skye's face, Anna wished she could take the words back about her mum not arguing or talking back to her. But it was too late, and Skye pushed open the door and gave Anna a wave as she turned and walked up the driveway towards Bec's front door.

* * *

As they soaked in the warmth of an outdoor heater on the deck of Jardin Tan, in Melbourne's Botanical Gardens, Anna had to curb her laughter at how wide Bec's eyes grew as she explained what she and Skye had uncovered that morning.

'That changes everything,' Bec said. 'We have to find out who sent that letter.'

A surge of gratitude went through Anna at the 'we' reference.

'I wish we had something like that about Chris,' Bec said. 'As much as I wouldn't want to know someone had killed him, it would be heaps better than living with him killing himself. What did your mum say when you showed her the letter?'

Anna had come straight from Willowridge to Jardin Tan, where they were both enjoying their first cocktail.

'It was good and bad,' Anna said. 'It made her feel better, I think, that she was remembering correctly, but then she couldn't remember why she had forgotten about it back then. She was so distraught when Dad died and so overwhelmed with grief, I think she put it out of her mind altogether.'

'That would make sense,' Bec said.

The two women sipped their drinks and continued talking as the sun slowly sank behind the trees.

'How did you go with your mum this week?' Anna asked. 'You're dealing with a lot right now.'

'And it feels like a lot,' Bec said. 'It makes me miss Owen even more than I normally do. I'm used to having him to turn to. He always knew the right thing to say or the questions to ask to get me thinking about what I really wanted. I'd give anything for him to still be here.'

The two women lapsed into silence, and Bec was grateful when Anna reached across and squeezed her hand. It was one of the many things she liked about Anna – that she didn't push her to discuss her feelings or feel she had to comment on something because Bec opened up to her.

As the temperature dropped, they decided it was time to leave while it was still light enough to enjoy the beauty of the gardens.

'It was good of Zara to go with Skye to the park today,' Anna said as they walked back towards the exit and car park. 'It's great to see they've made friends so quickly, too. It's not easy at that age to find someone that you really click with.'

'It's been great for all of them,' Bec said. 'Zara's worried things will change when Skye gets placed with a family. That they might not let her catch up with us.'

Anna frowned. 'We're aiming to find her a family she fits in with and who will listen to what she wants. I can't imagine they'd do that.'

Bec glanced at her sideways. 'Still not thinking about taking her on yourself?'

Anna shook her head. 'I'm still a no.' She sighed. 'I have a lot on my plate with my mum at the moment, but if I'm really truthful, I couldn't bear to invite her into my life and then lose her.'

'I understand, but I just don't think it's the same as what you went through with Maisie. Why don't you come back to mine for some Thai takeaway and a glass of wine. I'll see if I can change your mind.'

Anna smiled. 'Thai and wine, yes. Change of mind, no.'

20

Samara knew telling Bruce about her visit to Rebecca and the children wouldn't go down well. He'd been so angry the last time they'd discussed it, if you could call the heated argument a discussion. But, one thing she would say about her relationship with her husband was that they'd always been honest with each other.

She waited until she'd put dessert on the table, Bruce's favourite chocolate torte.

He put down his wine glass and smiled as she placed the bowl in front of him. 'Wow, that's a treat.' His smile turned to a frown. 'I didn't miss anything, did I? It's not our anniversary or your birthday, or mine for that matter.'

Samara smiled at him, unable to muster the energy to laugh. 'No, nothing special.'

Bruce sank his spoon into the torte, closing his eyes in pleasure as he put the first spoonful into his mouth. He swallowed and opened his eyes. 'Amazing as usual.' He reached for a second spoonful, his spoon hovering in the air. He looked up at Samara. 'Is this an attempt to sweeten me up?'

She cocked her head to one side, eyeing him carefully. Yes, she supposed it was. 'Not sweetening you up necessarily, but making what I'm about to tell you easier to digest.'

Bruce put his spoon down, picked up his napkin and wiped the corners of his mouth. He sat back in his chair expectantly. Samara had seen this pose many times over the years. Any time she or one of the kids had something to tell him, he took on an edge of defensiveness.

She cleared her throat. 'I saw Rebecca and her children on Wednesday.'

Bruce picked up his wine glass and took a sip. That was progress at least. She'd expected him to hit the roof.

'They live in Camberwell and the kids are lovely,' she said. 'Twins, like Rebecca and Chris. Very different from each other, but they resemble Rebecca and Chris at that age. They're sixteen,' she added. Instead of anger, all she could see in her husband's eyes was pain. She swallowed before speaking again. 'Rebecca and her husband set up a successful business. It's called Reclaim and it helps people, including young offenders, get trained and find employment. It also offers creative outlets, which Rebecca's in charge of. You remember how good her drawings were, well she's made that part of her career. They had an office in Sydney, but she closed that when Owen died and they moved back to Melbourne.' She knew she was rambling, but considering Bruce had suggested he didn't want to know anything about Rebecca and had banned her and the kids from the house, this seemed like a very different reaction tonight.

Bruce put down his glass. 'I don't know if I can do this, Samara.'

'Do what?'

'Have her back in my life.'

'I'm not asking you to do that. I'm telling you that I saw her and the children; that's all.'

Bruce closed his eyes and Samara reached out and put her hand over his. 'I know this is hard for you, that it's been hard since it all happened. When we dreamed of having a family, this wasn't what it looked like in any shape or form.' Tears filled her eyes as she thought back to the excitement of finding out she was pregnant with twins. Of Bruce rushing out to get them baby-sized AFL football jerseys for Richmond, the team he supported, and wrapping her in cotton wool for the entirety of the pregnancy.

Bruce opened his eyes and Samara's heart contracted when she saw the raw pain in them. 'I only ever wanted the best for both of them – you know that, don't you?'

Samara nodded.

'Chris ending his life... I don't know what to even say. I had no idea how to handle it. I was devastated and angry and guilty.' A tear rolled down his cheek. 'I should have known he was that low. I should have helped him. Saved him.'

'We both should have,' Samara said. It was the first time since Chris's death twenty years ago that her husband was finally talking about it.

'You did,' Bruce said. 'You tried to get me to listen and I told you that you were making more out of it than you should. That he was just going through a phase and would snap out of it.' He met her eyes. 'I'm sorry, Samara, I really am. I know how ineffective those words are, but I want you to know I've never forgiven myself.'

'You should have talked to someone, to me even at the time. It would have helped you. Helped us.'

Bruce squeezed his eyes shut again. 'I couldn't. The only way I could deal with it was to push it away. The same with Becca. As hard as it was losing her, having her gone was easier in some ways. Easier to compartmentalise and focus on other things to try and, I don't know, I won't say forget because that wasn't what I needed; I just needed a way to cope.'

Samara wiped her eyes.

Bruce took a deep breath. 'How was Becca?'

Samara couldn't help but smile. Bruce had insisted on calling Rebecca, Becca, moments after she was born. Said he thought Rebecca was too formal, especially for a small baby, and he'd called her that ever since. Samara on the other hand, had refused to shorten her favourite girl's name. It was Rebecca, not Becca or Bec.

Bruce continued, 'she must be finding it hard since her husband died. The kids, too.'

'Yes, I think she's struggling as any of us would be. But she's also raised two amazing kids who look like they'd be there for her and she for them. It wasn't a long catch-up and the kids were around for some of it, so there was only so much we could discuss.'

Bruce nodded.

'I intend to continue seeing her and the children if they're happy for me to be in their lives,' Samara said, 'and I'm telling you because one of things I've loved most about you and me, is that no matter what's happened over our lifetime together we've always been honest with each other. If you don't want to see them, that's fine, but I intend to, and I'd like to become part of their family if we're not going to invite them to be part of ours.'

Bruce picked up his spoon and had another mouthful of torte. Samara had no idea what he was thinking or feeling.

'I'm having coffee with Rebecca tomorrow so I can talk to her without the kids around,' she added, picking up her own spoon.

They finished their dessert in silence, and Samara stood to clear the dishes.

Bruce held up his hand. 'You go and relax; I'll do that. You did all the cooking.'

Samara smiled. 'Thank you.' She turned to leave the kitchen.

'And,' Bruce said, causing her to turn back to face him, 'it doesn't have to be tomorrow, but I'd like to see Becca. Could you tell her that and perhaps invite her here whenever she's ready to visit. And tell her I'll understand if she chooses not to, but I would like to see her.'

She nodded, hoping the surprise she felt wasn't showing too broadly on her face. If Samara had guessed how this discussion would go, it wasn't like this.

* * *

Anna had enjoyed her afternoon drinks, which had turned into a takeaway dinner at Bec's house with Skye, Zara and Hugo joining them. They'd all ended up playing poker, which had brought a lot of laughs and bragging rights for Skye, who'd cleaned up.

Now, as she lay in bed the next morning, listening to the early Sunday morning birdsong, she smiled thinking about Skye. The teenager had slotted into her life, and in turn, they'd both slotted into the Sampsons' lives. It was as if they'd all known each other for years. She'd made a lifelong friend in Bec – of that she was sure.

Her phone rang, and her heart raced a little as Kieran's name flashed up on the screen. She quickly answered it.

'Hey you,' his deep voice glided down the phone line. 'Good sleep?'

'It was,' Anna said. 'Where are you and what time is it?'

'London. The crew went out for dinner and we just got back to the hotel, so I thought I'd call you and also ask a favour. How are you?'

'Good,' Anna said, and went on to tell him about finding the letter in her father's belongings and Skye's idea of posting it to the school's Facebook group.

'Do you think it's a good idea? Won't it bring up all the hurt and trauma again?'

Anna was about to say of course it was a good idea, but she realised Kieran was also protecting himself. He was involved with her again for the first time since Jake's death, and now she had the potential to reignite all the hurt they'd both been through.

'I think not doing something would be more difficult than doing something,' Anna said. 'I live with the hurt and trauma every day. Sure, it's duller now than it was years ago, but it's still there. This might all come to nothing, but I think I need to find out if I can.'

She was met with silence. 'Kieran?'

'Sorry, yes, you need to do what feels right for you.'

'I do. So, tell me, what's the favour?'

'I forgot to water my plants before I left. Would you mind terribly popping over and watering them?'

'Of course I will, although it'll seem strange going to your place for the first time without you there. Text me your address and I'll stop in before work tomorrow.'

Two hours later, she found herself repeating her words to Marty that the search for the letter writer might all come to nothing but she needed to at least try.

'You definitely need to find out if there's anything to this.' Marty had greeted her at reception on her way into Willowridge, and she'd ended up telling him the full story about Xavier and the letter and then showed it to him.

He'd let out a low whistle when he'd read it. 'No wonder your dad was looking for answers,' he said. 'What did Kieran say?'

'He said he knew nothing different about the accident than I did. He left soon after it happened and he cut ties with everyone at school, so there was no reason for him to hear any of the news. Jake and he were tight, but the other guys they hung around with were friendly but not friends in the same way. Once he lost Jake, he wouldn't have had any reason to stay in touch with anyone.'

'It's strange that whoever wrote the letter pointed him out, though.'

'Whoever wrote it probably knew they were friends,' Anna said. 'Honestly, I don't know what to think, other than I like Skye's idea of putting it in the Facebook group. I only hesitated because of Kieran's reaction, which I think is about it stirring up more hurt for him. His wife died not that long ago, and more grief is the last thing he needs.'

Marty rolled his eyes, making his thoughts about Kieran clear. 'This isn't about him; it's about finding out the truth and setting the record straight for Jake. What are you going to tell Lyn?'

'Exactly what I told you, other than the Kieran bit. I'll leave that out. I'm not sure she really understands Facebook, but I'll do my best to explain how it all works.'

'If you need any help explaining, let me know.' Marty grinned. 'I spend far too much time on Facebook.'

Anna raised an eyebrow. 'You don't seem like a time waster.'

'Well, turns out I am. Send me a friend request and you'll see the random content that I post about.'

'Deal,' Anna said. 'Now I'd better go and see Mum. How's she been the last few days?'

'Actually, kind of surprising,' Marty said. 'She's been more present than usual.'

'Really?'

'Yeah. I think having something to focus on has kept her more grounded. She's been asking about it constantly, but she's not drifting off the way she normally does.'

'Hopefully she'll calm down a bit once we tell her we found the letter,' Anna said. 'Although I wouldn't be surprised if she wants it posted to Facebook immediately and then asks every ten seconds if there's been a response.'

Marty laughed. 'I would probably be checking every ten seconds too, if I'm honest. I do that when I post regular stuff on my page. Love that dopamine hit.'

Anna shook her head with a laugh as she started towards her mother's room. She looked back over her shoulder at Marty. 'I must say I'm intrigued about this Facebook addiction.'

'Well, I think you should explore your curiosity.' He grinned, his dimples deepening. 'Send me a friend request when you find me.'

***

Bec wondered what had possessed her to agree with her mother's suggestion that they move their café coffee catch-up to her parents' house. She'd been adamant that she wasn't going to see her father, but her mother's phone call explaining what had happened the previous night had stirred something in her, and now here she was driving down the driveway of what had once been her childhood home. She had to admit, she was curious to see what they'd done with it. It had been rented out for the time they were in Canberra, but they'd been back for a couple of years now.

She wondered if her father would really be there or whether he'd make up an excuse at the last minute and avoid seeing her. Her question was answered as she neared the house; the sight of her father coming out of the front door caused a ripple of nerves to course through her. She was aware this could go many ways. Probably one of two, really. A civil catch-up or a shouting match and no return invitation, which might, in fact, be her preference.

She was shocked when she stepped out of her car to find him beside her. He opened his arms, and without thinking, she stepped into his embrace. He hugged her tightly, a silent conversation that felt like a multitude of apologies going between the two of them.

Eventually, they pulled apart, and she stood back and took in his appearance. He'd always been a handsome man, and now, in his late sixties, that hadn't changed. The grey in his hair made him look distinguished, and overall, he looked fit and healthy.

'It's good to see you, Becca,' he finally said, a smile playing on his lips. 'Those words feel incredibly inadequate after twenty years.'

Bec's eyes filled with tears, the anger and resentment she'd felt towards her father for years seeming to disappear, or at least be put to the side for a moment. He was right; it was incredibly inadequate, but what did you say after all this time?

'Come inside. See if you recognise the place. Your mum's in the kitchen, cooking all your favourite cakes from the smell of it. A benefit of having you back in the fold.' He winked at her, and it transported her to when she was a kid.

* * *

She was ten, maybe eleven, and the house had been humming for weeks with campaign chaos – flyers on the kitchen table, signs being painted in the garage, and strangers coming and going with clipboards and loud laughter. Her dad had decided to run for council and, as far as he was concerned, they were all in it together.

Bec sat cross-legged on the kitchen floor, licking icing from a wooden spoon while her mum bustled between trays of muffins and cakes. Lemon drizzle, chocolate hazelnut, raspberry and her favourite, caramel slice – sweet treats, or bribes, for the stream of volunteers and curious locals who popped in to offer support.

Her dad swept into the kitchen, his shirt sleeves rolled up, tie loose, the ever-present campaign grin on his face. He dropped a kiss onto her mum's cheek, swiped a still-warm muffin and winked at Bec as he passed.

'Couldn't do this without the best team behind me,' he said, voice warm and full of pride for his family. 'Especially my secret weapon.'

Bec beamed at him, licking caramel from her fingers. In that moment, he was her hero, the man who was going to make the town better.

* * *

The memory faded as quickly as it had come, and Bec blinked away the sudden sting in her eyes. How did they go from the incredible family unit they were when she was younger to being completely broken?

She allowed her father to guide her into the house with his hand placed lightly on her back. She had to smile when he opened the door, and her senses were hit with the inviting smell of baking. She breathed in and couldn't help but let out a sigh.

'It's like coming home from school,' she said, causing her father to smile.

'The rest of the house might not feel that way,' he said.

And it didn't.

'Wow,' Bec said as her father led her into an open-plan living, dining room and kitchen. It had all been separate rooms when she was growing up.

'Rebecca!' Her mother's delight was genuine and again

brought tears to Bec's eyes as she stepped into her mother's arms for a hug.

'It looks and, more importantly, smells amazing in here,' she said when her mother released her.

She saw a look pass between her parents, and relief settled in her mother's eyes. No doubt she'd been worried about how her father was going to receive her, and vice versa.

The one thing that Bec couldn't help but notice when her father gave her the tour of the house was the lack of photos. There were none of her and Chris. She felt hurt on one level, but also understood. She certainly didn't have photos of her parents on display in her house which her mother probably noticed when Zara had insisted on giving her the tour of their home.

'I'm very sorry about your husband,' her father said as he took her into a more feminine room. It was set up like a library or a study. 'Your mother's getaway,' he said, with a conspiratorial eye-roll. 'But back to your husband, it must be very difficult for you and the kids.'

'It is,' Bec said. 'He was fine one day, went off to a conference and never came home. An aneurysm we didn't know existed. It was awful that it happened when he was away too. None of us were with him.' She shuddered at the memory, turning to look at her mother's bookcase. Her heart lifted when she saw a line of photos of her and Chris from when they were babies, right through until they were teenagers. They hadn't been forgotten.

Her father cleared his throat. 'These are the only photos on display. I'm sorry about that. I found it too hard. After Chris died and you left, I was angry. In fact, I think I've remained angry all this time to deal with the loss.'

Bec squeezed his elbow. 'I get it, Dad, really, I do. We haven't put our family photos back out yet since moving from Sydney. It's easy to say we haven't unpacked everything, but I think we all know looking at Owen's photo every day would be too hard.'

He nodded, and she was surprised he'd given her a glimpse of his more vulnerable side. He sniffed the air and tapped his nose, exactly like he had when she was a kid and the cake was coming out of the oven. 'Come on, you, let's go and make some coffee and see what Mum's made.'

It was over coffee and lemon drizzle cake that Bec learned more about her father's activities since leaving politics.

'I wanted to do more than I was able to in the government position,' he said. 'I'd been lucky along the way to have met a lot of well-connected people with money to invest, which is why I started my own consultancy. When I was a politician, I did my best to get as much money into certain portfolios as possible, but there was a limitation on what I could do. In the private sector, I've been able to concentrate on private support services for things like mental health.'

Bec was glad she didn't have any cake in her mouth when he said this, or she probably would have choked on it. Instead, she cleared her throat. 'Mental health?'

He nodded. 'I got more involved in the health sector when I was the Minister for Health. I'm not sure if you've seen anything about my political career, but I did quite well in the end.'

'I've seen a bit online,' Bec admitted.

'Your father's managed to do a lot of fundraising and investments for the mental health charities,' her mother said, 'as well as the private sector. Places like Beyond Blue and Men's Hotline.'

Bec had to let this sink in. She'd always blamed her parents for Chris's death, and now she realised they blamed themselves too.

'From what your mum's told me, and I've since seen online, your business is one that our investors would seriously consider reviewing if you're looking to expand at any stage. It's impressive what you and Owen have done.'

Bec smiled. Hearing the pride in her father's voice was something that she still enjoyed. 'Thank you. It's doing well too. I have a business partner, Damien, and right now I think we're content with how things are going. We've downsized, if anything, by closing the Sydney office.' She thought for a moment. 'Reclaim doesn't need investment, but my friend, Anna—' she turned to her mother '—she's the one who ran the session at Echoes the other night – the business she works for definitely needs an injection of funds.'

* * *

Bec felt a weight lift from her shoulders as she drove away from her childhood home. The catch-up had been very different from what she'd expected. She'd been apprehensive about seeing her father and wondered if it would be an awkward, forced catch-up. But it hadn't. She had to remind herself that before Chris had gone off the rails, they'd all been a close-knit family. She knew how proud her parents had been of both her and Chris, and that they would do anything for their kids.

That was a point that always stuck with her. They *would* do anything, so why hadn't they done something for Chris?

She thought about the conversation and the surprise, followed by a sense of pride, she felt for her father's business dealings. He was making a difference now, perhaps to make up for his guilt over Chris. It was her reason for Reclaim, so it made sense to her that he would want to do something like that to help others. He'd also spoken about his clients and their focus when it came to investing. She'd talked at length about Hopefield and the support groups Anna ran, and he said he would be interested in a tour of Hopefield if Bec wanted to arrange it.

She couldn't wait to tell Anna.

* * *

Anna was still smiling when she pushed open the door to her mother's room and stepped inside. She was sure Kieran was wrong when he'd said that Marty liked her, but having that seed planted she found herself looking at him through a different lens. She'd never given much thought to his personal life, not because she wasn't interested but because it seemed inappropriate when his involvement with her and her mother was in a professional capacity. He was lovely and attractive, so she would assume that he would also be happily attached to someone.

'Anna.' Her mother switched off the television, her smile broad as Anna approached to hug her. It was on days like this that Anna really missed her mum, because this was the woman she remembered and who remembered her. If her mother hadn't turned to alcohol all those years back, this is who she might see every day and who would most likely be living in her own home rather than being in care.

'What's the news on Xavier?' she asked as Anna sat in the armchair across from her.

'Well,' Anna said, taking the letter from her bag, 'Kieran and I saw him on Friday night. He remembered that Dad had been upset about a letter he'd received from someone after Jake's death.'

'That's right,' Lyn said, clasping her hands in her lap. 'There was the letter. We didn't know who it was from.' She frowned. 'Your father never let me read it. He mentioned something about Kieran though. That the letter made him worry about Kieran and he wanted to find him and talk to him. At that stage his parents didn't know where he was. It was after Dad died that Kieran's mum told me he'd settled in Adelaide.'

'Kieran doesn't know anything,' Anna said. 'He only knows what we were told about the accident when it happened. He didn't keep in touch with anyone from school, so he didn't hear any gossip or other information. The letter only suggested that he might. Here—' she held it out to her mother '—read it for yourself.'

'You're right,' Lyn said, 'the letter doesn't say Kieran knew anything, and in fact suggests whoever wrote it was worried something might have happened to him. I wonder who these guys are the letter refers to?'

Anna went on to explain her plans to upload the letter to the school's Facebook group. Her prediction to Marty was correct.

'Facebook,' Lyn said. 'I'd forgotten about that. I used to love looking up people and seeing what they were now doing. I never really used groups though. Does that mean you'll put a copy of the letter in the group, and everyone you went to school with will see it?'

'If they're Facebook users and belong to the group, then yes. I'll add a few sentences reminding people of who Jake was and what happened and see if anyone comments or messages me.'

'What are you waiting for, then?' Lyn said, pointing at the letter. 'Put it up now.'

21

Bec didn't get a chance to call Anna after the catch-up with her parents on Sunday morning. She'd arrived home to find Zara and Hugo in a heated debate about whether ancient Egyptians really performed brain surgery or if that was something exaggerated in documentaries. It was exactly the kind of argument Owen used to jump at, pulling books off shelves or loading up some obscure article on a website to settle it once and for all.

But he wasn't there, and she had no idea of the answer and really wanted to get out of the house. So, Bec suggested a trip to the museum. One of Owen's favourite places.

Ironically, if he'd been the one to suggest it, he would've been met with groans and eye-rolls, probably a dramatic 'absolutely not' from Zara and a mumbled excuse from Hugo about homework. But when Bec asked, both had said yes.

She knew why. Not an interest in ancient medicine, or even proving that they were right, but their dad. A way to be near him, to sit in a space he had loved. She smiled, thinking of how she'd shush him when they visited the Museum of Sydney as he read every plaque on every exhibit in a loud booming voice as if he were a tour guide.

After the museum visit, they'd gone out for burgers and chips at the pub down the road. 'Dad's favourite food,' Zara had pointed out after declaring herself the winner of the initial argument about the Egyptians.

It had been a lovely afternoon, and Bec had felt close to both kids and to Owen at the same time. It made her realise they needed to do more things that reminded them of the fun things they'd done together. To this point, she'd been actively doing her best to avoid any places that would leave her with tearful memories.

Now, as she sipped her coffee at her desk mid-morning on Monday, she found herself distracted from planning the creative sessions she had booked in for the week and instead picked up the phone and found Anna's number.

Bec briefly explained the visit to her parents' the previous day.

'How are you doing?' Anna asked. 'That's a lot to deal with on top of everything else you have going on.'

'It was strangely nice,' Bec said. 'I get the impression that Dad found it easier when I wasn't there. Out of sight, out of mind worked well for him when he was trying to cope. But it didn't feel as awkward as I thought it would. It's small steps for now, but we'll see. I'm open to seeing them again and having them involved with the kids, which I really didn't think I would be. Now, what I really wanted to tell you about was my dad's business.' She went on to explain what Bruce did. 'He'd be very interested to come and learn more about Hopefield and see if there are any opportunities to assist with investment.'

'Really? That's incredible. Thank you!'

Bec shared with Anna more about her father's business and

what she'd learned about his investment interests the previous day during her visit.

'I said I'd speak to you and then put him in touch if you were interested.'

'Interested?' Anna laughed. 'That would be an understatement.'

'I'll let Dad know. Now, more importantly, what's happening with the letter and the school Facebook page? Have you posted anything in the group yet?'

'I did yesterday,' Anna said. 'So far, there've been comments from a few people who remember the accident, but didn't hear anything unusual at the time. I'll keep an eye on it and hopefully we'll hear something more useful.'

After a few more minutes of chatting, they ended the call, Bec saying she planned to be at Echoes the next night with her mother and Zara accompanying her.

* * *

Anna ended the call with Bec and clicked on the Facebook icon on her computer. There were another four comments on the post, but again, they were people saying hello without offering any information.

She sighed, wondering if it was a wild goose chase. She hated to get her mother's hopes up, and her own hopes, too.

Isabella's assistant poked her head around the corner of Anna's door, breaking into her thoughts.

'Isabella asked if you had time to go and meet with her. She wants to discuss the Echoes group.'

Anna smiled. She loved Isabella's idea to expand the group, even considering other cutbacks, and had already started mapping out a strategy for this. She stood and collected a folder of papers from the edge of her desk. 'Of course. I'll head down to her office now.'

Isabella was on the phone when Anna arrived at her office door, and she smiled and pointed at one of the mismatched armchairs across from her. Anna sat down, placing the folder on the chair next to her, admiring, as she often did, Isabella's taste. Her office was simple but inviting. Sunlight streamed through the blinds, casting soft stripes across the bookshelf that sagged with folders and community reports. It wasn't fancy, but it felt lived-in and welcoming.

Isabella finished her call and sighed. 'These cutbacks are a nightmare. I don't know how we're going to do half of the programs if they really cut the budget to this extent. It's closer to two million dollars that they're talking about.'

Anna wasn't sure how to respond to this. It would certainly mean staff cutbacks.

Isabella forced a smile. 'Don't worry, you'll be the last to go if that's what you're thinking.'

Anna's cheeks heated, embarrassed that she could be read so easily.

'Now,' Isabella said, 'I'd still like us to think about expanding the Echoes group. While my original thoughts were that it'd leave us with a good customer base once our funding was reinstated, I'm beginning to realise we might not get funded again unless we show that we're doing something above and beyond the norm.'

'And you think Echoes ticks that box?'

Isabella nodded. 'Definitely. Have you given it any thought since we last discussed it?'

Anna picked up the file and passed it across the desk. 'Yes, there's a document in there that outlines my ideas for two new weekly sessions. You'll see the rationale for the time of day and the target audience, plus the costs involved with running a session.'

For the next half an hour, the two women discussed Anna's recommendations and began mapping out a strategy to get at least one of the sessions running within a month.

'This might be too premature to mention,' Anna said, 'and it might not come to anything, but a friend of mine is doing an introduction to her father for me. He runs a company that invests in mental health organisations in the private sector, and he has clients who like to make sizeable donations to organisations across the board, private and government. She's told him about Hopefield, and he's apparently agreed to come and meet with us. I'm expecting a call from him in the next day or two.'

A flicker of hope crossed Isabella's face. 'That'd be great if he had some people interested in us. Do you know what his company name is, or his name?'

'His name's Bruce Langford, but no, I don't know his company. I got a call from my friend about it just now. I haven't had a chance to google him.'

Isabella frowned. 'That's a familiar name. Not the politician, Bruce Langford?'

'He was in politics,' Anna said, 'but then retired and started his own business.'

'He did a lot of good things as the Minister for Health,' Isabella said. 'It would be amazing if he took an interest in Hopefield. Let me know when you hear from him. I'd like to be part of the initial meeting and tour.' She grinned. 'He might be our knight in shining armour. Fingers crossed anyway.'

Anna returned to her office, conflicted by her feelings. On the one hand, she was worried the centre might be shut down or partially shut down, but on the other, she was pleased to be able to expand Echoes. She was also nervous, but hopeful that Bruce Langford might be able to help.

* * *

Following the surprisingly successful catch-up with her parents, Bec extended an invitation for them to come over to the house the following weekend, but on mentioning this as she sat down with Zara and Hugo for dinner that night, she was quick to discover this wasn't soon enough for Zara.

'What do you mean we have to wait until Saturday?' Zara demanded. 'I'd like to see them sooner.'

'What's the rush?' Bec asked, genuinely curious.

'I don't know,' Zara said, 'I've got this feeling that I need to meet my grandfather, like something's going to happen and if I don't meet him soon, I never will.'

Bec frowned. 'Like something will happen to him?'

'I don't know,' Zara admitted. 'But there's this weird feeling in me that something's going to happen. I can't explain it; it's there. I don't know if it's a premonition or what it is, but it's been there for ages, and now I know they exist and they live not far away, I need to see them, to meet them.'

Bec nodded. While she knew Zara was impulsive and had no patience, she still had to be careful in dismissing her daughter. If her father had an accident or suddenly died, she'd feel terrible that she had stopped a meeting. 'Okay, I'll call them after we finish eating and see if we can do it earlier.' She turned to Hugo. 'How are you feeling about your new grandparents?'

'Good,' he said. 'It's nice to have more family. As long as you're okay with them, then I'd like to see more of them.'

'Is it strange to go from hating them for all these years to saying they're okay?' Zara asked.

Bec nodded. 'Very strange. My dad changed after Chris died. I'm realising now a lot of that would have been grief, but it was really in the couple of years leading up to his death that I couldn't understand Dad's behaviour. It was like he didn't care that Chris was struggling. He'd get angry with him rather than being supportive or encouraging. It was really unlike him, but it made Chris worse, and that's why I blamed Dad for his death.'

'Do you still blame him?' Hugo asked.

Bec thought about the question. Sure, her dad had been nice to her the previous day, but that didn't change anything about his behaviour leading up to Chris's death.

'Yes,' she finally said. 'I do blame him. But seeing what he's done with his career both in politics and now in the private sector to try and prevent as much suicide as possible, I can see that he's done everything he can to try and make amends. I can't fault him for that. We lost Chris, but he's probably saved thousands of lives through his work and funding of health centres.'

'Will you forgive him?' Hugo asked.

'That's a tricky one. I'm not sure I can do that. But a lot of time has passed, and I'd like them in our lives, so I'll need to work out what that's going to look like.'

After they'd finished their meal and stacked the dishes in the dishwasher, Bec had retreated to the room she used as a study and called her parents.

Bec jumped in fright, not expecting Zara to be eavesdropping as she came out of her study. 'Zar! You nearly gave me a heart attack.'

Zara grinned. 'Sorry, I wanted to know what they said.'

'They're going to both come to the Echoes group tomorrow night, and we're going out after for dinner at Sophia's. So, if you want to meet him, then you can, or you can wait until the weekend as originally planned.'

'They're both coming? Is this their way of finally dealing with Uncle Chris's death?'

'Maybe,' Bec said, 'but I think Dad mostly has plans to visit Hopefield and meet Anna, so I thought he might also be interested in seeing Echoes. He's got a business that could see some money go to the centre, which it sounds like they could use. So possibly he's looking for ways to deal with Chris's death, but it's more likely research for the business.'

'That's good,' Zara said. 'Skye mentioned that Anna's really stressed about the centre losing funding and even needing to close.'

'Hopefully it won't come to that,' Bec said. 'Anyway, if you want to come tomorrow, I'll be leaving around five thirty. I want to get there early to introduce Dad to Anna.'

'Yeah, I'll come,' Zara said. 'Skye's going too. Okay, I'm going to finish my homework. Thanks, Mum.'

Bec smiled at the rare thank you from Zara before making her way back to the kitchen to flick the kettle on. She'd spoken with her father, who'd launched straight into an update of his conversation with Anna. He sounded quite enthusiastic about Hopefield and was looking forward to joining her mother and the rest of them at the Echoes support group the next night.

22

A million thoughts rushed through Anna's mind as she read and reread the message she'd received via Facebook. She and Skye were sitting in the cosy couch area of the apartment, having finished eating a delicious basil pesto chicken pasta dish created by Skye. Skye was reading and Anna was trawling through the comments on her Facebook post, hoping she'd get someone to remember something.

As they sat in silence, Anna was willing the minutes to speed up so she could speak to Kieran. She was amazed at how much time she was spending thinking of him.

She looked across to Skye, who was sitting on the couch, her head in a book, and she smiled. It was hard to believe this was the same girl who'd turned up at Echoes with Bec a few weeks earlier.

Skye looked up. 'Are you okay?'

'Yes, why?'

'I don't know, but you've been sitting there for ages, not doing anything. I can read in my room if you want to turn on the TV.'

'I'm waiting for Kieran to call,' Anna admitted. 'I'm finding it hard to concentrate on anything else. I want to tell him about the message I received today. See if he remembers this guy, Cameron, who we went to school with.'

'Did he respond to your Facebook message? The Cameron guy.'

'Yes.'

Skye put down her book and, much to his annoyance, lifted Smoko off her legs so she could sit up properly and turn to face Anna. 'What did he say?'

'I'll read it to you if you like?'

Skye nodded, her eyes lighting up with anticipation.

> Hi Anna, it's Cameron Turbot. You might remember me as that smart-arse always getting detention at school. I remember you as that kind, cute chick who always sat in the second row in English. Although my attendance was random, so that might have been every other week on the day I happened to attend.
>
> I hope life has treated you well and better than it did when you lost Jake.
>
> I saw your message on Facebook and wanted to let you know that I wrote the letter to your father.
>
> I'd be happy to meet and discuss in person. I'm heading away until early July, but I'm happy to catch up then. I do have more information than I gave your dad. Feel free to get in touch.

'He's then listed his number,' Anna said as Skye took the information in.

'Wow, he definitely knows something else,' Skye said. 'I'm assuming you'll meet with him?'

'Of course. It's frustrating – it's so long away.'

'You could text him; you have his number. You don't have to do it in person, and he said he's heading away, not that he's gone yet.'

Anna thought about the suggestion, and it was true; she could do that. 'I don't know. I think maybe I should respect his timeframe.'

'Why?' Skye asked. 'This means a lot to you but might be something casual for him. You could always text and ask if it's possible to chat, and if not, no problem, you'll catch up when he's available in July.'

Anna nodded. 'I'll think about it. I guess there's part of me that really wants to know what he has to say, and then there's another part of me that's a bit scared too.'

She found herself repeating similar words to Kieran an hour later when he called.

'Cameron Turbot?' He gave a low whistle. 'I remember him. He was nuts, always in trouble with the police. He did heaps of drugs too, back then at least. He was one of those guys most likely to end up dead in a ditch or behind bars.'

'Well, he's not dead,' Anna said. 'I didn't have much to do with him back at school. Jake knew him better than I did. He said he was okay, but I should stay well away from him. That he didn't trust him.'

'A pretty good sum-up, I'd say. Hopefully, he's changed in the last twenty years, but I wouldn't count on it, and I wouldn't count on anything he has to say being of use. He was high as a kite pretty much every day. Even if he remembers something, proving it wasn't a hallucination might be difficult.'

'It can't hurt to talk to him,' Anna said.

She was greeted with silence.

'Kieran?'

He let out a long sigh. 'Sorry, I'm struggling with bringing all of this up again. It's taken me so long to deal with Jake's death. Ignore me, though; this isn't about me. I want you to know that if I seem a bit distant or not as supportive as I should, it's not deliberate. It's just hard.'

Anna closed her eyes. On the one hand, it was so wonderful that he'd loved her brother so much, but there was part of her that felt this was also his opportunity to be there for her, step up and give her the support he hadn't when Jake died. 'It's no problem,' she found herself saying. 'I'm not asking you to be involved, I'm telling you what's going on. I need to find out what happened that night, for my sake and for Mum's. If it's exactly what we were led to believe, then nothing lost, nothing gained, but if something or someone else was involved, I want to know. Now, let's talk about something nicer, like when you'll be home, and I can see you.'

* * *

Bec was pretty sure she was having an out-of-body experience the next afternoon when she got home early, wanting to prepare herself emotionally before going to the Echoes session. *Preparing herself emotionally* was really ensuring she had time for a glass of wine and to sit in the garden, one of the places she found she could think and sometimes talk to Owen about her problems, or the stresses of the day.

'You're home early,' Hugo said when she'd walked through the door after four and was raiding the fridge for wine.

So much for not drinking through the week. She'd have to address that another time. 'You still coming tonight?' she'd asked him.

'Is Skye?'

'I think so.' She paused. Was he still interested in Skye? It could be problematic moving forward if he were. 'Hugo,' she said gently, 'I don't think it would be a good idea to hope you might get involved with Skye. She's still dealing with her own grief, and she's Zara's friend. It could get very awkward.'

The friendly smile he'd been wearing was replaced with a look of dejection. 'What if I'm in love with her?'

She stared at her son. He was sixteen, and he might think he was in love, but it was unlikely to last. But she could hardly say that to him and crush his heart.

He started laughing. 'You're trying to work out what to say, aren't you? Don't worry, I was only joking. I'm not in love with Skye, but I'd like to see her. She said one of her friends is having a party on Friday night and she might be able to get me and Curtis an invite. There will be lots of girls there.'

Bec let out a sigh of relief and then laughed. That was more like it from a teenage boy. 'Okay, good. Now, how are you feeling about meeting your grandfather?'

He shrugged. 'If you're okay with us meeting him, then I am. I was only against them if you didn't want them back in your life.'

She pulled him to her and gave him a hug. 'Thank you.'

'For what?'

'For looking after me. Dad would be very proud of you, you know. The way you've stepped up is amazing. It wasn't expected of you, but I'm incredibly grateful. You let me know if you're struggling at any time, won't you?'

He nodded. 'I've...' He stopped, his eyes downcast in the way he acted when he was little and was debating whether he should tell her something or not. 'I've found this guy at the gym who's been helping me.'

'Helping you?'

He nodded again. 'Yeah, with the Dad stuff.'

'How's he helping you?'

'By listening. Letting me punch stuff, making me lift weights to exhaustion. He lost his dad when he was my age and then lost his kid and wife in a car accident about ten years ago. He knows how to deal with grief.'

'How awful for him,' Bec said.

'It was, but he's a great guy. Everyone calls him Mortar.'

Bec frowned.

'You know,' Hugo said, 'mortar like you use to build a house. He keeps everything and everyone stuck together. You're not going to crumble if Mortar's around.'

'How long have you known him?'

Hugo blushed. 'Since I joined the gym. But don't worry, he's not some weirdo, he's a genuine guy.'

'Is he a psychologist or a counsellor?' Bec asked. 'Do we need to pay him?'

Hugo laughed. 'No, he's a big guy who has time for others, no strings. I don't know if you've ever met anyone that you can just be around and you feel better for it. They're calm and have their shit together and you hope you'll be like them one day.'

Bec nodded. He'd described his father, and from what she'd seen of Hugo the past few months, himself. She wondered if she could go to the gym when Hugo was at school and see if this Mortar guy was there. Thank him. Because, if it was his influence that had made Hugo grow up so much and handle his father's death with the maturity he'd shown, then she owed him a big thank you.

'I'm wondering if I should change the catch-up venue tonight. It seems a bit weird you and Zara meeting your grandfather for the first time somewhere public.'

Hugo leaned forward and kissed her on the forehead like she'd done to him a million times. 'Don't stress. We'll say hi and then have dinner later. It'll be fine.'

As the words left his mouth, her phone pinged with a text. She picked it up from the island bench.

> Hi Darling, Mum here. So nice to be able to say that again! This feels like a rather awkward way for the family to meet. I wondered if we could pop into your place for half an hour before we all go to Echoes?

Bec let out a sigh of relief that they'd had the same thought.

She sent her mother a quick text agreeing it was a much better idea and suggested they come at five.

'Everything okay?' Hugo asked.

'Your grandparents are going to come here first. Can you be ready around five, and we'll do the introductions and then all go to Echoes?'

'Sure, I'll let Zara know. She'll probably need at least an hour to change her clothes a hundred times.' He rolled his eyes as he said this, causing Bec to laugh. Having twins of different genders was interesting. They saw the world so differently, yet in most instances, she found she could relate to them both.

23

Anna didn't usually go home between work and Echoes on a Tuesday, but she wanted to check on Skye. Skye had originally said she'd make her own way to Echoes that night and mentioned that Zara had invited them both out to dinner with her growing family afterwards. Anna wasn't sure that Bec had signed off on that invite. It seemed strange to invite other people when it was the first night her children would meet their grandfather. Anyway, she'd already decided she'd pull Bec aside to check it was fine with her.

But after three, Skye had messaged to say she wasn't going to Echoes or the dinner. That she was fine, but felt like a night with Smoko.

While it was a reasonable statement, something didn't ring quite true for Anna, so she decided to dash home and check that Skye was okay before she went to the meeting.

The moment she opened the door to the apartment and heard sobbing coming from Skye's room, she was glad that she had. She knocked quietly before entering the teenager's space. Skye was curled up on the bed, at first Anna thought in the foetal position, until Smoko's head popped up and looked at her. He was curled up in Skye's arms. Anna's heart melted. Thank goodness the cat had been here for this, when she hadn't. She'd been expecting it for some time and had been surprised that Skye had appeared to be coping so well; she knew she wouldn't be herself. She didn't cope when she lost her dad, and she was a few years older than Skye at the time.

She didn't say anything, just sat on the bed next to the teenager and gently rubbed her back. She flinched initially and then relaxed. Anna could hear her trying to curb her crying, control it for Anna's sake, but she didn't want her to do that. Getting it out would help.

'Just cry,' she said softly. 'No one's expecting you to go on as if your world hasn't been shattered. The person who loved you more than anyone, even before you were born, is gone. It's a massive loss and one that, if you cry out every tear in your heart, it won't fix. It might help a little, though.'

Skye's body convulsed as she let go, no longer trying to hold back.

Anna lay down next to her and encircled her with her arms as she cried. She closed her eyes, her own emotions welling up as she thought of her dad and Jake.

'You know,' she said, her voice still barely a whisper, 'it hurts so much because we loved them so much. And while it sounds like a cliché, and probably is, I would go through the pain I have in losing Jake and my dad again, if it were the choice between not having had the years I had with them and the memories of how much we loved each other.'

Skye nodded as she cried, and Anna pulled her closer. She hadn't told Skye yet, but she'd found the perfect foster family for her. They'd fostered five children previously, but now four had left home, leaving just one girl slightly older than Skye. In meeting them she'd fallen in love with their gentle natures. But right now she wasn't sure she was going to be able to give her up. She'd gotten under Anna's skin and felt like she belonged right where she was. The problem, though, was that the foster family would be better for Skye than she would.

* * *

Bec looked at her mother and mouthed 'wine' the moment she opened the front door. She could see her own anxiety reflected in her mother's eyes about this rather impromptu meeting. How different it would have been if they'd been meeting newborn twins, the excitement, the celebrations; instead, her father was meeting his grandchildren sixteen years later.

She ushered them into the kitchen where Hugo was waiting, dressed in a fresh pair of jeans and a neatly ironed shirt, his hair slicked back with some kind of hair product. His wobbly smile belied his otherwise calm exterior as Bec introduced him to her father.

Bruce held out his hand. 'I'd hug you, but I'm not sure any sixteen-year-old boy is after a hug from some old man he doesn't know.'

Hugo laughed, the tension broken immediately and shook his grandfather's hand. 'Beer?'

'Now you're talking,' Bruce said. 'You going to join me?'

Hugo looked to Bec, who only hesitated for a split second. 'One okay. He's only sixteen, Dad?'

Her father turned to face her. 'Becca darling. How old were you when I had to come and pick you up from Sally Ross's house? Do you remember that?' He turned back to Hugo. 'I had to carry your mother out of the house and hose the vomit off her and the full interior of my car, when we got home.'

Hugo's eyes widened, and he turned to Bec. 'How old were you?'

'Oh, I don't know. It was a long time ago. Twenty-one or something.'

'You left home at twenty, so that's a lie,' Hugo said.

Bruce laughed, the deep, infectious belly laugh Bec had always loved as a kid. She joined in. 'See, this is the real reason I kept you parent types away from my kids all this time – I knew you'd tell them all my secrets.'

'What secrets?' Zara asked, striding into the room with her usual cocky confidence, which disappeared as soon as she locked eyes with her grandfather. 'Oh, hi.'

He walked around and hugged her, and Bec was as surprised to see her hug him back. 'It's lovely to finally meet you. As for the secrets, I'd better not say any more.'

'Mum got trashed at fifteen and—' Hugo hesitated and looked to Bruce. 'What should I call you?'

Bruce smiled. 'Granddad would be nice if you feel comfortable with it, otherwise Bruce is fine.'

Hugo nodded and continued. 'And Granddad had to carry her out of her friend's house covered in vomit.' He grinned at his twin. 'And then he had to hose her down.'

'I was not fifteen,' Bec said.

'She was sixteen,' Samara said. 'And it happened once and once only. I don't think she ever had another drink while still living under our roof.'

Bruce snorted. 'That's a likely tale. I remember…'

'Dad!' Bec said, and he stopped and laughed again, causing them all to join in.

'Now,' Samara said, 'speaking of drinks, where's that wine you mentioned, Bec?'

Bec nursed her glass of wine for the next forty-five minutes, listening to her father ask her children question after question. Her mother looked across to her at one stage, slightly raising her eyebrows. It was obvious that she'd been as worried as Bec as to how this might go.

'I'll meet your friend, Anna, tonight?' Bruce asked, finally including Bec in the conversation.

'Yes, I'll introduce you. I believe she's looking at building on these sessions at Echoes to prove to the government how popular and needed they are, and hopefully, with the next round of funding, they'll get some of what they lost back.'

Bruce nodded but didn't comment.

'What?' Bec asked. 'What's with the sceptical look?'

'Unfortunately, some of the public sector centres like Hopefield are going to feel the effects of budget reallocation now and moving forward.'

'You said public sectors. What about private?'

'Private companies are different because you're talking with boards and shareholders. Agendas are different. Those out to make money will follow the cutback-type models, but then there are those that are being run for altruistic purposes. They're the ones that, with the right investors, are more likely to survive.'

'Boring,' Zara said, with an exaggerated yawn. 'How about we talk about interesting stuff, like how many times Mum had to be picked up out of the gutter when she was Hugo's and my age.'

Samara laughed, quickly covering her mouth when she appeared to realise it wasn't appropriate to encourage her.

Bec, however, rolled her eyes and stood. 'While I'm not agreeing with Zara that this is boring, I am realising we need to get to Echoes. Anna won't be very impressed if we're late.'

* * *

It was as if time had stood still as Anna continued to hold Skye. The teenager had stopped crying and now lay, occasionally whimpering, in Anna's arms. Smoko remained firmly attached to Skye's front and, between the two of them, Anna hoped she was feeling the love they were trying to convey.

Mid-whimper, Skye suddenly sat up, shaking Anna off and causing Smoko to give an unimpressed yowl.

'You're going to be late. It's Tuesday.' She turned to Anna, her eyes red and her cheeks tear-stained. She was a mess.

Anna reached out and stroked her hair. 'I'm not going anywhere. I'll call Isabella and ask her to take the session tonight.'

A flash of horror crossed Skye's face. 'It's in fifteen minutes. You can't drop it on her that late. Come on, I'll wash my face and pull myself together, and we can go.' She reached down and gently stroked Smoko's head. 'Thanks, boy. You knew exactly what I needed, and you too,' she said, turning to Anna. 'Sorry. I don't know where that came from. I thought I was okay.'

Anna pulled her to her and hugged her tightly. 'That saying that grief comes in waves isn't a myth; it's the best way to describe it. Unfortunately, waves tend to come in sets, too. Some people say they come in sets of seven, but I think that's a bit of a myth. For me, the waves have continued for twenty-two years when it comes to Jake. They're smaller sets now, and they don't dump on me in the same way as they did in the early days, but I still have my moments. And the thing I learned is that you don't fight it, you accept that it's part of the process, part of being human. As painful as it may be, there's something quite beautiful too. I kind of see the depth of our pain reflecting the intensity of our love.'

Skye smiled and pulled away from Anna. 'As wise and beautiful as that is, we're going to be late.'

24

Bec checked her watch. It was already after six, and there was no sign of Anna. The chairs hadn't been put out, and people were milling about, murmuring amongst themselves. She was wishing she hadn't brought her father tonight; it was hardly showing Anna or the centre in the best light. He and her mother were looking at the range of posters on the walls, talking about the centre's offerings with Hugo.

'Skye messaged,' Zara said, 'she had a complete meltdown, and Anna's been looking after her. They'll be here in a couple of minutes.'

'Oh no, is she okay?'

'I think so. She said Anna was amazing. Held her while she bawled her eyes out. I'm surprised they're even coming, but Skye said she made Anna come. Anyway, let's get everything set up.'

Bec didn't have a chance to respond; Zara was already moving across the room.

'Hey, you guys,' she heard her daughter say, pointing to a group of three men in their forties. 'Give me a hand to put the chairs out, would you. And you,' she said to Clare Fleming, who was standing on her own by the door, 'could you go and get the urn filled up in the kitchen and check that everything's ready for the supper? Take someone with you to give you a hand 'cause of your arm. And, try not to yell at that woman over there,' she said, pointing at Bec, who wished the ground would swallow her up at that exact moment. 'She's not as bad as she seems.'

And with that, Zara went and started shifting the chairs into place.

'She's so like you,' Bruce said, approaching Bec. 'Knows her mind. She should consider politics.'

Bec laughed. 'I'll leave that for you to discuss with her.'

Bruce looked across to where Hugo was now standing, talking to a boy around his age. 'And he's a real credit to you, Becca. They both are, but there's something about Hugo that tells me he's going to do great things.'

'You can tell that after less than an hour around him?'

Bruce nodded. 'I can.' He sighed. 'I wish we'd seen them grow up.'

Bec didn't respond. She was feeling guilty about how she'd handled things, but didn't want to get into that, not now.

'But,' Bruce continued, 'I think you might have done the right thing keeping them away from me.'

'What? Why?'

He paused, seeming to be choosing his next words. 'You blamed me all those years ago for Chris's death, and you weren't far off the mark. I think in some ways you were right, and I was responsible, and if I told you why I thought that you'd probably leave again, or certainly refuse to have anything to do with me.'

Bec stared at him. Something had happened in the years leading up to Chris's death. She never knew what, but he'd been affected deeply by something.

'Do you know what happened to him?' she asked now. 'I don't

mean him dying, I mean whatever it was that happened a couple of years earlier. The thing that sent him off the rails?'

Pain flickered through her father's eyes as he considered his response. 'It's not something I can talk about,' he finally said. 'One day, perhaps, but even then I'd say it's unlikely. It's too painful.'

Bec stared at him. He knew why Chris had killed himself but wasn't going to share the information? 'Does Mum know?'

He shook his head. 'And I'd rather she never did. All I will say is it won't be beneficial to any of us if I share the details. It'd be more likely to destroy both you and your mother, and while I know you don't think I protected Chris all those years ago, I did my best, and I've done my best since to protect your mother. If you'd been around, I would have done the same for you. If I tell you, you'll see your brother in a very different light.'

Bec wasn't sure what to make of this cryptic discussion, other than it sounded like Chris had done something that her father was choosing not to share. While she was curious, would she even want to know, after all these years? She wasn't sure she could take any more pain right now. After losing Owen, she was at capacity for what she could handle.

Her father squeezed her arm. 'Just know I loved both of you. You were my world back then, and I hope you'll let me back in now so that both you and the kids can be part of my world again.'

'As much as I'd like to believe that was true, I was there, Dad. I don't know what Chris was supposed to have done, but leaving him to get high and suffer to the point of killing himself isn't what I'd call loving someone.'

Her father flinched and his face paled. Bec wasn't looking to hurt him, but she also wasn't going to let him rewrite the past. She left her family for a reason and that reason was believing her father could have saved Chris if he'd given him the attention he needed during the period before his death.

She was open to having her parents back in her life, but not with lies tarnishing Chris's reputation.

Bruce cleared his throat and nodded. 'You're right. I let him down terribly.'

Bec stared at her father, surprised at this admission, but didn't say anything. He'd spoken the truth and she wasn't going to soften it for him.

'Sorry,' Anna hurried into the room with Skye close behind her, signalling to everyone to take their seats.

* * *

Anna was feeling out of kilter after doing her best to comfort Skye and then rushing to the centre. She was pleased to see the teenager gravitate to Zara and felt her heart squeeze a little when Zara immediately threw her arms around Skye. It was exactly what she needed.

She searched the room for Bec, finding her sitting with her mother and a man who Anna assumed was Bec's father. She gave her a quick smile before launching into the evening's session. It was one of the many times she was glad she was an over-organised person. She'd planned the session the previous weekend, so was able to run it on autopilot to a degree.

She welcomed the new people to the group and explained the format of the night. 'I know there are a few people who want to share their stories tonight,' she said, 'so we'll start with that and see how we're tracking before we have our tea break. Now, who would like to go first?'

Jack Morrison was the first to speak. He spoke of how the sudden loss of his sister had left him angry with the world and withdrawn from his family. It wasn't until he began volunteering at a local animal shelter – something his sister had always dreamed of doing – that he found a way to feel connected to her again. 'It doesn't take the pain away,' he said, 'but it gives the pain somewhere to go.'

Next was Sharon Ellis, who spoke quietly about losing her dad during lockdown. 'We didn't get to say goodbye properly,' she said. 'No funeral, no hugs, just a TV screen to watch his funeral on. I felt like I had to push my grief down because no one else could carry it with me.' Her voice cracked. 'Five years have passed since he died, but I still struggle with it.'

A lot of nods followed Sharon's admission.

Anna was surprised when Clare Fleming got to her feet and looked briefly around the room. They had a one-on-one scheduled for Thursday, but Anna hadn't had a chance to check up on Clare's situation to see if there were any updates.

'I know some of you were here a few weeks ago,' Clare said, 'when I first came and when I shared my story about the hit-and-run accident that killed my husband.'

The room fell silent.

She took a deep breath. 'Yesterday, a woman turned herself in to the police, saying she had been the driver of the vehicle. She couldn't live with what she'd done and was ready to face whatever consequences that might bring.'

A gentle murmur trickled around the room.

'How are you feeling?' Anna asked. She was surprised Clare was choosing to share this information with the group before they'd discussed it.

Clare remained silent, but the concentration reflected on her face suggested she was giving real thought to her answer.

'I'm not sure,' she finally said. 'At first, I wanted to kill her if

I'm honest. I was so angry that she'd done this, but then I learned a little more about her.'

The room remained silent, all waiting for Clare to continue.

'She's only thirty. Had her first baby six months ago and has suffered from postnatal depression since. The night she hit our car, she'd been contemplating taking her own life. She was driving to Brighton, and planning to throw herself off the cliff. Apparently, there's a popular suicide spot there.'

You could have heard a pin drop.

'But then the accident happened and it woke her up. Made her realise that her baby would grow up without its mother and that her husband loves her, as do her parents and family. She hadn't been able to pull herself out of the hole that depression has gripped her with.'

'Why didn't she stay at the accident scene?' One of the regulars asked.

'From what the police have told me, she freaked out. She didn't realise Ned was dead, but she couldn't handle it either, and she fled. She didn't tell her husband or anyone else what had happened. She said someone must have hit her in the car park at the supermarket, as she didn't know how the damage to her car had happened. She found out a few days ago from a Facebook post that the accident had been fatal, and that's when she realised she had to come forward.'

'What will happen to her?' Skye asked. 'And to her baby?'

'I don't know. The part of me that wanted her in prison now is hoping she gets help.' Clare took a shuddering breath. 'My sister had postnatal depression. You can't understand it unless you've been there yourself or watched someone very close to you struggle with it. I guess the main thing for me is that while she shouldn't have been on the road in her state, she wasn't drugged or drunk, but she was in a very desperate place.'

'Surely fleeing the scene would be considered a calculated action?' Someone from the back said. 'I think she should be punished regardless of how low she was.'

A murmur went around the room as everyone shared their opinion on the matter.

'She does need to be punished,' Clare said, 'I guess my point of sharing tonight was to tell you that finding out what happened has brought a sense of peace to me. I can now concentrate on grieving for Ned and trying to let go of my anger.' She gave a wry smile in Anna's direction. 'Something for you to deal with on Thursday.'

Anna smiled. 'That's good news, and you're right, it will now be time to concentrate on Ned. Thank you for sharing, Clare.' She glanced at her watch. 'We've time for one more and then we'll have a tea break.'

* * *

'You okay, Dad?' Bec noticed her father looked paler than when they'd arrived. While she felt she'd done the right thing in standing up for Chris, there was still a part of her that felt bad to have hurt her father with her words. But she wasn't going to apologise or change what she said. And now, listening to other people's confronting stories, she wasn't sure whether it was what she'd said to him earlier about Chris or what he'd since heard that had affected him.

The last speaker had been an older man who'd spoken about losing his daughter to suicide. His quiet words and the way he clutched her photo the entire time had left the room heavy with emotion. Bec had found herself squeezing her mother's hand at one stage, knowing that this story would hit close to home for all of them.

Her father forced a smile. 'I'm fine, Becca, I wasn't expecting people to be so open about their situations. They're all a bit too close to home.'

She nodded. 'Why don't we go and find ourselves a cup of tea. Anna usually allows about twenty minutes for the break. If she's free, I'll introduce you.'

They stood and made their way to the break room. Zara and Hugo were already there with Skye, inspecting a rather delicious-looking brownie slice one of the women had brought with her.

Bec organised cups of tea for her parents, smiling as Anna made a beeline for her. The two women hugged before Bec introduced them.

'That was very powerful,' her mother said. 'I didn't realise that someone else's story would affect me so much.'

Bruce put an arm around his wife's shoulders and squeezed her. 'It brings it all back, doesn't it?'

Samara nodded.

He reached out a hand and shook Anna's. 'Bec's told me a lot about Hopefield. I'm looking forward to a tour and identifying possibilities where my clients might be able to assist.'

'It would be incredible if that was an option,' Anna said. 'As I know Bec's told you, we've lost a substantial amount of funding with the announcement of the state budget. Several of our in-person services will be affected.'

'Which is awful,' Bec said. 'Look at how much everyone's getting out of other people's stories. You're not going to get the depth of emotion in a virtual session or online. Everyone was on the edge of their seats earlier when Clare spoke. Poor woman. Imagine going through what she is.' Bec wished she could swallow her words as quickly as she'd said them. 'Sorry,' she added for Anna's benefit. 'I know it's close to what happened with your brother, isn't it? And with everything going on and finding out more about that accident.'

Anna smiled. 'That's fine. It might all come to nothing, and we find out that the story of what happened with my brother was exactly as the police said at the time. Now, I'd better go and get ready for the second half.' She smiled again at Bec's parents. 'Lovely to have met you, and I'll look forward to chatting more at the end of the session.'

'We're having dinner at Sophia's after,' Bec said. 'You and Skye should join us.'

Anna looked from Bec to her parents and back again. She still felt this should be family only.

'Yes, do,' Samara said. 'It looks like Zara and Skye would enjoy that, and it'd be a good chance for Bruce to learn more about Hopefield.' She looked at her husband. 'Wouldn't it, hon?'

Samara nudged Bruce when he didn't respond. He looked like he was a million miles away.

'Sorry,' he said, 'what did you say?'

'That it'd be nice for Anna and Skye to join us for dinner tonight.'

He nodded. 'Yes, of course.'

* * *

Zara practically hugged herself as she looked around the table at Sophia's. She had grandparents, and they were chill. While she understood why her mother left, it was hard to believe that these people, who appeared so lovely, were the monsters her mother had made them out to be. She'd be lying if she didn't say she felt a level of anger towards her mother. They could have been in her life from when she was born.

She took a deep breath, trying to remind herself to be grateful that they were here now, even if they had missed out on sixteen years. Her grandfather was speaking to Anna about her job. He sounded so professional and intelligent. She was sure she'd learn a lot from him.

'You okay?'

She turned to Skye, who was next to her.

'Only you look kind of weird. Like you're happy and mad at the same time.'

Zara laughed. 'That sums me up perfectly. But this shouldn't be about me. How are you?'

'A lot better,' Skye said. 'I think I needed to cry. I imagine you're the same about your dad? It creeps up on you every now and then.'

Zara shuddered. 'It does, but I can't imagine losing my mum. I don't know how you're coping so well.'

Skye gave a strangled laugh. 'I'm not. Ask Anna.'

* * *

After they'd eaten, Bec excused herself and went in search of the bathrooms. She was finding it hard to comprehend having her parents back in her life. She'd slipped back into feeling comfortable with them very quickly. If she didn't have two sixteen-year-olds sitting at the table, she could easily believe that she'd last seen her parents months ago, not years.

She came out of the toilet stall to find Anna at the sink washing her hands. 'Thanks so much for coming with us tonight.'

Anna frowned. 'You don't need to thank me. I was worried it might be an intrusion on your first night with your parents and the kids coming together. That's why I came to find you in here. It's a bit hard to talk privately around the table. I wanted to check you're okay.'

Bec smiled. 'Thank you. And no, it's perfect. Dinner needed to be diluted.' She turned and looked at the toilet doors. One was closed. She pointed at it and mouthed 'Skye?' to Anna.

Anna shook her head. 'No, she went to the bathroom on the other side of the restaurant. Said something about checking out a picture her mum had really loved that was hanging on the wall near there.'

'Okay, good. I was saying dinner needed to be diluted, especially after that last woman who spoke at Echoes. I think she messed with Dad's head. I guess because she was speaking about the woman in the car crash wanting to commit suicide. It makes me wonder what, if any, counselling he's had. He's the type to *get on with things,* so probably didn't have any.'

Anna nodded. 'He's old-school, so quite possibly didn't get any help. It's not too late, though, as we all know. He's coming to tour the centre on Thursday, so I'll see what I can find out then and perhaps steer him towards some counselling.'

'That'd be great, thank you. And more importantly, how's Skye doing? It sounded like she had a rough night.'

'She did,' Anna said and sighed. 'I'm not sure what to do to be honest. I've found a family who I think might be perfect for her, but...'

'But?'

'But I'm not sure. She's a beautiful girl and I don't know that I'm ready to just hand her over.'

Bec raised an eyebrow. 'You're thinking of keeping her?' She smiled. 'I'm guessing that's not the right terminology, but you know what I mean. You'd foster her yourself?'

* * *

Skye was about to flush the toilet when she realised Bec and Anna were in the bathroom talking about her.

Her heart contracted when she heard Anna say she'd found a family that would be perfect for her. She loved living with Anna and Smoko, and having Zara and Hugo close by and Bec too. It wasn't the same as her mum being there, but she felt safe with them. Loved even, although it might be a bit early to say that. But she knew that she didn't want to go to live with strangers. Even though Anna and the Sampsons had been strangers only a few weeks ago, there was an instant connection. One that she knew you didn't have with just anyone.

She leaned against the back of the toilet door and listened as Bec spoke.

'You're thinking of keeping her? I'm guessing that's not the right terminology, but you know what I mean. You'd foster her yourself?'

Skye held her breath. Anna had said it was only a temporary arrangement, but had she changed her mind? They got along so well. She could imagine living with her. Would love to in fact. She willed Anna to say what she wanted to hear.

'No, definitely not.'

Skye closed her eyes, a sharp pain stabbing into her chest.

'Why not?' Bec asked. 'I know what you said about your last experience but that was totally different. Skye's not going to be taken off you. You've fallen in love with her like we all have. It's a no-brainer.'

'Easy for you to say,' Anna said. 'I'm afraid to live with the constant fear of losing her. And then there's my work – I can't give her the stability she deserves. My hours are unpredictable, and I barely keep myself balanced most days. She needs certainty, not someone who might let her down without meaning to. The truth is, as much as I care about Skye, I'm not the person who can give her that.'

Bec snorted. 'I disagree and I'd say it would be good for you too. Give you someone to help take your mind off your mum and Jake. Get on with living a little. With your counselling background you're exactly what she needs.'

Tears ran down Skye's cheeks as she listened to Anna justify why she wasn't going to let her stay with her.

'It wouldn't be good for her,' Anna went on to say. 'She needs a family who can show her how to trust the world again. And if we're honest, I think that's you, Bec. You and your kids – you've already given her a place where she belongs. You're the one who can give her the future she needs, not me.'

Skye found she was holding her breath again. It wasn't something she'd even considered. She'd hoped Anna would want her to stay, but as a fallback plan it wasn't a bad one. In the short time she'd known them, she loved Bec and the twins and she knew both Zara and Hugo loved her.

Bec remained silent and Skye willed her to say of course she'd have her to stay. But instead the silence was eventually broken by a wry laugh. 'I've told you before there's no way I'm in the right place to take on more responsibility. I struggle to get out of bed every morning and pretend all's fine and I'm dealing with losing Owen. At some point I'm likely to crack and everyone will see that I'm not as alright as I'm trying to make out. I can't offer Skye a home and then do that to her.'

'Why not? If you do crack, your kids might actually benefit from seeing that, and we'll all be here for you. And the kids having each other would make a huge difference. Skye and Zara's friendship is helping both of them and who knows what will happen if she does end up with another family. She's old enough to have a say in who she sees and what she does, but you never really know how that's going to turn out.'

Silence filled the bathroom. She only needed one of them to say she was welcome to live with them. And it would only be for a couple of years until she was old enough to be on her own.

Minutes passed before Anna spoke. 'I'll talk to Skye tomorrow about the foster family I've found. While I think you'd be the perfect family for her, they're a good second option.'

Skye crumpled against the toilet door as she heard the door to the bathrooms open and the two women leave. She could just make out Bec's voice as they left the bathroom: 'we have to remember that she's not...'

That she's not what? Our child? Welcome? Our problem? Skye could only imagine the end of that sentence. Her stomach cramped and within seconds she heaved into the toilet.

25

Anna made herself a cup of tea and took it through to the lounge room and sank into her favourite cream corner chair. Skye called it a night as soon as they'd arrived home from the dinner. She'd hardly spoken through dessert or on the drive home. Anna asked how she was and got a shrug. It wasn't unexpected after the state she'd found her in earlier. She sighed, rubbing Smoko's head as he climbed onto her lap and moved himself around to get the best position possible. The foster family she'd found looked like they'd be a good fit for Skye, but the thought of telling her wasn't something Anna relished. And especially not after finding her so distraught.

Her thoughts shifted to Bec's parents. She couldn't imagine having been in Bec's shoes all those years ago and walking away from her family. She'd give anything to have her parents alive and well and together.

Her phone pinged with a text.

> Hey Anna, where's my friend request? Just kidding. Wondered how you're doing and whether you've reached out to Cameron. I know your friend thinks you shouldn't, but for both yours and Lyn's sake, I think you should. Anyway, not my place, but I wanted you to know you have my support. Enjoy your night. Marty.

Anna smiled that he'd cared enough to reach out. He really was a good guy. She knew Kieran would prefer she leave it all alone, but she couldn't. Her mother was her priority, as was Jake. If something needed to be put right about his death, then she'd do everything possible to make that happen.

She gave thought to what she wanted to say and then punched out a message on her phone.

> Hi Cameron. Thanks so much for getting in touch. I'd be keen to talk to you if you're able to make some time. I know you're heading away soon, but I would be very appreciative if you have some time before that to chat.

She then provided her contact details and pressed send.

She sighed as Smoko dug his head into her leg and purred as he continued to sleep. She sometimes found it hard to believe that so many years had passed since Jake's death, and here she was, still fixated on it.

She sipped her tea, eliciting louder purrs from Smoko as she stroked his head, when her phone lit up with a text. It was Cameron Turbot.

> Hi Anna. I can catch up on Saturday if you're free. I don't take off until Sunday. Any time between 11 and 3 will work for me. Let me know where best to meet. I'm living in St Kilda. I don't have a car but can catch public transport if it's not too far. CT.

Anna sent a quick text back confirming eleven as the meeting time and suggested a café she liked on Barkley Street.

A thumbs up came back, causing a nervous ripple to run down her back. What, twenty-two years later, was Cameron Turbot going to reveal?

* * *

Bec sat at her desk on Wednesday morning, skimming through the accountant's report that Damien had forwarded to her. The business was doing well, and she was relieved that it appeared selling the Sydney arm had been beneficial.

'Hey,' Damien said, slipping into the seat across from her. 'How's things? Are you feeling okay about the weekend? It'll be weird to celebrate without Owen, but I feel like we need to do something.'

He was looking at her in a way that suggested she was supposed to be aware of something. She clasped her hand over her mouth as recognition dawned on her. It was Owen's fiftieth birthday on Sunday, and she hadn't planned anything.

'Oh my God, I completely forgot,' she said now. 'How could I forget something so important?'

Damien smiled. 'I'd say it's more likely you blocked it out than forgot. Were you thinking of doing something for it?'

Bec nodded. 'Yes, maybe I'll do something at the house. Small, but at least acknowledge it. Are you free on Sunday?'

Damien nodded. 'Of course, let me know what you need. I'll warn you now, I'll probably get very drunk. Owen and I were supposed to be going on our golfing weekend in July to celebrate both of our birthdays.'

'Are you still going?' Bec asked.

He shook his head. 'No, I cancelled it. We'd planned it for ages, and I can't imagine doing it without him.'

Bec reached across the table and squeezed his hand. 'And that's why he loved you so much.' She took a deep breath. 'Okay, Sunday afternoon. We'll have a BBQ out the back of my place. I'll get lots of drinks and all his favourite food.'

'Should we do a cake?' Damien asked.

'Will that be weird when he's not here to enjoy it?'

Damien shrugged. 'The one thing I know about Owen is that he'd hate to see us missing him like we are. He'd want us out having fun and getting on with life. I'd say we try to make it a fun party for the sake of the kids, too. Give them a happy time that relates to their dad rather than it being a sad occasion.'

'They might be a bit bored,' Bec said. 'They're not supposed to drink, and standing around isn't all that much fun for them. And I don't know that many people. I guess I could invite my parents and Anna. Do you have any friends who might have met Owen and would want to come? You guys did some social stuff when he came down from Sydney on work trips, didn't you?'

Damien nodded. 'A couple. I'll see if they're free. And as for Hugo and Zara being bored, I've got an idea.'

* * *

Anna did her best to shift her thoughts from Skye to Bec's father's impending visit to the centre later that day. She was finding it hard to get the teenager out of her mind. Skye had hardly said a word since Tuesday when she'd found her cuddled up to Smoko before the Echoes session. She'd tried talking to her but she'd politely shut her down each time with one-word answers and no initiation of conversation. She knew she shouldn't read too much into it when the most likely explanation was that Skye was missing her mum.

And now, as she sat at her work desk and scrolled through her emails on Thursday morning she'd be lying if she said she wasn't nervous about Bec's father visiting the centre. She wasn't one to put all her eggs in one basket, but she didn't know many other people who were positioned to help them. Not that there was any guarantee that he'd be able or willing to, but it was a start. She'd invited Isabella to join them for the tour, and she couldn't help but notice the extra effort her boss had gone to. Her tailored navy suit was freshly pressed, her hair smoothed into a sleek low bun, and even her heels looked like they were brand new.

Bruce arrived at two and Anna was quick to do the introductions before she and Isabella took him on a tour of the centre. Anna was pleased that Isabella was accompanying them as she was able to quickly answer Bruce's questions related to the finances of the centre.

'You've built a very good community here,' Bruce said. 'I did some research before I came, and you rate very well. It's a shame that you're not a private business. Funding would be a lot easier. Being government, we'll be looking at donations rather than investments. I do have a few clients that I may be able to get interested.'

They continued talking as Isabella explained the development of the centre.

'Would you like a coffee?' Anna asked after Isabella had

shaken Bruce's hand and left them under the guise of needing to get on with some work. 'There's a lovely café next door.'

Bruce nodded. 'That would be good. I'd like to talk to you more about Echoes and your expansion plans.'

Ten minutes later, having placed their coffee orders, they sat across from each other at Willow and Grind, a warm, light-filled space with hanging plants, timber tables and a gentle hum of conversation that added to the atmosphere.

'I'm very impressed by the work you're doing at Hopefield,' Bruce said, as their cappuccinos were placed on the table in front of them. 'What made you go into that line of work?'

Anna found herself telling Bruce about her brother's death and the lack of support available for her family. She couldn't help but notice him shifting awkwardly in his chair as she spoke of the impact on her parents. 'I'm sorry,' she said gently. 'I know about your son, and I know you understand what I'm talking about. I doubt you or your wife were offered much support back then either.'

'There was support, but I wasn't open to it. I buried my head in the sand. It was my coping mechanism. Not a good one obviously, when you see the impact it had on Becca and my wife. Samara's not the woman she was. Losing Chris and then Becca nearly killed her. She stuck by me. Why, I can't imagine, but she did.'

They spoke for a little longer about their respective losses, but Anna could see Bruce getting more uncomfortable with the topic so she turned the conversation back to Hopefield. 'Do you think there'd be any likelihood of financial support?'

Bruce nodded slowly. 'I'd like to bring in one of my finance guys and look at the books, and a few other elements on how the centre is run from a business point of view, but from what I've seen so far, yes, I think we'll be able to do something to help.

Perhaps not cover the entire shortfall of what you've lost in funding, but we can certainly make a start.'

Anna found herself relaying Bruce's words to Kieran later that evening when he called.

'That's fantastic news,' he said, the delight in his voice genuine. 'You haven't told me much about Bec's father. What's his business? I'd be interested in looking it up.'

Anna gave Kieran the details.

'Langford?' Kieran said. 'As in ex-politician, Bruce Langford?'

'Yes. Why, do you know him?'

She was met by silence.

'Kieran? You okay?'

He cleared his throat. 'Yes, I'm fine, sorry. Not a fan of some of his politics, that's all. But if he can help the centre, that's great news.'

'He's done a lot to support mental health services,' Anna said. 'Losing his son has had a much bigger impact on him than Bec realises.' She sighed. 'It's not easy, is it, dealing with the fallout from death and grief.'

She was met with more silence and could have kicked herself. Of course, it wasn't easy, and he'd not only suffered more than his fair share, but he'd also made it very clear he didn't want to talk about it.

'Kieran?'

'I have to go. Sorry, Anna, one of the guys is at the door.'

'You'll still be back on the weekend?'

'At this stage, most likely. I'll call you when I land.'

Anna stared at her phone as the call ended, uneasiness settling over her. If she wanted any kind of future with Kieran, she'd need to do a much better job of censoring her words around him.

* * *

Bec wasn't sure how her parents would feel about an impromptu visit but decided to test the waters. She needn't have worried. As soon as she pulled to a stop in their curved driveway, the front door opened, and her mother appeared, a tentative smile on her face.

'Rebecca, is everything okay?'

Bec smiled. 'Yes, I wanted to ask you something, so I thought I'd drop in rather than call. I hope that's okay?'

Relief filled her mother's face. 'Of course it is. Come in for a cuppa or a glass of wine. You're welcome to stay for dinner too if you like.'

Bec shook her head. 'Yes to the cuppa, no to dinner. The kids will be expecting to be fed. They're annoying like that.'

Samara laughed. 'Yes, I do remember feeling similarly at times when you were growing up.' Her laugh died. 'Mind you, I regretted all of those thoughts when it was no longer an option.' A shadow passed over her face as her thoughts retreated.

'Becca!' Her father's booming voice broke into their thoughts, and her mother seemed to recompose herself. 'To what do we owe this pleasure?'

'I wanted to invite you to a birthday celebration on Sunday. Sorry for the late notice, but I only decided to do it today.'

'Whose birthday?' her father asked.

'It would have been Owen's fiftieth. I wasn't planning on doing anything, but my business partner, Damien, who was also Owen's friend, talked me into it. I think it'll be good for the kids if we do something fun and positive. It's been a pretty sad time since he died.'

'We'd love to come,' her mother said before her father had a chance to respond. 'I'll cook up a storm so you don't need to do anything. Come on in, and you can give me a list of all your favourite foods and Owen's and the kids. It'll be lovely to be involved.'

Bruce winked at Bec as they made their way inside. 'Your mother will have the whole thing organised in a matter of minutes.'

'I wasn't expecting you to do the food,' Bec said, 'I just hoped you'd come.'

'Nonsense,' Samara said. 'It'll give me a purpose for the next few days. Now, I'll pop the kettle on and then we can go and sit by the fire. It's quite chilly today.'

Bec was halfway through her tea, enjoying the crackle of the open fire and the smell of the burnt wood and eucalyptus smoke, when she asked her father about his catch-up with Anna.

He paled at the mention of it, and Bec's heart contracted. She was beginning to realise how harsh she'd been towards both her parents. They'd suffered enormously over Chris's death and still were. She saw how much the words that were shared on Tuesday at Echoes affected him, and it was quite likely the topic of suicide had come up again during his visit with Anna, or that she'd in fact asked him about his situation.

He cleared his throat. 'The centre's very impressive,' he said, 'as is your friend. I'm finding it hard to get the thought out of my head of why she's working in that field, if I'm honest. She told me about losing her brother.'

'She went through a rough time as a teenager,' Bec said. 'Which you still see traces of in her day-to-day dealings, as to how affected she was. But, as horrible as it is, it's also what makes her so good at what she does. It's why the Echoes group is so successful, too. She has the empathy that's needed.'

Her father nodded. 'I think I'll be able to get support from some of my clients in the form of donations. Leave it with me.'

Bec enjoyed chatting with her parents and felt a slight tug of disappointment when she'd finished her tea and saw from the mantel clock in the lounge that it was close to six. She'd need to get going and start thinking about dinner.

She hugged her parents as she said her goodbyes and thanked her mother for the offer of help with the food for Sunday. She drove away with mixed feelings. Happy to have reunited with her parents, but sad at the thought of a party for Owen when he wasn't here to enjoy it.

26

Anna studied Cameron, finding it hard to believe this shell of a man was the broad footballer from their teenage years. She had no idea what he would have to say as she sat across from him and ordered coffee.

'It's so strange seeing you,' she said. 'I've seen a few friends from school since we all left, but didn't really keep in touch with anyone.'

'Is that because of losing Jake?' he asked.

She dipped a teaspoon in her coffee and stirred it, considering her answer. In the end, she nodded. 'It was easier to stay away from everyone who knew him. It was too painful to see people and have them want to talk to me. Especially after Dad died too.'

Cameron nodded. 'I get that.' He sighed. 'You're probably wondering what I've got to say and why I look like this?' He gestured to his gaunt body.

'Definitely intrigued as to why you wrote the letter and what else you might know, but the rest you don't have to share.' It was obvious to Anna he'd been through a difficult time, or perhaps even something quite serious on the health front.

'I got out of prison a few months ago,' Cameron said.

Kieran's words played over in Anna's head: *I remember him. He was nuts, always in trouble with the police. He did heaps of drugs too, back then at least. He was one of those guys most likely to end up dead in a ditch or behind bars,* and she did her best not to react. She frequently met people through her work who'd served time.

'I went off the rails through my twenties and the start of my thirties. If I'm honest, it was pretty much once we finished school. Got away with most things. But it all caught up with me five years ago, and I got put away. Served my time and am adjusting to being back in the world.'

Anna waited for him to continue.

He took a deep breath. 'One of the things that happened while I was in prison was a pretty nasty battle with cancer.'

'I'm sorry,' Anna said, genuinely sad that his appearance was a result of illness.

He gave a wry smile. 'My punishment, I guess. I'd say I deserve it, and I think you'll agree with me when I tell you why I'm here.'

'I'd never say that,' Anna said. 'You were punished for what you did, I wouldn't wish ill health on top of that.'

Cameron evaded her eyes, tapping his fingers on the tabletop, causing a nervous flutter to shoot through her. She couldn't imagine anything he could have done that would have affected her and made her want him sick or dead.

Eventually, he met her eyes. 'Well, I've been lucky that it appears I won the battle with cancer, but seeing your Facebook post made me realise that maybe one of the reasons for not dying was to be able to make up for some of the things I've done along the way. One being what I did to you.'

'Did? I can't imagine you did anything to me. I hardly knew you. You were friends with Jake, but not me.'

'It's what I did to Jake.'

'Oh,' Anna waited, having no idea what to expect.

'I was there the night Jake died.'

'There? Where? At the party?'

Cameron shook his head. 'No.' He took a breath. 'I was in the car with Jake.'

Anna's heart rate quickened. 'But they only found Jake. They found Jake dead with the car smashed into the tree.'

'I know,' Cameron said.

Anna stared at him, unable to form words. This made no sense. 'But you were never mentioned.'

'I left the accident scene,' Cameron said. He cleared his throat. 'Actually, that's not exactly true. I was removed from the accident site.'

'Removed?'

'I hit my head when we smashed into the tree and was knocked out. But I was okay. I came around later. I had no idea then that Jake was dead. All I knew was we were hit by a car and then hit the tree.'

'Hit by another car?'

Cameron nodded, and Anna waited for him to continue.

'When I came to, I had a massive headache and was in a room with some very scary, threatening guys.' He closed his eyes briefly. 'They started grilling me. What caused the accident? Did I see the other car or the driver? What did I remember?'

'Did you remember any of that?'

'It was all very vague at the time. I don't know who it was, but from what went down, it was someone who didn't want to be caught.'

Anna shook her head. 'I don't understand. Why didn't you come forward? You knew it was a hit-and-run? To this day, no one has ever been charged.' Panic was rising in Anna. She wasn't sure why, but it was coming on strong.

Cameron nodded again. 'I know, and if I could turn back time, I would.'

'Okay,' Anna said, hearing the tremble in her voice. 'What happened? Who were these guys, and why didn't you say anything?'

'I don't know who they were,' Cameron said, 'other than they worked for someone with a lot of money. They used a combination of threats and bribes on me.'

'Threats and bribes?'

'Yeah, we'll break your legs and pretty much destroy you, alongside a huge amount of money to keep your mouth shut.'

'Really? They paid you?'

Cameron nodded.

'A lot?'

He nodded again. 'Enough that if I'd been clever, I could have made something of myself.'

'So, telling me is to clear your conscience?'

'Partly. It was only seeing your Facebook post that made me realise you'd never known the truth. That whoever was involved in the accident got away with it.'

'But if you didn't know who they were then, I'm not sure we'll be able to find out any more than what you've shared,' Anna said. 'If you were the only witness and you didn't see who was driving the other car, then it's probably a bit pointless bringing it up with the police now.'

'Not necessarily,' Cameron said. 'The thing is, it wasn't just me in the car with Jake that night.'

* * *

Bec was pleased to have something to look forward to, even though Owen's absence at his own birthday party was likely to trigger all sorts of emotions. She was grateful that her mother had taken over the cooking, which left her to elicit Hugo and Zara's help to tidy up the garden and house.

With the party the next day, they'd been working for a few hours, and the garden was gradually being transformed from an overgrown area to an inviting one. She had two outdoor heaters that she'd asked Hugo to get from the garage as a chilly night was forecast.

As they were checking that the heaters worked, Bec's phone rang and it was Damien. 'I've got a surprise. Okay if I bring it over now?'

Bec had agreed, and half an hour later, Damien arrived with a delivery truck and an incredibly strong-looking husband-and-wife team.

Damien grinned as they opened the back of the truck. 'Remember that idea I mentioned? Well, here it is. Hopefully, no bored teenagers at the party tomorrow.'

A pool table with a blue felt top was strapped into the back of the truck.

'It's really heavy,' Damien said. 'Is Hugo home? We'll need at least one more set of muscles.'

Bec called for Hugo to help and watched as the four of them moved the pool table into place out the back of the house. The large undercover outdoor area was perfect for it.

'Cool,' Zara said, coming to inspect it after the delivery people left. 'I love pool.'

'Do you know how to play?' Bec asked.

Zara rolled her eyes. 'Of course. Remember Jen in Sydney? Her family had a table. We played all the time.'

Bec turned to Damien and impulsively hugged him. 'Thank you. This is amazing. Tell me what I owe you and we can sort it out.'

'Absolutely not. This can be my birthday present to Owen. We used to play pool quite a bit when he'd come down from Sydney.' He laughed. 'He said it was one of the more manly things I did. Drink beer and play pool.'

Bec smiled. 'You gave as good as you got in that department.' She used to quietly enjoy the way Damien would tease Owen about his ultra-masculine ways, throwing in the odd comment about how it all felt a little too textbook to be natural. Owen never missed a beat – he'd shoot right back with jabs about Damien's flair for the dramatic and taste in shoes. It was their thing, and she imagined it was one of the many things Damien was missing about his friendship with Owen.

Damien rubbed his hands together and looked around the yard. 'Okay, put me to work. We need to turn this place into party central.'

* * *

Anna's mind was racing as she drove away from St Kilda after her meeting with Cameron. She felt like she'd been punched when he told her who was in the car that night. It made no sense. She'd questioned him, thinking perhaps he was making it up or hadn't remembered correctly, but as he said himself, why would he come forward now to tell her what had happened and then lie? There was no benefit to him. He was trying, while far too late, to do the right thing.

She'd planned to go and visit her mother, but after what he'd told her, she needed to sort out her thoughts first.

A text appeared on her phone.

> Hey Anna, checking you're still good for tomorrow? Bring Kieran and Skye, of course. It would mean a lot to all of us if you could be there. I might need some moral support. Bec x

Anna found herself bypassing her Prahran turn-off and continuing towards Camberwell. She needed to talk to someone, and while Bec had a lot to deal with right now, she knew she'd be a good sounding board.

Fifteen minutes later, she was knocking on Bec's front door. She could hear laughter coming from the backyard and Zara shrieking, she assumed at Hugo. She smiled, hoping Skye was with them. She'd still been in bed when Anna left to meet Cameron, which was unusual as she was normally up early. But she'd had a big week, so Anna hadn't disturbed her.

'Anna!'

Bec's smile was wide when she opened the door. 'Are you replying to my text in person? Come in.'

Anna followed her through to the kitchen, watching as Bec picked up the kettle.

'Coffee?'

'Yes, please, and sorry to turn up like this.'

'Don't ever be sorry. I love people who drop in. Means we're good friends, well, in my opinion at least.'

Anna nodded. 'Is Skye here?'

'No, is she supposed to be?'

'She mentioned she might come and help you set up. She's been pretty down all week so might choose to have a day to herself.' She sighed.

'You okay?'

The concern in Bec's eyes brought a lump to Anna's throat. No, she wasn't.

'I caught up with a guy I went to high school with. He was there the night of my brother's accident.'

Bec frowned. 'There? As in, he saw what happened? I thought you said there were no witnesses.'

'That's what we were led to believe. Turns out he was in the car with Jake. From what he remembers, they were run off the road and hit a tree. He was knocked out, and when he came to, he'd been moved from the accident scene.'

'Moved?'

'Some guys moved him. Older, rough. Threatened him and then bribed him.'

Bec's mouth dropped open. 'What?'

Anna went on to repeat what Cameron had told her.

'So let me get this straight. They threatened him and then paid him off so he wouldn't say who'd caused the accident in the first place?'

'Yes. But he didn't know who caused it. He saw the other car but not the driver. And the car was nothing unusual, a Commodore, which half the boys at school were driving. Could have been any of them, if it was even another student.'

Bec was silent, absorbing everything Anna had told her.

'I guess he was young at the time,' Bec eventually said. 'No excuses for not coming forward, but a payout at that age was probably quite appealing and preferable to having your legs broken or whatever else they threatened him with.'

'He took it,' Anna said. 'Interestingly, he went off the rails. He says now he thinks it was a combination of grief and guilt that had him doing all sorts of crazy things. He eventually ended up in jail.'

'What are you going to do about it?' Bec asked. 'Will you go to the police?'

'I'm not sure. There's more to it.' She took a shaky breath. 'There was someone else in the car with them. Someone who Cameron thought would have spoken to the police after it happened. He had no idea that we didn't know. He assumed that the other person had chosen to leave him out of the mix when he spoke to the police. It was his only explanation for why they never came after him.'

'Who was with them?'

Anna closed her eyes.

'Anna?' Bec promoted gently. 'Who was it?'

Anna opened her eyes. 'Kieran.'

* * *

Bec stared at her friend. 'What? Kieran?'

Anna nodded. 'According to Cameron, he was in the car with them and might well know who was driving the other car.'

Bec shook her head. 'But that doesn't make any sense. He would have spoken to the police.'

'Cameron said the guys who threatened him were scary. He assumed, because of Kieran's connections with our family, that he would have talked, but he didn't.'

Bec wasn't sure what to say. 'I'm not sure coffee's going to cut it,' she finally said. 'Do you want something stronger?'

'Yes, but I won't,' Anna said. 'I'm going to have to confront Kieran and find out the truth from him. I'm amazed he's pursued anything with me now, if he's hiding what happened all those years ago.'

'When's he back?' Bec was aware that Kieran was away for work.

'Tonight, but he acted quite strange on the phone yesterday when I told him I was catching up with Cameron. Now I know why.'

'There might be a reasonable explanation,' Bec said, trying to give Kieran the benefit of the doubt. 'I can't begin to imagine what it might be, but hopefully there is one.'

27

Anna couldn't imagine what a reasonable explanation was either but had left three messages for Kieran the previous night and two texts. Now, as she sat sipping a cup of tea early on Sunday morning, she sent another text.

Call me, please.

She frowned at her phone. The *Delivered* message wasn't showing like it usually did with text messages.

'You okay?' Skye asked, walking into the kitchen with Smoko slung over her shoulder like a scarf.

Anna couldn't help but smile at the sight of the two of them. Smoko was going to miss her as much as she would. She still hadn't broached the subject of the foster family. She would, eventually. She was trying to get her head around it herself, and the best way to raise it with Skye.

'Anna?'

'Oh, sorry,' Anna said, realising she hadn't answered Skye's original question. 'I can't get onto Kieran, that's all. He was supposed to be home yesterday. He might still be in the air as my messages aren't delivering.'

Skye peered at her phone. 'Did you have a fight?'

Anna hesitated. They hadn't, but it was quite possibly what was coming. 'Not exactly, but he might be avoiding me. He didn't want me to catch up with Cameron, the school friend who messaged me from the Facebook post.'

'Why not?'

'It's a long story, but having now met up with Cameron, it appears Kieran didn't want me finding out a few things that happened all those years ago. That's why I think he could be avoiding me.'

'If he's avoiding you and your messages aren't delivering, he might have blocked you,' Skye said. 'Easy way to tell. What's his number? I'll message him from my phone. If it delivers, we'll know he's blocked you. I'll say, it's Skye and to please call you.'

Skye's message showed the 'delivered' status as soon as she sent it, while Anna's remained undelivered. 'Sorry,' Skye said. 'He's blocked you. What did he do back then?'

'I'm not completely sure,' Anna said. 'But from what I learned yesterday, Kieran knew more about my brother's death than he ever let on. It makes more sense now why he disappeared the way he did. It also makes sense why he's been so guilty all these years. The one thing that doesn't make any sense is why he's tried to start something up with me again.'

'Maybe he thought if you hadn't found out in the last twenty years what he did, that there'd be no reason you'd find out now.'

Anna nodded slowly. That could be the explanation.

'Can you go to his house and confront him?' Skye said. 'You know where he lives, don't you?'

* * *

Samara had known it wouldn't be a big crowd, but even so, the quietness of the gathering surprised her. Rebecca, the children, Skye, Hugo's friend, Curtis, Damien, and a couple of Damien and Bec's staff. That was it. It was understandable as they'd only been back from Sydney a few months, and hadn't had time to build the kind of community that usually filled a backyard for a fiftieth. Not that this was ever going to be that kind of celebration. It was Owen's birthday and he'd been gone only a few months. She hoped it would be a nice day and that Rebecca would be able to laugh and enjoy it. She wasn't sure she'd be able to in her position, but her daughter had proven to be more resilient.

She stood inside the sliding door, taking it all in. She couldn't help but smile at the good-natured arguing that was coming from the kids at the pool table.

The only thing that didn't sit quite right was how strangely Bruce was behaving. He wasn't enjoying the party in the way she'd expected he would, and she couldn't think of any logical explanation for his mood. From everything he'd said, work was going well, and he had seemed delighted to be back in touch with Rebecca and to have met the grandchildren. But he'd seemed off since earlier in the week. She couldn't pinpoint when or why, but there was something going on.

She shifted her gaze from him back to her grandchildren.

'It was Damien's idea,' Rebecca had explained when they arrived. 'Owen loved pool and always wanted a table, but we didn't have a big enough space in the Sydney house. We don't have space inside here, but this outdoor undercover area is perfect.'

From the fun her grandchildren were having, it appeared Damien had been right on the money. *Her grandchildren*. She had to pinch herself that she was really at Rebecca's house and was being invited into her grandchildren's lives. She'd honestly never thought this would happen. What had surprised her the most was Bruce's change-about. He'd always been so adamant that he would never have anything to do with his daughter again, yet he'd thrown his arms open to her, literally.

But now, as she looked across at him, there was an odd expression on his face which she couldn't work out. She'd questioned him the previous day as to whether he was okay, and he'd done his best to brush it off as nothing. 'Feeling a little off, that's all,' he'd said. 'Nothing a good night's sleep won't fix.'

But it appeared it hadn't, and he was now onto his third drink, and they'd only been here for an hour.

She switched her attention to Rebecca. It was her daughter she should be worried about today. To have lost her husband so young was incredibly sad. Mind you, she seemed to be coping well. She was laughing as she talked to her business partner, Damien, and a friend, or perhaps a work colleague, who had arrived with him. She was pleased that Rebecca seemed to be surrounded by good people.

She picked up a plate of sausage rolls and thought she'd make herself useful and hand them around.

'Is Skye coming?' she asked Zara when she offered her granddaughter the plate.

Zara nodded, smiling her appreciation as she helped herself to a sausage roll. 'I can't believe I have a gran who can cook. Yes, she'll be here soon. She sent me a text earlier to say Anna was going to see someone on her way over so Skye was catching the bus.'

* * *

Anna decided she couldn't wait until after the party to see Kieran.

She needed answers before she drove herself mad trying to figure out what he'd seen and why he'd now returned.

Skye insisted she was fine making her way to Bec's and shortly after Anna found herself on the way to Port Melbourne, and Kieran's apartment. She wasn't expecting him to be home, or to answer the intercom to her if he was, but she needed to try.

She pulled up outside the apartment block, having been here earlier in the week to water his plants. Her heart was thumping. She couldn't begin to imagine any scenario where Kieran could have been convinced to walk away from Jake, or her, for that matter. She needed to hear from his mouth what happened. Cameron, of course, could have made the whole story up, but that seemed unlikely, as what did he have to gain from doing that?

She buzzed the intercom for his apartment and waited. Her backup plan was to wait at the entrance until he came or went. He couldn't avoid her forever. Much to her surprise, the door to the complex clicked open.

Her heart thudded as she took the lift to the fifth floor and stepped out directly across from Kieran's apartment. Maybe he was expecting someone else and had buzzed her in without looking? No – there was a camera. He knew it was her.

The door opened as she reached it.

'Hey.'

Kieran stood in the doorway, unshaven and pale, with bloodshot eyes and a sag in his shoulders that hadn't been there the last time she saw him. He looked terrible.

'Are you okay?' She couldn't help herself. While she wasn't expecting an easy conversation, she also wasn't expecting him to look so dishevelled.

'I forgot you had my address,' he said. 'Come in.'

She followed him into the modern apartment and through to

the open-plan kitchen and living area. How had he forgotten she had his address? He'd only given it to her a week ago in order for her to water his plants.

'Coffee?'

'No thanks, just an explanation.' She was doing her best to keep her anger at bay.

Kieran motioned to the couch area, and Anna sat down.

'You saw Cameron?'

She nodded.

Kieran ran his hand through his hair. 'And he told you he was there that night?'

'And that you were. Is it true?'

Kieran nodded slowly. 'We were both in the car with Jake.'

'How could you? He was your friend. I was your girlfriend. You knew what happened and you ran away?'

'It wasn't quite like that. All I know is that someone else caused the accident, and they made it impossible for Cameron and me to stay around.'

'Cameron told me they threatened him and then bribed him. Did they do that to you, too?'

He nodded. 'They thought I knew who caused the accident and didn't believe me when I said I didn't. We were hit by another car, and that's what sent us into the tree and ditch, but I didn't even see the car.'

'Cameron thought you might have seen the car and the driver, which is why he told me to speak to you.'

'I didn't, but the guys who pulled me from the wreck thought I did. I don't know who they were. They appeared almost as soon as it happened. Pulled me and Cameron out. Cameron was unconscious, but I wasn't. I'd hurt my arm, but nothing serious. They took us to an old house out in Footscray. That's where they threatened me. Said if I didn't keep my mouth shut, they'd hurt me in ways I couldn't even imagine.'

'That's awful.'

'They were terrifying, Anna. I mean, terrifying. I've never told anyone what happened that day, not even Paige.'

'Tell me now.'

He stood up and walked over to a drinks cabinet and poured himself a whisky. He held up the bottle to her, but she shook her head.

He knocked back the dark liquid, refilled the glass and sat back across from her.

'We left the party around eleven. Jake had been hoping to hook up with Christa, but she'd blown him off and gone off with someone else. He was pretty upset about it, so I said I'd go home with him. I'd planned to stay at your place that night. We picked Cameron up when we saw him walking home. He was drunk, swerving all over the road, so Jake stopped, wanting to make sure he was safe. That was the only reason we were on that road. It was to take Cameron home.'

'We weren't far from his place when a car came up fast behind us. Jake was swearing, calling the guy a dickhead. The next minute, the car went to overtake us but was so close that it must have clipped the back of Jake's car and sent it into a spin. It all happened so quickly.' He shuddered. 'The crunch of metal was horrific. I've never heard anything like it before, and then everything went quiet, too quiet. I called out for Cameron and for Jake but got no answer from either of them. My arm was trapped between the seat and the side of the car, so I couldn't get out. About ten minutes later, a car turned up. It was the guys who got me out. I thought they'd call an ambulance and the police, but they didn't. They said...' he hesitated '...they said Jake was dead, and they carried Cameron to their car and walked me to it. I told them to call for help, but they told me to shut up and do what I was told.' He closed his eyes, his face contorting with pain.

'They took us to the house, and that was the last time I saw Cameron. They made it clear that we were not to speak to each other ever again, and then they took me off to a separate room. They questioned me a bit about what had happened and what I'd seen. I was honest with them, told them there was a car, but I didn't see it or the driver. One of them punched me hard in the gut. Told me if they found out I was lying, that they'd do a lot more than that. That's when they threatened me. They told me I had to leave town and never return. They gave me directions on where I needed to go once I left, and that there would be payment waiting for me. That they weren't looking to ruin my life, that in fact they'd do everything possible to make sure I succeeded.'

'Hold on,' Anna said. 'I saw you the next morning. You came over after you'd supposedly heard the news about Jake.' It was the last time she'd seen him.

'I did. For me, I was saying goodbye, but you didn't know it. It was the hardest thing I've ever had to do, Anna, I swear. But I couldn't trust these people. I truly believe they would have hurt me. Probably killed me.'

Anna was trying to take all this in. 'Where did you go?'

'I went to some guy's house in New South Wales. He put me up for a night and told me I needed to keep silent about the accident and the guys who'd threatened me. He also said I'd be paid a substantial amount of money to move somewhere other than Melbourne and to keep my mouth shut. I didn't want it, but I was told it wasn't optional. That I would accept it. I think they thought if I accepted it then I was less likely to go to the police because I was now part of it, if you know what I mean. The guy that night was quite decent. Said that things happen sometimes that we have no control over, but I should move forward. Take what was being offered and use it for something beneficial.'

'And did you?'

He nodded. 'It paid for my flying training. I had to do something to honour Jake, and that was what I did. There's no way I could have done that otherwise. It cost a lot.'

'So you took the money and never looked back?' Anna could hear the bitterness in her voice.

A tear rolled down Kieran's cheek. 'All I did was look back,' he said. 'I was racked with guilt and remorse for leaving the way I did, but I didn't know how to fix it. I thought about going back a few times and going to the police, but then I was worried about what they might do. These weren't people you mess with, Anna. To this day, I don't know who they were protecting, but they were powerful, and they had money. I'm assuming they gave Cameron the same as me, which was five hundred thousand dollars.'

Anna's mouth dropped open. 'They paid you that to keep quiet?'

'And it kills me to this day that I took it.'

They sat in silence for a moment before Anna stood. She picked up her bag and headed for the door. She stopped and turned to face him. 'Why did you get back in touch?'

'I missed you. I've missed you and Jake every day since the accident, and I've felt guilty every day since. I wanted to make it up to you somehow.'

'By pretending to like me? To want to date me?'

'It wasn't pretending. I did want to be with you. I do want to be with you.'

'Even with all of the guilt you say you're experiencing?'

'Yes.'

'Do you think you would have told me the truth if Cameron hadn't contacted me?'

He couldn't meet her eye.

'Someone should have paid for Jake's death,' Anna said. 'If I go to the police now, are you willing to tell them what you've told me?'

His eyes remained downcast, and he didn't respond.

She turned and walked out of the apartment, letting the door click shut behind her.

* * *

Bec had been worried she'd find Owen's party overwhelming and that she'd really struggle to keep it together, but she found it quite the opposite. Hugo was laughing and genuinely enjoying playing pool with Curtis and whoever else was game to take them on. Right at this moment, that was her mother, who – much to everyone's surprise – was very good at pool.

'You all think I was only ever a mum and wife,' Samara had said after wiping the table with Hugo, 'but I had a life before all of that, too, you know. I went to pubs and played pool and did all sorts of things that might surprise you.'

'Really?' Zara said. 'I'd like to hear about that.' Bec was pleased to see Zara rejoining the group. She'd been texting Skye to see where she was and then getting worried when she wasn't getting a response. Bec had assured her that Anna and Skye would appear soon.

Samara laughed at Zara's enthusiasm to hear her stories. 'Rack the balls. If you beat me, I'll tell you one of my secrets.'

'You offering the same, Dad?' Bec had asked her father, who looked a million miles away.

'What's that, Becca?'

'Mum's offering to tell one of her secrets if Zara beats her at pool. I was asking if you were offering the same?'

He sighed. 'No, I don't think that would serve any of us too well.'

'You okay?' Bec might not have spent much time with her father over the past twenty years, but you couldn't miss the fact that he looked defeated.

He managed a smile. 'The last few days have brought up a lot from the past; that's all. Don't get me wrong, I wouldn't change having you, Hugo and Zara in my life, but it's reminded me of a lot that happened all those years ago.'

'With Chris?'

He nodded. 'Hug your kids each day, Becca. You never know when your last time will be or what regrets you'll end up with if they're suddenly gone.' He shook his head, his face turning red. 'I can't believe I said that, today of all days. I'm so sorry.'

Bec smiled. 'It's okay. Owen would have said the same. He forced hugs out of both of them every day if they weren't forthcoming. He was a big believer in showing us how much he loved us through his actions.'

'He sounds like he was a great husband and father. I wish I'd met him.'

'I wish you had too. You would have liked him. He was a Tigers supporter too, so you had that in common.'

'Good man,' her father said, as he did about any fellow Richmond Tigers supporter. AFL had a huge following in Melbourne, and it was unusual to meet anyone who didn't follow it religiously. 'Where's your friend, by the way? Anna? I thought she'd be here today.'

'She will be,' Bec said. 'She had to see someone first.'

'There she is now,' her father said as Anna stepped out of the back door into the yard.

The strain on her face immediately told Bec that things hadn't gone well.

'I'll go and check she's okay,' she said to her father. 'Can I get you another drink?'

'No,' her mother answered on his behalf. She waggled a finger at him playfully, but Bec could see the concern in her eyes. 'I've been watching you, and that's at least your third drink. Come over and beat your grandchildren at pool and take a break from the beer.'

Bruce put his beer down and reached for her hand. He winked at Bec. 'I don't think it was number three, but beating the grandchildren has a nice ring to it.'

Bec watched as they made their way to the pool table, and she turned to face Anna.

'Everything okay?'

Anna shook her head. 'I might need a drink.'

Bec led her inside and found a bottle of Sav Blanc in the fridge and poured Anna a glass.

'It's like something out of a movie,' she said after Anna told her what Kieran had confessed. 'I wonder who was being protected?'

'No idea,' Anna said. 'But they should have paid for what they did. I'm not sure what to do now. I guess I could go to the police, but I doubt Kieran or Cameron will tell them the truth. Cameron might, but Kieran, I'm not convinced he will. And I'm not sure what they could do now anyway. Neither Cameron nor Kieran know who caused the accident; they know it was a hit-and-run, rather than Jake being responsible.' An image of Clare Fleming came to mind when Anna referred to the hit-and-run.

'I don't know what to suggest either,' Bec said. 'Perhaps let it settle for a few days. See how you feel. You could ask a lawyer for some legal advice around it.'

'That's a good idea,' Anna said. 'I might do that. And I must decide what to do about my mum, too. She's still very agitated, and I do at least have a partial answer for her now as to what happened. I think she'll want more than that, though. She'll want someone to pay for what they did.'

'I'd have to agree with her on that,' Bec said. 'Someone's enjoyed twenty-two years of freedom after they caused Jake's death. There's nothing fair about that.'

'There's not,' Anna said, 'but it's also not what we're here for today. This is all becoming about me when it should be about you and Owen. Let's go out the back and celebrate this birthday. I'd better say hi to Skye.'

Bec frowned. 'Skye's not here. Zara's been texting her trying to find out where she is. She hadn't had a response ten minutes or so ago. I assumed she was coming with you.'

'She was going to make her own way here as she didn't want to come with me to Kieran's,' Anna said, pulling her phone from her bag. She called Skye's phone, which clicked straight to voicemail.

She looked to Bec. 'This doesn't feel right. She should have been here ages ago. Let's go and see if Zara's heard from her.'

* * *

Zara knew sending another message to Skye was pointless, but it didn't stop her. Her gut feeling was that something was very wrong. She and Skye were usually in constant contact and this was unusual.

She looked up as her mother and Anna approached her, the concern on their faces making her stomach flip. 'Has something happened?'

Her mother shook her head. 'No, Anna assumed she was already here. I just wanted to see if you'd had any luck tracking her down?'

'No, but something's up. She's turned off location sharing on Snapchat so I can't see where she is. She normally always has it on.'

'Why would she turn it off?' Anna asked.

'Because she doesn't want to be found,' Zara said. 'Did you have an argument or something?'

'No, nothing at all. She's been a bit off since last Tuesday when she had that meltdown. She seemed better immediately after it but then since we got back from having dinner with all of you she's been acting quite differently.'

'Did you or Hugo say anything to upset her?' Bec asked.

Anger surged through Zara. Of course her mother would think it was her fault. 'Of course not,' she said. 'Why would you even think that?'

'I'm not blaming you or Hugo,' Bec was quick to say, 'just trying to find out what might have happened.'

'We should look for her,' Anna said. 'But I don't even know where to start.' She met Zara's eyes. 'Do you know any of her friends? Is there someone you'd suggest we start with?'

Zara nodded. 'Just one girl, Mya, but I've already messaged her. She said she hasn't heard from Skye for over a week. She checked with the other girls Skye's friends with and they all said the same.'

'She was missing her mum the other night,' Bec said. 'Maybe we start there? Go to the old house. Do you know where it is?'

'And the park her mum loved,' Zara said.

'And what about the friend of her mum's that was supposed to have guardianship of her?' Bec said. 'Is there any chance she would have come back from Yemen or wherever she was?'

Anna shook her head. 'No, I would have been notified by the department.'

'Why?' Zara said. 'How would they know she's back? She might not even know that she's supposed to look after Skye.'

'Good point. I'll call and see if there's any news from the UN about Erin. Rule her out at least. It's Sunday so there's no point trying that until tomorrow when they're back at work. In the meantime, I'll go to her old house and see if anyone's seen her there and then to the cemetery. I'd better go home first, in case she's cuddled up with Smoko and has no idea what the fuss is all about.'

'We'll come with you,' Bec said.

'Absolutely not,' Anna said. 'It's Owen's party, you need to be here.'

'I'm coming,' Zara said. 'If Dad was here he'd insist the party be stopped and we all look for Skye.'

'He would,' Bec agreed. 'Let me quickly tell everyone what's happening and then we'll go.'

28

Anna crossed her fingers as she put her key in the lock of her Prahran apartment, hoping that they'd find Skye curled up with Smoko. Smoko came running the moment she opened the door, and she scooped him up and hurried into the apartment.

'Skye?' she called as she made her way to the teenager's bedroom. She pushed open the door to find the room empty. Anna turned to Bec and Zara who'd followed closely behind. 'She's not here.' She was about to close the door when she stopped and took another look around.

'What's wrong?' Bec asked.

Anna stepped into the room. 'All her stuff's gone.' She'd left everything neat and tidy, but there were no traces of Skye.

'There's a notepad on the desk,' Bec said, pointing to it. 'Check if it says anything.'

Anna picked it up to find a very brief note. '"Thanks for everything, Anna." That's all it says. No explanation. Nothing.'

'I can't believe she took off and didn't tell me,' Zara said. 'I thought we were, like, best friends.'

'She probably thought you'd tell Anna or me,' Bec said, 'and it appears she's decided to disappear.' She turned to Anna. 'Did you tell her about the foster family? Did that scare her off?'

'What foster family?' Zara asked.

'There's a family who are keen to meet her; that's all,' Anna said. 'And no, I hadn't told her about them. I had planned to this week.'

Zara frowned. 'I bet she found out. That would make perfect sense. She said to me heaps of times that she wasn't going to some randoms and she'd take off before that happened.'

'I can't see how she would have found out,' Anna said. 'I haven't had any discussions from home about it and there's no paperwork; it's all digital. She doesn't have access to my computer to be looking up that sort of thing.'

'Have you two talked about it?' Zara asked, the accusation clear in her voice.

Anna looked to Bec. 'I told your mum last week that there was a family interested.'

'When?'

'I guess it was at dinner after Echoes. But it was when the two of us were alone, not at the table.'

'Oh no,' Bec said, her hand covering her mouth. She looked to Anna. 'Remember there was someone else in the bathroom when we had that conversation.'

'Jesus,' Zara said, 'and you asked me if it was me or Hugo who said something to upset her. Let me guess, you had a full-blown discussion about her lovely new family. No wonder she went weird that night and has now disappeared.'

Anna closed her eyes, thinking back to the discussion. 'It was a lot worse than that.'

'A lot worse,' Bec agreed.

* * *

Skye hugged her knees tighter, her chin buried into the bulk of her jacket. She'd layered on almost everything she owned, two T-shirts, her hoodie, and the oversized jacket Zara had once lent her and never asked for back, but the chill still seeped through. The wind whipped across the sand of Brighton Beach in bursts, rattling the wooden stilts of the beach hut she'd crawled under for shelter. She'd tried the doors on at least twenty of the colourful beach huts but they were all firmly locked. She wished she'd thought to bring a blanket.

She pulled her hood further over her face and shut her eyes, trying not to think, but the harder she tried, the more the thoughts crowded in. Anna didn't want her. Bec didn't either. No one did, other than maybe some random strangers who she definitely didn't want. She had no one and nowhere to go.

Her chest squeezed at the thought of her mum. She missed her so badly. Why did she have to die? It was so unfair. It was just the two of them, not like Zara and Hugo who lost their dad but still had their mum and each other. At least if she'd had a sibling they'd have each other to call family.

She shrieked, scrambling backwards as something cold and wet brushed against her hand. Her heart was thumping as a small white dog appeared out of the shadows, its curly fur thick and woolly so it almost looked like a lamb. It nudged her knee with its nose, its tail wagging slowly.

'Hey,' she whispered, half laughing at her fright, half relieved it wasn't someone else finding her. She reached out, her fingers sinking into the dog's coat. It was warm in parts and wet in others. 'Where did you come from? You weren't silly enough to go swimming, were you?'

The dog gave no answer, only shuffled closer and plonked itself against her side as though it had already decided they belonged together. Skye wrapped her arms around it, grateful for its warmth. It smelt a little salty, and stinky, but she didn't care.

'Guess it's just you and me, little Lammy.' She rested her cheek on its back. The steady rise and fall of its breathing quickly turned to gentle snores.

Hot tears slipped down Skye's face, wetting the dog's fur. She pressed her eyes closed, her chest aching as her thoughts returned to her mother and all that she'd lost.

29

Anna was on the phone to her contact at the UN about finding Skye's guardian early on Monday morning. After failing to find any trace of Skye at her old house or the park they'd gone straight to the police station and reported her as a missing person.

The police had been excellent. Getting as much detail as Anna, Bec and Zara could provide. They were already checking the places Skye might turn up: train stations, shopping centres, and Skye's favourite places, which included the beach and botanical gardens. They'd also promised to reach out to Skye's school first thing Monday morning to contact her friends.

There would be efforts to pull CCTV if needed, and they'd try tracking her phone.

Anna sighed as she ended the call. As unlikely as she knew it would be, she'd held some hope that Erin might have returned to Australia and Skye was with her. But no, the UN couldn't release any details other than to say the situation of Erin Clarke remained unchanged.

Tears welled as Smoko rubbed around Anna's heels. She was

devastated to think Skye might have overheard her and Bec. To have lost her mum and then overhear that neither her nor Bec were willing to give her a home was awful.

Her phone rang as she did her best to push away this thought and concentrate on where Skye might be. It was Marty.

'This is a friendly call, not about your mum,' he said immediately, knowing she'd be worried to see his number.

Anna did her best to inject some enthusiasm into her response. 'Not about Mum?'

'Nope. Well, it probably will end up being a discussion around her, but no, I wanted to reach out and just say hi. How have you been?'

Anna wiped her cheeks, and forced a laugh. 'Not great actually.' She went on to tell him about Skye.

'What can I do? I can be there in twenty minutes if you want to go searching for her.'

A lump rose in Anna's throat. He'd do anything for her and she hadn't even noticed he existed as anything beyond a carer for her mum until now.

'Thank you, but the police are onto it and I'm not sure there's a lot we can do. I don't know her friends from school so I really don't have any place to start. What you can do is distract me for a few minutes. I know you said this wasn't about Mum, but I do have some updates for you.'

Marty let out a low whistle when Anna had finished telling him about Kieran and what she'd found out.

'Wow, so the boyfriend was a lowlife after all. I thought he probably was.'

Anna couldn't help but smile at the delight Marty was failing to mask in his voice. The one thing Kieran had been right about, it seemed, was that Marty was interested in her.

'I should come in and tell Mum, but I need to find Skye first

As much as I want to get Jake's named cleared, it's not urgent, whereas finding Skye is.'

'I meant it when I said I'd come and help you find her. See how the day unfolds and call me if you plan to go out looking. I'll be your driver.'

Anna gripped the phone a little tighter, grateful for the unexpected phone call and support.

* * *

As she emptied the dishwasher after dinner on Monday, Samara reflected on the past few weeks and how she once again felt like she had purpose back in her life. It was a stark contrast from the existing she'd been doing for years. To have Rebecca back as part of the family and two beautiful grandchildren was more than she could ever have expected. She wished she'd found her years ago.

She knew Bruce was feeling the same way, although she'd seen over the past few days that he was also struggling with his demons from the past. She thought back to the months that followed Chris's death and how she hadn't been able to get close to him. His grief had been as raw as hers, but instead of bringing them together, it had driven a wedge between them. Bruce had been angry with Chris. Furious even that his son hadn't come to him for help. That he hadn't seen how much he was struggling, even though both Samara and Bec had seen and had pointed it out to him.

Bruce came into the kitchen rubbing the back of his neck as she put away the cutlery.

'Any news of Skye?'

'No, I spoke with Rebecca earlier and they're all still very worried about her.'

'Poor kid,' Bruce said, continuing to rub his neck. 'I hope they find her soon. Have we got paracetamol?'

'Top cupboard,' she said, nodding towards it. 'You okay?'

'Headache. Should have listened to you yesterday and stopped on the beers. Had a few too many.' He gave her a tired smile. 'Becca was very touched by the cake you made. It's a shame that Skye disappearing meant we never got to eat it.'

Samara smiled, remembering the look on her daughter's face when she'd arrived with the fiftieth birthday cake she'd made for Owen.

'It's perfect,' Bec had mouthed, taking in the rich layers of chocolate, the colourful swirls of icing, and the playful sprinkles Samara had added after hearing he had a sweet tooth and a good sense of humour. She hadn't known him, but she'd wanted the cake to feel like a celebration, not a sad moment that he wasn't able to be here to celebrate.

'I'm sure Rebecca and the kids will enjoy it.' She watched her husband open the cupboard, pop two tablets from the foil, and wash them down with a glass of water. He paused for a second, gripping the bench to steady himself.

'You don't look well at all,' she said, noting the grey tinge of his skin. 'Why don't you go and lie down. I'll bring you a cup of tea.'

He nodded, smiled at her gratefully and shuffled out of the room.

She slid the cutlery holder back into the dishwasher and shut the door as a loud crash echoed from the hallway.

'Bruce?' she called, already moving.

There was no answer.

* * *

Bec was getting ready for bed when her phone rang. She, like Zara and Hugo, had been sick with worry about Skye. The twins had taken the day off school, and she from work, and the three of them had spent the day driving to different locations Skye had mentioned to Zara as being favourite places. But they'd had no luck. 'I'm sorry I gave her that money,' Zara had said. 'I never thought she'd disappear without telling me where she was going. I honestly thought I'd just be keeping her secrets for her. That you'd be mad with me but I'd know she was safe.'

'It's not your fault,' Bec had said. 'Anna and I are the ones to blame if she overheard our conversation.' She'd shaken her head. 'I can't believe we did that. And at least she has some money so hopefully she's using it to stay somewhere and not just sleeping on the streets.'

Now, Bec grabbed the phone hoping there would be news of Skye, but saw her mother's name on the screen.

'Hi, Mum, still no news.'

'That's not why I'm ringing, although that's not good to hear.'

Bec frowned, her mother wasn't at home. There were all sorts of strange, clinical noises in the background. 'Everything okay?'

'No. I'm at the hospital.'

Bec's heart began to pound.

'It's your father. He's okay. He's had a mild heart attack and is undergoing surgery. The doctors have assured me it's standard procedure and he'll be fine. I thought you should know.'

Bec's heart pounded faster, remembering how Zara had said just a few days ago that she'd had a feeling she needed to meet her grandfather sooner rather than later. She couldn't lose her father now that she'd got him back into her life. But if she did, she needed to be there to say goodbye. 'What hospital are you at?'

'St Vincent's, but don't come down; there's nothing you can do.'

'I can be there for you. No arguments. I'll let the kids know, and I'll see you soon.'

She ended the call and quickly exchanged her pyjamas for the clothes she'd only just taken off. Her mind whirled. What if she lost him too?

She hurried to Hugo's room first and then to Zara's. She repeated what her mother had told her, trying to keep the panic from her voice. The twins insisted on accompanying her to the hospital.

Less than thirty minutes later, the three of them hurried down the corridor of St Vincent's. They found Bec's mother sitting in a waiting area, looking very pale. She jumped up the moment she saw Bec and put her arms around her first, and then the twins. 'They said he'll be fine,' she assured them. 'They're putting in some stents now, and then he should be on the road to recovery.'

'He didn't look well yesterday,' Bec said. 'I thought there was something wrong. I should have said something.'

'I thought the same,' Samara said, 'but then I thought it was too many beers on top of feeling maudlin about the past. I'm afraid it might be some time before they'll let us see him.'

It was close to three hours by the time Bruce was brought back to the room. Samara sat down in the chair next to him and grabbed his hand, while Bec, Hugo and Zara stood on the other side of the bed.

'Is he going to be okay?' Zara asked when one of the nurses came in to take his vital signs.

'He should be,' she replied. 'Best to ask the doctors, but from my understanding, everything went to plan, and it was quite straightforward.'

They pulled up chairs next to the bed, and after half an hour, Samara suggested that Bec take the twins home. 'It's late and it's school tomorrow,' she said. 'He's going to be okay. I do appreciate the visit. I'll call you in the morning with an update,' she promised.

Bec stood and hugged her tight before leaning over and kissing her dad on the forehead. 'That was quite a scare, Dad,' she said. 'No more of those, thank you. I can't have not seen you for twenty years and then lose you.'

'I think you're going to lose me.' The words came out as a soft murmur but were incredibly clear.

Bec looked to her mother, whose alarmed eyes reflected her own. 'Should we call the doctor?'

'No,' Bruce said. 'Not lose me to death. Just lose me. I need to tell you something. About Chris.'

Samara patted his hand. 'Not now, hon. You need all your strength to recover, then you can tell us anything you need to.'

Bruce's eyes fluttered shut, and his breathing deepened.

'He's been struggling the past couple of weeks,' Samara said. 'Something happened back then with Chris that he blames himself for. He's managed to leave it locked up for years but having you all back in our lives has brought it up again.'

'Do you think it caused the heart attack?'

'What, you coming back into our lives?'

Bec nodded. How awful would that be?

'No, the heart attack was building for years. His heart was broken when Chris died, and then you left. If anything, I would have expected this a long time ago.' She leaned forward and hugged her daughter. 'You go and get some rest. I'll call you in the morning, and once Dad's up to it, he can tell us whatever it was he wanted to say tonight. And let me know if there's any news of Skye.'

30

Tears of relief ran down Anna's cheeks as she hurried through the front entrance of Prahran police station. She was grateful she'd been at home when Detective McDonald called ten minutes earlier to say Skye had been found. She was also grateful she lived so close.

She spoke to the officer manning the reception area and was quickly shown down a long corridor to a private room where Skye was waiting with Detective McDonald.

Anna's heart contracted at the sight of Skye. She was filthy, her face pale and her eyes red-rimmed. Anna could only imagine what she'd been through the past three days. She walked straight to her and drew her into a hug. Skye didn't hug her back, just stood stiffly in her arms.

'I'll give you both a moment,' the detective said, leaving them alone.

Anna pulled back. 'I'm so sorry. Bec and I should never have had that discussion.'

Skye shrugged, the hurt in her eyes at odds with the casual

gesture. 'Why not? It's how you both feel. You weren't being dishonest; you just didn't know I'd heard.'

Nausea churned in the pit of Anna's stomach. 'And I'd give anything to be able to take back the fact you heard us. We only want the best for you, and finding a nice family is part of that plan. There are lovely people out there. Families like the Sampsons who you might come to love as much as you do Zara, Hugo and Bec. Don't forget, you've only just met all of us and none of us were thinking about fostering. The families who are registered to foster have given it a lot of thought and know it's something they're keen to do.'

Skye rolled her eyes. 'Like the families that abused Mum when she was a kid and the one that wanted me as their live-in babysitter. I think you've got a very unrealistic picture of what the system's really like.'

Anna indicated to the table and chairs off to one side in the small room. 'Sit for a minute. I want you to hear a few things.'

Skye reluctantly sat down and folded her arms across her chest. The protective gesture and hurt in her eyes tore at Anna's heart.

'I've worked with the system for close to twenty years, and yes, I know there are some bad stories, but overall there are amazing people doing everything in their power to help kids like you. They want to give them a good home and a loving family. They're not out for anything more than sharing their love and their lives. That's the sort of family I want to find for you, Skye. One that you'll be part of forever, not just the next couple of years until you turn eighteen and can do whatever you like.'

A tear rolled down Skye's cheek. 'But what if they're not good to me? Or I don't feel like I belong? At least with you and Smoko I feel safe. You don't expect me to be anyone but me.'

Anna reached across the table, her voice soft but steady. 'I know you feel safe with us, and I'm glad you do. But don't you want more than just "safe"? A chance to have siblings, maybe even a father figure, and all the things you've missed out on? Feeling secure is important, but settling for something that's just okay might not be what you deserve. And Skye, I'm on your side. If we place you somewhere and it doesn't feel right or if the family isn't kind or you don't fit in, I'll make sure you're moved. You won't be left somewhere that isn't good for you. I care about you, a lot, actually.'

'You promise?' Skye said. 'That if I call you and say I need to leave you'll make that happen?'

'Definitely,' Anna said. 'And you'd come back with me and Smoko while we find a family that you want to be part of. To start with, when we find a maybe family, we'd just have you spend a few hours with them, perhaps two or three times a week. While I said I generally only do temporary fostering, there is no rush for this. I want you to be happy where you end up and if that takes longer than normal that's absolutely fine.'

Skye nodded.

'But,' Anna said, 'I need you to make a promise to me before we leave here.'

'What promise?'

'I need you to promise to give this a go. To not disappear the minute something feels hard and you don't like it. That if things don't feel right you'll talk to me. That we work together to get the best possible solution and life for you. That we make your mum proud knowing you're not only being looked after and loved, but that you're happy.'

Skye closed her eyes briefly, and took a deep breath. She reopened them and nodded. 'Okay, I promise and I'm grateful, Anna, for everything you've done and are doing for me. I'm not your problem, but I do appreciate your help.'

A lump rose in Anna's throat. 'You're not a problem, Skye. You're a beautiful, generous and loving girl who's been served up a raw deal and I'd like to help you if you'll let me.'

Skye nodded again. 'I would.'

Anna stood and came around to Skye's side of the table. 'Proper hug this time.'

Skye smiled, stood, and this time circled her arms around Anna. Anna pulled her tight and squeezed her.

After a few minutes they pulled apart, their cheeks wet with tears.

'Let's get out of here,' Anna said. 'We need to ring the Sampsons and let them know you're okay. Zara's out of her mind with worry, as are Bec and Hugo.' She turned towards the door, stopping when Skye reached for her arm, and turned back to face her.

'Wait a minute. There's a slight complication.'

'Oh?'

Skye nodded. 'You're doing so much for me already, I know that, but there's something I need you to help me with and I'm not sure I can leave unless you agree.'

* * *

Anna shook her head as she and Skye drove away from the Prahran Police Station. There'd been a number of forms to fill in and a kind but firm talking-to for Skye by Detective McDonald about asking for help rather than taking off another time. She'd explained how much time and worry went into finding someone who disappeared, and how every missing-person report meant police were pulled away from other emergencies. Anna wasn't sure it was the most compassionate approach for someone who'd run through desperation, but from Skye's pained expression, she could see it had hit home.

When the detective was finished, she'd put an arm around Skye's shoulders, her voice soft. 'They just want you to be safe, you know. So do I. And like Detective McDonald said, if you can't talk to me or Zara or another friend, Kids Helpline might be something to consider.'

Now as she pulled to a stop at a red light, she glanced in the rear-vision mirror at Skye, still shaking her head. 'I can't believe I agreed to this.'

Skye grinned. 'Me either, but thank you. Do you think Smoko will be okay?'

'I'm not sure,' Anna said, 'but we'll work something out.' She pressed the button for her window and opened it a crack to let in some air. 'The one thing I will say is before we do anything else, both you and Miss Lammy need a bath.'

Skye curled her arm around the little dog, pulling it to her, and Anna couldn't help but smile. From what Skye had told her, the dog had befriended her the first night and hadn't left her side.

'She even chased this drugged-out guy who was asking me for money,' Skye said. 'Bared her teeth and all. If she wasn't so cute she'd probably be scary. The guy moved on though.'

Thank God, Anna thought hearing that. While Skye had had a couple of uncomfortable days roughing it, at least nothing bad had happened to her.

'She is cute,' Anna agreed, 'but will be considerably cuter once she's clean. Now, I'd better ring Bec so they know you're safe.'

She called Bec's number from the car and her friend picked up immediately.

'Anna, any news?'

'She's with me,' Anna said. 'Safe and well, other than a bit dirty.'

'Oh, thank God,' Bec said. 'Zara, Hugo,' she shouted. 'Skye's been found.'

Anna glanced in the rear-vision mirror, seeing a small smile on Skye's lips at the relief they heard in Bec's voice.

They could hear commotion at Bec's end as Zara and Hugo joined Bec wherever she was. 'Where was she?' they heard Zara say.

'Hold on,' Bec said. 'Let me talk to Anna and then I'll fill you in.'

'Sorry,' she said. 'I had to let them know. They stayed home from school again today, and me from work, so we could drive around the streets again. We've been out of our minds with worry. Where was she found?'

'Hey,' Anna said. 'How about a I call you a little later with the details. Skye's with me now and we're just heading home so she can have a shower and get cleaned up.'

'Why don't you do that and then come to us for lunch?' Bec said. 'We all need to see her. To hug her and tell her we're sorry.'

Anna glanced at Skye again in the mirror, tears filling her own eyes as she watched the teenager wipe away a tear. She was glad she'd left Bec on speaker and Skye had heard the relief and love in her voice. 'What do you think?' she asked Skye. 'Are you up for it or would you prefer some time to yourself?'

'I'm up for it,' Skye said. 'As long as Lammy can come too.'

'We'll be about an hour,' Anna said to Bec. She glanced again in the mirror at the dirty pair in the back seat. 'Actually, maybe a little longer, we've got a fairly extensive cleaning job to tackle first.'

* * *

Anna couldn't help but laugh as she poked her head into the bathroom to find Lammy sitting patiently in the bath tub enjoying the sensation of being shampooed by Skye.

'She'll be the best-smelling dog in town,' Anna said. 'That is my good shampoo, you know.'

Skye, freshly showered and in some of Anna's clothes while hers went in the wash, grinned. 'I know. She's been living pretty rough so I thought she deserved a treat. Look how much dirt's on her. She'll be sparkling when I'm finished. How's Smoko?'

'Still under my bed,' Anna said. 'We'll try and introduce them again later.'

'Look how good she is,' Skye said. 'I thought dogs went crazy and ran around the house all wet spraying water everywhere when you tried to wash them.'

'Some do,' Anna said, thinking of Pickles, the scruffy dog she'd had growing up, and the showers of water he'd managed to spray them with. She frowned.

'What?' Skye asked.

'I'm wondering if someone's missing her. We should take her to the vet and get them to check for her microchip.'

'And give her back?'

Anna smiled gently. 'If she has a family and a home then yes. But otherwise, we can give some thought to the best arrangement for her.' She laughed. 'And yes, I already know what that is and that you're now a package deal.'

'Let's do the vet thing on the way to Bec's,' Skye said. 'Just so I know.'

Anna nodded. 'I'll go and google if there's one on the way.'

* * *

'She's here!' Zara's voice was filled with excitement and relief as a car pulled into the driveway.

The front door flew open and Bec could hear the twins rushing out to meet Skye. She'd told them both to give Skye some space, that they didn't know how she'd be feeling and might not be ready to just slip back into their friendships. She should have known better of course when it came to Zara.

She hurried to the front door in time to see Skye step out of the car and Zara practically knock her over with the intensity of her hug. She smiled as Skye laughed and said something to Zara before pointing into the car. Hugo didn't stand back, he pulled Skye to him and hugged her so tight it brought tears to Bec's eyes to see how much he cared.

She met Anna's eyes as her friend pushed open her door, and wasn't surprised to see her own tears reflected in them. Happy tears at least.

Zara squealed and laughed as the three teenagers peered into the back seat. 'She's gorgeous!'

Bec moved closer to the car, wondering what they were looking at. She smiled as a little white dog with a very new-looking bright purple collar and lead jumped down from the back seat and stood next to Skye.

'My turn,' she said, putting her arms out as she reached the group of teens. Skye moved into them and she hugged her tightly. 'I'm so sorry you heard what we said. We all love you dearly; I do want you to know that.'

Skye nodded and Bec hoped she believed her. She stepped back and looked at the dog. 'And who is this?'

'Lammy,' Skye said. 'She found me at the beach the first night I left and protected me.'

'We just went to the vet to check her microchip,' Anna added. 'Her owner died a few months ago. His family had contacted the central microchip registry to let them know she'd gone missing and said if anyone found her, they'd either like her rehomed or, if that wasn't possible, put down.'

'Can you believe that?' Skye said. 'That they'd have her put down. At least you're only trying to rehome me, not put me down too.'

Bec was relieved to see a smile playing on her lips. 'Are you going to look after her?'

Skye nodded. 'Yes. She's officially registered to me now.' She turned to Anna. 'Thank you, again, for doing that. It means a lot. She needs a family just like I do, and at least we've now got each other.'

'Let's take her to the back garden,' Hugo said. 'We can let her off the leash and throw a ball to her.' He frowned. 'Unless she needs to rest and be fed?'

'I think she'll be okay,' Skye said. 'I fed her lots the last few days, which I need to thank you for, Zars. That money fed both of us. I will pay you back.'

'Don't be silly, it was your emergency fund. If I ever need one, I'll ask you for help.' She raised her eyebrows. 'And living with Mum and Hugo means I'll definitely need to escape at some stage, so start saving. I prefer five-star accommodation to roughing it on the streets by the way. Now, let's take Lammy out the back so she can explore and you can tell us all the stuff that happened that Anna and Mum aren't allowed to hear.'

Bec and Anna watched as the three of them took Lammy through the gate at the side of the house that led to the back garden. Once they were gone, Bec turned to Anna and hugged her.

'How are you? This hasn't been an easy few days.'

Anna returned her hug with a squeeze. 'For any of us. But thankfully she's back. I was able to have a good talk to her too. I think I finally got through to her that there are decent people in the world and that finding her a foster family could take time but she'll have plenty of say in who she ends up with.' She sighed. 'Mind you, now we're rehoming a package deal so have to find someone who'll take on the dog too.'

'It looks like they were meant to find each other,' Bec said. 'At least she wasn't completely alone. Now, come inside and we'll put the kettle on and start thinking about some lunch.'

31

'I'll just need to give Mum a quick call,' Bec said, as Anna settled herself on a stool at the island bench and she switched on the kettle.

Laughter was coming from the back garden and Bec glanced out of the window to see Lammy go tearing past after one of Hugo's tennis balls. She quickly filled Anna in on what had happened with her father the previous day.

'That's awful,' Anna said. 'You should have let me know.'

'You had enough on your plate,' Bec said, 'and it all happened last night. There's nothing you could do.'

She spoke to her mother quickly, telling her Skye had been found and then asking for an update on her father.

She ended the call and popped teabags into two cups. 'Dad's doing well,' she said. 'It's quite amazing what they can do these days. Mum said he's likely to be allowed to go home tomorrow afternoon. Then it's just getting used to medications and taking it easy for a few weeks.'

'That's a relief.' Anna shuddered. 'You've only just reconnected. Imagine losing him that quickly.'

'I know,' Bec said pouring boiling water into the cups. 'Although he made this weird comment last night that we were going to lose him.'

'He thought he was going to die?'

'No, he was quite specific that he wasn't dying, but we were going to lose him. I have no idea what he meant. Hopefully it was just the drugs talking.'

* * *

Bec was glad when the working week ended. Having missed Monday and Tuesday due to the situation with Skye and then her father, it had felt like a long week playing catch-up on work. Her father had been discharged on Wednesday and was now resting comfortably at home. She, Hugo and Zara had been to visit the previous afternoon, giving the twins an opportunity to also see her childhood home.

'It's weird,' Zara had said, 'that a few weeks ago I didn't even know him and now I really care about him. I guess that's what it means to be family.'

Now, late on Friday afternoon, Bec drove up the driveway of her parents' Canterbury house on her own. Her father had asked her to visit without the kids. There was something he wanted to talk to both her and her mother about.

She hugged her mother who met her at the front door and followed her through to the cosy lounge room. Her father was sitting in an armchair, his eyes closed, a book on his lap.

Bec looked to her mother and lowered her voice. 'He's asleep. Should I come back later?'

Her father opened his eyes and smiled. 'Not asleep, just resting. Come in and sit down.'

Bec leaned down and hugged her father before sitting in one of the two armchairs across from him. 'How are you feeling?'

'I've felt better,' he admitted, then sighed. 'But it's not to do with the heart attack. I need to speak to you and your mum, and what I need to tell you isn't easy.'

Bec glanced at her mother, who gave her a look that clearly said *I have no idea.*

'Should I make some tea?' her mother asked.

'You and Becca might be better with something stronger, but tea would be nice for me, thank you.'

Unease uncurled in Bec as she watched her father. Something wasn't right and it wasn't related to the heart attack. He'd been like this at Owen's party and she wasn't sure that she wanted to know why.

Her mother returned a few minutes later with cups of tea for all of them and sat down next to Bec.

'You don't need to do this now,' Bec said. 'It's been a big week. Why don't you just recover and then fill us in.'

He cleared his throat. 'No, this is long overdue and I need you both to know that I've never forgiven myself for what I'm about to tell you.' He hesitated, looking from Bec to her mother, before taking a deep breath. 'I did something awful when Chris was alive. My intentions were good, while very misguided. I've spent years convincing myself that I only ever had Chris's best interests at heart and that he would have been ruined if I hadn't stepped in and helped him. But the reality is, I was protecting myself too.'

Bec glanced at her mother. Samara looked as unsure as she felt.

A tear squeezed out of the corner of her father's eye. He reached out, taking each of their hands in his. And then he told them.

32

Bec operated in a daze following her father's revelation on Friday afternoon. She wasn't sure what to do or what to say. Her mother had stood up when her father had finished talking and walked out of the room. She hadn't said anything and hadn't looked back. Bec had sat staring at her father and eventually stood and followed her mother's footsteps.

There was nothing to say to him. She'd had her father back in her life for a short time, and now he was gone again. She would never speak to him again.

Her mother had been waiting outside the front door for Bec and had put her arms around her as soon as she'd reached her. They'd walked to Bec's car in silence. Eventually, her mother turned to face her.

'I don't know what to say or what to do.'

'I think we need some time to process what he's told us.' Bec shook her head. 'I can't believe it.'

'I can,' her mother said. 'I never thought...' Her words petered off as they both considered the enormity of his confession.

'I need to go,' Bec said. 'Work out what I'm going to do. I imagine you're going to do the same.'

Her mother nodded. 'I'm not sure I can ever look at him again, let alone be under the same roof.' She sighed. 'Just as things were looking good. We had you and the kids back with us...' A tear escaped the corner of her eye. 'I was feeling happy for the first time in two decades, and now this. I don't want to lose you again, Rebecca.'

Bec stepped forward and hugged her mother. 'You won't. The kids and I are here, and that will never change, and there's a spare room if you need it.'

Now, four days had passed since her father's confession, and she'd only spoken to her mother briefly since. They both needed time to come to terms with what he'd told them, and they needed to do that separately.

As she sat at the kitchen island deep in thought her phone pinged with another text from Anna. She hadn't responded to any messages since Saturday and had only sent one quick one to Damien the previous day to let him know she needed to take a few days off work.

> Hey Bec, hope your dad's doing better. Not expecting to see you tonight, but if you do make it, let's go out for dinner or a drink after. I'm sure you could use a friend right now. A x

Bec didn't respond.

'Can we go to Echoes tonight?' Zara asked, appearing in the kitchen and breaking into Bec's thoughts. Bec hadn't told Zara or Hugo what had happened. They were excited to have their grandparents in their lives, and she was dreading telling them that they were about to lose their grandfather again. There was no way she would allow any of them to have a relationship with him moving forward.

'You can,' Bec said. 'I'm a bit tired. Hugo might want to go with you, or Skye will probably be there.'

'You need to come,' Zara said.

Bec raised an eyebrow. 'Need? Why's that.'

'Remember that crazy lady who you said shouted at you the first time you went?'

'Well, I'm not sure she was crazy, but yes, I know who you mean.'

'I bumped into her outside Anna's work yesterday when I was waiting for Skye. She's planning to apologise to you. She wanted to check if you would be there. I promised her you would be.'

An uneasy feeling unwound itself in the pit of Bec's stomach. 'You shouldn't promise people on my behalf. I really don't want to go tonight.'

'Pretty please,' Zara said. 'It's a big deal for her to apologise. I think she's very stressed about it, and her anxiety will get even worse if she has to wait another week. She's been through such a hard time, Mum.'

Bec wanted to say no, in fact she felt like screaming that she was going through a hard time too and needed to be left alone, but she couldn't do that, and she also knew Zara well enough to know that she'd push for an explanation, and the truth wasn't something Bec was ready to share.

In the end, she agreed to go, but made it clear to Zara that she was leaving as soon as it was over. 'If Skye or Anna asks us out after, I'm not up for it tonight, okay? You can go with them, but I'm coming straight home.'

Zara had looked at her strangely but reluctantly agreed.

* * *

A week had passed since Skye's return and Anna was relieved to see that she'd settled back into school and routine and had even asked a few questions about foster families that indicated she was perhaps more open to the idea. The family Anna had thought might be a good fit for Skye had taken on another teenager, making them no longer available for Skye, and Anna and Skye's caseworker had to go back to the drawing board trying to find a good fit.

'She's lucky to have you,' Ivy West had said. 'Not many temporary carers will extend their fostering period like you have.'

Anna was committed to finding Skye the right family and home, and she was truthful when she'd said there was no hurry. Her concern currently had shifted from Skye to Bec. She knew her friend was going through a hard time with her dad recovering but it was unlike her not to respond to messages. She'd asked Skye to check with Zara that she was okay, to which Zara had replied that she was acting weirder than usual. Anna suspected that Bec was feeling overwhelmed with everything she was dealing with right now, which was understandable. She'd leave her for a few days and reach out again later in the week.

For that reason, she was surprised when Bec slid into a chair towards the back of the room, as she got started with Echoes that night. She'd seen Bec's mum earlier and now saw Zara and Hugo sitting with Skye.

The session got underway, and Anna did a quick recap on the guest speaker from the previous week, reminding the group of the links she'd shared to some interesting resources that they might get value from.

'Now, if anyone has anything they'd like to share tonight, the floor is open.'

'I would.'

Anna was surprised to see a very pale Bruce Langford

standing at the back of the room. She looked to Bec, who was shaking her head and appeared to be muttering under her breath. To Bec's right, Samara's face was set in stone.

'Why don't you come and sit down, Bruce?' Anna said. 'You've had a big week on the health front, and I'm not sure you should be here, let alone standing.' She pulled a chair across to the front of the room, and he made his way to it and sat down. He closed his eyes briefly, the pain in his face difficult to look at.

'Are you sure you're up to this?'

He opened his eyes and looked directly at her. 'This is something I should have done two decades ago. It's way overdue, and there's nothing I can do other than explain and then leave the consequences to come my way.'

Anna frowned. She had no idea of what he was talking about and wondered if he was confused after his operation. She assumed Bec or Samara would be up here with him if they felt he shouldn't be speaking.

'Okay, well, the floor's yours.'

'Thank you.' He lifted his head and looked around the room, his gaze stopping on Bec and Samara briefly before moving away.

'For those of you who don't know me, my name is Bruce Langford. I'm a former politician, having started in local council back in the early 2000s and eventually holding a federal seat. Some of you may recall I was the Minister for Health for a period. Following my retirement, I started a business called Mindvest. I work with investors to seek out organisations that specialise in mental health and look at ways to invest and assist their growth.' He shook his head. 'I'm not sure why I'm telling you any of that as it isn't directly relevant to my reason for being here tonight.'

Anna found her gaze constantly going to Bec. Her friend was so pale that Anna was worried she might be sick. She expected

Bruce was going to talk about his son, and that would of course have Bec on edge. She was dealing with enough grief with Owen's death; she didn't need the emotional trauma of her brother's passing to be reignited.

He cleared his throat.

'I was blessed forty years ago to have twins, Christopher and Rebecca. Becca and her children are here tonight, along with my wife, Samara. We were a tight family when the kids were little. Very close. Had each other's backs and I knew how lucky I was.'

He paused, looking over at Bec and Samara, both of whom were looking at the floor.

'The family helped me run for local council, mayor and then state and eventually federal government. We were in the public eye and we all were careful to be respectful of that and do our best within the community.'

He took another deep breath, and Anna wasn't sure if it was his heart or what he was sharing that was causing the issue.

'That all changed in 2003 when my son, Chris, had an accident. He'd been drinking, and he hit another vehicle with his car. He was okay, not injured, but—' he turned and looked at Anna '—he ran another vehicle off the road.'

Anna drew in a breath. No. It couldn't be and if it was, surely he wouldn't do this here?

Bruce's voice was shaky. 'The accident happened not far from our house, and Chris came straight home. He was drunk and crying and told me what happened. I honestly can't imagine what possessed me, but in that moment, I saw his life flash before my eyes. My son in prison, everything he'd worked for gone in an instant. I also saw my own career dissolve before my eyes. The headlines flashed in front of me. *Politician's drunken son causes fatal accident.*' He dropped his head, unable to continue looking at Anna.

'Yes, the other driver was killed, not that Chris was aware of that initially.'

A murmur circled the room, and Anna noticed for the first time two police officers standing in the doorway of the centre. Had Bruce told them he was going to confess?

Bruce continued. 'It gets worse. I went crazy in that moment. I knew a couple of guys who I could get to do anything for me. They owed me, and they paid up. They went to the scene of the accident to discover two other teenagers in the car with the boy who died.'

Anna looked at Bec, who met her eyes briefly.

She mouthed, 'I'm sorry,' before looking away.

Fury rose in Anna. Bec had known what her father was going to say. She'd let him do this publicly and she hadn't spoken to her first. A chill ran through her as Bruce met her eyes, seeming to read her mind.

'My family were not aware I was going to speak tonight. The reason I'm doing this here is I doubt my wife or daughter would have agreed to sit in the same room as me.'

But they knew. Bec knew sometime before tonight and hadn't told her.

Bruce continued. 'They took the boys from the scene and ensured they never told anyone what had happened. They were paid off to leave town. The alcohol my son had been drinking was planted in the car, and I believe may have been forced into the driver's mouth.'

An angry whisper was starting around the room. Anna's stomach churned, and she thought it was highly possible she would be sick, but she pushed the nausea down and held up her hands. She was surprised to hear herself speaking. 'Let him finish.'

Bruce closed his eyes. 'The authorities didn't question the

accident. It looked like the driver had drunk before he drove, lost control and hit a tree, killing himself. That was how the accident was recorded. I was guilty, but I was relieved. This wasn't going to hurt my family in the way I had thought it would. Ultimately, it hurt a lot more. My actions that night were the catalyst for what would end up destroying my family.'

'You should have been destroyed,' Clare Fleming called out. 'And you should have gone to jail.'

'You're right on both accounts,' Bruce said meeting her eyes to address her before continuing with his story.

Anna thought there was a good chance she might vomit. He'd not only covered up for his son, but he'd had Jake set up to look guilty in the process.

'Chris changed overnight,' Bruce said. 'He wanted to go to the authorities and turn himself in, but I wouldn't let him. I convinced him that ruining his life wouldn't bring back the boy who'd died, and it would kill both his future and my career. He got angry. Ultimately, he did what I said, but to cope, he turned to drugs. Instead of going to university, he sat in his room getting high, and he moved into a level of depression that, within two years of the accident, led to him taking his life. My son killed himself. And I've never forgiven myself.'

Silence filled the room, only for a few moments before someone spoke. 'You've never forgiven yourself, yet it's twenty-two years later. Is this your confession, or did you go to jail like you should have years ago?'

'This is my well-overdue confession,' Bruce said. He had to raise his voice to be heard over the angry murmurs that were circulating in the room. 'It's taken a heart attack and several other factors to make me see that I can't live another day with this on my conscience. A lot of people suffered because of the decision I made that night, and it's not something I can live with any more.'

He turned to Anna, raising his eyes to meet hers. 'I'm sorry. I know that's completely inadequate, but I also want you to know it's true. Back then, I was doing everything I could to protect my family and my career. Unfortunately, that cost was borne by your family.'

The room fell silent and all eyes turned to Anna as Bruce's words sank in.

'Now, for the first time in years,' Bruce said 'I have a chance to have my daughter in my life and to get to know my grandchildren, and I know I don't deserve that. Why should I get that when your parents missed out? I've lived a life of privilege, which I abused. I am truly sorry, Anna. Bec and Samara only learned the truth a few days ago about what happened that night. I can assure you, our lives colliding now is pure coincidence.'

Anna stared at him, stunned. Words wouldn't form. Her mind was a storm of disbelief and fury. Anger shot through her so fast it made her hands tremble. She wanted to tear him apart. What he'd done to Jake, to Kieran and Cameron and of course to his own son and family. It was unthinkable. And the fact that he got away with it? That was the worst part. She imagined he'd paid off a lot of people to make this happen.

The sharp echo of footsteps broke the silence in the room as the two police officers moved towards Bruce. He stood and sought out Zara and Hugo. 'I'm sorry to not be the man I want to be for the two of you. From everything I've learned about your father, I'm glad that you had a role model who you can be proud of and emulate, as I'm obviously not that man.' He held out his hands as the police officers reached him.

'That won't be necessary, Mr Langford,' one of them said, taking him by the arm. 'As you called us here, we don't see you rushing off. We'd like you to come down to the station with us so we can learn more about what you've shared here tonight.'

Bruce turned to look Anna in the eye one last time. 'What you've set up here and at Hopefield is a credit to you and the love you had for your brother. I'm so sorry I changed the course of that night. I know that it wouldn't have changed the outcome for Jake, but you should have had the truth from day one, and he shouldn't have had his reputation tarnished. I truly am sorry.'

Anna didn't respond.

The room fell silent as Bruce Langford was walked out by the police.

* * *

Bec stood and made her way over to Anna on autopilot. She wasn't sure what to say or do, but she knew she needed to see her friend.

Anna turned to her, her face white with shock.

'I'm so sorry,' Bec said. 'I don't know what else to say. I had no idea until a couple of days ago, and then I couldn't speak to you. I was trying to work out what to say. I had no idea he'd be here tonight. Mum and I are both still in shock. I don't know what to say or how I can prove that my friendship with you has been genuine. I...'

Anna put her hand up to stop her. 'Bec, stop. I know all of that. I need to get my head around what your dad said, but I know our friendship's the real thing. Don't forget, you blamed your father all those years ago without knowing what he'd done. You left. You did everything right. I don't blame you at all. But I am going to need some time to process this.' She looked for Skye, who was standing next to Zara, the shock on her face a reflection of Anna's.

'Skye and I are going to leave. Would you mind putting the chairs back and locking up for me after the session?'

Bec nodded and watched as Anna put an arm around Skye and the two of them made a beeline for the exit.

She turned to Zara and Hugo and walked forward, drawing them into a hug.

'I'm so sorry,' Zara said, 'so sorry.'

Bec pulled back and looked at her daughter. 'It's not your fault.'

'I shouldn't have tried to find them. It is my fault.'

'Oh, Zars,' Bec said, 'you finding them means Anna finally has closure on what happened to her brother, and my father is going to get what he deserved twenty-two years ago. You did nothing wrong.' She pulled her daughter to her and held her tight.

33

Ten days passed before Anna was ready to talk to Bec. She'd sent her a few messages, assuring her they were still friends; she just needed some time. She knew from the responses that Bec was dealing with her own demons of learning what her father had been capable of all those years ago and now truly understanding what her brother had been through. It would no doubt cost her a lot in therapy sessions.

Now, late on Friday afternoon, she'd arranged to meet Bec for a drink at Somewhere, a cosy bar that had popped up in Prahran a few weeks earlier. She arrived a few minutes early, and Bec hurried in shortly after she sat down and leaned down and hugged her tightly. She didn't need to apologise again; the hug said everything she needed to. Anna didn't blame Bec for any of this, and that was one thing from tonight she wanted to ensure her friend understood.

'How are you?' Bec asked after they placed their wine orders.

Anna smiled. 'Surprisingly good. It's been a huge shock, but it's been good too. Mum has had some closure, as have I. Things that didn't make sense now do. The reality is, Jake would still have died that night; nothing your dad did was going to change that. We still would have lost him.'

Anna thought back to the conversation she'd had with her mother a week ago. She hadn't been able to talk to her straight away; she had so much to come to terms with and wanted to have some information from the police before she did speak to her. From what she learned, both Cameron and Kieran had been questioned, and Cameron had contacted her to let her know that he and Kieran were not in the clear. The police were looking at whether they'd perverted the course of justice by not coming forward at the time and what the consequences of accepting bribes would be.

While Kieran had been put in a difficult situation all those years ago, he'd also seen his best friend die and had agreed to leave Melbourne. She shuddered each time she tried to put herself in his shoes. There's no way she could have made the same choice, no matter what the consequences may have been.

She'd been pleased that her mother had been completely lucid when she explained what had happened and that Bruce Langford was going to pay for his role in tampering with the accident as well as for bribing Cameron and Kieran.

'He should be in jail,' her mother had said.

'From everything I understand, he will be,' Anna had replied. *'It's waiting for the legal process to begin. Regardless of what happens to him, he's lost everything.'* She went on to explain how he finally had Bec and her children in his life, and they'd now cut him off. *'Bec also told me that he's moved out of the family home. His wife wants nothing more to do with him.'*

It had been bittersweet to see her mother relax and smile about justice finally being served but then have tears rolling down her cheeks as she pointed out that it wasn't going to bring Jake back. Her son was still dead, and nothing was going to change the pain of that.

'I imagine this has been harder on you and your mum than on my family in some ways,' Anna said. 'How's your mum doing?' Bec's eyes filled with tears at the mention of her mother, and Anna put a reassuring hand on her arm. 'It can't be easy for her.'

'It's not. Chris might still be alive if Dad hadn't taken this all upon himself to *handle*.'

Anna nodded. The same thought had gone through her head on more than one occasion. If Bruce had allowed his son to face the consequences it was quite likely he'd have served time and continued with his life after.

'And the kids? How are they coping?'

'Zara's gutted,' Bec said. 'She feels responsible for bringing them back into my life. I can't seem to get through to her that learning all of this has been a good thing. He can't get away with what he did. It's bad enough that it's taken this long.'

'One of his investors reached out to the centre,' Anna said. 'I've handed them on to Isabella, but from everything she's said, it sounds like we're going to get a large injection of funds via a donation.'

Bec raised an eyebrow. 'How do you feel about that?'

Anna shrugged. 'At first I wanted to say no way, but I've come around to the idea. I'll never forgive him for what he did, and I'm glad he'll get what's coming to him, but I also won't be silly and say no to an opportunity that can help a lot of people.'

The women sipped their drinks, and the conversation gradually turned to other topics. Anna was pleased that they'd found their natural rhythm again. As hard as it had been since Bruce's confession, she didn't want to lose Bec's friendship. She'd always thought the fact they'd both lost brothers explained their connection, but now it was so much more.

'How's Skye going?' Bec asked. 'I know Zara said she seems a lot happier, and she and Lammy have been visiting us a fair bit, but I'm never sure if she's just putting on a brave face.'

'She seems to have relaxed,' Anna said. 'Lammy was the best thing that could have happened when she ran away. She adores that dog and it's very mutual. I think she sees herself in her. Without a family, they need to stick together. We've finally had news about her mum's friend, Erin. It's good and bad unfortunately.'

'Good and bad?'

Anna nodded. 'It's been confirmed that she's alive, which is the most important thing. I was worried Skye would be dealing with another loss. She was captured and held hostage in Yemen, but she's been released and is expected back in Australia next week.'

Bec stared at her. 'What does that mean for Skye?'

'Relief, mostly,' Anna said. 'Just knowing she's alive is something. But she won't be able to take Skye on. I haven't been told much, but it sounds like she's been through an awful ordeal and almost certainly will be dealing with PTSD. She'll need time and space to recover. Even if she wants to take Skye, I doubt child services would see her as a suitable guardian right now. It could take years before she's ready.'

'Oh no,' Bec said. 'Poor Skye. Is she okay?'

'Better than expected,' Anna said. 'Her focus has been entirely on Erin, worrying about her, asking what she can do to help, what Hopefield might be able to offer in terms of counselling when she's back. When I explained that Erin wouldn't be able to take her on, she said she understood. She just hopes she'll get to see her again. Said her mum would have wanted that.'

'She's incredibly mature for her age,' Bec said.

Anna nodded. 'She is. And I think it's important we keep reinforcing that she's loved and wanted here, no matter what happens with her placement.'

'The twins and I will do our best to make sure she knows that.'

'Me too,' Anna said. She took a sip of her drink and replaced it on the table with a sigh. 'Kieran contacted me last week.'

Bec's mouth dropped open. 'Really? I thought he would have stayed well away.'

'He wanted to tell me again how sorry he was and how much he loved Jake and me.'

'And?'

'And I told him that twenty-two years of doing nothing about the situation told me exactly how much he loved us. I realise he was threatened, but it wasn't like he turned up wanting to confess and make things right, even after all this time. He's not the man I thought he was, and I don't want anything to do with him ever again. Marty thinks—' Anna hesitated.

A smile played on Bec's lips. 'What does *Marty* think?'

Anna blushed. 'He thinks I was mad to have let him back in to start with. But I think he was just jealous.'

'I think that's a pretty good summation. Now, what's happening with this Marty of yours?'

Anna imagined her cheeks were crimson by now. Out of all the unpleasant surprises of the last few weeks, Marty had been a very pleasant one.

'We had a drink the night I told Mum about Bruce and what had happened. He's lovely, Bec. Attentive, funny, the whole package. We're having dinner tomorrow night.'

Bec smiled but didn't say anything right away. 'You like him,' she said finally, her tone light.

Anna laughed softly. 'Yeah. I do. He's been there for me for years, when I think back to how he was with Mum. Can't believe I was so blind.'

'He could have asked you out,' Bec said. 'It doesn't sound like he was exactly obvious about it.'

'No,' she said, unable to hide her smile, 'but I'm glad he finally did.'

EPILOGUE

A month had passed since learning of her father's betrayal, and life had settled back to a more normal routine. Bec was pleased that her mother had slotted into her family so quickly and that she was doing her best to cope with the situation around her father. She'd made it abundantly clear that Bruce was never to step foot in her house again, not that it looked like he would have the option, with the lawyers suggesting he'd be serving time.

Now, as she stood in her bedroom, her overnight bag packed, Bec did her best to push thoughts of her father from her mind. She had more important things to worry about today.

She took a deep breath, picking the urn up from Owen's bedside table. Was she ready to do this? No, she wasn't. Would she ever be? Probably not. But she knew she needed to do it for Zara and Hugo. Give them some closure and hopefully a nice memory of a beautiful area where they knew their father would have loved to be.

She wondered how Skye was feeling this morning. When the trip had been planned, and Zara had suggested that Anna and Skye join them, Skye then confided in Bec that she planned to bring the urn with her mother's ashes in it and would decide when they arrived whether she was going to scatter her in the same location.

For Bec, it was more than saying goodbye to Owen; she felt like it was saying goodbye to Chris again. Now that she knew everything, she understood more about her brother and his choice. She shivered, as she did each time she thought of what he'd been through.

Bec stared at the urn, its intricate design so beautiful. She had to remind herself that the urn and its contents weren't Owen. Owen was in her heart. He was there every day and in everything she did. He was in Hugo's and Zara's hearts. A day wouldn't pass without one of them, if not all three of them, thinking about him, missing him and remembering how much love he'd brought them.

What was in the urn was part of the process. Scattering his ashes signified her letting go of some of her grief. Not all of it, but a little part. A little part that would remind her that she was healing. She'd miss him forever, she'd never forget him, and she'd continue to love him, but she would be okay, and that's what this trip would remind her.

* * *

Bec stood with the urn pressed gently to her chest. They'd found a stretch of the Murray River tucked away from the main tracks. The water level was low, revealing worn tree roots and half-buried driftwood at the bottom of the steep riverbanks. Hugo and Zara stood either side of her.

Anna, Skye, Lammy and Samara hung back a little to give the family space. Skye was quiet, her shoulders hunched slightly, a small tin clutched in one hand, Lammy's lead in the other as she gazed at the river.

Bec stepped closer to the riverbank. She opened the lid slowly, the breeze lifting strands of her hair as she held the urn aloft.

'Travel safe, my love,' she whispered.

She scattered the ashes in a gentle arc. The breeze caught them, and the pale dust danced across the surface of the river before settling into the current. No one spoke. There was no need.

A few minutes passed before Skye cleared her throat, handed Lammy's lead to Anna and stepped towards them.

'I brought my mum,' she said. Her voice was quiet but sure.

Bec turned to her. 'You don't have to—'

'I want to.' She glanced at the river. 'I looked it up last night. The Murray runs for over two thousand kilometres. She always wanted to travel, so I thought maybe she could start here. I'm not scattering all of her ashes. Eventually, when I'm old enough to leave school and travel, I'll take her with me and leave a little of her in the places she never got to see.' She paused. 'It feels like something she would have liked.'

She stepped forward and tipped the tin slightly. When she was done, she didn't speak. Just stood and watched as the river carried her mother away.

'We've lost so much,' Bec said gently, breaking the silence. 'Owen. Chris. Jake. Your mum.'

'We've found each other, though,' Zara said. 'We lost Dad, and you lost Chris, but now we have Gran and we have Anna and Skye. We're pretty lucky.'

'We are,' Bec agreed. Her voice caught, and she glanced at Anna, who, along with Samara, had moved closer to them.

'I feel really lucky,' Skye said, 'to have met you all. And to

Anna for looking after me. It's been a lot longer than you said I could stay and I appreciate that and that you kept your word about me having the decision on a family.'

Anna turned to Skye, her expression softening. 'I've been waiting for the right time to tell you this, and while this might seem like a strange moment, you'll see that it's not. This is the start of a new chapter for all of us, and part of your chapter is that I've found you a new family. A permanent placement.'

Skye looked at her, eyes narrowing. 'Hold on. You what? We had a deal, remember, that I get to meet them, spend time with them and ultimately decide.'

'They're nice people. They've got room, and they want you. It's a good home, Skye. I know in my heart they're your people.'

Skye blinked. 'I've just scattered my mother's ashes, and you think this is a good time to drop this on me?'

Bec reached for her hand. 'Anna wants what's best for you. We all do.'

Skye shook her hand away. 'I think I need to get out of here.'

'Oh, for God's sake,' Zara said, 'would someone put her out of her misery. You two are dragging this out ridiculously. Just tell her or I will.'

Skye's eyes widened and she turned to Zara. 'Tell me what?'

Bec reached for her hand again, and this time she didn't push her away. 'We want you to be part of our family.'

Skye's mouth dropped open, and she looked to Anna, who nodded in confirmation.

'You complete our triplet set,' Zara added. 'What are the chances you were born when you were and it not being a sign? If you weren't one of us before, you are now.'

'But you said you didn't want me,' Skye said looking to Bec. 'When you were speaking to Anna.'

Bec shook her head. 'No, I said I didn't think I had the

capacity to give you what I thought you needed. I'm dealing with my own loss and was worried I wouldn't have enough in me to make sure you felt loved and cared for. When you ran away, I realised what a huge loss it would be for us if you were gone. In a short time you felt like part of the family and I started questioning why I wasn't ready to just open my arms to you. When I questioned myself I realised that I was ready. Zara and Hugo love you like a sister and I'd like the opportunity to love you like a daughter. I'll never replace your mum, but I'd like to be the person you know has your back and will do anything for you.'

Tears filled Skye's eyes and she seemed unable to speak.

'But,' Zara said, 'unfortunately, you'll have to put up with Hugo.' She rolled her eyes, lightening the mood. 'And you have to take over most of my chores.'

'Zara!' Bec said.

'God, Mum, she knows I'm kidding. Only some of the chores, like an equal split between the three of us, but sorry, you would still have to put up with Hugo.'

'We'd love you to be a Sampson,' Hugo said, ignoring his sister, 'not change your name or anything, but be an honorary one of us.'

Skye swallowed. 'Until I'm eighteen?'

Bec placed a hand on her arm. 'I'm not giving up any of my kids at eighteen, you included. No, this is signing on for life. If you say yes, you're family and that's it.' She smiled as Lammy gave a gentle bark, reminding her that she too was part of the package. 'And Lammy comes too, of course.' She looked at her mother. 'I'm not walking away from family ever again.'

Samara wiped her eyes.

'Say yes,' Zara said, nudging Skye.

Tears ran down Skye's cheeks as she looked from Zara to

Hugo and to Bec. 'Thank you. I can't believe you're going to do this.'

'Ironically I had to fight Anna for you,' Bec said. 'Even after everything you heard us say, she was also giving serious thought to snaffling you.'

'Really?' Skye said, looking to Anna. 'But all those things you said to Bec?'

Anna nodded. 'I know, and you've made me question all of those things. I was protecting myself and my heart rather than opening it to you. Bec made me realise how much richer my life is with you in it. And I want you to stay in it, Skye. While you'll live with the Sampsons, I'd like you to consider me a really good friend. Kind of like an aunt, I guess. One who loves you and will do anything for you.'

'I don't know what to say,' Skye said, clearly overwhelmed.

Bec wrapped an arm around her shoulder and drew her close. 'Don't say anything. Right now, we've got everyone here – your mum, Owen, and all of us. It might not be the most conventional family, but it's ours. We had no choice in those we've lost, but we do get to choose each other – and that's what makes us family.'

* * *

MORE FROM LOUISE GUY